The Eagle in Green Man's Clearing

A. L. O'Connor

This is a work of fiction. All of the characters, names, incidents, organizations, and dialogue in this novel are either the products of the author's imagination or are used fictitiously.

Archway Publishing books may be ordered through booksellers or by contacting:

Archway Publishing
1663 Liberty Drive
Bloomington, IN 47403
www.archwaypublishing.com
1 (888) 242-5904

ISBN: 978-1-4808-8055-9 (sc)
ISBN: 978-1-4808-8309-3 (hc)
ISBN: 978-1-4808-8308-6 (e)

Library of Congress Control Number: 2019916870

Print information available on the last page.

Archway Publishing rev. date: 11/15/2019

THE EAGLE IN GREEN MAN'S CLEARING

Dedicated to my parents, because of them I was presented to the glories of the Roman Empire from our time in Izmir, Turkey. There I was introduced to Ephesus, Roman aqueducts, a Roman hospital, and Roman chariot stadium ruins. And our equally exiting time in Lakenheath, England where I experienced the glories of the British Isles. Mom and Dad you are the best.

Acknowledgements

I would like to acknowledge my husband Mike, who's patience and perseverance in his business allowed me to work unimpeded for the last four years doing the writing and research on this project. It was enough for me to get two books out of the first initial submission!

I'd also like to dedicate this book to my daughters Marie and Ann. They patiently let me write my book, sometimes at the price of me not attending a school function or being attentive to their friends when they came to the house for entertainment.

I'd like to acknowledge and thank my editing team Anne and Tracy. These two gave me undying encouragement, thoughtful remarks, and good pointers for my story. Anne would always talk about the themes in each chapter and would give me ideas to further the plot. Tracy was my moral compass, speaking on how each character needed to have a complete personality, good and bad, to make them believable.

CELTIC CHARACTERS

Pronunciation of the Spellings of the Celtic Names

Bh is the breathy (v) sound
S is the (sh) sound when in the middle or at the end of the word
Mh is the (v) breathy sound
Dhgbh is the (v) breathy sound
Dh is the (v) breathy sound
Dh is the (h) sound
Nn is a short (n) sound

Edana
Edana is the oldest child from the union of Ardan and Bebhinn, her brothers are Carrick and Ailbe. She meets, falls in love and marries Quintus Agricolanus.

Bebhinn (Bay-vin)
Bebhinn is the mother of Edana and Ailbe, wife to deceased **Ardan** and **Carrick**. She is a trained healer from the Iceni tribe where she was apprenticed and trained by the druids.

Ardan
Ardan is the Father of Edana, Carrick, and Ailbe.

Carrick
Brother to Edana and Ailbe, son of Bebhinn and Ardan.

Ailbe
Youngest son of Ardan and Bebhinn. He is also a favorite of the gods and is able to foresee things before they happen. His hounds' name is **Cabhan** (Kevan). He becomes Miach apprentice and makes his own druid's bag for his accoutrements that he will gather as a druid.

Cathmore
He is the paternal uncle to Edana and Ailbe. He has a large farm closer to Gosbecks with his wife **Meara** and daughters **Aine** and **Flann** who are good at singing and frequently sing during their festivals.

Meadghbh (Maeve)
Best friend of Edana, Her father **Rumo** and brothers, **Caolan** and **Addis** and sister **Brenna.** Meadghbh's mother is **Eimear (Ee-mer)** she is hard working and kind.

Brenna
She is the older sister to Meadghbh and since they lost their father and brothers has had to marry an older man **Ferdia** whose first wife's name was **Aideen.** Dark headed Ferdia has smaller sons **Fintan, Daire**, and **Aengus.**

Eilis (Ay-lish)
The youngest of Edana's friends and the most timid, she is very pious and follows religious ceremonies with the utmost respect. She's an only child of two very hard working parents who have their own business selling tartans and scarves. Her father is **Ronan,** her mother's name is **Fingula.**

Sadhbh (Sav-een)

She is the easy going and confident friend of Edana. Her father **Declan**, the Gosbecks smith lost his arm in the rebellion and brother **Addis** killed also considered a leader. Her mother **Etain (e-tain)** and younger sister **Lavena** are also on the Romans notice to lose their smith.

Niamh (Neev)

She is the neighbor to Edana with her large farm on the ridge closest to theirs. She has three daughters and her parents living with her. Her fathers' name is **Drust,** mother's name is **Ealga (ale-ga)**. Her husband **Galahaut** and son **Adair,** her daughter's names are **Aibhlinn (Av-leen), Cliona (Klee-ona), and Nola.**

Miach (My-ax) Daly

He is Gosbecks resident druid, very clever and wise.

Iollan ((ul-an)

Gosbecks best drummer, played at the Samhain festivity. His wife's name is **Gormley.**

Lorcan

Gosbecks best piper, dad is the innkeeper **Oisin** and mother is **Grania**.

Aedan

The young Celt that was forced into interpreting after the Boudicca's rebellion.

Kearney

A handsome red-headed piper that is the second best piper playing in Lorcan's band.

Oisin (oish-**een**)
Name of the tavern keeper in Gosbecks, his wife is **Grania** and son is **Lorcan** the piper.

Dahy
The butcher for Gosbecks his wife is **Muirne** (mir-ne).

Glendon
Another drummer that plays with Iollan during ceremonies, his wife's name is **Aileen.**

Fintan
Friend of Kearney and another piper

Murtagh
Friend of Kearney, he is a drummer.

Gearoid (**gar-roid**)
Friend of Kearney he is also a drummer.

Conor
Owner of the musicians' cart.

Niall
The only lyre player in Gosbecks.

Eamon
Eamon and his wife **Ida,** their sons **Eirnin** and **Hugh.**

Carrick
Carrick and his wife **Darcy**. Their children are **Garret, Cathal** and **Kalin.**

Lachlan
Lachlan and his wife **Neala**, they have four children, **Aideen, Lee, Dalaigh, and Bairre.**

Gerard
Gerard and his wife **Hannah** are neighbors to Ferdia and Brenna.

Malachi
Seller of tartans and scarves.

Alwyn Rhys
Leader of the Ordovices and grandfather of Cai.

Owain ap Gruffudd
Cai's father and husband to **Margaret Siddons** who are riding with Cai to Gosbecks. He is the son of Alwyn Rhys. He spends a lot of time getting the family settled in Gosbecks.

Cai
Wife of Grex.

The O'Shea
The head of the druids.

The O'Nialle
On the high druid counsel. He represents the South cardinal direction.

The O'Connor
Another high druid on the counsel. He represents the East cardinal direction.

The O'Reilly
Another high druid on the counsel. He represents the West cardinal direction.

The MacNair
The O'Nialle chooses the leader of the druids up in Skerrabra in the Orkneys for the high druid of the north.

Aobh (Aov) **O'Brien**
Leader of the Stonehenge druids. The O'Nialle chooses him to become a high druid of the west. He becomes **The O'Brien**.

Cian (Ki-an)
Envoy form Boudicca to talk to Gosbecks about joining the rebellion.

Enda
Envoy from Boudicca to talk to Gosbecks about joining the rebellion.

Nuala (Noo-la)
The mother of **Caddoc**. She is an Ordovices and is married to **Sextus** who is a veteran and a guard at the carcer.

Phelan (Fwail - awn)
Glass maker with experience in the glass making factory in Camulodenum. His wife's name is **Meryl**.

Aderyn
Mother of **Bryn** who has the coughing sickness. She also comes to Bebhinn at the bath house to get her son cured. Her father **Newlin** also has the coughing sickness. Aderyn's mother is **Bronwyn**. Her husband's name is **Darius** who is an architecti working on the buildings in Gosbecks.

Carys
Mother of **Folant.** Her husband's name is **Felix** and is working on building the Principia. She is an Ordovician.

Aednat (ey-nit)
The widow who houses Gaius Catulus while his villa is being made.

Hugh
Bartender for the veteran's tavern.

Tadhg (Ti – gue)
He is the cook for the veteran's tavern.

Eimear (ee-mer)
The curly haired blond waitress at the Wet Dog.

Tierney
The farmer who with his wife **Liadan** had a little girl that Bebhinn delivered. The little girls' name is **Einin (ey – neen).**

Anlon
He is a sunny dispositioned bee keeper that sells honey at market day. His wife **Eachna** (eck-na) works with him.

Tyree
Young farmer that loses his farm due to his inability to pay his taxes. His wife's name is **Brigid.** They have two small children a boy and a girl.

Denzel
Carter that takes the message of the massacre of the druids on the Isle of Mona to the town of Coria up in northern Britannia in the area ruled by the Brigantes.

Cloda

Cloda is a small widow with several children that are all middle aged and able to help her around her farm. She has twin daughters **Aideen** and **Chevonne**, they are 13. She also has two younger boys **Malachy** who is 7 and **Lee** who is 9.

Tyree

Miller for Gosbecks. His wife's name is **Nara**.

Gerrit

He is *a Gallus* gladiator and comes from the Trivantes tribe. He is large and shows his appreciation for returning to Britannia by staying in Gosbecks after they get there.

CONTENTS

CHAPTER 1
BRITANNIA

*P*iss *and pestilence. Does this gods forsaken land ever stop drowning in rain? Where is the sun?*

Quintus Agricolanus rubbed the rain out of his eyes and looked at the landing site for his century of soldiers from the Tenth Legion. The landing site was a green embankment on the far side with no planking to hold back the mud. The bank just ran in rivulets of mud into the river. They had come up the river since making landfall in the early spring morning but saw no work going on, which was unusual in the normally busy wharf in Londinium. Quintus had been told the landing site was still in disrepair from the previous storm that lashed the area. Seeing the lack of finished wharves and cranes to unload his cargo told him this was true.[1] He had been told that the wharves in Londinium[2] formed the busiest and biggest place

---

[1] http://cncrane789.over-blog.com/2014/02/ancient-roman-cranes.html, https://en.wikipedia.org/wiki/Roman_technology

[2] http://www.mola.org.uk/publications/londinium-new-map-and-guide-roman-london

to unload from the continent. All he saw were several wharves with storm-wrecked quays that jutted out into the River Thames. No cranes were working in sight. He rubbed his face again and smoothed the rivulets of water out of his handsome, curly, dark-brown hair and large brown eyes. The driving rain was making it hard to breathe; the rain kept blowing at an angle into his face as he wiped his large nose. Did the rain have an ulterior motive to make him look like a drowned wharf rat?

Despite the rain that just kept coming, Quintus tried to keep presentable as befitted his rank of centurion.[3] Quintus looked at his helmet with the transverse plume of silver horsehair that had wilted in the rain. He looked down at his leather, embossed cuirass and the leather greaves on his shins. His shoulders were covered with leather guards, and he had strips of leather hanging down his arms and groin. Around his neck was a thick brass torque, and on his cuirass hung medallions that showed his awards for valor in battle. He looked over his shoulder at his blue cloak with the yellow border that showed his rank of centurion. Finally, he picked up his vine stick cudgel that also was a signifier of centurion rank. His shield was leaning against the bench with all the other shields.

Joining the military had been a foregone conclusion for Quintus. His grandfather and Faber were centurions in the Roman military. Quintus remembered the tales his grandfather told him of fighting in Gaul and Britannia under Caesar. He fought in the same legion that Quintus was in currently, the Tenth, and fought against the Nervii in the battle of Sabis in Gaul. The deciding point in the battle took place when the Tenth Legion was able to attack from the rear and route the Nervii, winning the battle for Caesar at the last moment. His grandfather's original centurion, Marcellus Drusus, was killed during the battle when a Nervii slashed his throat.

---

[3] http://www.dictionary.com/browse/centurion, https://en.wikipedia.org/wiki/Centurion, https://images.search.yahoo.com/yhs/search?p=Centurion+Uniform&hspart=att&hsimp=yhs-att_001

Witnessing the blow, his grandfather jumped into the fray and rallied his soldiers. Due to his quick thinking, he won the day for the Tenth and for Caesar. After the battle, Caesar promoted him into the centurion position in recognition of his good work. It was the proudest day in this grandfather's life. Growing up, Quintus heard this story frequently from his grandfather. It was one of the reasons Quintus put in for serving in Britannia. His grandfather was one of the first Romans to fight in Caesar's invasion of Britannia, and he always told Quintus to go back to where it all began. So fighting in Britannia had always been a dream of Quintus's. He wanted to follow his grandfather in glory.

Looking at his own *Contuberium,*[4] Quintus was proud to have them with him on this new venture. There was Fullo, his closest confidant and fellow Apulia native from Italy. His light-brown hair, blue eyes, and handsome face made him irresistible to the ladies. The man next to him was Bundarus, whose large body dwarfed Fullo's and whose large, bald head resembled a rock ballista[5] from a war machine. Bundarus was the soldier's soldier who followed every protocol to the letter. Next to Bundarus sat Rufus, the tall, red-haired Roman from Potentia, Picenum.[6] His height and long reach made him dangerous on the battlefield. In the next bench was Faber, the large, dark soldier who resembled Vulcan.[7] His background as a smith allowed him to be promoted into the engineer corps. He would discuss any of the war machines with everyone. Sitting next to him was Coriaro, a fellow war machine enthusiast. Coriaro turned and nodded to Quintus and gestured to the bank with a shrug. On the other side of Coriaro sat Titus, a stocky, shorter version of Coriaro. Titus was renowned for his sense of humor and played pranks on his fellow soldiers. Titus also looked

---

[4] http://dictionary.sensagent.com/CONTUBERNIUM/en-en/
[5] http://www.merriam-webster.com/dictionary/ballista
[6] https://en.wikipedia.org/wiki/Potentia_(ancient_city)
[7] http://www.merriam-webster.com/dictionary/Vulcan

at Quintus and smiled, his hazel eyes crinkling in the rain. Last but not least was the little Sicilian Grex, who was the squad's lead tracker and scout. Grex was small and dark with a face like a ferret.

This was the group Quintus was closest to in the army; they worked well as a unit and knew one another's strengths and weaknesses.

Quintus turned and looked at the embankment where they were expected to disembark from their trireme.[8] The tired-looking wharf was stuck out haphazardly into the river. The boat captain moved them in closer, slowly inching them close to the wharf. He yelled out to the sailors in the back of the boat, "Get her straightened out! She's coming in too fast to the port side."

"Ay, ay captain," they chorused back to him as they moved the oars to straighten the boat out. Soon the boat pulled up to the dock slowly, and one sailor jumped out to secure the boat. As soon as they were tied off, the soldiers rose as one and gathered their equipment as efficiently and quickly as they could. Then they turned to Quintus and waited for him to tell them to disembark.

Quintus stood up and grabbed his vine stick cudgel, and then he waved it above his head to get their attention. "Follow me! Take your equipment, and only set it down where I say so."

The soldiers began to get off the boat in an orderly fashion, following Quintus in a singular line. Out on the wharf was waiting the quartermaster from ships that had made their landings earlier. The grizzled soldier met up with Quintus, who introduced himself. "Seems you finally made it with your men. How many in this boat? I'm Lepidus Piso, by the way."

"There are fifty in this boat, with the remaining ten on the following boat." Quintus turned and waved at the other boat coming in. "They have our mounts in that boat."

---

[8] https://en.wikipedia.org/wiki/Roman_navy, http://military.wikia.com/wiki/Trireme

"So you have only sixty in your century? Do you have more coming?" the quartermaster asked.

"We are down a number from our last battle in Gaul. I have another boat coming in with replacements later today or tomorrow," Quintus replied.

"Well, we'll get you bunked up as soon as you're unloaded. I'll take you to the main fort as soon as you're ready. Just follow me." The grizzled quartermaster[9] nodded to Quintus.

Quintus just nodded his acceptance and moved off to get his group ready. He went back to the boat to see how many were left to get unloaded. Presently, they were all unloaded from the boat and moved to the bank next to the wharf. Each soldier had loaded his pack and stood at attention for Quintus to inspect.

Soon after perusing his soldiers, he turned to the quartermaster and signaled they were ready to follow him to the main fort. The grizzled soldier took off, and the group followed him in an orderly line.

They walked away from the wharves and into Londinium, the main destination for Romans in Britannia. As they passed the docks and moved into the larger town, Quintus got his first look at the land. The rain continued unabated, but the residents were used to the downpour. They moved about without pausing. The sight of more Roman soldiers was also part of the norm because other than the tavern keepers coming out to look, the residents ignored them. They were led past the docks and to the right of the town where a large Roman fort had already set up. The soldiers inside were moving in their orderly fashion, obviously with duties to perform.

Then Lepidus Piso led them to the main building, called the Principia, in the middle of the fort,[10] where all the governing took place. The soldiers began to file in behind Quintus and set down their shields but did not lose their attention and stood quietly. The

---

[9] http://www.dictionary.com/browse/quartermaster
[10] http://historylink101.com/2/Rome/roman-army-forts.htm

quartermaster turned to Quintus and said, "At the back of the fort is your barracks. The last building on the south side. You'll stay here until you get word from Governor Gaius Suetonius Paulinus."

"Do you know how long until we hear from the governor? I am under the impression he will want us to join him as soon as possible," Quintus said.

"Could be he'll have you go to him in his current location, which is on his way to the druids' sanctuary in Mona. We'll send a messenger forthwith and get that to him as soon as possible. We've been having trouble with these religious groups, and the governor wants to end the problem as soon as possible. You'll have to deal with me in his absence."

"It was the same with the Gauls and their druids. They fomented problems with their religion. Is it the same here?" Quintus looked at the quartermaster.

"I guess so. They've been spreading dissent at the number of Roman troops lately. They don't want us here in their land so it is not surprising they would foment more distrust amongst themselves. Nothing that we haven't run into before," the quartermaster shrugged his burly shoulders. "You'll have time to get your men to the barrack and mess hall. The mess hall is located next to the Principia. We have another cohort of engineers stationed here and they will be joining you for the meal. If you follow me you will be dismissed as soon as we get to your barracks." The quartermaster turned and gestured to Quintus to follow him out to the barracks. They followed him to the barracks, out into the now lessening rain and to the south side of the fort.

"Does it rain like this all the time?" asked Quintus.

"Pretty much, it is coming up on spring time and it will rain more during the planting of crops. This is a pretty dreary country," the grizzled quartermaster said as he strode forward to the barracks.

Quintus shook his head: "Will it get any warmer during the spring? It seems pretty wet and cold now."

Lepidus Piso smirked and said jokingly: "You expecting the sunny climes from southern Italy? It will warm up in the summer but don't expect the sun much. Maybe the reason the local Celts are so grumpy is they never get to see the sun much here. Not that I blame them. I could use a little sunny weather now and then." They got to the barracks building and the quartermaster just smiled and waved the soldiers inside. "When you've gotten the men settled come out to the mess building and to have your midday meal." With that he turned and left the building retraced his steps back to the Principia to fill out the paperwork for the new arrivals.

"Alright you lot go pick out your areas of bunking within individual *Contuberium,* then when you're done line up at the front for the midday meal," Quintus belted out loud enough for everyone to hear. The soldiers separated in an orderly manner into their *Contuberium* and started getting their bunks. Quintus turned to his own *Contuberium* knowing they would have gotten the best spot as befitting his rank which was at the front of the building. Fullo had already reserved his bunk next to the main door, the first place a centurion should be. The barrack was well made with stone walls and stout timbered floors, the roof tiled in red terracotta. There were rows of beds lined up and down the building on both sides of the walls. Windows were scattered throughout the building with stout shutters pulled shut to keep out the rain. Interspersed down the center aisle stood stoves for heat, one to cover every eight beds or per *Contuberium.* Quintus' men were in the process of setting up their beds with the usual ribbing going on. "Don't get too close to Coriaro, you know how he smells, coming from the smelly tanner section of the *subura* that he did," Fullo said cheekily to Quintus. Quintus just shook his head.

"Better to stay away from your piss smell Fullo! I know your dad as a fuller used to bleach the togas of the uptight, upper crust with piss. Wasn't that the reason you went into the military?" Coriaro rejoined.

"We should put both of you together and save everyone's nose.

Put you right next to the door to let the smells drift out and away from us," laughed Titus.

"Neither one smells of their pre-military jobs of tanner and fuller, I will sleep next to them with no problem," Bundarus rumbled calmly as he stashed his belongings next to his bed, he wiped his bald pate with a part of his cloak. "Plus the end should be the centurion's bed not Coriaro or Fullo's."

Titus just laughed again. Rufus grinned and set his pack next to Bundarus': "Is it permissible for me to bunk next to you Bundarus or am I breaking Roman protocol?"

Not seeing anything incorrect Bundarus just gestured to the bunk and grunted in the affirmative. Grex set his pack next to a bunk on the opposite side and next to Titus. Faber and Coriaro set theirs down there after thus making up their *Contuberium*. Once they had claimed their bunks they turned to Quintus. Quintus indicated with his vine stick cudgel and waved it to the door to assemble the soldiers for the midday meal,. Meanwhile the other soldiers had also found their bunks filed in line behind them. Once outside they made their way to the mess building in two lines, following Quintus in quickstep time.

When they arrived at the mess hall they lined up at the cookpots to get their dinners then took their seats at the large empty tables surrounding the room. The quartermaster Lepidus Piso had waited for Quintus to arrive with his century to sit down before he spoke to the troops: "As you can see we have a new century that landed today and will be leaving soon to join the governor. They come directly from Gaul and will need help getting their bearings here in Britannia. They'll need for you to show them around Londinium. You need to advise which taverns are clean and charge fair prices, which ones to avoid due to previous problems," at this the quartermaster pointed to a burly light haired engineer,: "and which that loser started recent problems. We'll talk about the money to be dispensed to the tavern owner shortly, thank you Lucius," a loud guffaw at that quick aside from the fellow engineers at that table. "That being said we'll require better activities than fighting within the tavern premises, right Lucius? Or do you need some cooling off in the carcer?"

"I need to talk about the growing unrest in the countryside outside of Londinium. It seems the local druids are stirring up bad feelings focused on Romans and have started fomenting distrust among the locals. The countryside while it is beautiful is strictly off limits from here on out. The last two forays we held were met with sullen and muttering villagers and some rock throwing by young kids. The locals were not to be trusted. When we stopped to deal with the unrest they formed an unruly mob of farmers that yelled our men down, brandished their farm implements of scythes, shovels and hoes. The small group of twenty men made it back to the fort but only with the quick thinking of the centurion Aulus Capito who was able to double time it back before the mob could attack. He still needs to write up the report," the grizzled quartermaster looked at a square dark headed man on the right side next to Lucius. "I'll need that before the end of the day today, Aulus." Aulus nodded. "No more small training exercises until the next shipment of cranes arrive by the end of this seven day period for you lot. If the newly arrived century needs to stretch their collective legs and do an exercise they will need to take plenty of men, a *Contubernium* of eight men is too small; maybe at least half of their century should go out in mass to prevent another episode out in the countryside. How does that sound Quintus Agricolanus?" asked Lepidus Piso

Quintus stood and said "That would suit us just fine for exercising; we'll go out with no less than forty men at a time.[11]"

"Good that should keep you from any problems and get your men fit for the governor. All that easy time in Gaul should be taken care of on your trips out in the area. It'll get you familiar with the people. Do you have anyone who can communicate with the Celts?

---

[11] http://www.pbs.org/empires/romans/empire/soldiers.html

I understand the language is close to what they speak in Gaul," Lepidus Piso said.

"I have some of the ability to speak with those in Gaul as do several of my men. I guess we'll just have to see when we get out in the countryside to find out for sure," Quintus answered.

"Good, do that as soon as you can, maybe tomorrow after your rounds are made and see the rest of your men back from the boats, I understand they'll be in later today with all of your mounts, as soon as it arrives I'll let you know," the quartermaster said.

"Right and we'll be ready for the mounts when they come," Quintus smiled and sat back down.

Lepidus Piso turned to the group on the right: "Alright you lot, now back to the nuts and bolts of the day, we still need the planking up on the banks at the wharves. The rain will make it tough but I'm sure you engineers will figure a way around the problem. I'd like it done before the cranes get floated here; the wood needed for the planking we can unload from the docks. I might requisition some of your men Quintus to help set up the lumber on the wharves. Is that alright with you?"

"We'll be there where you need us, how many men do you need?" Quintus said.

"I'll need a good twenty of them to start with. The rain looks to be slacking off so maybe we'll get the job done sooner," the quartermaster replied.

"I'll have twenty lined up as soon as we're done," Quintus allowed, and singled out the men: "Come to me when you are done with your midday meal men."

"Good, now back to eating and we'll get some work done today. Aulus get with Quintus after the meal to tell him about the areas to avoid when exercising his men later. That is all," with that Lepidus Piso grabbed his food and sat down next to Quintus for his midday meal. He started to shovel his meal into his mouth as quickly as possible. The men sitting around him did likewise and the only sound was of the men slurping up their stew.

After the midday meal the twenty men from Quintus' century were selected and marched off with the engineers. Quintus left his century to follow Aulus Capito, the centurion for the engineers. They discussed the problems in the countryside while Aulus showed him around the fort. "The Celts are not organized, they tend to get into groups and talk about us as if we are another warring tribe. The area is mainly governed by the Trinovantes tribe but there are traders from other areas such as the Atrebates and far west is the warlike Catuvellauni. Each tribe fights the other for trade routes and land on a regular basis. In the middle are the druids or their priests. They could be male or female and often are one of the fighters in a skirmish, or at least the instigators causing the problem."

"Are the druids identifiable by dress or insignia?" Quintus asked.

"Not as I can tell, the all dress similar to each other with long hair and beards. The only way I've been able to identify them is by their speech. They are usually very well spoken and versed in their laws. They don't have any writing so everything is done by memory. Some of the laws must be made up on the spot they are so convoluted,[12]" Aulus said.

Quintus laughed at that: "That also makes them harder to find. Do they have temples for worship?"

"Not buildings like we have but there are clearings in the forest that I've heard they go to and worship," Aulus answered. They were both outside of the mess building and went to the main road, the Via Principalis. Quintus could see the fort because the rain had finally abated. The fort was well positioned and laid out with all

---

[12] https://images.search.yahoo.com/yhs/search?p=Druids+of+the+Isle+of+Mona&hspart=att&hsimp=yhs-att_001, https://en.wikipedia.org/wiki/Anglesey

of the buildings made of stone and timber in a grid pattern. There was a perimeter stone and stockade fence that was stout with four gates to be entered, set out on a north, south, east and west grid. The largest was on the north side and had stout towers on either side of the gate. They walked to the gate and up onto the wall through the towers. Aulus gestured to the empty fields around them set in lush countryside: "This is pretty much all our land that you see, the fort followers are located just over there to the south side of the fort, closest to the barracks. There is a lot of comings and goings between the two areas from the south gate that needs to be watched. The granary is supplied with grains from the surrounding area farms and shipments from the wharves. From the wharves we get the main amount of goods for fort living, oils, wine and foodstuffs. Otherwise the shipments coming in from the wharves are for building. You heard Lepidus Piso talk about the cranes on the way for construction[13]. "

Aulus gestured past the wharves in the distance and further to the west where the docks cleared out to more fine-looking stout buildings with thatched roofs in the distance. "See the main road over there, leading into the fort? That is the main road we use for our exercise parties, and for the incoming legions from the hinterland. The governor is located far west of here and will be staying there for the foreseeable future since he has his hands full of warring tribes in the area. It appears just when he makes a treaty with one tribe there are three more that pop up with their wants and needs that supersede the first one. I don't know how he does it. I would just go insane from the uncertainty!"

Quintus looked at Aulus: "How long have you been here in Britannia?"

"I've been here in Londinium since last summer," Aulus said.

"So you've here been for several seasons? How was the summer

---

[13] https://www.heritagedaily.com/2018/01/10-roman-forts-britanni
https://www.youtube.com/watch?v=ODUeICqyaHI

then in this dreary country?" Quintus gestured to the sodden landscape.

"It was fine, still rainy but there was some warmth to it. Far too brief for my liking but then I'm from Ostia[14] on the coast just south of Rome. Those were the sun drenched summers I would prefer, not the bleary watery ones you get here. The sun doesn't shine as much here," Aulus looked at the drenched landscape as well. Then he shrugged and said: "But what can we do, I have many years left until I retire, I'll just bide my time and build more wharves, cranes and roads for Rome." Quintus looked at Aulus and nodded his agreement. "What else can we do but build for Rome."

They finished their tour of the fort and returned to the *Praetorium*[15] building back in the middle of the fort. "I need to finish my report for Lepidus," was all Aulus said and left Quintus at the main door. Just then a runner came up to him with the news: "The horses and the last bit of our troops just pulled in, the quartermaster sent me to come get you."

"Alright let us go," Quintus replied and they left in a hurry to return to the wharves. At the docks the mounts were just being unloaded. They were being lead off towards the grassy banks which flanked the wharves to be calmed down. The soldiers with the mounts were also the ones who took care of them normally. Using their quiet voices and caresses they calmed the horses as they reached dry land. After being on board the ship the horses were very impatient and restive and needed to stretch their legs. They did several pirouettes as soon as they got to the wharf. They looked eagerly at the fresh grass on the banks. Their eagerness showed they had been on- board the ships too long. Quintus saw his dark brown mount and moved forward to deal with his gelding taking

---

[14] https://images.search.yahoo.com/yhs/search?p=Location+of+Ostia+In+the+Roman+Empire&hspart=att&hsimp=yhs-att_001 http://www.roman-empire.net/tours/empire/ostia.html

[15] https://en.wikipedia.org/wiki/Praetorium

the halter from the soldier who had it. Quintus spoke soothingly to the fidgety horse, calming him down as quickly as he could. The handsome gelding listened to his master and was soothed. He kept prancing around in circles as Quintus walked him over to the grassy banks for feeding. The other horses were eating the grass enthusiastically, since it had been a long time since they had gotten fresh green grass. The quartermaster strode up to Quintus: "I see that is your mount, he's a fine one. When you're done seeing to him we can move the mounts over to the stables back at fort. I think they are fine for now."

"Have the men also unloaded? I need to talk with them first I'll follow you to the stables with the horse," Quintus answered.

"They are standing right over there," Lepidus pointed over his shoulder at the embankment at the waiting soldiers standing in loose formation.

"Good, I'll get them ready to follow us up to the stables, give me a moment," Quintus motioned to one of the men holding the horses to take his dark brown gelding. He went over to the men in the group who were waiting patiently for him. Quintus quickly talked to them about following the horses to the stables and getting their bunks in the barracks hall at the back of the fort. Then he returned to the horses and got the halter back for his beautiful gelding. He turned and indicated to the quartermaster he'd follow him. Lepidus turned and yelled to everyone to follow him to the fort. They moved through the wharves to the well laid out Roman fort with as little disruption from the horses as possible. The stables where located next to the main gate located on the north side in two spacious buildings. They were two long buildings made of stone, hard-beaten earthen floors and stout lumber roofs. Inside there were spacious stalls on both walls running the length of the building, the tackle room and grooming supplies had its' own room at the end of the building. Once they got to the stables the main grooms led the horses into the stalls and stayed with them, getting bedding laid down.

The rest of the soldiers waited for Quintus to lead them to their barracks which he did as soon as he had put his gelding up in a stall, laid out the bedding and gave the dark gelding some soft words of encouragement. After Quintus came out the soldiers followed him over to the barracks then into their room. "Get your men into their *Contubernium* and set up your sleeping area. When you're finished we'll go out to the parade ground with the other men of the century and get lined up for the sign off on our transfer to Britannia. I want to get a visual on all of my soldiers." The men nodded and departed to finish their bunk assignments. When they had all reseved their bunks they met up in line and followed Quintus to the parade ground. Quintus walked up to the front of the parade ground and his soldiers fell into line behind him and onto the parade ground. They spread out into formation standing at attention.

Quintus moved to the front and got to his position for addressing the troops: "Men, we are in our new home for now. The governor of Britannia will be notified of our arrival. We will be leaving here to join him at his location to the west. In the meantime we will be doing our duties here at the fort in Londinium which means we will be assisting the engineers in constructing new replacement wharves and cranes. We'll also be performing our military exercises to get into readiness for later military maneuvers. There is one item to report to everyone. Unrest in the countryside is due to religious druids fomenting their dislike of the Roman presence in Britannia. When we go out we need to take at least half of the century to make sure we have no problems. There is nothing like showing the might of Roman soldiers to put fomenting dissenters on the run." The men laughed at this in agreement..

"We'll be frequenting the businesses here in Londinium which supports the fort. There are several taverns that we should avoid altogether. The ones closest to the fort are cleared for our use. Beware of the one called 'The Black Cat' they are known to overcharge for wine and ale. I hear just next door is the 'The Sailor' which is known for their nice looking women in the tavern and for other sorts of fun. I don't want to hear of you lot getting too rowdy with the hangers on, remember this is not a permanent fort for us." Quintus looked around at the men lined up with squinted eyes. "We need to leave here with a good report from the quartermaster Lepidus Piso. Should I hear anything not conducive to good soldiering I will personally put you in the carcer to slow you down and dry you out." There were several groans from some soldiers, the ones that had spent time in the carcer in previous forts. "That is all I need tell you for now. Those of you who have just arrived the mess building in located at the front of the fort. Just buddy up with the other soldiers and they'll show you. The layout of this fort is just like any other well laid out fort in the Roman army. You know the drill one military fort in the empire is the same as all of them." Quintus then saluted the soldiers and took his leave.

Fullo was by his side quickly: "So do we have your leave to go meet some of the fine women here in Britannia? The fellows of your *Contuberium* just spent all this time from midday meal until now helping the quartermaster set up more planking on the wharves. We could do with some relaxation and perhaps companionship."

"We just got here and should be the first to volunteer to help Lepidus Piso with more duties. You know that is how things work wherever we go Fullo. Especially our *Contuberium* is always the group that needs to be the first one in line for more work. We have to be the best and let the others go to their relaxation first. We'll be able to relax later when we are a little more established," Quintus said with an exasperated look on his face. "Why do you always do this every time whenever we get to a new fort? You know better."

Fullo shrugged his shoulders, "I got to ask don't I, hoping that one time you'll be lenient? There will be a time when we will need to wait for our own relaxation. You always work us the hardest. You should see Faber and Coriaro talking with the engineers, they can't wait for the time to get off duty and sit down with the engineers. Faber alone was asking about their war machines already."

"Yes I can just imagine him questioning the engineers. He has been out of control ever since that stint in our last fort with the ballista engineers. I thought he would request a transfer to work with the engineering corps and leave us altogether," Quintus said.

"Ha, maybe they both will but I doubt it. Coriaro would keep him here with our *Contuberium* intact. He can't stand the thought of leaving us. Besides who else will he be able to fight about our aromatic beginnings?, His from the smelly tanners section of the subura in Rome and mine from my Faber's fuller factory in Apulia[16]. We both had it hard before we got into the military." Fullo laughed.

"Then why do you always fight with him so much? If there is anyone who will wind up in the carcer it would be you two," Quintus asked

Fullo just laughed harder: "You know that is just the way we get out our pent up energy."

Quintus shook his head: "You better be careful of the good looks you are so proud of. Coriaro just might break your nose and it'll set with a great big kink just like his did from your last fight. Or maybe he'll just give you a scar on your pretty face, wouldn't that just be what you need."

"Now you're just being mean, my handsome face is what makes me so popular with the ladies. You need to get your manhood rubbed by some of the lovely natives here in Britannia. Care for a quick drink with me?" Fullo asked.

"No, now get going and volunteer some of your extra energy away to the engineers. Or if you can't find anything to do go help the mounts get accustomed to their new stalls. There is always plenty to do around a fort, find something. I have to go to meet up with Lepidus Piso to fill out the new paperwork." Quintus cuffed Fullo's arm as he walked away. Quintus went back to the *Praetorium* building and made his way through to the quartermasters' main office in the front. Inside he met Aulus Capito who had just finished his report on the events in the countryside.

---

[16] http://www.historyfiles.co.uk/KingListsEurope/ItalyApulia.htm

"Quintus come in and sit down," Lepidus showed him a table and stout four legged stool to sit on. "I have all of your scrolls ready for your examination. It is the regular information given to all centurions that come into Britannia. There is an intelligence report for you to read about the zone and especially the area where the governor is. The war like Ordovices[17] directly to the west of us that has a lot of particularly mean bunch of rabble-rousers you need to learn about. Originally they were in power over Camulodunum[18]. That changed after a few years of infighting between the tribes and the two hereditary kings in the midst, it seems the brothers couldn't rule jointly. The governor has had to deal with this lot on a daily basis." Lepidus got up and moved to a large wooden cabinet on the floor. He withdrew a large map of Britannia and spread it out on the table for Quintus to see. The map was a good representation of Britannia with the Roman enclaves clearly marked. It showed Londinium, Camulodunum and the small towns and villages that were surrounding both and had established trading with the Romans. The traders were key to any outpost to the Roman Empire, especially the ones still experiencing growing pains like Britannia was. Quintus was impressed by the long reaching goals of the Roman office in Londinium. They had a network of trade based on the surrounding areas and tribal agreements concentrating on natural trade routes such as the river systems. The picture was still evolving since the Romans were still negotiating with the surrounding tribal areas and agreements were being made. Quintus did not relish the political portion of these negotiations but realized it was part of building up a successful and profitable province for the empire.

"See the ever changing agreements made by the governor with the surrounding tribes? They change on a whim and will be renegotiated with new parties every time a new negotiations proceed

---

[17] https://en.wikipedia.org/wiki/Ordovices
[18] http://www.britainexpress.com/History/roman/camulodunum.htm

as we move further into Britannia. The tribes all want a bit of the Roman trade and Roman money. The oldest agreements have been with the Trinovantes simply because they are the tribe which governs Camulodunum and Londinium our two largest and most established settlements. Camulodunum also has the first settlement of veterans from the years of working in Britannia. The colonia was established and has about 400 veterans already living there on farms." Lepidus pointed out the area and circled the surrounding established farms on the map. "Camulodunum is the largest Roman city in Britannia. It will be even larger as soon as the temple to the emperor Claudius is finished. We plan to expand the colonia and open more throughout Britannia. I have a few senior officers that will be retiring soon and they will be moved into the colonia. I expect you will also get a farm if you stay longer, by the gods I might be retiring here as well as soon as I'm done with my service. The land is fertile here and it will be a pleasure to farm after all the years I've put in the military. Of course I might trade it all in for a place in Africa but the size of farms there are getting very small and hard to get so I think I might just stay in Britannia." Lepidus beamed at Quintus and rubbed his hands. The lighting from the lamps on the table showed the dark lines on the map with the names of the tribes and their areas of influence. Quintus couldn't help but see there was a lot of Britannia that wasn't filled in. It just depicted the bare outlines of an incomplete coastline, especially when you moved to the northern areas.

"Do we know how many tribes are in Britannia?" he asked.

"No, we only have estimated half of them. The far west and far northern areas are still being explored and trade negotiations are still being held to get trade started. I don't relish the governor's job. He will be spending half of his time in trade talks with Roman companies and Roman tax men and the other half with the new tribes. There seems to be a lot of the tribes in the area all jockeying for positions to trade with Rome.," the quartermaster said. Quintus just nodded. "One thing to be aware of in Britannia is the role druids play in the normal everyday life of the villages. They are the intelligent elite and hold a lot of sway in the Celts life. Do not cross them.. The grief they can cause is not worth the time it will take to unravel all the bad blood which they foment."

Quintus looked at Lepidus for a moment and thought about what the grizzled quartermaster was saying. If the druids were currently agitating against the Romans it might be an indicator of worse relations between the Celts and the Romans. It could also mean there was something they did not want the Romans to have. Quintus asked: "Are we watching the druids influence the Celts or are we seeing something new and more troublesome between us and the Celts?"

"That I do not know but that's very perceptive that you recognize it. I'm sure you'll get the information from the governor when you meet with him." Lepidus said. He then turned and got the intelligence report for Quintus to read and put it in front of him. "Take your time and read all of the report, the more you know about the Celts in Britannia the better off you'll be." Then Lepidus turned and brought two more lamps over to the table showing that he intended for Quintus to read all of the report right now in his office. Quintus pulled the report to him and began to read. Fortunately the office was large and airy with windows on three of the walls with shutters thrown open to let in light and the soft spring weather from outside. Lamps were strategically located on several of the tables and chests in the room. The floors were laid with native textile rugs that showed some skill, colorful with ochers, yellows and some greens shown throughout the alien circular designs.. It was a very official looking office for the quartermaster of a large Roman military fort. Quintus turned his attention back to the report and started reading and read until the sun started sinking in the west. Outside s soldier blew the horns for evening meal.

Lepidus walked back into the office and said: "Why don't you stop reading the report and go eat the evening meal with your century. The report can be read tomorrow, just come when you are ready to resume your analysis. I would rather you read and retain the information which you won't if you are hungry."

"The report is thorough but there are still a lot of empty places where the military simply doesn't seem to know the answers. Questions pertaining to why the Celts seem to be so upset about what the Romans are doing in their trade agreements. Are we not explaining them in clear detail so they can understand?" Quintus asked.

"I'm sure the governor will explain a lot to this to you. For me I'm far enough away from the frontier so it doesn't affect me and my operations here in Londinium. We have very good relations with the Trinovantes here." Lepidus answered. "Now go eat your end of day meal with your men."

Quintus nodded and got up to leave the room but before he left he asked Lepidus: "If the druids are fomenting problems in the villages surrounding this fort, how can you be so sure that you don't have problems like the ones in the west where the governor is?"

"Because this is the second oldest fort in Britannia, we've been here since Caesar invaded Britannia. The only older settlement is Camulodunum. They have the biggest settlement of Roman families, military forts and of course the colonia where military veterans have been given farms to retire to." Lepidus proudly told Quintus. Quintus nodded and left the office. He felt that the quartermaster really didn't answer his question. Shaking his head in bewilderment he made his way to the mess hall to meet up with his century.

The mess hall was spacious and laid out to take a good 200 men at a time with rows of large wooden tables set up to feed the legionaries. There were large windows with shutters pulled back to let in the surprisingly soft spring air from outside, metal sconces holding torches set between the windows to light the room. The room rumbled with the deep voices of the soldiers, interspersed with a laugh and the clink of eating spoons as the men ate their evening meal of hardy stew. The mess hall slaves were dishing out the meal with typical military skill as the soldiers continued to fill past the cookpots. Inside the mess hall Quintus saw his century had taken up two rows of tables at the back, the same tables they ate at previously. He lined up to get food and walked back to the tables taken over by his century. Stopping to greet soldiers as he went to an opening at the end of the table Quintus found his *Contuberium* and sat next to Faber and Coriaro on the end. "Did you have a productive day? Where'd they put you both to work?"

Faber nodded and in his deep bass voice said: "We worked with the engineers out on the wharves, there seemed to be the most need there. It was satisfying to work with the engineers when they designed a method to increase the stability of the wharves in anticipation of the cranes coming in seven days. They calculated the weight needed to unload ships at the docks and how to get the slaves to move the cranes accordingly. Remember they use the wheel system to move the cargo from the ships with the cranes. Slaves turn the mechanics by walking within the moving wheel at the back, they use that energy to lift the crane arm up and out to the ship and back again[19]." Faber was so impressed with the crane system he tried to explain the system to Quintus who had no interest in the engineering aspect., He was just interested in how it got done and was just interested that the cranes were working. He felt confident at trusting the engineers do the calculating and design work that they were trained to do.

Coriaro was also enthusiastic about the work the engineers were doing to shore up the embankment that was running in muddy runnels toward the river making it impossible to unload the cargo from ships. "They are setting the embankment with wooden stakes. Then will be filling in the stakes at the base with rocks and stone to make the embankment solid and not a muddy quagmire that impedes the loading and unloading of ships coming into the port. In the next seven days they should have the main embankment shored up."

---

[19] http://greaterancestors.com/ancient-ro

"Good to know the engineers are moving forward with repairs on schedule. Did you also have an opportunity to talk about siege machines which I know you have a keen interest in speaking with them about their tactical benefits?" Quintus asked.

"Not yet," said Faber "We're going to meet with the engineers we worked with later tonight. We'll ask about them then."

"Can we ask for some relaxation in the taverns with the engineers?" Coriaro enthusiastically asked.

"Since you already volunteered to work with them today I think it is appropriate for you to go have some relaxation with them," Quintus said.

Fullo heard them discussing the engineers and piped in: "So we *all* get permission to go to the taverns tonight? What about you Quintus, do you think you might also want to see the town with all of us?" Titus and Rufus were also listening to this discussion. Grex and Bundarus were the only ones still intent on eating their stew.

Quintus smiled and just shook his head: "You all can go to the taverns tonight, I have more work to do with the quartermaster first thing in the morning. I will need my wits in the morning without sporting a heavy head in the morning from the previous night's drinking. Plus I want to check on my gelding Boreas[20] in the stables."

"I suspected you would use the horse as an excuse rather than getting to better know the night life around this fort," Fullo laughed, "I'll check out the taverns with their ladies and give my report to you in the morning."

"Just be careful in your amorous engagements, you will still be needed in the morning at first light. I don't want a report later on that you let yourself get taken by more than one of the fine ladies at the tavern." Quintus grinned.

Grex took the opportunity to interject: "I'll go with you to the

---

[20] http://www.theoi.com/Titan/AnemosBoreas.html

stables; I need to check on my mount as well. I don't have a strong enough connection with him yet since he is young and silly still."

"What about you Bundarus? Are you coming with us to the taverns or will you go to the stables with Quintus and Grex?" Fullo asked.

"I would like to see some of the night life here in Britannia, I'm going with you lot to the taverns." Bundarus rumbled and smiled, his eyebrows waggling.

"Fine, all you guys just be ready for the first call at dawn and no complaints about your heads. Remember to stay close to the fort and don't go tavern hopping, save your selves for later trips with a day off when you've earned it," Quintus said. The men going to the taverns quickly cleared their bowls and left together in a group, Fullo giving Quintus a smile in thanks for letting him go. Quintus and Grex finished their meal and cleared their bowls next. They gave their bowls to the kitchen slaves to clean and left taking the *Pretoria* road directly to the stables near the largest *Porta Pretoria* gate on the north side. Quintus asked Grex about his new gelding as they walked into the stables. Grex shrugged his shoulders as they walked up to his stall: "Look at how proud he is standing there showing off his gray hide. The grooms did a good job rubbing him down. I'm proud to pick this little gelding but he has a flighty disposition that needs to be worked with.." The little gelding came up to them at the gate and pushed his nose out with curiosity to see who had come to him. They smiled as the horse blew into Grex's hands and accepted the little bit of bread Grex offered him.

"Do you always offer him treats? Kind of bribing him to look kindly upon you?" Quintus asked.

"Of course. He is not used to me yet but I want to make a good impression with him," Grex smiled as the gelding looked at him for more tasty treats, snuffling his nose into Grex's hip pouch for more. "What about your horse Boreas? You have had him for a while now and he is definitely your horse."

Quintus smiled as he looked at the dark, bay gelding, which had heard their voices and stuck his head over his gate to look at who came into the stables. "He is always attentive to my will when I ride him. We have a good connection as horse and rider. He has seen me through a lot of tense situations in Gaul and I hope to keep him busy in Britannia. It takes time to build a good rapport between the rider and his mount. The effort a good horse gives his rider is well worth the effort put forth by the rider to build that rapport. I'm glad you are taking the time to build a good bond with your mount. It shows you have a good regard for a legionnaires tools."

"I've always had a good relationships with the animals in my care. Back in Sicily I had a flock of sheep and goats that I kept. They aren't as intelligent as horses but they respond to care more than you realize. I had a lead ewe that I raised from a lamb. She would have followed me anywhere and the rest of the flock followed her. It made the work easier than it could have been. Sheep and goats are flighty, silly herd creatures that have a tendency to wander off when they spy good forage. I can't tell you how much their wandering honed my tracking skills to where they are now. There were many a time when a few would wander off and it would take all my skills to find them. Also keeping them safe from wolves kept my tracking skills sharp. The wily wolves would test me in my ability to keep the flock safe, especially at lambing time. Wolves are smarter than you think, they test your limits."

Quintus looked at Grex, never having thought about wolves as particularly smart. "What do you mean 'test your limits'? What would they do when hunting sheep or goats other than singling them out and attacking?"

Grex smiled the corners of his weather beaten eyes and mouth crinkling in amusement. "During the lambing season there is not a lot of sleep to be had but if you're a good shepherd you learn to sleep lightly. Wolves are smart and cunning hunters and in lambing season they would follow us and lie in wait at night around the flock on several sides. When a ewe would go into labor they would create a diversion in one side of the flock but would actually go after the new lamb which was their original target. It took me awhile before I realized what they were doing. The last time they tried this I stationed my herding dog on one side of the flock, I took the other side. One night there were about five ewes that were set to drop their lambs so I stayed close by them as much as possible. Pregnant ewes were uneasy because they are in labor with the lambs. One ewe moved off to the side which is what sheep do when they are getting ready to drop a lamb. On the far side of the flock I heard my dog bark and take off in pursuit of a wolf it had scented too near the flock. Here is where wolves are so cunning, while the ewe that was getting ready to drop her lamb moved to a rocky ledge that seemed to be easily defendable by the sheer drop on two sides. The other two sides had large rocks and scraggly bushes. The wolves moved into position by the scraggly bushes and rocks out of my sight. The ewe went into labor and as the way of sheep gave birth rather quickly. I was on my way to get to her when I saw two wolves move in and take the new lamb as soon as it hit the ground. They stole the lamb with a quick, stealthy nab of the neck and escaped. I was amazed at how they worked as a team to keep my dog busy going after one wolf yet still keeping their attention on their real target which was the ewe that was giving birth. I saw them work as a unit and became a grudging admirer of them. The resident wolf pact and I understood each other very well."

"I had no idea wolves were so cunning. That took an amazing amount of coordination between the wolf pack members." Quintus said, shaking his head in amazement.

Grex nodded: "That wolf pack and I had the same range area. We learned from each other. The two dominant members were grey, lithe and very sneaky. They took my measure just like I took theirs. Never underestimate you enemy."

"Sounds like you used this experience when you scouted our foes in Gaul. You always amazed me with your powers of deduction when tracking our adversaries," Quintus said.

Grex shrugged his shoulders and ran his hand over his sharp

face. "I learned from those wolves that the enemy is just as clever as I am in their own way. It is my job to see all the possibilities in tracking foes intent on our demise, to deduce the ultimate goal of the enemy. Is the foe making a move to the most obvious direction because they are fleeing or is the intent actually a feint and they will circle around behind you to come from the rear?"

"Yes, I see that the wolves trained you well. They made it easier to see all the possibilities of your foes tactics. I will remember this conversation. If we run into any enemies here in Britannia I will look to you for any clues as to their intent. I suspect with this unrest in the villages from the druids inciting dissatisfaction that we'll need to think in terms of your wily wolves," Quintus supposed.

"You could be right, or it might be they are just mad that the Romans traders offer more money to certain tribes, leaving out some of the disgruntled tribes with less advantageous trade agreements. Or it might be the simple fact that we are their invaders," Grex said.

〽〽〽〽

Fullo and his group went to "The Sailor", the tavern with the best looking women. They went into the dark interior that was already loud with soldiers taking their leisure. Inside the tavern it was smoky and crowded with soldiers who obviously knew where the good looking ladies were. The interior was very masculine and filled with tables and stools crowded together within the room. There was little room to maneuver between the tables and mass of bodies. Attractive barmaids managed to avoid the soldiers, swaying and twirling away from them to avoid getting groped by the randy soldiers. At the back was a long table where the fat, sweaty tavern owner was pouring drinks as the barmaids called out the orders to him.

"I just got an order for five more ales, Captain," A blousy red haired barmaid yelled out.

"Aye, I'll get it right now," replied the tavern owner who liked to be called Captain in 'The Sailor' in keeping with the nautical theme despite never having even gotten on a boat in his life. Fullo turned to the last empty table and grabbed a stool. The others followed his lead and filled the last stools except for Faber who was looking around the room.

"I want to find the engineers; they are supposed to meet us here at The Sailor. Let me go into the tavern and look around," Faber rumbled in his deep bass voice. Fullo just nodded and waved him on. He was looking at the barmaids and liked what he saw, especially the loud, buxom, red head. He tried to get her attention with a raised hand to get her their drink order.

A different but equally attractive dark haired barmaid moved up next to him and said: "You're in my section of the tavern, I'll take your order." She smiled in an alluring way and stood with her hand on her hip as she waited for his order. "I see you must be new to Britannia, where are you from?"

Fullo smiled in appreciation, he told her: "We are newly arrived from Gaul to Britannia. This is the first time we've been allowed to go out for drinks. We'll have six orders of wine for me and my companions." She smiled and turned on her heel to go back to order the drinks. Fullo watched her walk away with a smile. "I love when she walks away with that perky sway of her bottom."

"Fullo it doesn't take you long to move on the ladies, I'll wager you'll make your move on her before Faber and Coriaro get in embroiled in their conversation with their engineer friends," Titus laughed.

Rufus snorted and said: "I'll get in on this wager, I say Fullo is the first to leave with a barmaid tonight."

"But we all know he'll be the first to leave, I wager that I'll get a barmaid before Fullo," Coriaro said.

"Ha, I'll take that wager Coriaro, you smell too bad for the ladies. There is no way they'll take you over me," Fullo turned back to the table.

"It is a wager I'll take then. Let's see if your piss smell doesn't turn them to another better looking soldier like me," Coriaro sneered.

"I'll be the arbiter for this wager between you two," Bundarus smiled and in his ponderous way waved at them both. "No fighting, you heard Quintus this afternoon." Titus and Rufus just laughed.

"Like that will happen Bundarus, we are talking about the fighting smelly guys in this *Contubernium*," Titus smirked. Rufus just laughed.

"No they'll follow orders and keep it clean, no fighting between them," Bundarus rumbled.

"Or they'll try to give each other another broken nose, I think this time it will be a worse one for Coriaro because Fullo is too vain about his looks. He'll fight dirty," Titus said with a guffaw.

"No I think Fullo will get a cut on his big lips for trying. Is this the new wager or are we going to stay with who gets a barmaid first. What if it is me that gets the barmaid?" Rufus asked

"So this is the new wager? What if Bundarus gets the barmaid, or Faber you know he is always the sneaky one with women, he'll just over power them with his big, bulky, smith-muscled body. What say you Bundarus?" asked Titus.

"This sounds like a wager that will be fun. I feel like my chances are just as good as Fullo's chance to get a barmaid. And The Sailor does have the best looking ones," Bundarus waggled his eyebrows again.

Fullo smiled and said: "The bet is on, the first soldier of our *Contuberium* that leaves with a barmaid will be the one to win the wager. I'll put a quadrans down for it."

"Save your money for the drinks, we'll each put in an uncia, the winner will take the lot, which of course will be me," Coriaro grinned.

Later that night Fullo collected his money as he sauntered out of the tavern with the serving girl on his arm.

"Funny how it's always Fullo that gets the girl." Bundarus growled. Titus and Rufus just laughed.

CHAPTER 2
THE ISLE OF MONA

Gaius Lutatius Catullus was a handsome young *Tribunus Laticlavius*[21] in the Tenth Legion of Britannica. He sported light brown, curly hair and brown eyes and had a pleasing face. He has been in the legion only five years but had built a reputation for being harsh but fair minded. Gaius Catullus got his reputation fairly, by measuring his responses to questions and hearing out all sides of the issue before getting to his decision. As *Tribunus Laticlavius* he was the most important tribune. His ranking was directly below the general Gaius Suetonius Paulinus and was the first person Paulinus turns to for his orders to be issued. Gaius Catullus did the best he could and frequently went beyond. When Paulinus asked for a report on his legion's usage of grains Gaius Catullus included all of the commodities supply chains in the report as well. The information was much appreciated by Paulinus because of the intertwining knots of tribal preferences were included. Working

---

[21] http://dictionary.sensagent.com/tribunus%20laticlavius/en-en/
https://en.wikipedia.org/wiki/Tribunus_laticlavius

with the Celts was a landmine of bickering and complaints. If you hadn't include several sources of commodities then the legion ran into the problem of not getting that particular commodity such as grain. The gorgon knot of tribal influences colored everything in the legion. It mattered because of the men traditionally had their families pushing their tribal influences in every decision. Gaius Catullus was savvy enough to look into the recommendations of his soldiers first and could easily get the answer that way.

Nero's temporary happiness with Gaius Catullus' family worked out well. Because of his family's vast wealth and patrician status Nero had happily put Gaius Catullus forth for the *tribunus laticlavius* position in Paulinus' army. The emperor had the final say as to whether a high ranking tribune would be placed in the army. Because of Nero's good word Gaius Catullus found the way hassle-free. He had little experience in the army but used his contacts to learn as much as he could. He relied on the top level centurions for the daily running of the legions. His *Princeps Pila* was the best he'd ever worked with and learned as much as possible while serving in Gaul with him. He could rely on his expertise to get the daily grind of the legion moving in the correct manner and direction. Taking his expert opinion Gaius Catullus learned through asking questions on the complex interrelated relationships for each item. For example asking the question on what was the best grain supplier the answer was long and winding. The *Princeps Pila* answered with a long roundabout answer he had to extricate all of the lines of the answer. It turned out that the centurion Quintus Agricolanus knew of the best and most reliable line of grain was to be had by a certain supplier who was also the father-in-law of a certain low level legionary. That low level soldier had the best family for delivering grain on time. Without getting to the bottom of every question Gaius Catullus wouldn't have been half as capable as he was. He understood that the different relationships within the legion made the whole legion run smoothly. In other words not a decision could be made without the information from the centurions.

When he was transferred to Britannia and placed under the guidance of General Paulinus, Gaius Catullus got his first true experience. Under Paulinus he had the authority to do so much more. The Britannia's Celts were an unruly mess and a lot of the commodity lines of refurbishments had to be negotiated. Gaius Catullus had the dubious advantage of negotiating each of them. He learned quickly who was to be trusted and which supplier was to be avoided. There was no *Princeps Pila* to rely upon so he relied on the lower level centurions to get his information correct. For the most part he was able to negotiate appropriately and did an exceptional job of it. But he did miss the old *Princeps Pila* from Gaul who was able to give his faster and more up to date information than the lower level centurions did.

Gaius Lutatius Catullus the *Tribunus Laticlavius* was getting his officers ready for this next battle. The young and handsome tribune turned his head to regard the other two men in the tent. His curly brown hair dripped with water from the rain outside. The other two men returned his regard. The Island of Mona[22], which was the druids' epicenter was getting a battle royal. The druids[23] ruled Britannia from this small rural island. It didn't even have a building on it proclaiming its supremacy. There was nothing but a nondescript bloody alter in the middle of a forest. There were plenty of trails bisecting the island and showing where the most important places were but nevertheless there were no buildings. Everyone

---

[22] https://en.wikipedia.org/wiki/Isle_of_Man https://images.search.yahoo. com/search/images;_ylt=A0SO8w8JFn1XflUAcS9XNyoA;_ylu=X3oDMTEy NnAzdnZ2BGNvbG8DZ3ExBHBvcwMxBHZ0aWQDQjIyOTFfMQRzZW MDc2M-?p=The+Isle+of+Mona&fr=yfp-t-s

[23] http://www.timelessmyths.com/celtic/druids.html
https://en.wikipedia.org/wiki/Druid
https://images.search.yahoo.com/search/images;_ylt=AwrSbgNRFX1Xg K4Aj.FXNyoA;_ylu=X3oDMTEyNnAzdnZ2BGNvbG8DZ3ExBHBvcwMx BHZ0aWQDQjIyOTFfMQRzZWMDc2M-?p=Druids&fr=yfp-t-s

knows that the sacred site for Romans is the Optimus Maximus[24] located in Rome which had a grand temple to show it. The Optimus Maximus was dedicated to Jupiter Maximus the supreme deity to all Romans. The temple was opulent with the different marbles inlaid surrounding the elaborate alter. The lamps alone costs 70,000 sesterces to keep lit on a daily basis. The amount of slaves that it took to keep the temple clean was enough to impoverish the Catullus family which was rumored to be one of the richest families in Rome. They had a massive villa on the Palatine hill, right next to the emperors palace. Nero was lavish in his blandishments for his toadies. The parties alone cost dearly to throw. Many of Gaius' family members were regular attendees to these lavish parties. It kept Gaius in the forefront of the emperors opinion which was very favorable at this time. It was always a good thing to be considered a favorite with the emperor. Nero's parties were getting more elaborate and dangerous each day. The most recent one alone cost three million sesterces. At this rate he would bankrupt the government. There was no end in sight as he was becoming more unbalanced. Now he was building a theater that cost the government and would soon bankrupt the government if he continued at the same pace.

Gaius Lutatius Catullus, the *Tribunus Laticlavius,* was getting his officers ready for this next battle. "I think we should do well if we stick to the war plan and keep in formation. These Celts don't fight with any plan. They just get into a circle and start wielding their long swords. With no plans just acting like the Gaulic bezerkers[25]. If we keep them compressed into a smaller area they won't have any room to wield their long swords. They will effectively be deemed outclassed."

---

[24] http://www.thehelicon.com/2012/jupiter-optimus-maximus/
https://images.search.yahoo.com/search/images;_ylt=A0SO8oauFn1X0qgAHCBXNyoA;_ylu=X3oDMTEyNnAzdnZ2BGNvbG8DZ3ExBHBvcwMxBHZ0aWQDQjIyOTTfMQRzZWMDc2M-?p=Temple+of+Optimus+Maximus&fr=yfp-t-s
[25] https://en.wikipedia.org/wiki/

"What about the cavalry?" queried Gaius Saterninus Raberius his light brown hair and blue eyes flashing. "When do you want to deploy them?" Raberius was the auxiliary commander for the cavalry and kept his men at a strict level of readiness. He was a tough commander and rarely gave out compliments to his men except when they deserved it. To get any compliment from him was to be valued.

"Hold until the Celts get surrounded by their own eagerness to fight. They'll want to rush in to engage us." Gaius Catullus said.

"Hold on the left flank or the right?" Raberius asked. Raberius governs the auxiliary Scythian horsemen[26] with an iron fist and was proving it just then.

"Hold on the right. I'm reserving the left for the infantry. We have a lot of Germanic infantrymen that make a swift demise of any enemy. They are all over six feet tall with long reaches. There is a reason they are used as the Emperor Nero's Praetorian Guard[27]." Gaius Catullus said.

"Agreed." Raberius said.

"So the infantry is to be positioned on the right flank. What about in the middle?" Marcus Lentulus Hortensius asked, his wet black hair dripping into his dark eyes. He was the tribune in charge of all the infantry. At this time of the empire the infantry was a mix of Roman and foreign infantry men. The Germans in the army were given Roman citizenship if they joined the army and fought in the wars. This was done so that they could get land at the end of their service.. Marcus Lentulus Hortensius was an affable man that got along well with his troops. They loved how approachable he was. Many tribunes in this position weren't so. Marcus Lentulus Hortensius was the exception.

---

[26] https://images.search.yahoo.com/search/images; ylt=A0SO80hYGH1 XhIUA6vdXNyoA; ylu=X3oDMTEyNnAzdnZ2BGNvbG8DZ3ExBHBvcw MxBHZ0aWQDQjIyOTFfMQRzZWMDc2M-?p=Scythian+Calvary&fr= yfp-t-s https://en.wikipedia.org/wiki/Heavy_cavalry

[27] https://en.wikipedia.org/wiki/Praetorian_Guard

"Put the infantry that is primarily Roman in the middle. They will make short work of anything in their way. Their forward motion and fighting with their shields up and chopping with their swords will make the obliteration of the enemy a forgone conclusion." Gaius Catullus smiled and looked down at his maps strewn about the table. "We need to fight here," he pointed to a bowl shaped indention on the Isle of Mona. It was still in the heavily forested area. "The heavy forest will impede our battle but it's not like we don't have the right experience, we do. It will impede their ability to flee. The Germanic infantry is used to fighting in the Black Forest. They'll be able to negotiate the trees and make it our victory. The forest will make it that much harder to use the cavalry Raberius."

"It makes it difficult but not undeliverable. We can still do what is needed," Raberius murmured in his sure way.

"That's good to know." Gaius Catullus smiled.

They all looked at the map on the table. The braziers giving off a dim smoky light. Around them the slaves that acted as scribes scribbled on their wax tablets to keep the general abreast of the military planning. Normally, the General Gaius Suetonius Paulinus would be present in the war council but he was delayed by bad weather. The infernal wet weather had bogged down his carts. The message to continue with war planning had just come in earlier by courier. Gaius Catullus said: "Since the general has given his command to continue with the planning portion of this endeavor, let us conclude with the auxiliaries staying in in reserve. That way if we need to fortify a flagging flank or the middle they will be able to come in and bolster them. The cavalry will stay out of sight until needed. At this point I don't think there will be much need for them but keep them in reserve to be safe."

"Understood," rumbled Raberius.

"So you think this will be a melee. Just a bunch of barbarians fighting in mass?" Hortensius asked, unsure of hearing about the Celts for the first time and recognizing the benefits this type of fighting would give the Roman legionnaires. He knew that the Celts fighting style would be easy to conquer by keeping in formation. If the Celts lose the space to fight they will not be able wield their long swords. The tight knit legions will be able to inexorably move forward chopping with their smaller swords. They'd be able to move forward and crush the Celts in the middle. If the Celts in the back keep moving forward, it would be a very successful tactic.

"Yes I do. I've fought in Gaul and that is exactly what they did there. While the Celts in Gaul are different they probably fight the same here as they did there." Gaius Catullus pointed to the maps on the table. "We fight here and finish off the druid menace once and for all. The druids are the mouthpieces of dissent. We cannot let this continue. We must stamp out their barbarian vitriol before it gets disseminated throughout Britannia. They are the ones that go throughout the tribes and tell them that the Romans are not to be trusted. We need the local tribes to be peaceful and not fighting like they have been."

"So the druids are their priestly caste? They educate the local peoples and teach them to fight against us?" Raberius queried. Marcus Lentulus nodded as he leaned forward to hear from Gaius Catullus.

"Yes. They keep the way open for discontent and internal fomenting of the dissenting peoples. They egg on the locals to fight against us instead of accepting Rome peaceably like the Trinovantes have. Cesar was smart to negotiate with them." Gaius Catullus smiled. "It also helped that they were the governing tribe over Londinium. The Trinovantes are a reliable client tribe. Around the Isle of Mona there it is the Beaumaris, Caernavon and the Ordovices."

"And that the treaty made the Trinovantes rich beyond their heathen minds," smiled Marcus Lentulus Hortensius. Gaius Catullus barked with laughter. Just then a very wet centurion came rushing in.

"Pardon the interruption but the general just rode into fort," the centurion saluted the tribunes in the room.

"With this infernal climate it will take him time to get situated. We're pretty much done here so why not get something to eat and a little wine to drink?" He hailed the slaves waiting in the foyer. "We want some wine, onions and olives if we still have them. Bring in capons too. And some walnuts as well." The slave in his short dun colored tunic ran off to do his bidding. He returned shortly with a wine ewer and another dun colored tunic wearing slave bringing in the food. The wine was poured and delivered to the tribunes, delivered with practiced ease of longtime servitude. The slaves went to the foyer and stood to await further instructions.

"Now we'll get the lay of the land." Gaius Catullus said to the other two tribunes. He took a thoughtful drink of his wine and grabbed some olives mixed with onions to eat. He munched on the olives while he thought about the upcoming battle.

Presently a slave came into the command tent. "The general is coming and wants some wine to start with then he'll be ready for your report." The waiting slaves quickly poured wine into a large goblet for the general as he strode into the room. Gaius Suetonius Paulinus arrived. He was a tall patrician general, his dark hair was clipped short and his grey eyes scanned the room, alighting on the table with maps strewn over the surface. He impatiently wiped off his brow of the rain water that trickled into his eyes. "A towel," he barked. One of the dun tunic dressed slaves dashed forward with the linen towel. He handed it to the general then took the towel from him once he'd finished.

"Gaius Lutatius Catullus, Gaius Saterninus Raberius, Marcus Lentulus Hortensius." He nodded to each of them. "Give me your report on the battle plans." He fixed Gaius Catullus with a sharp look. "Let me know what we need to do to get the druid scourge wiped off the earth."

Gaius Catullus told him what they had already discussed. "We will fight in this bowl here," he indicated the indentation on the map in front of him. "We will take them in a formation according to Roman army tactics. Raberius' horse to take up the left flank, the Germanic infantry to take the right. In the middle we'll set the regular infantry."

"Sounds like a sound idea, very much by the book," the general looked at the map. "It looks to be heavily forested. Will you be able to negotiate the area?"

"Yes, We feel confident that we can,' Gaius Catullus answered.

"My Germanic infantry is well versed fighting in heavily forested areas. It is similar to fighting in the heavily forested parts of Germania. We are well versed in fighting in this type of place." Hortensius took a big gulp of his wine. "They are ready," he asserted.

"What about the cavalry? Can they fight in a heavily forested area?"

Gaius Raberius stepped forward. "They have experience fighting in Germania. They will be able to fight here with no problem."

"Then let's not wait. Get your men ready for the assault." Paulinus turned and took a handful of olives and walnuts to snack on. "We'll get this done as soon as possible. When we finish up here with dinner get your horse and men in position. It is only midafternoon. The sooner we get this battle over with the better." He sat down to eat. "Let's eat quickly since it is already midafternoon." Soon he finished his lunch and tossed down his wine. "Let's go."

〽〽〽〽

The head of the council of druids looked at the other men outside in the glen. The O'Shea said: "We've all had the same dream. We have a problem with the advancing Romans. They are like locusts that come and raze our crops. We know that they are amassing on the island. But to what end? My dream says they are looking for our annihilation. They will be fighting with all their might and in a strange formation. With cavalry and infantry. We also need to change our fighting style, not to get bunched up in the middle and make sure our men have plenty of room to wield their swords. We need to meet them head on to turn this scourge!" He stood there with his eyes wide and his abnormally long fingered hands holding his staff next to his body in a defensive manner. His long white hair and beard glistening with the droplets of water on them. They all stood outside in the rain. The druids were all amassed in a group open to the elements. Better to worship their gods that way.

The O'Connor stepped forward. "We need to prepare for the upcoming battle. All must be armed. All must be ready to fight these interlopers." His ruddy complexion growing even redder with his talk as he got excited. "We need to fight with all of our assets. I say we get the female druids up and chanting a spell to get rid of the Romans. Maybe the "Be Gone Menace" prayer, or the Death Prayer sent up to the *Morrigan*[28]."

Then The O'Shea stepped forward and agreed to the singing of the prayers. He was tall and lanky. His gray eyes stared out of his skeletal face making him all that more scary to look at. "They are eerie sounding prayers and will instill fear in the Roman army. They will turn tail and run away. It is a good step to take, well done."

The O'Nialle stepped forward. The smallest of the four counsel of druids he was also the most warlike. He moved his sodden salt and pepper hair out of his eyes and spoke. "We need to be blood-thirsty in this battle. The Roman army is looking for our annihilation. All strikes must be to cleave the heads of our enemy from their bodies. *Nuada*[29] is crying to get out his sword and decimate the infidels. The *Morrigan* is ready for their eyes to be plucked out of their dead bodies. You are right O'Shea that we need to change our fighting tactics. We need to disseminate the order that the

---

[28] http://www.goddess-guide.com/goddess-morrigan.html

[29] http://www.godchecker.com/pantheon/celtic-mythology.php?deity=NUADA https://images.search.yahoo.com/search/images; ylt=AwrBTze7HX1XMQYA9Q5XNyoA; ylu=X3oDMTEyN3UxdnFkBGNvbG8DYmYxBHBvcwMxBHZ0aWQDQjIyOTFfMQRzZWMDc2M-?p=Nuada&fr=yfp-t-s

fighters are not to be grouped so close so that they can wield their swords more effectively. I think we'll be able to fight the Romans. Woe be to their names and their children's names." He turned to the waiting assistant druid and gave the order for the women druids to start singing.

The O'Reilly stepped forward. He was the youngest of the high druids on the council and his long black hair fell to his mid back. He was tall and gaunt but was the most contemplative of the council. He preferred to spend his time ruminating on the gods and their meanings in nature than in war. He was the most reticent of all of them in this endeavor. "Do we really need to do this? The Roman war machine is world renown for their successful tactics and aggression."

The O'Shea just looked at the O'Reilly with a withering look. "It must be done. They are coming to us and we must retaliate."

With that the druids broke up and ran to their weapons cache[30]. The women druids started their prayer and sang it to *Nuada* and the *Morrigan*. The sound was eerie, lots of moaning and gnashing of teeth. Occasionally they would rend their cloaks and strip down to their skin despite the chill in the air. The rain continued to pour adding a despairing atmosphere to the whole picture. They lined themselves around the inner lake of the island. It was small but was deep and sacred to *Arnemetia*. They ringed the lake and clasped their hands. Their cries were very discordant and frightening.

The rest of the druids painted themselves with woad pigment in swirling glyphs on themselves. They stripped down to their loin cloths. The more woad pigment they put on themselves the more likely their prayers would be answered by the Celtic gods. They prepared several war chariots. They painted their horses as well, mostly on their flanks and legs, the places that horses were most

---

[30] http://www.weapons-universe.com/Swords/Ancient_Celtic_Weapons. shtml http://www.weapons-universe.com/Swords/Ancient_Celtic_ Weapons.shtml http://www.ancientmilitary.com/celtic-warriors.htm

vulnerable to injuries. Their spells would block any spear thrusts against them. Pretty soon a rising mist cloaked the field. The druids were ready for the Romans. They stood there in the preternatural gloom and waited. Word was disseminated to all those fighting to not get bunched up and to allow for plenty of space to wield their swords. The fighters smiled at the bit of intelligences from the druids. They were sure to win now.

回回回回

The Romans came upon the eerie scene. Some of the horses were restive from the moaning and chanting. The wispy fog and heavily forested areas made for shadows that caused the horses to spook easily. It took the cavalry time to settle down their horses. The eerie moans and yells made it even worse for them to keep the horses in check.

"Keep in formation!" barked Gaius Raberius. He was also discomfited by the strange chanting that the druids did. "Keep on the flank like you are supposed to! No frittering away like a bunch of women. You are soldiers first and foremost!"

The infantry was also disconcerted by the moaning and chanting. They started to murmur among themselves. Until Quintus told them to shut it and stay in formation. "Quit acting like a lot of girls with their under garments in a twist. Be men and be soldiers! Get back in formation."

Fullo turned to Quintus and said under his breath with a smirk on his face. "You got to be kidding me! A bunch of naked women moaning and yelling will need to be fucked and then killed afterwards for the stupid chanting."

Titus grinned and laughed uneasily. "That's the way to look at the skinny bitches up there ringing the lake. Just a bunch of women looking for some nookie."

"Hush and keep your places in formation," belted out Bundarus. He was always the first to keep everyone's eyes on the battle at hand. He had an uneasy feeling that today would be his last day on earth. He had his auspices read before leaving Italy. The oracle said he'd be killed by a Celt. "Keep in line and watch yourselves."

"We will," murmured Rufus. He also had an uneasy feeling about this assignment. They were told to kill all of the druids and not keep any for slaves. The druids were deemed too dangerous even to make them into slaves. "Pity we can't keep the women. They'd make decent bed warmers. We'll just have to rape them all and then put them to the sword."

"Pity to lose the money from not selling them as slaves," Faber muttered as he looked out over his shield. All of the *Contubernium* was in line in the middle of the formation. They were all in the front of the formation so they would definitely see action. Faber looked over at Coriaro who gave him a nod of determination.

Coriaro said: "I'm looking forward to getting some of the women to shut up that infernal caterwauling. My head is beginning to hurt over the stupid chanting."

Grex grinned and said: "I will personally fuck the daylights out of the women after we kill the Celts standing there with all those silly blue men[31]. Look at them they are just standing there and glaring at us."

"Quiet you sods. Be prepared to march forward as soon as the signal is given." Quintus felt sweat run down the back of his neck at the time. He was also feeling uneasy just like everyone in his *Contubernium*. But he couldn't show it being their centurion. He had to follow orders. Just then he saw the signal and he called to those around him. "Shields up and move forward now." They began to move slowly forward to engage to enemy. Just as they started

---

[31] https://www.google.com/search?q=Celts+with+woad+designs+painted+on+them&tbm=isch&source=univ&sa=X&ved=2ahUKEwjdjKHAvK3kAhVOIqwKHRR-C0sQsAR6BAgIEAE&biw=1034&bih=630 https://loraobrien.ie/celtic-woad-an-authentic-resource/

marching the Celts let out bloodcurdling yells and began to run at the line of Roman soldiers.

The Celts were the first to draw their swords and started wielding them in great arcs. They crashed into the line of soldiers and started hacking with abandon. The first line of infantry on the right went down under the onslaught. Their heads cleaved from their shoulders. At the first heads cleaved from Roman soldiers the Celts redoubled their effort and pressed forward. Infantry soldiers took the place of the fallen comrades smoothly with no let up, they just moved up and replaced those lost in line. Getting closer however worked against the Celts as they bunched up preventing them from doing the wide swings needed with their long swords. They began to run into the inexorable movement of the Roman line of shields. The Roman infantry then used their shorter *pila*[32] to start fighting in short jabs. Using their gladius[33] they also slashed and jabbed at the druids. Inexorably they began to decimate the Celts.

Paulinus turned to Gaius Catullus. "Just as I predicted. They are losing now and will be quickly silenced from now on." He preened in the saddle on the top of the ridge. Gaius Catullus smiled. He also felt uneasy when they first began. The druid women started keening even louder now that the Celts had engaged the Roman army in battle. It sounded horrible to hear. All he wanted to do was go down into battle and subdue the caterwauling women. He signaled to his retinue to go to battle. Paulinus nodded his approval. "Go down and stop that infernal whining that those women druids are doing. Kill them all!"

---

[32] https://romanmilitary.net/tools/pilum/ https://images.search.yahoo. com/search/images;_ylt=AwrBTz9kIn1XDKwAcIZXNyoA;_ylu=X3oDMT EyN3UxdnFkBGNvbG8DYmYxBHBvcwMxBHZ0aWQDQjIyOTFfMQRz ZWMDc2M-?p=Roman+Pila&fr=yfp-t

[33] http://www.strongblade.com/history/romangladius.html https://images. search.yahoo.com/search/images;_ylt=A0LEV19AI31XbNcAwmNXNyoA;_ ylu=X3oDMTEyN3UxdnFkBGNvbG8DYmYxBHBvcwMxBHZ0aWQDQjIy OTFfMQRzZWMDc2M-?p=Roman+Gladius+History&fr=yfp-t-s

Gaius Catullus turned his charger for the battle and made his way up the right flank. The Germanic infantry quickly made room for him while they mowed down to the Celts on the right flank. The close set trees didn't deter them at all. Gaius Catullus quickly made his way to the women druids and started to finish them. He stabbed the first one with his javelin from horseback. She died instantly. Her fellow druids broke off their chanting and started screaming as more Germanic infantry followed Gaius Catullus' lead. They started grabbing the naked women and started raping them. They finished quickly and then killed them.

Seeing this the O'Shea saw the actions of Gaius Catullus and the Germanic infantry men. The O'Shea moved his war chariot towards them at full speed, knocking the Celts in the middle from their bunched up area. He roared as he drove his team. "Space yourselves for the fighting so you can wield your swords!" The Celts turned and started to spread out like they were supposed to do in the beginning. Gaius Catullus' horse heard the loud roaring and shied. The abrupt movement unseated Gaius Catullus who went crashing to the ground making him lose his *pilum* and *scotus* or shield. He also lost his sword which fell from his hands and out of his reach. In reaction to the unseating the closest Germanic Infantry moved to shield him. At this time Quintus and his *Contuberium* had reached the same area. Quintus saw the O'Shea wheel his war chariot[34] and come back to mow down Gaius Catullus. He heaved his *pilum* which clove through the wheels of the O'Shea's war chariot. The chariot abruptly turned sideways as it crashed into more Celts taking them out as well as taking out the O'Shea. All of them killed. As Gaius Catullus stood up he was in the sights of the O'Connor. The O'Connor turned and swung his long sword from his war

---

[34] https://en.wikipedia.org/wiki/Celtic_warfare https://images.search. yahoo.com/search/images; ylt=AwrBT7xWJH1XQhcAJDVXNyoA; ylu= X3oDMTEyN3UxdnFkBGNvbG8DYmYxBHBvcwMxBHZ0aWQDQjIyO TFfMQRzZWMDc2M-?p=Celtic+War+Chariots+With+Iron&fr=yfp-t-s https://en.wikipedia.org/wiki/Scythed_chariot

chariot at Gaius Catullus cleaving him in the buttocks, all the way to his hips. Gaius Catullus cried out and fell like a marble pillar knocked over by an earthquake, suddenly and without warning. Quintus saw the whole thing and got out from behind his line of *scutum*[35]. He left his relatively safe place and rushed to the scene. He engaged The O'Connor in hand to hand combat, at a disadvantage because The O'Connor was still in his war chariot. He hacked at the horses, clipping their legs rendering them lame. They screamed in pain and reared as much as they could, quickly getting entangled in their tresses. The war chariot twisted and fell over. The O'Connor leapt from the war chariot and landed on his feet. He took the forward momentum and pressed Quintus. Quintus parried the blows and found an opening when The O'Connor pulled back his arm to do another wide wielding slash of his long sword. Quintus took advantage of his stretched out swing to stab at his belly, then he jerked the sword upward. The O'Connor stopped with a surprised expression on his face and quickly keeled over. Quintus then turned to the other Celts that had descended upon him. Two blue painted Celts wielded their swords at Quintus at the same time. Quintus parried the blows with his *scutum* and *gladius*. He managed to knock one of the Celts to the ground with his sword thrust and pushed the other over. Then he leapt in to stab the first one with his sword. He knocked the other with the edge of his scutum and broke his neck.

The O'Nialle rode his war chariot into the fray around Quintus. He engaged him with pounding, slashes from his long sword. Quintus had a hard time recovering. He quickly turned and shoved his *pila* into the spokes of the war chariots' wheels ending its momentum forward and quickly made it possible to fight with The O'Nialle, one on one,. Quintus was at a disadvantage of having the Celt fighting from higher ground. They parried back and

---

[35] http://www.historynet.com/roman-gladius-and-scutum-carving-out-an-empire.htm http://romanobritain.org/8-military/mil_roman_soldier_shield.htm#.V30ltM_6u70

forth, slashing, meeting their swords with *scotum*, with *gladius* and long sword, sparks flying. At one point The O'Nialle leaned far out of his war chariot and ended up stepping down from it. They continued to fight. Parry, thrust, long overhanded slashes from the O'Nialle. Short jabs from Quintus. Eventually Quintus got up under the shield held by The O'Nialle and pierced his ribs. The O'Nialle quickly backed up. The wound wasn't life threatening but it was bad enough to hurt. The battle was winding down and the druids were getting the worst of it. The O'Nialle looked around in dismay and saw what was going on. He quickly made the decision to run and departed the battlefield. Quintus let him go and turned his attention to other things.

To the side entered The O'Reilly in his war chariot. He wasn't as sure of what to do so he just pressed forward and began to engage the soldiers. The soldiers cut his horses' Achilles tendons and rendered them lame. The horses screamed in pain and tried to bolt but to no avail. The war chariot upended dumping out The O'Reilly. The soldiers converged on him and quickly took him out, killing him quickly.

◇◇◇◇

The immediate area around Gaius Catullus was cleared as the rest of his *Contuberium* caught up with Quintus and surrounded the tribune. They saw how grievous his wounds were. "We need to get the surgeon over here as soon as possible," Bundarus ground out. He quickly took off in the direction of the onsite surgeon unit where the surgeon was held in reserve just for this type of thing. The surgeon was Egyptian of the best caliber because everyone knew that Egyptian doctors were the best with the most up to date techniques. Amenhotep, the Roman surgeon returned with Bundarus and went to work on Gaius Catullus immediately.

"You have a broken hips and a nasty slash on your buttocks. We will need to get you to my tent to get the blood under control.

You're losing too much out here." Amenhotep said in his quiet efficient way. He shook his head that had elaborately braided hair, the braids tight to his head and streaming down his back. There were colored beads and bells interwoven in his braids that made a musical sound when he tossed his head which he did on a regular basis to get his braids out of his face. He expertly recruited Rufus and Bundarus to pick up Gaius Catullus by the shoulders and follow him in the midst of the fighting back to his surgery tent. Once they got him there after a few close calls. He asked them to lay Gaius Catullus on his stomach. He got to work quickly to staunch the blood pouring out of the wound. Gaius Catullus was grimacing from the pain.

"Can't I have some medicine for the pain?" he gasped.

"Let me get the elixir mixed and I'll administer it to you," Amenhotep murmured quietly. The din of the battle could clearly be heard around them as well as the injured being brought to the surgeon's tent. Their moans were just as loud as the ruckus of the battle. Amenhotep quickly turned and mixed his potions. He returned with a deep red syrup for Gaius to take. "This is extract from poppies. It will make you feel much more comfortable. Take it." Gaius quickly drank down the elixir. Then Amenhotep went to work as soon as Gaius' face smoothed out his grimace.

"That is powerful stuff. I think I'll go to sleep now." Gaius' eyes rolled back into his head as he passed out.

"You can return to the battle field. I have a lot of work to do with this ones wounds." He turned to Gaius and probed at the sword gash. He lifted the muscled to align it with its other side. As soon as he released it the wound gaped open again. The bleeding was still copious and he had to get it under control. Rufus and Bundarus quickly exited the surgeon's tent and went back to the battle. Meanwhile Amenhotep got out his instruments that he used for Cesareans extractions and grabbed a small pump that is used to stop blood loss. He affixed the round pad to the area which started to pull out the blood. He left it on as he worked the pump with his foot. He stamped on the pump which pulled out more of the blood.[36] Amenhotep did his for several more times before he quit. Then he revaluated the wound. The blood was clean and no longer dark and dirty looking. Amenhotep then put the muscles back into alignment and proceeded to stitch it up. He put in one hundred closely spaced stitches, half of them within the muscle itself. He used sheep sinew to stich the muscle together and more to adhere the skin.

When he was done he turned his attention back to the broken hips. He aligned the hips as well as he could making sure they were square and his legs were the same length. Then he got a brace to immobilize Gaius Catullus' hips and back. Amenhotep knew Gaius Catullus would recover but it would be months before he could return to full strength. He'd be bedridden for a minimum of six months if not more depending on his recovery. Now the thing to watch for was infection. Amenhotep poured honey all over the stiches. He quickly bandaged up the wound. He'd look for signs of the wound being tainted which was his greatest worry. Not to mention that this patient was a high level officer in the army, just under the General Paulinus. His responsibility was quite high to keep him well.

General Paulinus witnessed what happened to Gaius Catullus but also saw the quick work that Quintus did and how his *Contubernium* came to Gaius' rescue. He made a note to himself to reward Quintus after the battle was over. Which it seemed to be finishing up as the last of the druids were being decimated. Raberius' cavalry had entered the battle. They arrived from the left flank and mowed down the druids as they came in. It was a devastating blow to the Celts. They were razed from the earth with overwhelming efficiency. One moment the Celts were fighting with the infantry then the next they were laying on the ground after the

---

[36] https://www.jems.com/articles/supplements/special-topics/putting-clamp-hemorrhage/stop-bleeding.html

cavalry came through. Not a single one moved. The death rate was impressive. Soon there were no more druids in the eerie afternoon. It took three hours. Once the dead were tallied up only twenty-four Romans had lost their lives. There wasn't a single live druid left on the Isle of Mona.

⌧⌧⌧⌧

General Paulinus went to the surgeon's tent to check on Gaius Catullus. He was informed that Gaius was seriously injured but was expected to live barring the wound festering. He'd be out of service for the next six months minimum. Amenhotep informed the general that he would need extensive physical therapy to regain his mobility. "He has broken his hips. This is serious but it is not life threatening and can be healed. He needs to be immobilized for a minimum of six months. After that he will have to go through therapy to regain his muscles."

"When will he wake up?" asked the general.

"I gave him enough poppy that he'll sleep through to the morning. I hope to keep him sedated for the next week because of the pain," Amenhotep answered. He threw back his head and his braids tinkled musically. His tunic was stained brown from all of the wounds he'd been tending to. "For the most part there are only thirty-three wounded, including Gaius Catullus. That is pretty good considering the ferocity the Celts fought. It was as if they knew the plan was to decimate them."

"Yes I know what you're talking about." Gaius Suetonius Paulinus smiled. "They were no match for our military might though." He wiped his face with an already sodden handkerchief.

Amenhotep said: "Here my lord, take one of my dry towels to wipe off the pounding rain from your head." He handed a linen towel to the general.

"When will we be able to move the wounded?" the general asked.

"It would be better to go ahead and build a fort here or on the far shore line. There are twenty of the wounded that will need to convalesce and do it laying down. Best not to jostle them around." Amenhotep turned away to wash his hands out of a silver ewer. Silver having natural antibiotic properties and were universally used by the Roman army surgeons. "Excuse me, I need to boil my instruments now in cow's urine[37]. They must be kept clean."

"Carry on and good work." Then the general paid Amenhotep fifty sesterces. "You'll get a quadroon if you get Gaius Catullus out of danger of the wound festering."

"Thank you my lord," and Amenhotep pocketed the money. Amenhotep was saving up his money to buy back his freedom. He had amassed a lot so far so when he did buy it back he would be able to set up a practice in Rome. But practicing in Rome was an expensive business. He needed to amass more wealth to get his practice up and successful[38]. He hoped Gaius Catullus recovered well. Gaius Catullus was from an extremely wealthy family. It would be best to have him as a patron if he cured him. As a patron he'd be about to ask for more money as was the intended result of patronage. He'd have to spend close attention to Gaius Catullus to make sure that happened and make sure he followed his physical therapy exercises when he gets out of his brace. After six months of reclining the muscles will atrophy and need a lot of specific exercises. Amenhotep was already formulating the exercise regime he'd be in his head for Gaius Catullus.

"Keep me informed of when he is awake. I have a lot of work for Gaius Catullus to do even from the surgeon's tent. We have a lot of mopping up to do. Plus it will keep him from dying of boredom." Paulinus smiled and turned to leave.

"As you say my lord," Amenhotep bowed and turned to his

---

[37] https://www.youtube.com/watch?v=h1UqDkUJgvc
https://www.youtube.com/watch?v=k_5T3ErCqBo
[38] https://www.crystalinks.com/romeslavery.html

instruments. He began to boil the vat of cow's urine. Then he threw in his scalpels and needles that he used to sew Gaius Catullus up. He got back to his work as soon as the general left. He changed his tunic and threw the soiled one into the fire.. It needed to be thrown into the fire for cleanliness. After he had donned another undyed woolen tunic he felt better. "I will feel much better when we have built a bathhouse on the fort." Each Roman fort that was built included a bathhouse for the soldiers and that included a place for all soldiers to bathe on a daily basis. This included the seriously wounded which were under Amenhotep's care. When the bathhouse is built, Amenhotep would be assigned a small room for his medicines and will have all those who can get in the bath take a bath. It was considered hygienic for the wounded to take the baths. All Roman army surgeons adhered to this principle. Consequently they rarely had cases of festering wounds. Only the most egregiously wounded tended to get them. The ones with stomach wounds were the most likely to get the raging fevers. The surgeons knew to flush out all wounds with clear antiseptic water from the silver ewers. The recent wounded slept under Amenhotep's careful and watchful eye.

回回回回

The general then sent for Quintus and his *Contuberium*. They arrived still filthy from their battle. He smiled. "I want to congratulate you all for your quick thinking in regards to Gaius Catullus. You saved his life with your heroic actions. Quintus, I witnessed you personally killing eight Celts, including the leaders in their war chariots. I am promoting you to *Princeps Pilus*[39] of the legion for your heroic endeavors. Your *Contubernium* will be singled out as helping you in your rescue of the tribunus laticlavius, the leading

---

[39] http://military.wikia.com/wiki/Principes

tribune in the army. Because of your heroic endeavor he is going to survive barring the wound festering. Well done Quintus."

"*Princeps Pilus*? The first centurion of the legion? Am I worthy?" Quintus was stunned. He was only thirty-five and only had seventeen years' experience. Usually the *Princeps Pilus* was a veteran with over twenty-five years' experience and were grizzled veterans in their fifties.

"Your heroism is the reason for the promotion. You saved the *Tribunus Laticlavius*. You'll do fine as *Princeps Pilus*. There are plenty of centurions that can help you with decisions. I will have the ceremony later when we build our fort." Paulinus smiled again and quickly dismissed the men. He had a lot of work to do.

The *Contuberium* turned in unison and departed the tent. "*Princeps Pilus*! That is a mighty high position for you Quintus! I don't think anyone saw that coming," Fullo pounded Quintus on his back.

Quintus stood there with a bemused expression on his face. He looked at his *Contuberium* with a questioning look. "I didn't even stop to think what I was doing. I just reacted to the battle as it happened. I didn't even register that it was the *Tribunus Laticlavius*. I'd never even met him before."

"But he is the highest ranking tribune in the army. Just saving him alone will do it," rumbled Bundarus. "You saved the only person lower than the general in the army's hierarchy. Like the general said well done."

"Good on ya," said Grex. The other members of the *Contubernium* congratulated Quintus. Some more than others.

"You made the best action when you sent your spear through the tire spokes of the first Celtic leader's war chariot. Then you turned around and sent another spear you found on the ground into the second war leader. He was dead before he hit the ground. His chariot took out an additional four Celts. No wonder Paulinus promoted you to *Princeps Pilus*!" Faber gushed.

Coriaro added. "You deserved the promotion. I don't think I've seen you do so much in battle before today." He took the time to pat Quintus on the back just like Fullo did.

"Thanks, I think. It will mean more work to be done," Quintus unhappily said.

"But you are the man to do it," Fullo agreed. "We'll get no greedy sycophants getting rich over our ideas."

"Yes, and you'll save the best farms for us when we all retire," Titus smirked.

"I will be in the position to do that," Quintus agreed, nodding his head. He warmed up to the idea. "I can get all of us the best farms available. Just wait and see."

"That's the ticket," Titus laughed.

"You are the best centurion ever! I like you even better than Manlius Ahenobarbus. And he single-handedly fought off five Gauls during a battle. You out did him," Coriaro laughed with glee.

"Yes you did!" Faber said enthusiastically. "You outdid Manlius." He laughed with everyone in the *Contubernium* including Quintus as he began to like the fact that he did well during the battle.

"Now don't let it go to your head. You need to think sharp like you normally do for the next battle," Bundarus murmured in his ear. "I want you to do well for the next skirmish because you know there will be more." Quintus sobered up quickly after that. He knew that he needed to think straight for the rest of his term as *Princeps Pila*. He'd have to weigh all of his decisions, doing it quickly as each situation arose. He knew the enormity of the promotion that was thrust upon him. He quickly smiled and laughed with the others but he felt the gulf of authority widening between he and his *Contubernium*, wider than it was when he was just a centurion of the third degree like he was before. He'd be responsible for more than just his century of men. Now he'd be responsible for the whole legion. With everyone's problems the other centurions would come to him for help and guidance. The decision making alone had multiplied exponentially. Where they would build a fort would fall to him.

The next day Gaius Catullus finally woke up about midday. He was in pain but did not want to be knocked out by Amenhotep's elixir. He called Amenhotep to his bedside. "I need to talk with the centurion who saved me."

"Do you have pain? Would you like an elixir that is not as strong as the dose I gave you yesterday?" Amenhotep's braids tinkled musically as he moved his braids out of his face.

"No, I am in pain but it is bearable. I'd like my meal and then to talk with the centurion."

"As you wish my lord," Amenhotep disappeared then reappeared with his gruel for dinner. "It's not your usual dinner fair but it is filling and will get you ready for the meeting. The centurion's name is Quintus Agricolanus."

"Thank you. I'll speak with him as soon as I finish with my meal."

Amenhotep helped feed him as he laid there, spooning the gruel into his mouth as soon as possible. Gaius Catullus ate it quickly, feeling absurd that he would be spoon fed by the surgeon but relented in this situation. He finished and told Amenhotep: "I'm ready for the interview with Quintus Agricolanus."

"As you wish my lord," Amenhotep said and cleared his meal from the bedside. "Do you wish for some wine to be present while you talk?"

"Yes, that would be good," Gaius Catullus laid back and grimaced from the uncomfortable position. His backside hurt. Laying on his stomach was not conducive to talking with the dignity he was used to. "Is there any way to get me on my back?"

"No my lord, you have a grievous wound on your buttocks that is still bleeding. I will need to bleed it again later this afternoon," Amenhotep told him. "I need to give you more elixir of poppy for that procedure."

"Is that your way of telling me it will hurt like a motherfucker?" Gaius asked.

"Yes my lord," Amenhotep brushed his braids back again with his hand and smiled at Gaius Catullus' effort to find something amusing about his wound. He turned and left the tent to send a meeting request to Quintus Agricolanus. It was sent and presently Quintus showed up at the tent. He was clean and recovered from the battle. He came in and sat by Gaius' head where Amenhotep showed him. He made himself comfortable on the small fort stool, not sure how this interview would go. Amenhotep came in with a pitcher and goblets for the wine. He poured for Gaius but asked Quintus if he wanted some. Quintus shook his head. After giving Gaius his wine, Amenhotep stepped back to allow the two men to talk.

"I understand you saved me on the battlefield. My thanks to you," Gaius started out saying. "You and your *Contuberium* saved me. I have heartfelt gratitude for that act of heroism. Now I can talk to you about the acts you performed for me. I understand that you have been promoted to *Princeps Pila* by the general who witnessed your acts. That is quite the promotion for you."

"Yes my lord, it is a great honor for me," Quintus murmured still having a hard time believing it.

"I think that I can help you with this promotion. Just listen to my counsel and I'll steer you through the pitfalls and problems that are part of the promotion. You will be responsible for a lot more now than you have been before." Gaius grimaced and motioned to Amenhotep to give him more wine. After several gulps of his goblet he returned to his meeting with Quintus. "I would like to know more about you. Where do you come from? Do you have experience in farming?"

Quintus nodded. "I come from Apulia[40], near Luceria and yes I

[40] https://en.wikipedia.org/wiki/Apulia https://images.search.yahoo.com/search/images;_ylt=AwrTHQreK31X7SsAiFVXNyoA;_ylu=X3oDMTEyNn AzdnZ2BGNvbG8DZ3ExBHBvcwMxBHZ0aWQDQjIyOTTfMQRzZWM Dc2M-?p=Apulia+Region&fr=yfp-t-s

have experience farming. My father has a small farm that I helped run until I joined the army. I have experience with the vineyard, the orchard and the farming that were on the farm."

"You talk about it as if it was in the past. Does your family still own the farm?"

"Through poor management and failing crops we had to sell off the farm to the tax assessors." Quintus bowed his head, not letting Gaius see the pain in his face. Poor choices of his older brothers were the reason they had to sell the farm. His brothers had drunk up most of their shares of the farm and made poor business choices in Luceria. They were the reason the farm was sold to the tax assessor for nonpayment of taxes.

"I can tell there is more to the story, but that is for another time. I can help out if you need the money. I am very rich and owe you a life debt. But tell me of your *Contuberium*. What are they like?"

"I have a strong *Contuberium*. It is made up of strong members. I have two specialists in war machinery, Faber and Coriaro. I have a master scout in Grex. The others are strong in the ways of the army. Bundarus is the soldier's soldier. He can quote you army regulations without a problem. Fullo, Titus and Rufus are strong soldiers. They are always willing to do the utmost to further the army's orders. They do it without question. Rufus is a farmer from Picenum[41] in the north. Fullo is from Apulia but is not a farmer. He would like to invest in some businesses when he retires. Titus is by trade a carpenter from Ostia[42] south of Rome and will probably go into business as well. They are all very important to me."

---

[41] https://en.wikipedia.org/wiki/Picenum https://images.search.yahoo. com/search/images;_ylt=AwrSbgXgLH1XWQkAkfhXNyoA;_ylu=X3oD MTEyNnAzdnZ2BGNvbG8DZ3ExBHBvcwMxBHZ0aWQDQjIyOTFfMQ RzZWMDc2M-?p=Picenum+Roman+Republic&fr=yfp-t-s

[42] http://www.ostia-antica.org/ https://images.search.yahoo.com/search/ images;_ylt=A0SO8ypQLX1XffwAkaJXNyoA;_ylu=X3oDMTEyNnAzd nZ2BGNvbG8DZ3ExBHBvcwMxBHZ0aWQDQjIyOTFfMQRzZWMD c2M-?p=Ostia&fr=yfp-t-s

"They sound like a fine group of soldiers. I can help with those wishing to go into farming and any of the others who wish to invest in businesses as well. I like to hear about entrepreneurs in the army especially when we retire. There are great ideas to be made out there in the marketplace." Gaius motioned to Amenhotep for more wine. After a few more gulps he resumed his questions. "Is a farm your wish for in retirement?"

"Yes, I want a farm and would like to get one with a small orchard. We grew peaches on my farm in Apulia. I would like to grow them again in this new land of Britannia." Quintus smiled thinking back on the times when he had great memories in the orchard with his grandfather Marcus Agricolanus. His grandfather told him great stories about Britannia when he served under Julius Caesar. His greatest wish was to return to Britannia and his first love from this place. When it became obvious that Julius Caesar wasn't returning he retired to Apulia and took up his life as a farmer. He instilled in Quintus a desire to go to Britannia in his stead. Unfortunately he neglected to tell Quintus about the infernal rain that Britannia was famous for. He knew now.

"Then it's good that you are a *Princeps Pila*. That will be part of your job to parcel out the land to the retiring veterans. The other part will be to get everyone to the final place in one piece." Gaius drank some more wine. "Of course with a large number of retiring veterans and their families coming it will be an easy enough job not to worry about skirmishes along the way."

"Do you think it will be a large number?" Quintus asked.

"Most assuredly it will be a large number." Gaius Catullus said with conviction. "The veterans will be a legion size and their attending families will increase the number by a full third if not more."

"I did not know that. That makes it sound like a daunting undertaking." Quintus gulped, feeling queasy at the thought of such a grand effort to settle the veterans.

"Feel better that it will take years before we get to that time.

You'll have plenty of experience up until then to get you prepared for the undertaking." Gaius took some more wine. "Now I think that I've satisfied my curiosity of you and you may leave. I've got a procedure to endure with my surgeon and I am finally inebriated enough to take it."

"Thank you sir. I'll leave you to the capable hands of your surgeon," Quintus stood and made his way out of the tent. He felt a little sick over the new revelations that Gaius Catullus had imparted over the duties that lay ahead for him. There was a lot more to being *Princeps Pila* than he thought. He bemusedly made his way back to his tent. There was a lot to think about.

Back in the surgeon's tent Amenhotep brought the elixir to Gaius Catullus. He waited until Gaius had drunk the elixir down then helped him to void his bladder. "It will make the procedure that much more successful if it is empty." Amenhotep told Gaius. When the elixir had worked Gaius' eyes rolled back of his head and he passed out. Amenhotep went to work. He opened up the stitches then applied the pump device to Gaius' buttocks and drained the blood. He did it three times until he had a fresh blood that was clean. Then he stitched up the wound again and bandaged the area. Amenhotep continued to his hips to make sure they were still in alignment. He then checked for fever which Gaius had none. Satisfied with his work Amenhotep stepped away from Gaius Catullus. If he could keep the wound clean Gaius would be home free. He made sure to get some more watered wine set out for Gaius Catullus then left him to sleep off the poppy elixir. He checked on him periodically during the time Gaius slept.

回回回回

Quintus tried to think about all of the problems he could foresee over his promotion to *Princeps Pila*. Every time he could think about possibilities he got even more worried. There were so many small things that he had no experience doing. He hoped he would be able to work with Gaius Catullus. He seemed to be a good fellow. Time will tell.

"How'd your meeting with the tribune go?" asked Fullo.

"It was brief but good. He said he'd back you for your future business dealings. He said he'd back everyone in the *Contubernium*. Apparently he has more money than Midas had," Quintus said. He still had a perplexed look on his face. "He also said that I'd be responsible for a lot more than I thought. All of the retiring veterans and their families will be my responsibility. I will be doing this in a couple of years. The thought of being responsible for the their whole welfare is daunting. I don't think that any new items could be seen as me taking responsibility for doing them. I don't think I've got the ability to do that."

"Sure you do. I've seen you think things through and come up with great ideas," Fullo enjoined. "You will be fine at doing the duties of *Princeps Pila*." He smiled and cuffed Quintus on the arm.

"I think your hope is misplaced. I am a simple Centurion of the Third degree not *Princeps Pila* materiel." Quintus smiled sheepishly.

"Nonsense. You are the one who will be best for the job." Fullo said knowingly. "Think of the one who bested the Celts yesterday, that was a strong leader."

"That was the heat of battle. Anyone of you would have done the same."

"But we didn't. You did. And acted heroically in doing so," Fullo saw that Quintus was feeling worried about his new promotion . Now that he'd had this advancement thrown at him he felt that he was unworthy of it. Quintus was simply unsure of his decision-making for the new job. Fullo felt for him. "I know you are really unsure but do what is natural. In the next jobs make sure you follow regulations. Make sure you go with the army's decision making strategies."

"That is what Gaius Catullus said. He said I'd be fine and with experience I'll get the hang of it. I don't know how though. I'm just following orders on a regular basis. Not looking to do the more important things." Quintus looked down and folded his hands. "I guess that I'll make the decisions as best as I can. I have Bundarus to ask if I have any questions pertaining to regulations. He seems to know so much. I can always use his expertise when I need it." But he felt that was wrong. He needed to go up the hierarchy in the army before he relied on his *Contuberium* for answers. He'd just have to rely on the guidance from Gaius Catullus. Plus he will use his own innate ability to make decisions. Up until now he'd never second guessed his ability. He squared his shoulders and made the decision to move forward with his best efforts. He had to rely on himself and he would stop second guessing his decisions. "I'm ready to move on. I'll be mindful of my promotion and take the steps to fulfill its mission."

"Well done Quintus. I knew you'd be able to move forward," said Fullo feeling relieved. He wanted the confident leader he had always known and admired. He wanted to keep that Quintus bolstered up

The other *Contubernium* members filed in the tent. "Did you get a chance to talk with the *Tribunus Laticlavius* Quintus?" asked Bundarus.

"I did have a brief meeting with him. He is a nice fellow. He knows that I've been promoted to *Princeps Pila*. He offered me help to continue moving forward with all the new jobs it will entail. He is going to be sidelined for a while due to his injuries. But I'll be in contact with him during his convalescence. I'll be talking to him more," Quintus said.

"He must be grateful to you for saving him," Bundarus reiterated.

"He's grateful for all of our assistance. He said he'd be willing to finance you all when we retire. He asked about all of you. I gave him a rundown of you individually. Hopefully I included all of the pertinent information," Quintus smiled. "I think I did."

"Why did he ask for our information?" Faber asked.

"Gaius Catullus wanted to thank each of you for saving him. He knows the *Contubernium* was key to his successful extraction from the battle. He wanted to hear about you as a unit and hear about your help to save him," Quintus explained.

"I think I understand. There was so much going on that day and it happened with such rapidity. We all worked as a unit under your command. When we saw what you did we moved to your aid. And saved Gaius Catullus at the same time," Faber reasoned. "It is a good thing that we all worked together as required to finish a good military maneuver."

"They all move together for a purpose. The military is a machine that works in unison when it is well commandeered and it was well looked after." Quintus grinned at this last bit of information. That was the least of his problems. He had plenty now that he was *Princeps Pila*.

冗冗冗冗

Back in the surgeon's tent Gaius Catullus was waking up from his procedure. He was feeling discomfort but it was more from his position on the bed and not the injuries. The uncomfortable position was grating on him. It was not a dignified position. As a patrician his dignity was what he wanted on a daily basis. "Are you sure I can't be turned around and recline on my back?" he asked Amenhotep.

"Not this soon my lord. You have a grievous cut on your buttocks that needs to be allowed to heal first before we let you recline on you back. If you turn over the wound might fester, and there are your broken hips. They need to be immobilized for a while. This is the hard part of healing. You must give your body the time to heal. The general will be coming over with more duties you can perform as you recuperate that can be done in a supine position. You can complete the duties here in the surgeon's tent," Amenhotep finished his explanation patiently. He moved back his braids from his face in an unconsciously beautiful motion, letting his braids tinkle musically, the bells in his braids ringing in unison.

"When will the general come?"

"Shortly, he just left a message asking to be told when you woke from the procedure. I just sent the message." Amenhotep just said. He turned and got the wine goblet filled for Gaius without even being asked. Gaius accepted the goblet with a pained smile. He gulped down the contents. Amenhotep refilled the goblet for him. Presently the general came into the tent..

"I am glad you're up. I've got several things for you to do while you're holed up in the surgeon's tent. There were several people that didn't fight the way they should have. But due to the atmosphere created by the druids they ran off. I need you to adjudicate their punishment. They were acting cowardly not according to the Roman army way. You need to make examples of these few men. I want them to see the futility of weakness," Paulinus sniffed dismissively. "There are three men in particular that needs to be flogged for sure." Paulinus smiled an evil smile. "I hate cowards. If it was up to me I'd put them to death but a cooler head needs to reign. I want you to put them in the carcer for sure. The length will be up to you."

"Yes sir, I will adjudicate their punishments. It will give me something to do instead of concentrating on my wounds,' Gaius Catullus ground out. He grimaced again as a twinge of pain rolled through his hips and buttocks. He swiveled his hips to get more movement to his lower half and got the twinge of pain from it. He was very hurt and was just realizing how injured he was. Gaius Catullus smiled but there was pain on his face. "Let me talk to these cowards and we'll see how far they get."

"That's the spirit! That is exactly what we need now. A man who can act even though he is prone on his surgeon's bed," Paulinus smiled. He stood up and dusted off his robes. He smiled at Gaius Catullus. "It is good to see you recovering from your wounds so well. I know it is still early but the surgeon has been top notch in his attention to you. That bodes well for a full recovery."

"Let us hope so, I do not like this lying prone all of the time. It is very demoralizing," Gaius Catullus said. He groaned and tried to move his legs but felt unbearable pain in his hips.

"Buck up young man! You'll get back on your feet and on your horse soon enough. I have no doubt. I think I have the thing for you, you just need to do some mental exercises while you wait for your body to repair itself. You need to keep your mind sharp while you convalesce." General Paulinus beamed. He made as if to pat Gaius on the back but took his arm away at the last minute not being sure where to pat him would be. He looked at Amenhotep for guidance.

Amenhotep smiled and indicated anywhere on his shoulders would be best by giving the general hand motions. He then tossed his braids to make a musical tinkling of the bells in his braids. The general nodded and lightly patted Gaius Catullus on the shoulder. Gaius smiled his acceptance of the pat. He wanted to thank the general for coming to visit him and allaying his boredom. He motioned to Amenhotep that he needed some more wine and Amenhotep deftly refilled his goblet and brought it to him. Gaius gulped it down with alacrity. He needed the taste of wine to get the pain under control.

CHAPTER 3
THE PEOPLE OF GOSBECKS

The morning sun just peaked over the top of the East Ridge. The day was bright with promise of an entire unencumbered morning for Edana without errands. She had finished her chores already. Edana loved mornings like this, the new sun bright, the trees showing their lush late summer growth and the wind sending rolling waves in the grass and sedges all the way to the shoreline of her favorite lake, subtle ripples on the water. She sprang forward from the ridge where she was looking at the morning beauty with such happiness.

The sun hit the lake making the light dapple in her eyes. She had to crouch among the sedges and move quietly forward to get to the edge, hoping to start fishing and getting the midday meal for mother, father, Carrick, and her little brother Ailbe. Ailbe wanted to come with Edana to the lake but at seven years old Ailbe was a hand full. His favorite saying was: "I'll do it myself!". Plus he was still nursing a cold, was cranky because of it and way too loud. He was now her mother's problem since he was running a fever and needed to be kept at home. Edana felt bad, mother needed a break.

Since she was a healer, the village needed her now more than ever. Her father and brother Carrick would be out in the pastures harvesting the wheat and barley. They would be too busy to help her mother with help in her care of Ailbe today.

"Curse the Romans to forever have *Morrigan*[43] on their shoulders!" Edana muttered as she reached her favorite spot to fish. She quickly baited the bone hook and threw the line out into the fish hole she knew always had mullet and perch. Quietly she waited, also glancing at the surrounding grasses and sedges and taking note of the wild onion she could pick for her meal. She saw cattail and water cress growing at the shoreline. Elsewhere Edana saw chickweed and field pennycress to pick further up on the grassy ridge[44]. "Thank *Mananon Mac Lir*[45] for the bounty," prayed Edana. Now if she could just catch some fish.

Looking over the lake with the morning sun dappling the waves, the sedges thick with dragonflies, Edana wondered how things could look so fresh and beautiful. The past years have been dark. Her Faber and brother were working hard to get the farm ready for planting but they were under the Roman yoke for taxes. "Roman scum!" she muttered. They had come to their lands back in her grandfather's time with promises of trade and wealth. Since then the only ones getting wealthy were small toadying men who agreed to ridiculous terms for trade which enriched only themselves and their families but not even the other members of the

---

[43] http://www.druidry.org/library/gods-goddesses/morrigan
[44] http://www.wildfoodschool.co.uk/urban/wfsurbanguide.pdf
http://www.artofmanliness.com/2010/10/06/surviving-in-the-wild-19-common-edible-plants/
[45] https://www.britannica.com/topic/Manannan-mac-Lir https://images.search.yahoo.com/yhs/search;_ylt=AwrT6VumDYFXYMMAZy8PxQt.;_ylu=X3oDMTByNWU4cGh1BGNvbG8DZ3ExBHBvcwMxBHZ0aWQDBHNlYwNzYw--?p=Manon+Mac+Lir&fr=yhs-att-att_001&hspart=att&hsimp=yhs-att_001

Trinovantes tribe[46]. The Romans were greedy and kept taking more crops, more cattle, more land, there were even rumors of enslavement from some of the smaller villages that could no longer afford the growing demands of the tax collectors. "The next time they come we might find ourselves out of land entirely," Edana mumbled, pushing a loose flying strand of her blond hair out of her mouth. She took the moment to braid her hair back from her beautiful smooth face, her grey eyes squinting in determination.

A tug at her line redirected her thoughts from her musings. She deftly hooked the fish and pulled in a large perch. "Good, something finally going right, thank the gods." Edana quickly unhooked the fish, set it aside and caste the line with more bait, knowing that fish were hungry this time of the morning. She settled back for more waiting and returned to her musings.

Her mother Bebhinn, the only healer in the area had her worried. She worked so hard as a healer for their village and surrounding areas. Her younger brother Ailbe was an unexpected blessing for mother and her said he was a blessing from the Gods, called him a Beltane[47] baby since he was conceived during that glorious celebration of rebirth. His birth was hard and they weren't sure he'd make it to his first year celebration because he was small and frail yet her mother never doubted it. But what a wonder he was as he proved to everyone by making it through that first tough year and blossoming into the little warrior he was now. Ailbe was still small and pale but no longer the frail baby he was that first year. Edana loved listening to his big stories. He loved to recount exciting things that happened during his day. Yes, truly a Beltane blessing.

Mother, Edana's heart stuttered a moment as she watched the dragonflies dance amid the cattails. The amount of skirmishes between Romans and Celts had been on the increase resulting in

---

[46] http://www.britainexpress.com/History/prehistory/trinovantes.htm

[47] https://wicca.com/celtic/akasha/beltane.htm
https://en.wikipedia.org/wiki/Beltane

the upsurge of men and women wounded and needing her medical expertise,. The meeting of the two groups was always tense but now it devolved into fighting outright. The ones that got the living daylights beaten out of them was the Celts. They simply were out- classed strategically. The Romans worked as a unit whereas the Celts tended to fight as individuals. The combined effort that the Romans performed tended to make their assaults much more successful than the Celts..

Edana's uncle came back from a skirmish between the Romans and the Trinovantes with significant wounds to his left arm. The one carrying his shield was smashed by a Roman cavalry man's sword. The downward swing had obliterated the small wicker shield of her uncle. By the end of the summer he had lost all movement in that arm. Through the tireless tending of Bebhinn he was able to keep the arm and not lose it as she feared but it was a lifeless appendage.

Other men also needed her healing expertise and took a lot of her efforts. Edana did not get to see her much the following months as more men returned home with injuries from the indiscriminate skirmishes with Romans. Most were cuts and broken arms or legs that needed tending but others were more serious sword swipes and spear jabs. The resident smith lost his right arm in a skirmish and almost died. Now the village did not have a working smith to fix even everyday objects for farming such as plows, scythes or axes[48]. Even some of the farmers that did return came without limbs so they did not have the ability to bring in their crops. More families had to let the land go fallow because there wasn't enough manpower to bring in the crops. That will make the coming winter particularly hard

---

[48] https://www.facebook.com/TheCelticForge https://images.search. yahoo.com/yhs/search;_ylt=AwrTca.6EIFXMYUA8aUPxQt.;_ylu=X3oDM TByNWU4cGh1BGNvbG8DZ3ExBHBvcwMxBHZ0aWQDBHNlYwNzYw--?p=Celtic+Smithy&fr=yhs-att-att_001&hspart=att&hsimp=yhs-att_001

because not enough grain and hay for the livestock had been put aside. If it is a harsh winter there will be famine indeed.

Four more fish were quickly caught bringing the morning's catch to five. Fishing done Edana quickly gathered the watercress and cattails from the lake side. Further up the hill she gathered the wild onion, chickweed, watercress and field pennycress for their midday meal. Wrapping the fish up and bundling and the greens in mats she quickly wove from the extra cattail leaves she turned for home. She carried the fish and greens as she headed over the rise and moved through the wood to their farm which was a good walk away. The late summer bounty was evident in the thick growth of the elms, chestnut and oak, Edana took note of the burgeoning chestnuts for later harvesting. When she crested the last rise she saw her farm laid out in the late morning splendor, the droplets from last night's rain shining from the leaves in the lining hedgerows of blackthorn, hazel and oak. The farm was large with several fields gleaming, their crops of barley and wheat glowing golden in the late morning light. The farm house itself was a curious round building with a long entryway, a thatched roof setting on top like a wizards hat and white stucco encircling the bottom[49]. It was snuggled within several large trees of oak, elm and larch. Beside the farm house was a gnarled shrubbery and small building for the chickens and ducks next to the farm house. Chickens ran around pecking at the ground in effort to find more food. She looked at her goats wandering in their high pasture close to the house she saw Ailbe who tended to them, steering them towards the inner milking shed that was located next to the chicken coop. *He must be feeling better* mused Edana.

---

[49] https://images.search.yahoo.com/yhs/search;_ylt=A86.J3aeEYFX8BYA6SgPxQt.;_ylu=X3oDMTByNWU4cGh1BGNvbG8DZ3ExBHBvcwMxBHZ0aWQDBHN lYwNzYw--?p=Celtic+Farms&fr=yhs-att-att_001&hspart=att&hsimp=yhs-att_001

"Enough dark thoughts of the Romans, time for the living now," Edana told herself as she trudged home.

"Edana!" Ailbe's happy but hoarse squeal met her as he saw her walking up on the lane, he rushed out in greetings. "Where did you go, what did you get, did you get blest by *Mananan Mac Lir*?"

"Yes five times over by the look of it., her mother Bebhinn said from the doorway of the farm house. "And I see you got some greens to go with the fish, very good," Her mother moved out from the house, her eyes looking tired in the morning light. Not surprisingly since she had been out all night at a birthing for their neighbor Liadan.

"How was the birth? You were gone since yesterday afternoon," Edana asked.

"The first child is frequently more difficult to birth but Liadan was blest with a new baby girl. Summer is always the best time for births, food is plentiful and the mother can recover quickly." Bebhinn replied. She sighed with fatigue and rolled her shoulders. Despite the heavy circles under her eyes Bebhinn looked good, her regal face smoothed as she looked at Edana. "I'm glad you were able to get the midday repast, I did not want to go searching for greens this morning with Ailbe, getting over hid cough. He's doing better but I didn't want to bring him outside to get wet in the damp grass. You know how he is." She lovingly patted his head despite his hand waving her away.

"I do know and that is exactly why I did not take him with me to fish! All his chattering would have frightened all the spirits and fish away."

"No I would have been quiet and helped you fish Edana!" Ailbe croaked. "I'm feeling much better and wanted to go with you," His showed her a disgruntled look at being left behind.

"Yes and wet, you can't help yourself around the lake without getting at least your feet wet, most likely all of you would be dunked in a thrice," Edana laughed. She loved her little brother no matter what mischief he'd get into, it was part of growing up.

They turned from the long entryway and went to the outside hearth where Edana unpacked the food. "Is there any news from the village?" Edana asked, looking at her mother.

"Not good news I'm afraid. It is said that large tracts of the fallow land has been given to some Roman veterans. Seems our village is now to be a new colonia[50] like Camulodunum. Word has it they are supposed to start coming within the next few seasons," Bebhinn said with a resigned look on her handsome face, she tucked her red hair shot through with white back behind her ears.

"What about the families that owned the land? Are they going to be paid for the loss?" Edana sharply asked, more upset because her best friend Meadghbh's farm was one of those left fallow since her father and brothers were killed in a skirmish with the Romans. Her older sister Brenna was just married to an older man in the hope that wouldn't happen this summer and her new husband would be able to help farm their land.

"Not that I know of but that is the Roman's strategy. They see the work put in and take the best without any recompense! I am so sorry for your friend's family," Bebhinn replied sadly. She reached up to smooth Edana's hair back from her face. "We will be fine though. There are more good people in the village that will help us,. Bebhinn said their unspoken worry of their own lands now. Last year's harvest was ruined because of all of the rain. Edana knew they also had the shadow of Roman greed looking at them. Their farm was one of the larger ones and butted up against a shallow meadow where their wheat and barley grew. Next year's tilling and planting will be very difficult this spring. Their plow was heavy and their oxen slow and difficult to lead. Unfortunately that will leave two more fields fallow. Her mother's plot of garden vegetables and medicinal plants took the remaining time between the two them to keep weed free and tended properly. Bebhinn's knowledge

---

[50] https://www.britainexpress.com/History/roman/colonia.htm
https://en.wikipedia.org/wiki/Colonia_(Roman)

of medicinal plants were known throughout the settlements in the area and in great demand especially now. Her supplies were low of agrimony to stop bleeding, comfrey for spreading on wounds and poultices for bruises, sprains and dislocations, vervain and feverfew for fevers and headaches and coltsfoot for coughs because they were needed on an almost daily basis. There never seemed to be enough time in the day to get all the chores done.

"If father and Carrick go away to fight, do you think we'd be able to keep up the farm?" asked Edana.

"No, our neighbors will help, we only have to ask," her mother replied smiling wearily.

Edana looked at her mother skeptically. Even if they asked there was so many men and women not returning home there wasn't that many able bodied people to help out. No one was able to come in and help, even their farms were feeling the pinch of not enough laborers. Families had to deal with their own farms and pay their own tax levies. Edana shook her head and focused on the midday meal preparation. Her mother was a hopeless optimist. Especially in these trying days it was hard to see her viewpoint without feeling bitter. Edana needed to be more like her mother in that respect.

"Edana, I want to have my fish grilled with the watercress! Let me help you do it" Ailbe interrupted her thoughts with a burst of childish energy, yes it seemed he *was* getting over his cold.

"Come my little man, I'll help teach you how to prepare the fish and of course you'll eat it with watercress, as well as the cattails, wild onions, field pennycress and chickweed, all to fill that bottom-less pit of your growing boy tummy!" Ailbe laughed and followed her to the fire pit outside. She made quick work of cleaning the fish and letting Ailbe pull the entrails out. Once they were ready she showed him how to arrange in the pan for grilling. Her mother had collected the greens Edana had picked earlier and was preparing them for cooking. The cattails, watercress, wild onions and field pennycress all entered a pot to be boiled together and she added salt and additional herbs for flavor.

Ardan and Carrick came in from the fields, sweaty and hungry. "I see you were successful in your fishing today." Ardan said.

"The fish were very hungry this morning. As soon as I put in my hooks with bait they took them," Edana said. "Now look at the bounty!" Ardan and Carrick both grinned. They dug into the midday repast.

When they finished the midday meal Ailbe deemed it particularly good because of his contribution to the preparations. Ardan and Carrick returned to their work in the fields. Bebhinn and Edana gathered their gear to start harvesting their garden. Most plants were ready to be harvested now and in the next few weeks and they needed to get a start on them before they had to harvest their grain at the end of the season. Since it was just the two of them to do it they were more hard pressed to do it all. In the garden with Ailbe also was a problem because he frequently interrupted them when he asked to help or to go do something more manly like hunt down rabbits for dinner. After an hour of his bugging Edana gave up and took him off to hunt. Her mother just laughed and continued her work.

Once out of the garden Ailbe danced along the trail and didn't stop talking: "Edana, there are always rabbits around the upper meadow beside the birch trees, we should go there first. They are probably eating the clover and dandelions up there."

"Yes we'll go there now but you must stop talking so loudly, you'll scare them all back into their burrows. We'll set snares on their trails to catch them where they go; you must pay attention to what I say because soon this will be your job. Watch were I set the snares." Edana said, as they trudged up the meadow to the warren. After about a mile they arrived as the upper meadow in time to see the rabbits dart down their burrows because of their approach and of Ailbe's cry of "There they are! I was right."

In exasperation Edana picked up Ailbe and tickled him, "Yes you were right, now let's lay some snares." She set him back down and went about to find the best places to set their snares and after two hours and set four. Ailbe was beginning to flag so Edana picked him up, put him on her back and trudged back home for a nap. Along the way she picked dandelions and clover for a summer salad later. When they got back home, she laid him in his bed for a quick nap and then headed back to the garden to her mother.

"We might have a rabbit dinner tonight. I'm not counting on it since the rabbits were terrorized by Ailbe's loud voice. But you never know, he is a Beltane boy so maybe *Mananan Mac Lir*[51] will bless us tonight." Edana told her mother as they met in the field. They worked in companionable silence for a while picking the ripening vegetables and herbs. At the end of the row they gathered their produce and herbs then headed back home. As they came around the bend toward home Edana caught sight of her uncle Cathmore, her Faber's brother coming up the lane, his long lanky frame loping up the drive as he hailed them. "Well hail Uncle! What news do you have for us this day?" Edana asked happy to see him.

Cathmore smiled at his favorite and only niece, "My left arm is still not working but I do well enough. The only news I have is we are planning Samhain's[52] festivities and need your service to be a mummer[53] to offer appeasement for those that have passed this year. It is an important job as there will be a lot of troubled spirits . We will need a good mummer to draw away the unwanted and malevolent spirits abroad that night Edana."

"That is a great service to be done Edana," Bebhinn said, "There will be an unnaturally large amount of restless spirits abroad at that time. The danger could be very real to you but if you do this the reward could be equally great."

"I never really considered being a mummer at Samhain, that

---

[51] http://manannan.net/whois/

[52] http://paganwiccan.about.com/od/samhainoctober31/p/Samhain_History.htm

[53] http://www.merriam-webster.com/dictionary/mummer

is usually a young man's job. Are there no others able to do it?" Edana asked.

"No there is not. Most of the men and boys who would normally do this are gone Edana." Cathmore smiled sadly, "We are asking the young women who are left like Meadghbh, Eilis and Sadhbh. All of them have agreed so far to be mummers. Be aware the danger is real. The sheer amount of the dead will be great but if your heart is pure and we offer the correct amount of appeasement the spirits will be satisfied and leave the land for their darker shores of the afterlife." Cathmore said urgently, "Please give this great consideration and give me you answer when you have thought about all the possible ramifications." He straightened his tall body and rubbed his left arm. The dangling arm looked much more withered than the last time Edana had seen him.

She looked at him and said" "What exactly are the ramifications?"

"The spirits will try to lure you away. Since the veil between the worlds are at their thinnest the night of Samhain, they will try to lead you astray and get you to do what is the wrong thing. Even lure you away to their domain of death and destruction," Cathmore murmured, his white blond hair looking even more drab than usual.

"What about the others who have already agreed, Meadghbh, Eilis and Sadhbh? Do they know all the ramifications too?" Edana asked.

Cathmore replied: "Yes, going mumming in pairs it is best. Two are harder to lure away than only one. I know all of the girls are your friends but if you agree that will make it an even number so two groups can go pacify the spirits instead of just one. You'll be able to cover even more area in the least amount of time."

"Then I will do it." Edana said.

Cathmore smiled: "I knew we could count on you. Now you must spend the time to create your mummers disguise so the spirits cannot see you as Edana but another of unknown origin. They cannot follow you in their rage at being killed back to your family.

I know that burdock leaves are particularly noxious to them so start gathering them now so they will be dried by the time Samhain comes around. Also sheaves of wheat make a good head dress for disguise. If you have any questions just ask me or your mother."

"I will do that Uncle. Do you wish to eat your end of day meal with us? I have some rabbit snares to check but I'm confident Ailbe and I set them in the right rabbit trails."

"Ailbe helped set the snares huh? I would like to see if they are correctly set and if he did get one I will share that with him," laughed Cathmore, "Perfect for a rather unexceptional day. If he has caught something we need to make him his own mittens from it as a trophy!"

"Shall we go now?" Edana laughed, strangely sure that Ailbe might be lucky and have caught at least one.

Off they trudged with Bebhinn staying to begin preparations for the end of day meal. Cathmore followed Edana as they made it back to the upper meadow and the rabbit warren. They walked through the farm to the outer pasture for the goats where the land lifted and was ringed by a stand of birch trees. The rise gave them the ability to look up at the warren sitting in a sheltered area, hidden by more hawthorn bushes. Sure enough, Ailbe had indeed caught four rabbits, one buck and three does, perfect for four sets of mittens, one for Ailbe, one for Edana, one for Ardan and one for Carrick. Dinner was a festive event and Ailbe was happy to know his idea for rabbit dinner came to fruition. "I was right!" Ailbe laughed and danced in the meadow as Cathmore and Edana got the rabbits. He did dizzying circles, his arms held out straight and scared all the rabbits away for good.

"I told you Edana, the upper meadow was full of rabbits! Maybe tomorrow we should look for ducks on the lake? Or deer in the forest?" Ailbe gleefully said between bites of his rabbit at dinner. Ardan and Carrick smiled enthusiastically.

"Ducks for sure but deer are for the big men to get, not little brothers," Edana giggled, "We can get up at first light and try to get the ducks with my sling."

"Ardan and Carrick do you want to go hunting tomorrow?" Asked Cathmore.

"Of course we do." Answered Carrick eager to get out of the boring job of fence mending.

"I can get the men from the village to go hunting for deer as well. Maybe your mother is right, Ailbe is indeed a lucky Beltane boy. We should take his ideas and see if we can get both ducks and deer tomorrow. Should we get both maybe he is on his way to becoming a druid!" Cathmore declared his smile big and kind as he looked at Ailbe. Ailbe glowed in the praise, not really sure what was so momentous about the comment but happy that he had his normally stern uncles attention.

"If we do manage to catch both ducks and deer on the same day that Ailbe claims we need to hunt, that would be a true sign, right Mother? Would the druids come to take Ailbe for training after that?" Edana asked anxiously

"I don't think so Edana, most of the druids are no longer around, or at least not up to their previous strength. The Romans razed Mona and put to death all of the druids there. The ones left are in hiding like Miach is. They will reassemble in another druidic stronghold like Salisbury or even as far to the north in the Orkneys."

"Don't mention the other places out loud Bebhinn. The Romans are looking for just this loose talk. We need to train ourselves for discretion at all times. You will never know when Roman tax men will be sniffing around. Gosbecks is a very fertile place. I expect we'll be seeing more soon. If not the tax levies there will be soldiers, not to mention the traders that come in with ties to Rome," Cathmore grumbled, looking worried. "They'll be here in the next few months, probably in the spring. There was more talk in the next village that another colonia will be set up in our area. That means more retiring Roman soldiers around, and worse they'll be here permanently, marrying into our tribe, taking our farms, bringing in their own goods and turning our people into Romans! We need to be prepared for this and not talk about where our beloved druids are." Cathmore breathed heavily in his ire, his forehead sweaty.

"They can't do that, not an entire colonia in our area, in Gosbecks!" Bebhinn looked worriedly at Cathmore, "We can't fight back there isn't enough of us around. I won't be able to continue as healer with their surgeons about."

"No we can't but this seems to be the Roman way, slowly integrate with the local tribes. They'll make it worthwhile with trade increasing and more foreign people moving into the area. Just look at Londinium and Camulodunum[54]. The tribes were lulled by the increase in trade, money flowing into the local economy and more and more Romans moving in. The same will happen here," he rubbed his head disgustedly. "I'm tired and will take my leave. I have a deer hunt to assemble in the morning." Cathmore smiled at Ailbe again. He stood to take his leave.

Ailbe giggled and hugged his uncles knees: "You will be successful in the deer hunt just like Edana will be in her duck hunt tomorrow. It will be a good day."

"As *Cernunnous*[55] and *Mananon Mac Lir* will it," agreed Cathmore giving Ailbe a one-armed hug.

The next day both Edana and Cathmore were successful in their respective hunts. Edana was able to down three ducks with her sling[56] at the lake and Cathmore and his assembled hunters were able to shoot two deer. It seemed Ailbe's prediction came to pass as foretold. Ailbe's fame as a favorite of the gods began that day.

文 文 文 文

The next day it was market day and Bebhinn, Edana and Ailbe got ready to go into Gosbecks. They got their satchels ready for the

[54] http://www.britainexpress.com/History/roman/camulodunum.htm
[55] http://paganwiccan.about.com/od/godsandgoddesses/p/Cernunnos.htm
[56] http://historum.com/ancient-history/26001-celtic-missile-weapons.html

items they would be buying. Bebhinn also brought her medicinal satchel that she always traveled with because she was the village healer. "Remember to get some pork for us Bebhinn." Ardan said as he and Carrick got ready to go out to start their workday.

Bebhinn nodded. "Do you have a preference for the cut of meat I get?"

"Bacon for sure. Maybe a good ham hock too." Ardan said thoughtfully. "I love pork and until our pig has piglets we won't have the opportunity to eat one."

Bebhinn smiled. "Cathmore has offered his pig to act as a stud if we needed it. We should ask for that service." Then she got Ailbe ready to leave with Edana and her. They said their farewells and took to the road. They followed the path lined with elm, oak and hawthorn. Interspersed was blackberry and crab apple shrubs. They continued walking until they reached a fork in the road. From the right they saw their neighbors coming round the bend. "Well hail Niamh, Drust, Ealga, Aibhlinn, Cliona and Nola! Off to market day I see. Looks like you are going to be getting something big, what with the cart you're bringing." Bebhinn sang out merrily.

Niamh smiled and waved. She was a strong matronly woman, dressed in a fine summery tartan of greens and golds. Her graying brown hair was loosely piled on top of her head. "We are after some lumber. We need to fix the roof on our cow barn from the last big storm. It blew off the shingles and some of the roof. Plus we need to have some in reserve for those unforeseen times."

"We all have those don't we?" Laughed Edana. "What else are you shopping for this market day?"

"We are looking for tartans! We've all grown out of our tartans. We'll need some new ones for winter which will be here before you know it. I'm looking forward to perusing the new styles from Ronan's cart. They always have the best ones." Aibhlinn said breathlessly. She smiled in anticipation.

Niamh rolled her hazel eyes. "Sure, we need new tartans for the winter. The ones from last winter are perfectly fine but they want something new. With these daughters of mine I'm sure it will be like this from now on."

"But Mother we need new ones. The ones from last year are old and have worn places in them." Cliona said. Aibhlinn nodded her head in agreement.

"What about you Nola? Do you need new tartan as well? What are you shopping for?" Looking at Niamh's youngest daughter Edana asked smiling.

"I don't need new tartans. I want some honey comb and some walnuts." Nola said jutting out her chin.

"I want honey comb!" Ailbe said grabbing his mother's hand. "And some nuts too."

"Well it just so happens I need to get some more honey for my medicines. So we'll make a pass at Anlon's cart. We might as well visit Ronan's cart as well for the tartans. I have three growing children that will need new tartans. Plus I just got some blood on my tartan the night before last when Liadan had her baby girl Einin. Tierney was over the moon to see his new daughter."

"A baby for Liadan and Tierney! How does the little Einin?" Ealga, Niamh's mother asked. She smiled as her wrinkled face puckered up around her eyes merrily.

"She is doing fine. It was a long birth but she arrived in time. Liadan was tired but happy. She looks like her father. She was born with his dark curly hair." Bebhinn smiled.

Drust, Niamh's fatherlaughed out loud. "Good thing she looks like Tierney. There was some talk that it wasn't even his because there was another man involved before they got married."

Niamh hit her father. "Hush that kind of talk! Liadan is a good girl. She was just seeing more than one person at a time to make certain she would pick the right person to marry. And she did." Niamh nodded her head.

"And how is it you know this Niamh?" Drust asked, a smile crinkling his eyes in anticipation of the answer.

"Why I asked her. I saw what was going on and was curious.

She mentioned that both Murtagh and Tierney were interested in her. She had to decide between them. She chose Tierney because he had a farm and Murtagh was still only a drummer. Not a good choice if you want to start a family." Niamh said triumphantly. She was a busy body but a kind hearted one.

Edana asked Bebhinn. "Could I also get a new tartan? I've worn out last year's tartan."

Bebhinn nodded and patted Edana on the cheek. "I was planning on it anyway, my love."

Just then they got to another fork in the road and came across Cathmore and his family. Cathmore walked with his wife Meara and two daughters Aine and Flann. Meara was walking by Cathmore with her hand on his shoulder. She was a tall stately woman with raven black hair that had a white stripe coming off her forehead. Her daughters were equally tall. Each had light brown hair and blue eyes. All four of them were renown around Gosbecks as the best singers in the area. Cathmore was known to have the best tenor voice. Meara and Aine had strong sopranos voices and Flann had a melodious contralto. They were in demand for all festivals and parties that were held in Gosbecks.

"Well hail neighbors! How goes your market day?" Niamh sang out.

"Good Niamh and Bebhinn. We are off to look for a bull for next spring. Our current bull is old and only sired one calf this year. We got only one and the little heifer is sickly." Meara said.

"You can always ask us too. We have a strong bull that serviced our cows this spring and we got twelve calves out of it." Niamh said kindly. "That is what neighbors are for."

"We need a bull nonetheless. For the future of our farm. Since I got this." Cathmore pointed to his left arm. "We have had a difficult time of it on the farm. We will have a tough time getting in all of the wheat and barley. Since last year was such a terrible harvest we owe a lot in back taxes. A bull will make it that much better for us in the long run." He trudged along with his staff. Meara still kept her hand on his left shoulder in solidarity.

"Everyone is in the same boat as you Cathmore due to the bad harvest last year. We owe a lot as well." Bebhinn said uneasily. Edana nodded.

"We ended up selling a lot of our cows to make up for the short fall on our farm. Good thing this year looks to be a better harvest than last years' crop." Drust said.

They all fell silent for a while they walked companionably on. Soon they came to the main road to Gosbecks. Traffic picked up significantly with many farmers, vendors and villagers coming into Gosbecks for market day. They moved into the stream of traffic. Walking along Niamh called out to some neighbors.

"Well hail Eamon and Ida. How goes it on this market day?" Niamh cried out waving to the stolid farmer with his buxom wife.

"We are faring well Niamh. We are in for the regulars like dairy items. I need more clotted cream and butter. We also need to get some farm implements. Our plow broke in two this past week. We've been limping along with just the shovels. Not good for the last minute jobs that we are performing." Eamon waved.

"Eirnin and Hugh are still back at the farm performing some last minute duties. They should be coming along later today." Said Ida as she smoothed back her graying brown hair. "They need more clothes. They just keep growing! Soon they'll be even bigger than their father." She squeezed Eamon's arm.

Niamh smiled and laughed. "If they are growing to be bigger than you Eamon then you'll have the largest men in Gosbecks helping out at your farm."

"I'm trying." Eamon shrugged his large shoulders. They waved and continued on into Gosbecks.

Soon the line of people walked all the way into Gosbecks. Market day was held on the commons which was located in the center of town. They followed the road around the smithy and the tavern into the middle of Gosbecks. Soon they arrived at the commons, a large green expanse that was square in shape. The vendors divided up into their specific trades and went to their designated areas. On the west side of the commons were the building goods like lumber and thatching materials. Also located here was the durable goods such as candles, lanterns, pots and pans, tinkers that fix and sharpen utensils for the kitchens and additional wood for implements on the farms. Located with the durable goods was the cart for weaponry, where swords, bows and arrows, slings, and daggers were displayed. On the north side was the clothes vendors such as tunics, trousers, tartans,boots, belts and shoes. On the east side was food stuffs such as the butchers carts, dairy carts, and farmers with their vegetables and grains for sell. On the east side was the specialty food carts such as nut sellers, beekeepers that sold their honey, and various baked goods. Also specialty items such as the musicians cart was located here. They displayed pipes, drums, and lyres for sale[57]. The musicians made their way to the musicians cart to see if they could afford new instruments and also to exchange musical ideas on new songs they've heard performed. In the middle of the commons was an expanse of green field. It was quickly filled up with the drovers that brought in their cattle for sell, with herders that brought in their sheep and goats. Herders that moved their pigs onto the green. Finally there were farmers that brought their chickens, ducks and geese for sell. The large flocks of geese and ducks being herded by younger children.

At this point everyone in Bebhinn's group decided to split up and go their ways to purchase their goods. Niamh and her family started off to the west side for their lumber. Cathmore and his family made their way to the cattle in the middle of the green. Bebhinn and her group went to the east side to the butchers carts to purchase their pork. As they made their way to the east side Bebhinn was hailed by several people as they passed by.

"Well hail Bebhinn, how goes your market day?" Called out Neala as she walked with her large family of four children and

---

[57] https://en.wikipedia.org/wiki/Ancient_Celtic_music
http://www.alisonvardy.com/harp-history.html

harried husband Lachlan. The children were all young, the oldest Bairre was only eight summers old.

"Good and well hail to you. I see you have the whole family here for market day. You must be shopping for clothes." Bebhinn said in return. Ailbe and Bairre smiled at each other as they were close in age. They both would rather play together than go shopping with their parents.

"Yes, we have to get shoes for Bairre and trousers and shirts for the younger ones." Neala said with exasperation on her face as some of the younger children wandered off since they had stopped walking to talk. "Everyone has been fine since the last time I saw you. Thank you for giving me some willow bark tea for the next time my children come down with a fever."

Bebhinn beamed. "Anytime you need teas for medicines just let me know. I'll let you go on now that I see you've lost the children's' interest since we've stopped. Off to the north side for you."

Bebhinn, Edana and Ailbe continued on to the butchers cart. When they arrived they hailed the large muscular butcher and his equally large wife. "Well hail Dahy and Muirne. We are here to get some pork. Some bacon and maybe a ham hock."

"Good morning Bebhinn, Edana and young Ailbe! So it's pork you're looking for? Good thing because I butchered a large pig just yesterday. I'll have the bacon and a ham hock ready for you in just a minute." The big bald man said. He turned and pulled out the selection of pork for Bebhinn to peruse.

Requesting it to be turned over Bebhinn inspected the meat closely. "It looks good Dahy. Just as I expected it to be. Please wrap it up and I'll take it. What do I owe you for it?"

Dahy scratched his bald head and looked pained as he tried to figure. "Well that's two pieces of prime cuts of pork. It will be about two quadrans[58]."

Muirne broke into the conversation at this point. "Dahy, there

---

[58] http://www.dictionary.com/browse/quadrans

is a better way for Bebhinn to pay for the pork. Bebhinn, Dahy has been complaining of pains in his back and shoulders from butchering the large pig and other animals. Could you just give us some teas to take care of this?"

Bebhinn nodded. "Of course! I brought my medicine satchel just in case for situations like this. Let me look to see if I can find the right ones." Bebhinn opened her satchel and started to rummage through the little leather packets. She began to pull out several. "I have here ginger, all heal, comfrey, yarrow and willow bark to make into teas for your a stiffness in your joints.[59] This should take care of your pain Dahy." She handed over the little packets to Muirne and Dahy.

Dahy looked relieved. "Thank you Bebhinn! That big pig was a bit much even for me. I'm sure I'll feel much better after all of this." He held the packets close to his chest as if they were made of gold.

Muirne smiled. "Thank you Bebhinn. I could even use some of this since I helped Dahy butcher the pig. And all of the other big animals that we need to do as well since we are the primary butchers for Gosbecks. We also butchered a deer from Cathmore's' last hunting trip. I hear we have young Ailbe to thank for that bit of good luck. I think he is going to be a top druid yet." She grinned at Ailbe who quickly ducked his head and hid from her behind Edana. Muirne and Dahy were big and intimidating to Ailbe despite their kind demeanors

"Let's go, off to see Ronan and his tartans. See you soon Dahy and Muirne." Bebhinn said as she waved goodbye. Edana waved as well, Ailbe danced on ahead anxious to get his honeycomb.

They all turned to the north side to get to the clothes area. There was a lively amount of trade going on at Ronan's cart, always a popular spot. Niamh and her family were looking over all of the tartans that Ronan had laid out for them. Ronan's wife Fingula and

---

[59] https://www.everydayhealth.com/pain-management/natural-pain-remedies.aspx

his daughter Eilis were pulling out more choices for Aibhlinn and Cliona to look over. Nola was standing off to the side looking bored, drawing circles in the grass with her right foot. Ronan looked up at Bebhinn, Edana and Ailbe. "Well hail Bebhinn! Are you looking for some tartans too? Niamh, Aibhlinn and Cliona are just finishing up their choices for winter tartans." Ronan was a short, round, dark headed man with a happy disposition. He was known as a fair vendor and as such was greatly respected. His wife Fingula was petite and birdlike in her quickness of movements. Their daughter Eilis was also petite with raven black hair and lovely green eyes. She smiled at Edana and waved.

"Well hail Ronan, Fingula and Eilis. We are looking for some winter tartans for everyone. I am looking for some working tartans for Ardan, Carrick, Ailbe, Edana and myself. We all seem to be needing new ones all at the same time. Carrick and Ailbe are growing so much. Ardan, Edana and I have just worn out our current tartans."

"That happens all of the time. Come look at some of the tartans we have displayed here." He turned to indicate his cart.

"I can get what want just let me know the color combinations," Fingula offered.

Niamh butted in. "There is a great black, blue and gray tartan[60] shot through with small green stripes. Here take a look." She handed over a length of tartan to Bebhinn who took it thankfully.

"Very nice. The wool is thick and finely woven," Bebhinn murmured as she stroked the material.

Edana was talking with Aibhlinn and Cliona. They were showing Edana the winter tartans that caught their attention. Edana was taken by a tartan of cool watery blues, purples and greens shot through with small black stripes. She lifted it up to show Bebhinn. "Mother, I like this one."

Bebhinn turned and looked at the tartan, admiring the

---

[60] http://www.lindaclifford.com/Tartan.html

harmonious combinations of colors. "I like that one too! It is very pretty. I'm always amazed at your ability to come up with tartans that are so beautiful Ronan."

Ronan looked happy at the compliment. "I have Eilis and Fingula to thank for the tartans. They both have the ability to combine colors in a pleasing way. Eilis came up with that particular color combination for that tartan."

"Did she? She has a very pleasant way of selecting and combining colors of yarn," Bebhinn complimented Eilis. Ronan and Fingula who nodded eagerly. "We'll take both of these tartans. Enough for all five of us. I think I'll also get another more plain one for my working tartan. I just came from a birthing that soiled by last tartan."

"Who had the baby?" Ronan asked.

"Tierney and Liadan had a baby girl. They named her Einin four nights ago." Bebhinn told them.

Fingula pulled out a smart looking green, brown and yellow tartan with small red stripes running through it. "What about this one?"

"Beautiful. I'll take it as well. How much do I owe you?" Bebhinn got out her money satchel that hung from her belt.

Ronan looked at the package of tartans. "I think we can do a trade. We will need to get some vegetables from your garden, enough for the next week. We'll need lettuce, turnips, celery, carrots and beets. I will also take some of your willow bark tea."

"Done. Come by tomorrow morning as the vegetable do best picked the before noon. I have willow bark tea right here and can leave it with you now." Bebhinn looked in her medicinal satchel and pulled out a small leather packet. After checking that it was the right kind she handed it over to Ronan. "You can always come get more if it is needed."

Ronan took the small packet and put it immediately into his pocket. "Thank you Bebhinn. Fingula and Eilis will be over tomorrow morning." Bebhinn, Edana and Ailbe took their packages and moved away to the east side for the honey. They continued walking through the busy market day crowd. There was continually people hailing Bebhinn.

An older woman stopped Bebhinn. Her husband recently died and she was quite lonely now. She looked up at Bebhinn because she was short and round. "Well hail Bebhinn, Edana, and young Ailbe. How goes your market day?" Aednat asked.

"It goes quite well. We are almost done. We just need to get some honey from Anlon and Eachna." Bebhinn answered her. "And how about your market day? Have you been able to get the items you need?"

Aednat fluffed her frowzy white hair with her hand. "I have so few things to buy today. I'm out mostly for the people. I've gotten the few things and am on my way to see the butcher's cart. I want to know what Dahy has to offer. Then I'm off to the musician's cart on the east side to see what is going on. Maybe I'll be there in time for their impromptu concert that they hold every market day. I want to hear it and maybe dance."

"We just came back from there. Dahy just butchered a large pig so he definitely has pork for sale. Does that sound good to you?" Edana told Aednat helpfully. She hefted the meat that was on her back in her satchel to show off their purchase.

Aednat chortled. "Looks like you got the biggest share of pork! There might not be that much left," Her wrinkles creasing in mirth as she laughed. "Are you planning on having a lot of company for dinner?"

"That was the request of Ardan this morning. He wanted to have pork. He asked for bacon and a ham hock which is what we got. Now it is just a matter of cooking it all up." Bebhinn smiled.

"Well then I think I need to hurry to the butchers cart. Goodbye everyone." Aednat turned and trotted off to the cart. Bebhinn and Edana both started to laugh. They moved off to Anlon's honey cart on the east side.

As they got to the cart the hailed Anlon and Eachna. "Well

hail Anlon and Eachna. How is your market day faring so far?" Bebhinn asked.

"Well hail to you Bebhinn, Edana and little Ailbe! Good to see you on this lovely, fair market day. What can I help you with?" Anlon, a sunny natured man that was tall and thin asked. His light blond hair and twinkling blue eyes matched his sunny disposition. His wife Eachna was also good natured and tall and thin like her husband but had brown hair and eyes. She looked up from her work with a customer and waved to them.

"I am in need of some honey for my medicines. A jar should do it for me." Bebhinn answered Anon. Ailbe's big eyes looked over Anlon's honey jars with eager anticipation of sampling the golden nectar. He crept as close as he could to Anlon's cart, his hands itching to reach out and touch the golden honeycombs.

Anlon seeing Ailbe's look laughed. "Would you like a taste of honey comb young Ailbe?" He asked and after shooting a questioning look at Bebhinn who nodded. He then turned and shaved off a bite of honey comb for Ailbe. He handed it over to Ailbe who eagerly snatched it away and popped it into his mouth. Ailbe smiled his thanks as the sweet honey dribbled down his chin.

"Thank you Anlon. It is wonderful!" Ailbe said after he had finished his honeycomb. Edana and Bebhinn laughed at the worshipful way Ailbe regarded Anon thereafter. "That's one way to get Ailbe to be polite to his elders." Giggled Edana as she ruffled his fair head. Ailbe just grinned.

"What do I owe you Anlon?" Bebhinn asked.

"I am in need for some willow bark tea and possibly some garlic, lavender oil, and plantain to make a paste for bee stings[61]?" Anlon asked sheepishly shrugging his shoulders. "My bees are normally calm if I smoke them enough but it never hurts to get more bee sting paste made up."

---

[61] http://www.motherearthnews.com/natural-health/bee-sting-treatment-zbcz1310.aspx

"I am glad you asked. In anticipation I packed just these herbs." Bebhinn pulled out her satchel and rummaged through the packets. She found the packets and the little vial of lavender oil and pulled them out. She smiled as she presented them to Anlon. "Make sure to remove the stingers. Just use the juice from the plantain leaves for the paste. Crush the garlic and use it that way. Also bind them all together with honey. Your bees create the best and most pure cure for their own bee stings." Bebhinn instructed.

Anlon smiled and took the packets and vial from Bebhinn. "Thank you! We try not to get stung but it happens from time to time." He waved merrily as Bebhinn, Edana and Ailbe moved off.

They turned to the musicians cart knowing they would run into Niamh and her family and Cathmore and his family there. They walked slowly over to the cart which had a large crowd around it in anticipation since it was getting close to midday meal time. Normally the musicians would put on an impromptu concert with instruments and singing every market day. Today was no exception as the musicians started to tune up their instruments. Lorcan, Kearney and Fintan started running trills up and down their pipes. The lyre player Niall got out his large curved lyre and started plucking the strings. He tightened some of the strings to get them into tune. The drummers Iollan, Murtagh, Gearoid and Glennon started to beat their drums in unison with the pipers trills. Soon the musicians started to play a known song "The Plea of Dauda's[62] Blessing", a rollicking happy tune to call all of the people to the musicians cart. It worked as more people started to gather around the cart, their hands full of purchases, their feet moving in time to the music. Soon the song ended and another was struck up.

"The Ballad of Siobhan" was struck up next and Cathmore, Meara, Aine and Flann stepped forward to sing the words of the ballad. Their harmonious voices making the crowd of appreciative

---

[62] http://www.irishcentral.com/roots/history/irish-centrals-top-ten-gods-and-goddesses-from-celtic-mythology-133143343-237789201.html

onlookers sway in time with the beat. Soon a few of the onlookers joined their hands and started to move in tandem and dance together. There were more and more people moving to the music and they created a moving chain of dancing patrons to the concert. The ballad ended and seamlessly was moved into an equally carefree ballads and jigs without ending. The audience just continued to dance in rings with clasped hands and dancing feet. Soon the people started to lag and began to drop out of dancing. The band then turned to some slower ballads and laments. The tired audience thankfully stopped moving, some sank down to their bottoms where they stood and gently moved from side to side. The first lament was "The Lament of Ciara" and sung by Meara, Aine and Flann. Their voices harmoniously coiling, drawing out the sad song until the end where Ciara is killed by her lover. In the audience some of the more sensitive members started to weep. Then Cathmore stood up to sing the "Ballad of Darragh". He sang the song in his clear tenor voice. When he got to the part where Darragh refused to sell his bull to Queen Maebh[63] the entire audience gasped knowing what the consequences would be for the refusal as they were all familiar with the story. The next few laments were sung by Meara, Aine and Flann. The last lament "The Lament of Caoimhe" was sung by Flann by herself. She had a lovely contralto that entranced the people in the audience. So taken by her voice were they that they seemed to feel the sorrow even more than the last laments. As soon as she finished the audience erupted in applause. A bag was then passed around for the musicians and everyone put money in it.

Cathmore collected his cut for his family and smiled. "Now we can purchase that bull." He felt much better about the day, the audience had been very generous. The musicians also were happy. Lorcan and Kearney turned and went to the musicians cart to turn in their money to complete payments on their pipes that they had taken out.

---

[63] https://www.britannica.com/topic/Medb

Lorcan smiled. "I am finally happy that I can get this pipe paid for. Conor the musicians cart owner will be relieved." He jiggled the coins in his pocket. "I even have money left for food and drink." Lorcan was a handsome, dark completed man with curly hair, a pointed jaw and nose, and merry brown eyes.

"So do I! Paying off the instruments is the best part of performing on market day. Plus I think I'll finally go talk to Eilis. You know Ronan's' daughter? I had a liking for her for a while now. What about you, who do you find to your liking?" Kearney grinned, waggling his red eyebrows up and down suggestively. He was a handsome man with ginger long hair and a masculine face.

Lorcan smiled secretively. "There is one that I'm very attracted to. Flann. But she is young and I'll need to wait a couple of seasons before I approach Cathmore with the request to court her. She has the best voice! And her looks are very pleasing. She is beginning to be a real looker."

They got over to Conor, the owner of the musicians cart. Conor was a tall effeminate man that could play all of instruments he sold. He was a temperamental man but also a caring one who frequently sold instruments to musicians and let them pay him back over time. It was good he did this because most of the musicians lived concert to concert. They frequently would come and stay at Lorcan's or Kearney's homes because they were the only ones that had houses. It worked out well because Lorcan and Kearney used those times to practice their songs then. They would come to the houses and practice until late in the night. Then everyone would get up late the next day and move to their next concert or festival. "We'd like to pay off our debts for the pipes you lent us." Lorcan and Kearney said in unison. They looked at each other and just laughed.

Conor laughed too. "Good to hear! Let's see." Conor looked down. "Both of you owe the same amount of four quadrans[64] on your pipes. Just pay up and you'll be clear of debt. Next time you

---

[64] http://www.dictionary.com/browse/quadrans

need anything you know where to come. By the way your concert was very good. I like how you kept everyone dancing first then slowed them down with the ballads and laments. That's good thinking, a good arrangement. I have some new songs for you and will play them for you both and I'll get with Cathmore later for the words. There is a new reel, new jig, new ballad and a new lament[65] for all of you to learn."

"Thank you Conor." Lorcan said with feeling. Kearney nodded liking the fact that they will get the new songs now. They'd be able to practice the songs tonight.

Iollan, the best drummer and Cathmore walked up to the cart. They heard the last interchange and were glad they hadn't left yet. "Let me get the other drummers to hear the songs." He quickly went back to the men and gathered them up.

Cathmore held up his hand. "I'm going to get my family too." And he left quickly to bring them back to Conor. " Conor has a new ballad and lament to teach us the words and melodies to. Come on." They all got up from the grass where they had sat down to rest and followed him over to the musicians cart. "We're ready now." Cathmore said to Conor.

Iollan and the rest of the musicians came up to Conor and everyone spread out around Conor. Conor quickly got his pipe and drum. "This one is called the Mummers Reel, it's about the scurrying mummers do on Samhain. He picked up his pipe and ran through a rollicking reel. Then he did the same with the drums. Then there is "The Ballad of Aisling". It is a long one about her father selling her to a lord that is notorious for cruelty but Aislings' beauty turns him into a good man. Then Conor piped the ballad out for everyone. He then picked up his drum and played it again. The drummers picked up their drums and played along. Then the pipers picked up their instruments and played along as well. Soon the song was done and

---

[65] http://www.oxforddictionaries.com/us/definition/american_english/lament

the musicians all congratulated each other on picking up the song so quickly. Then Conor sang "The Ballad of Aisling" for Cathmore and his family. His tenor was quite good and melodic. Cathmore and his family listened to it to the end and then they tried their hand at singing it accompanied by the pipers and drummers. Then Conor went on to "The Lament of Fiona" about the death of the most fair maid in the land. They went through the same steps and soon they were playing both the ballad and the lament without mistakes. Finally Conor played the jig on his pipe and all the musicians joined in the fray.

"Thank you Conor for your time. We now have two new songs for our concerts." Cathmore said.

"You are quite welcomed. Both of them will be wanted additions to your musical repertoires." Conor smiled. The musicians all disbanded. Some of the drummers staying to buy more drums. Others fingering through the hanging drums with envy.

Meanwhile in the audience several families started to break out their food from their satchels or carts and sat down to eat them on the grass of the commons. Bebhinn turned to Edana and Ailbe. "Let's go to the tavern and have our midday meal. I packed Ardan and Carrick's midday meal this morning and they took them along with them to the fields. We'll eat here at the tavern."

"Sounds good Mother. Lead the way." Edana said as she stood up and hefted the package of pork to her shoulder.

Ailbe stood up too and grinned. "I hope Oisin has that yummy deer stew! I really like his stew, it has a good broth."

"That's good to know. I'll ask Grania what herbs she puts in her stews." She stood up and herded them towards the tavern. It was directly to the south west side of the commons. The tavern[66] was a long rectangular building with a thatched roof. Inside it had a long low bar to one side and the earthen floor was filled with tables and chairs. The walls were decorated with blue, green and yellow

---

[66] http://www.nydailynews.com/life-style/ancient-bones-call-irish-celtic-heritage-question-article-1.2568277

glyphs of spirals, suns and leaves twining around the walls. The interior was dark as the only light came from burning rushes sitting on the tables. The interior was smoky and was already filled with patrons from the market day. Bebhinn, Edana and Ailbe moved among the tables until they found a free one in the back and sat down.

Presently Grania, the owners quick moving wife, came up with her bird-like movements. "What can I get you Bebhinn, Edana and Ailbe?"

"We will all take the meal of the day and three cups of ales." Bebhinn told her. "What is the stew today?"

"It is pork stew with summer vegetables." Grania said happily. "Dahy just butchered a pig yesterday. I made it out of pork shoulder."

"We got the bacon and a ham hock from the pig." Edana smiled. "I've been hauling them around all morning long. I can't wait until we get home and hang it up to smoke them."

"Smoked bacon is indeed a good thing." Grania smiled and turned to get their order. She stopped at several tables on her way back to the kitchen.

"Well no deer stew but the pork stew sounds goods." Ailbe puffed out his cheeks then grinned. "I can't wait to eat the bacon! Maybe tomorrow?"

"We need to let it smoke for a couple of days first Ailbe." Bebhinn said patiently. "Although I am looking forward to the bacon for sure. There is a lot of recipes we can make with bacon. Fresh beans cooked with bacon, fresh turnips sautéed in bacon fat with the bacon bits mixed in, and let's not forget deer steak lets wrapped in bacon."

Edana licked her lips. "And then there is the ham hock. There are lots of recipes that we can make with that. Ham and beans, ham cooked with beets, ham with mashed turnips and sautéed spinach. There's many more recipes. We also need to make up some mustard sauce."

Soon Grania retuned with their stews and cups of ale. They all started to eat their midday meal. The hum of the tavern droned on around them as the patrons all filled up on their meals. Toward the end of their meal the tavern suddenly quieted. In walked Gosbecks druid Miach. He was wearing his normal robes of brown tunic with a grey plaid tartan. He had his signature walking staff at his side. He was hailed by quite a few patrons. "Well hail Miach! How goes your market day?" Called out Ferdia. His wife Brenna sat next to him with their three boys. Fintan, Daire and Aengus. The boys were intent on shoveling their midday meal in their hungry mouths until they saw Miach and quickly stopped at the sight of the revered druid. Brenna was helping the youngest Aengus to eat turned her attention to Miach and smiled her salutations.

"My market day is faring quite well. I got the chance to do some shopping for boots that I needed." Miach smiled and ruffled young Aengus' hair. Aengus giggled.

Ferdia smiled big. "Could you come to my farm later and bless my fields? This summer is looking to be a much better one than last year. I've got much more wheat and barley in my fields. My garden is full to bursting with vegetables thanks to my new wife Brenna. Things are looking up over last year."

Miach beamed. "Certainly! I am glad to hear everything is falling into place for you. How about you Brenna? Are you as happy as Ferdia?"

Brenna blushed. "Yes Miach. It has been a lot of work but I am settling into work on the farm. The boys have been really good these past few months."

The oldest son Fintan stood up and shouted out: "Brenna has been cooking us our favorite meal, beef stew!" Daire and Aengus both whooped their agreements.

Ferdia chuckled. "As you can see Brenna has wormed her way into my boys hearts already with her cooking. Plus keeping the farm going with a partner is much more pleasurable than it was without one. I still miss my late wife but Brenna is fitting in nicely."

Ferdia looked at Brenna with adoring eyes. Brenna blushed even more.

"I can come out later this afternoon to bless your farm Ferdia. I'll leave you to enjoy your midday meal." Miach said kindly. He then moved on into the tavern. More people called out their greetings.

A childless couple sitting near the back waved him over. Gerard and Hannah were in their middle age, getting older but still able to have children. He was a stolid farmer and Hannah was a matron with a languid air. It had been Hannah's' sorrow that she had not conceived any children so far. Miach walked over to them. Gerard looked at him earnestly and said: "Could you also come to our farm today and bless us? Our farm is close to Ferdia's. We still would like to have children but the time is running out for Hannah." Hannah looked at Miach tremulously, her lip quivering as she threatened to tear up.

"Of course." Miach said. Then he laid his hands on Hannah's' as she grasp them thankfully.

"Thank you Miach, my druid." She whispered. Then the tears began to track down her still pretty face.

Miach said: "There is still time to try but don't be sad if the gods have deemed it not to happen. You can still mother the children in the neighborhood. Lachlan and Neala live near you and they have four children. They would be thankful for any occasional help you see fit to give them."

Hannah smiled quaveringly and nodded. "I'll do that. I do love those children. Neala needs help especially now that they are getting close to harvest time.

"Good. I will be by this afternoon to bless both of you." Miach smiled kindly then turned to go over to Bebhinn and her family.

He walked up to Bebhinn. "Well hail Bebhinn, Edana and Ailbe. How goes your market day?"

Bebhinn smiled. "It was good. We got all of our purchases and even had the opportunity to enjoy the concert at midday."

"I enjoyed the concert the best! That and the honey comb Anlon gave me. Mother needed some for her medicines." Giggled Ailbe.

"I enjoyed the tartans we got for the winter. Their colors are beautiful. We got tartans for everyone. For Ardan, Bebhinn and me for the winter and for working. For Carrick and Ailbe because they had grown out of their tartans." Edana enthused.

Miach nodded his head and smiled. "I'm glad you got exactly what you wanted then. I need to eat my midday meal then I'm going to Gerard and Hannah's farm for a fertility blessing and then a blessing of thanks for the abundance in Ferdia's farm. It is nice to do some of these blessings of abundance this year after our bad harvests last year. This year it looks to be a fruitful one."

Bebhinn agreed. "Our farm is very abundant. The wheat and barley in our fields are growing wonderfully and my pharmacopoeia garden is fruitful. I plan to get a lot of plants to store for my medicines this year. It is great after last year's bad harvest because of the rains. Plus we'll be able to pay off the taxes that are in arrears on our farm." She beamed at the good news.

Edana nodded agreement. "It has been very fruitful gathering wild plants and doing the hunting this summer. I had a great duck hunt the other day. Ailbe dreamed I would do well and I did."

Miach looked and the boy. Ailbe smiled and puffed out his chest with pride. "The gods have been blessing me with good dreams lately. I had one last night about some men who come to Gosbecks and change the direction we are going. I don't know who they are but they are good."

Miach stood quietly for a moment, his lips pursed. "I too am having dreams about strangers who come to Gosbecks and change the way we do things. The gods are not clear on what they'll change but just that they do. I, like you Ailbe, get the sense that they will change Gosbecks for the better. However some will not fare as good as others. I am thinking it will happen around the turn of the seasons."

"I get the same sense Miach. But my dreams are more positive." Ailbe said with a serious look on his young face. They could suddenly see the young man Ailbe would become in his visage. More serious and thoughtful in his burgeoning role of a druid

"Interesting." Was all Miach had to say about that comment. Then he cleared his face and asked: "Could I sit here and eat my midday meal?" He turned to Grania who had come over to take his order. He gave it to her for the same thing that Bebhinn had ordered. Then he turned to the table and pulled up a free chair. Grania returned quickly and Miach proceeded to eat quickly. Edana regaled Miach on how big her goat herd was getting. Bebhinn told him of the new baby Einin born to Tierney and Liadan. She also told him that it had been quite as far as sickness was concerned in Gosbecks.

"Good! The last thing we need is a new sickness come round Gosbecks. It looks like we will have a good harvest and a quiet winter. I am anticipating the new things coming after the harvest will keep us all intrigued." Miach said finishing up his midday meal. He then stood up and excused himself from the table. "Good morrow. Until later Bebhinn, Edana and young Ailbe." He gave Ailbe a sharp look of interest. And waved goodbye to them.

"Looks like Ailbe is doing even more other worldly things than Miach even predicted." Bebhinn said in an aside to Edana as they were getting their things together for the long walk home.

"I saw that too." Edana said and looked at Ailbe who was lovingly stroking the jar of honey in Bebhinn's satchel.

回回回回

When they finally got home they were able to hang up the pork above the hearth and Bebhinn began to get the hearth stoked up for the end of the day meal. They still had deer from the previous night so Bebhinn cut out steaks from the hind quarters and grilled them on the hearth outside. Edana went out into the garden and gathered fall vegetables of spinach, green peas and carrots. She then picked dandelion, nettles and plantain for a late greens salad.

Bringing them back to the outside cooking area she washed the vegetables and put them in bowls for everyone. Soon Bebhinn and Edana had the end of the day meal ready. They called to Ailbe to come and get ready to eat.

Ardan and Carrick walked in from the fields. They had washed off in the small pond near the goat shed and shook their wet heads. Smiling Ardan asked: "How was your market day?"

"Very productive. We got the bacon and ham like you requested and then we also got everyone tartans for the winter." Bebhinn smiled as she served everyone the deer and spinach, green peas and carrots. Edana put all of the fall salads out for everyone as well. Ardan and Carrick dug into the meal with gusto, each starving after working so hard in the fields. It was quiet as everyone settled down to eat their meals.

When he had finished Ardan leaned back and said: "What news from Gosbecks?"

Bebhinn crinkled her forehead. "Not much. Everyone was just about getting their purchases but no big news. The only thing of note was when we ran into Miach at lunch. Both he and Ailbe talked about dreams that they've been having. They are about men coming to Gosbecks that change it, some for the better, some not so much. Ailbe's' dream was more positive than Micah's'. I don't know what this means for us but it looks like it will happen around harvest time." Bebhinn looked at Ardan with an arched brow.

"Men coming to Gosbecks? What type of men? Will they be Trinovantes[67]? Or Cantulauvani[68]?" Ardan asked.

"They don't know, neither Miach or Ailbe was granted that information from the gods. Their dreams just said that the men

---

[67] http://www.britainexpress.com/History/prehistory/trinovantes.htm
https://en.wikipedia.org/wiki/Trinovantes
[68] https://www.britannica.com/topic/Catuvellauni
https://en.wikipedia.org/wiki/Catuvellauni

will come and make changes to Gosbecks for the better." Bebhinn bit her lip and worried it with her teeth.

"We'll find out at harvest time then." Ardan said.

Carrick had been listening to the exchange in silence. Then he raised up his head and said: "Maybe it will be a new tribe. Some other that is displaced and needs to come to our area to live."

"Mayhap. I don't know who it could be. We are small. Camulodunum[69] isn't that far from us and most of the important business goes there." Ardan mused. Everyone in the family just looked into the flames of the fire, thinking their own thoughts.

---

[69] http://www.britainexpress.com/History/roman/camulodunum.htm
http://www.camulos.com/gosbecks.htm

CHAPTER 4
BOUDICCA'S CALL TO ARMS

Morning dawned bright with the sun shining promisingly down on the earth. It guaranteed to be a clear warm fall day. Bebhinn got up early and started her daily chores beginning with drawing water for kitchen use. Soon she was met by Edana who also got up early. They both lugged in the jar of water and started cooking the morning gruel. Ardan, Carrick and Ailbe stumbled into the kitchen area yawning and wiping the sleep from their eyes. Ardan took some blackberry tea that Bebhinn handed him. Carrick ate a handful of blackberries to tied him over until the first meal of the day. Ailbe went out to start his chore of letting the chickens and ducks out of their coop. His dog Cabhan following at his heels. The chickens and ducks were already up and waiting for him to open the enclosure. When he did they spilled out and started to peck at the ground looking for insects to eat. Ailbe went and got the bag of grain to feed them. He began to throw out the seed .The chickens and ducks quickly went after the grain. He then went to refill the water bowls for the chickens and ducks. As soon as he finished he walked back to the farmhouse for the first meal of the day.

Bebhinn and Edana had the meal ready. They served the gruel with blackberries and clotted cream for everyone who quickly started eating the food. "What plans do you have for today?" asked Bebhinn to Ardan.

"We need to finish repairing the fence in the north pasture. The goats have broken through and are getting into the wheat field. We need to fix the hole." He said.

Carrick laughed. "The goats are all smart. They find one place to squeeze through and all of the rest of them follow. We need to close the hole as soon as possible. Faber and I have closed the hole but we need additional lumber to close it up properly. The goats have already eaten a good portion of the north quarter of the field. Busy little buggers that they are."

Edana stood up and took everyone's empty breakfast bowls. "Do you want some help? The goats are my responsibility."

"Sure. The more hands the quicker we can finish this chore." Ardan answered smiling. "We need to get the fence fixed anyway for the winter time."

"Then I will help you today. I was just going to help in the garden with mother but that can wait until tomorrow, right Mother?" At Bebhinn's nod she continued. "Let me get my things and I'll go with you." Edana said enthusiastically. Working on the fence in the north pasture was a lot more interesting than bending over and harvesting the vegetables and medicinal plants in the garden despite the time her mother put in at teaching her the medicinal properties of a lot of the plants. It was interesting but she wanted to do some physical work that required her muscles, like the work that Ardan and Carrick did. Plus she wanted to spend more time with Carrick. Her brother was so busy these days with the farm that they rarely had the time to do things together like they did when they were younger.

Carrick smiled at Edana. "It will be fun to have you out with us working on the goat fence.." He moved his fair hair away from his grey eyes impatiently, He was happy that Edana will be coming to work with him in the north pasture, he hadn't gotten the chance to work with her and was looking forward to listening to her running discourse that she regaled him with on a regular basis. Carrick motioned to Edana to go outside with him to gather their tools for the upcoming work. "We'll get the tools for building the fence back up. Some hammers and nails and additional lumber will be needed."

"Alright, I'll get the hammer and nails, you get the lumber," Edana said as she hurried to get the tools. She picked them up tucking them in her tool satchel that she brought. She would be the one to use them when the time came in the north pasture. They got the supplies together and made their way out to the courtyard where Ardan was waiting for them.

"Are you ready to work with us Edana?" Ardan asked again.

"I am ready! I'm looking forward to working with the two of you. I've not seen much of you except at mealtimes. I miss you too." Edana enthused. "Besides I need to tend to the goats anyway, that is my job." She smiled at Carrick who smiled back.

They all trudged out to the north pasture with their load of timber and tools. The early fall sun was peaking over the eastern ridge. Insects began to rouse in the beginning crisp temperature of the day began. The flowers along the edges of the pasture started opening their petals to the sun. The early fall fruit of apples and plums were ripe on the tree limbs promising a good harvest, plums ready to be picked sooner than the apples. They continued along. Fortunately the goats were all in the northern pasture and hadn't gotten into the wheat field.

"Let's get the fence more stable to keep the goats in the north pasture." Ardan said as he and Carrick dropped the lumber on the ground. Everyone gathered around to start the task of nailing up the fence in the northern pasture. They worked until mid-morning finishing the repairs methodically putting the lumber in the places needed. The goats began to wander over to see what the people were doing but once the goats satisfied their curiosity they quickly lost interest and meandered over to greener pastures. Soon the task was completed and they bent down to gather up their tools.

"Your extra hands made a difference Edana," said Carrick grinning at Edana. "We finished much quicker than we would have if you hadn't been here."

"Now we can take a moment to check the goats to see who is pregnant. I've been meaning to do this for a while now. They are all near us and I can already see that one little nanny goat looks pregnant." Edana said pointing to a brown and white goat that was grazing close by them.

"All right I'll look at them with you." Carrick said. He shrugged on his satchel containing tools and followed Edana over to the north pasture. They methodically made their way around to all of the nanny goats and felt their sides. "Looks like we have five out of seven of the goats pregnant, Edana."

"That is good news! We'll have plenty of nursing nanny goats for our use in Mother's ointments and elixirs when healing her patients. Not to mention more goat milk to drink for us and to make cheese. Also they will help new mothers that are having problems feeding their new babies." Edana said enthusiastically. She smiled big at the happy news. They were always looking to increase their herd of goats.

"I think now we can take a break and go fish for the rest of the morning." Carrick laughed. He was always jealous of Edana's ability to go fish for the family.

Ardan smiled and nodded his head. "I think it should be fine for you two to go fishing for the midday meal. It's early enough and we're done here. I am going to go help Bebhinn in her garden." Edana and Carrick smiled big and gathered their tool satchels. They took off at a lope for the farm house to get their fishing gear. Soon they got their equipment and headed out to the lake. They cast their hooks out into the water and waited for the fish to take their baits. The day was glorious. Dragonflies danced along the reeds at the edge of the inlet. Black water beetles skated the surface closer to the shore. There were some ripples caused by the fish under the surface further out in the lake where Edana and Carrick cast their lines. They looked at each other and grinned.

"Let's make a wager on who will be catching the first fish to-day." Carrick whispered.

"All right. I have the best bait on my line so I think I'll get the first fish." Edana sniggered. "I've found that the perch in this lake have a preference for pork which I brought in my bag."

"I've got the tried and true bait of a worm that is still alive and wriggling. It will get the attention of the fish." Carrick whispered. He jerked on his line to entice the fish. They settled down to waiting on the fish to bite and listened to the drones of the dragonflies. After waiting a few moments and jerking their lines occasionally Carrick whispered to Edana. "When are you going to get married? You are getting old enough to start pairing up with one of the available men here in Gosbecks. What about Meadghbh's brother Caolan? He has expressed interest in you before. Last Beltane[70] he asked to escort you but you turned him down. Or do you have your attention on someone else?"

"Caolan is interested in me?" Edana asked. "Caolan is nice but not for me. He is too outgoing and I didn't want to pair up with him last Beltane Plus I don't see him as a partner. He is more of a brother to me from all the time I spend over at Meadghbh's house. She is my best friend after all." Edana said looking down then twitching her fish line. "I don't find any of the young men in Gosbecks as interesting to me to settle down with."

"No one? There are plenty of the men in Gosbecks that find you very "interesting" as you say." Carrick squinted his eyes and looked at Edana. "Are you just still so interested in learning Mother's healing practices. What about Addis? He also expressed interest in you."

"Sadhbh's brother? He is so quiet when I'm there. He never

---

[70] https://www.britannica.com/topic/Beltane
http://www.sacredfire.net/festivals.html
https://en.wikipedia.org/wiki/Beltane
http://www.sacredfire.net/ritual.html

talks to me, always working with father Declan in the smithy. Plus he's too big and muscular for my taste."

Carrick chuckled. "He's quiet because he is blinded by your good looks. You make him tongue tied. But that's too bad that his physique doesn't match your ideal. There is also the musicians Fintan the piper and Gearoid the drummer. They've expressed interest in you."

"No musicians for me. Their means of support is too uncertain. Although I must admit that Gearoid is more to my liking in his looks." Edana considered.

"Oh ho, you like the tall and dark type of men. I'll look for possible men for you to meet. But seriously you don't have to marry. I like having you around the farm." Carrick reached out and patted Edana's shoulder.

"Thanks Carrick, I like being around the farm. The other reason not to marry just yet is I'm just not attracted to anyone in Gosbecks. There is a lot of information that I need to learn from mother about her healing. I have a good amount of knowledge of her pharmacopeia but there are still plants that I don't know about. Plus mother needs to take me on more healing trips when she gets the call to go. She's been taking me on some of them but not enough for me. I need to follow and assist her when she's healing her patients. The more patients I get experience with the better a healer I'll become." Edana felt a tug on her line and expertly set the hook. She then pulled the fish up to the surface. It was a good sized perch. "I win the wager! I was the first to land a fish."

Carrick pulled in his hook. The worm was drowned and hung there limply. "Can I get a bit of the pork for my line?"

"Sure here take some of it." Edana passed the bit of bacon to Carrick. She saved a little for her hook and rebaited it before putting her line back in the lake. They both settled down to wait for some more bites with occasionally tugging their lines to make them attractive to whatever was under the water. Both of them retreated to quiet contemplation of the gorgeous view of the lake on the late morning. The dragonflies droned nearby. Garganey ducks paddled around in the quiet eddies nearby, their striped feathers handsome in the late summer. Smaller drab Gadwall ducks also swam close by and kept to their own area looking for plants to eat. Red headed Pochard ducks swam in their own little area away from the Mallards. The drabber female Pochard ducks swimming next to the beautiful red headed males with their light grey backs and black fronts.

After several moments of quiet Carrick felt a fish on his line. He set the hook and brought in a brown trout. "You are right about the pork. This is a good sized brown trout on my line."

At about the same time Edana felt another tug on her line and pulled in another carp as well. Soon between the two of them they caught five fish, three carp, one brown trout and one perch. They then packed up their catch. Edana darted off to pick some cattail, wild onion and pennywhistle, and burdock on their way back to the farm house. Soon they had enough for everyone's midday meal. They came back to the farm house and Edana started to clean the fish and get them onto the fire to cook. Ailbe, Bebhinn and Ardan came up and met them at the outside cooking area. Soon they all sat down to eat their meal. "The fish were certainly biting I see," said Ardan around his mouth full of perch.

"Yes, we were lucky. Edana had the right kind of bait for us. Seems like the lake fish now have a taste for pork," Carrick grinned.

"Good for us that we recently got some pork then," Bebhinn observed. She smiled and continued to finish her midday meal.

"You should have let me come with you. I would have gotten more than both of you. Why don't you ever take me fishing with you Edana?" Ailbe plaintively said and looked at her with a worried face.

"I don't take you because you are too loud. You need to be quiet when you fish or else you frighten them away. But maybe next time I go you can come along, alright?" Edana said.

"Only if you are telling me the truth and not just putting me off to quiet me." Ailbe huffed.

"I'm not putting you off. I need to teach you anyway. You'll be able to provide for us soon." Edana answered. They all finished their midday meal in companionable quiet.

回回回回

Word came down to the people of Gosbecks that the most hated person from the Roman government, the publican[71] or tax collector Gnaeus Hortensius Aquila was going to come to make his rounds of the farms and business. Once a year he came for the preliminary determination of the future taxes for the upcoming harvest time. Gnaeus Hortensius Aquila was known to be greedy and nefarious in his business dealings. He was also a money lender who was willing to lend money to farmers who couldn't make the tax payments but with a catch. He levied such high interest rates on the money he lent so the recipients often found they couldn't pay back the loans and would lose their farms due to non-payment of the loan terms. He was also greedy in the amount of wheat he determined was the right quantity in payment for the taxes. Last harvest was so poor in Britannia that he didn't even come to Gosbecks knowing that he wouldn't get a good amount from anyone. He just sent his toady Fabius to log in the numbers of farms who couldn't pay their taxes last harvest. The numbers were about two thirds of the farms in Gosbecks were deficient on their taxes from the previous year. Those who did pay their taxes saw a lean winter and a tough spring. Now he was here to see that he got his levies back.

He came with a flourish as was his wont. He arrived in an ornately carved and painted red with white trim covered wagon pulled by two huge, matched, white dray horses because he was so overweight he couldn't sit a horse and no horse could carry him. The large wagon pulled up in front of Gosbecks only tavern. The

---

[71] http://www.unrv.com/economy/roman-taxes.php
https://en.wikipedia.org/wiki/Publican

tavern owner Oisin and his wife Grania both hurried out to meet the Roman publican.

"Well hail my lord. Good to see you back in Gosbecks," bowed Oisin. Grania bowed next to Oisin even lower than he did.

Gnaeus Hortensius Aquila had been traveling laying back on his side so he huffed hard and hoisted his great weight to a sitting position. He shouted to his driver. "Stool!" His driver jumped down from behind the horses and got out a large stool for Gnaeus Hortensius Aquila to use when he got out of the wagon. It was a large reinforced affair but beautifully carved and painted red and white to match the wagon. Gnaeus Hortensius Aquila moved his great mass to the edge of the wagon and raised himself to a standing position. His fat, bandy legs felt for the stool as he lowered himself down. Then he stepped out of the wagon and got to the ground after moving very slowly. At this time he let loose a large polysyllabic fart that lasted several seconds of varying noises. "Much better," he grunted. He straitened his handsome, snow white toga that looked more like a white sail on a ship than men's clothing. He moved his belt lower and felt for his beautiful apportioned knife. He pulled out a silk handkerchief and moved it up to his forehead to wipe off the beads of sweat that appeared after he got to the ground as if he had just walked a long distance. "Do you have wine in this establishment?" He asked brusquely as he made his way past Oisin and Grania walking to the door. He went inside and stood looking around for a place to sit. Finding the best table he moved to it and sat down.

"Yes my lord, I have good red wine for you." Oisin said obsequiously brushing his greasy hair back from his sweating forehead.

"Is it Falernian wine?" Barked Gnaeus Hortensius Aquila.

"I believe so. I bought it last time you came to Gosbecks." Oisin murmured looking at Gnaeus Hortensius Aquila dubiously, expecting to be hit. "From a Roman wines agent. I've been waiting for your return to serve it."

"Good. I'll take the Falernian wine then. That is the best wine to drink, a full bodied one with the right fruity grape undertones." Gnaeus Hortensius Aquila was mollified. "And while you're at it serve me some olives with onions in wine. And some freshly baked bread with olive oil to dip it in"

"As you wish, my lord." Oisin turned to Grania and she nodded her head turning around to get the food. Oisin ran to the bar to pour the wine for his Roman guest. They quickly pulled out the seat at the best table in the tavern and got him served. "Is there anything else you need my lord?" Oisin asked.

"Just bring me the most influential members of Gosbecks. I need to ask them about their taxes and what they will owe this time around. The weather has been good and I noticed good crops in the fields coming into town. I expect this year everyone will be able to pay up on their taxes and make up from last year's taxes that were in arrears." Gnaeus Hortensius Aquila smiled and then tackled his food starting with the olives and onions. Then he broke off a big piece of bread and dipped it in the olive oil, then ate a large bite. He took a deep swallow of the Falernian wine and smiled. "Good wine! *This is Falernian after all*. The bread is tolerable though, could be better."

Oisin smiled and nodded, relieved that everything *up to this point* seemed to be to his liking. "I'll be off to get the leaders of Gosbecks for you. Grania will stay here and wait on you if you need anything else, my lord." At Gnaeus Hortensius Aquila's nod Oisin darted out the door. Grania hovered just behind the bar in case she was needed. Soon the rest of the publican's retinue came in. They all found seats nearby the publicani but no one sat at his table showing their respect for him. Gnaeus Hortensius Aquila ordered more wine and more food. Grania kept him served as well as serving the other members of his retinue. Soon Oisin came back with several members of the leaders of Gosbecks. There were a small group of leaders that crowded around Gnaeus Hortensius Aquila's table, each looking slightly worried.

Gnaeus Hortensius Aquila made them all wait, taking his time finishing his food and drinking his wine. When he was finally finished he got Grania to refill his wine cup and to clear his food dishes. Once Grania came back with his wine he turned to the group and said: "I am here to assess the likelihood of recouping the losses incurred last year in taxes. Now looking at the crops in the fields it looks to me to be a much more successful growing season and you'll have ample crops to pay your taxes. That is good. There are a lot of your farmers that were unable to pay their taxes last season. Since they did not pay there will be a penalty levied on top of this year's taxes which they will be required to pay."

The first to step forward to speak was Ronan, the owner of a successful business in selling textiles and tartan clothing. "What about those that paid the taxes last year? Will they also be levied with this extra cost?"

Gnaeus Hortensius Aquila appeared to ponder this question for q moment. "That's a good question. Depending on how much we get from the farmers that are in arrears on their taxes you should not have to pay their portions. *But if there is a shortfall you all will be required to pay extra to make up this gap.*" There was an audible gasp from the leaders from Gosbecks at the proclamation. Gnaeus Hortensius Aquila folded his hands on his ample belly, looking completely satisfied with his answer despite the crowd's angry surprise and distress. He was anticipating this response and was used to their anger at being held responsible for everyone's deficits of taxes. He always considered this as one of the items that made his job as publicani so much more diverting. This chance to see the members of a group of barbarians under his influence understand the might of their Roman overlords.

Niamh, owner of a large and successful farm, stepped forward from the back. She was short but fierce in her stance with arms akimbo as she addressed the publican. "You know that we will all have to contribute then to the taxes for everyone. It was such a dismal last season. This year has proved to be much better but even then it doesn't look to be a great growing season. Everyone will still need to keep some of their crops for their own consumption for winter. You have guaranteed that everyone will need to pay extra taxes." There were angry cries of agreement in the crowd.

"That may be but the matter will still stand. Everyone will be paying into the taxes to make sure they are all payed for. Rome wants her cut." Gnaeus Hortensius Aquila looked self-satisfied and took the time to wipe his mouth after taking another swig of wine, he sniggered a little.

Declan the village smith with a missing arm stepped forward. "What about those that pay for all of the farmers that are still in arrears. Do they get any privilege for good intentions?"

Gnaeus Hortensius Aquila drank more wine then seemed to consider the question with a furrowed brow. "The answer is yes and no. Yes, you will be seen as a subject that can be counted on because you payed this seasons taxes. And no, because there is always next year's taxes to be gathered. You might have a bad year and fall behind on them." Gnaeus Hortensius Aquila turned and ordered more olives and onions from Grania who hopped up to get his food hoping they had enough olives and onions. She returned with them but also brought back some mixed vegetables in olive oil just in case the olives and onions didn't last. Gnaeus Hortensius Aquila smiled at the added food and quickly picked up a cucumber and ate it with relish.

Anlon the fair haired beekeeper for Gosbecks and owner of the honey cart called out a question.. "What about those that make their money selling goods? I've always paid my taxes even last year despite my bees having a hard time finding flowers last season. Do I have to pay additional money for a taxes shortage?"

Gnaeus Hortensius Aquila continued to eat. Then he wiped his fingers and mouth and answered: "The answer to that would be certainly you will be required to pay additional taxes to make up any shortfall. All of Gosbecks will be held liable for payment of taxes."

Miach stepped forward and asked: "So if we all pay our taxes will Rome be happy and leave Gosbecks alone?"

"Gosbecks is in a prime location. There are rumbles that there is plans in the future for a colonia[72] being built and veterans being retired to settle here with farms. I just don't have the timeline for it. It could be in several years or next year I don't know." Gnaeus Hortensius Aquila got extreme pleasure out of that bit of information that he dropped. *Let them chew on that for a while,* he thought. *It meant a greater Roman intrusion into Gosbecks.*

"How many veterans will be sent to Gosbecks? How big will the colonia be?" Miach asked perplexed and worried.

"It depends on how many retiring veterans they have. It could be fifty plus their families to one hundred plus their families. We're talking about one hundred to three hundred additional people coming to Gosbecks." Gnaeus Hortensius Aquila smirked at the looks of disbelief he saw. Now they will truly be uncertain of the changes coming to Gosbecks now that the Romans have come to Britannia. *Look at them squirm* he thought to himself and smiled even wider. *They have no idea how much things will change around here. Including their little village which will be built up and changed for the better. We will be getting rid of these awful round house monstrosities with their awful thatched roofs and barbaric method of heating with just a hole for a chimney in the roof.* He let that bit of information stew awhile longer.

"That means we will be outnumbered by Romans!" Niamh squawked. "Will they integrate with us or will it be the other way around?"

"I would imagine that you would need to accept their way of doing business. And you might want to learn Latin. You know, the language we Romans speak." Gnaeus Hortensius Aquila chortled at

---

[72] https://www.britannica.com/topic/colony-ancient-Roman-settlement http://www.livius.org/articles/concept/colonia/ https://books. google.com/books?id=XdSWklI_YRYC&pg=PA141&lpg=PA141& dq=colonia+in+Imperial+Rome&source=bl&ots=qT40TdkPMp& sig=XN9WGcFpfZhTng_FJqoe7UpOddI&hl=en&sa=X&ved= 0ahUKEwjcgda0rsbOAhVS1GMKHY8CCv0Q6AEIOjAE#v=onepage&q= colonia%20in%20Imperial%20Rome&f=false

their gasps. He decided to end this meeting at this point and stood up. His assistant Fabius jumped up with his scrolls and handed them to Gnaeus Hortensius Aquila. "I have all of the information here on the taxes that are in arears and their amounts. Come to my table tomorrow and we'll discuss how much you are responsible for this season. The meeting is adjourned." He then got up and went over to Oisin to settle his bill.

Oisin tabulated everything quickly. "Will my lord need a table set aside to hold your meetings tomorrow?"

Gnaeus Hortensius Aquila looked peeved. "Of course I'm going to need your best table for the next couple of days. What did you think I was going to do? Conduct my business in my cart? And have plenty of the Falernian wine ready tomorrow for the meetings. I don't want to have to ask for it when I arrive. Keep it flowing. I'm sure I'll have a lot of whining farmers and businessmen when they get their tax bills."

"As you wish my lord." Oisin said. He counted out the sestertius's in his hand for today's bill. *At least he pays well and will get me a fat profit*, Oisin thought. Grania went about cleaning up his table. She then got more orders from members of the publican's retinue as they continued to eat and drink.

The next day the publican and his retinue set up in the middle of the tavern. An unending line of farmers began to come into the tavern to talk to Gnaeus Hortensius Aquila, each with their faces showing their worry over their tax bills because they knew they will owed so much. Frequently when they were told how much they owed to Roman government they would cry out in anguish at the exorbitant amount. There were several smaller farmsteads that couldn't carry the bill so they lost their farms to Rome. But the larger ones seemed able to do better. One of these larger farmers that came in was Ferdia and his wife Aideen. They had a large farm that was quite prosperous and were just able to pay their taxes last year. They came into the tavern with confidence that they wouldn't have to be owing more to the publicani except for this season. But to their consternation they found that they would be owing additional taxes to help pay for the other farmers shortfalls.

"This is quite unforgivable. Why do I need to pay more to the Roman government when I paid my taxes last year?" Ferdia ran his hand through his dark hair in exasperation.

Gnaeus Hortensius Aquila just folded his hands over his ample stomach and smiled. "I know this is difficult for you to understand but there is a complex problem in Gosbecks. There are more farmers that cannot pay their taxes than can. The shortfall must be made up somehow and this is the most logical way to do it. To even out the difficulty I need to take the wheat from the larger farms that can afford it. Gosbecks will prosper and Rome will be happy."

Ferdia looked incensed. "I don't care about Rome being happy. I care about my family making through this next winter season. If we pay these taxes that you have levied on my farm there is a strong reason we won't be able to survive until spring. And it doesn't even leave us with seeds for the next growing season let alone enough food for our cows for the winter."

"Now, now, this is a perfectly reasonable amount that you can easily afford. Next season will be even more successful than this one." Gnaeus Hortensius Aquila placatingly waved his hands. He took the opportunity to take a swig of his wine before continuing. "It is just the way we must do this harvest season. You harvest the wheat and I collect the levies for Rome. It is as simple as that." Ferdia eyed the publican with disgust but said nothing. He gathered up his wife Aideen in his arm and they left with their bill on a scroll which they could not read anyway but was given to them as a formality.

Other farmers continued to come in and leave with bad news as well. Toward the end of the afternoon Niamh finally marched in with her husband Galahaut. "I hear that you are levying additional taxes even on those that paid last year. Why is that Gnaeus Hortensius Aquila?" She said.

Gnaeus Hortensius Aquila was displeased to hear Niamh say

his name and not to be addressed as "My Lord" as he was used to being addressed. "I am levying these taxes because there are still farmers that cannot make uithp their tax losses from last year. The amount of these additional taxes will still need to be paid from this year to make up from last year."

"Maybe if your lenient this year you would get more taxes that way. After all there is always next year's taxes." Niamh said with exasperation. She was getting mad at the publican and his short sighted ways.

The publican looked at Niamh with a punishing stare. "Rome needs her cut from the farmers, whether that is from their wheat crops, their cows, their vegetables they produce for sale or even timber cut down from their land. Anything that they can produce from their farms. I can get the taxes from them on an annual basis. Rome was willing to give everyone a pass last year because the bad weather effected so much of the country including the lands around Gosbecks. But now Rome is tired of waiting. Rome wants its taxes. Rome wants to be paid. So for you here is the taxes I am expecting from you." He handed a scroll to Niamh and Galahaut knowing that they couldn't read it. It gave him a feeling of superiority to hand out the scrolls.

"You know I can't read. Why don't you just tell me what we owe." She said with anger in her voice at his arrogance.

"I require the entire wheat crop from your northern field. It produces twelve bushels of wheat does it not?" Gnaeus Hortensius Aquila said with a wicked smile on his face.

He's enjoying this, thought Niamh. But she said: "Yes, that is about right. But the north pasture is my biggest growing crop of wheat. Could I include payments of lumber and vegetables like you listed off earlier? I can even include ten head of cattle."

"The ten head of cattle we'll take, and two pallets of lumber as well. Fifty pounds of vegetables we'll take but we will still need a minimum of six bushels of wheat." The publican listed off the cost of her taxes and sat back to see what she will say.

Niamh ground her teeth. "What about ten cows, three pallets of lumber and twenty-five pounds of vegetables with five bushels of wheat."

Gnaeus Hortensius Aquila was enjoying her bartering skills. "What type of wood are we talking about?"

"Oak, hawthorn and pine."

"Hmmm … Make that all oak and hawthorn and you have a deal." The publican said. Oak and hawthorn were much harder woods and were much more in demand than pine which tended to be too soft to do any building with that would last any amount of time.

Niamh and Galahaut stood up. They looked at Gnaeus Hortensius Aquila with abhorrence and left the tavern. Behind them came in Bebhinn and Ardan. Niamh caught Bebhinn's eye and just shook her head. "Barter your taxes with the publican. He is greedy today and is asking for a lot of taxes to be paid. If you offer additional goods he'll take it."

Bebhinn and Ardan came to sit down with the publican. He was ordering some appetizers of olives, onions and vegetables in a nice spicy wine sauce with more wine from Grania for his dinner. When he was done he looked up at Bebhinn and Ardan. "Ah, Gosbecks resident healer. How is business this year? Better than last year I hope."

"It is steady. Fortunately no one has been really ill. Just some births." Bebhinn answered him, surprised that he remembered what she did for a living.

"Good, nice to hear all that. Let's get down to business. For your taxes this year I will require twelve bushels of wheat or six sestertii[73] if you would prefer to pay by coin. Do you get paid for your services as a healer?' Gnaeus Hortensius Aquila asked her patiently.

---

[73] http://www.dl.ket.org/latinlit/mores/currency/currency.htm
http://www.ancient.eu/Roman_Coinage/

He folded his hands and waited for her answer knowing she got her payments in kind with trade goods and not coins.

"We'll pay the twelve bushels of wheat." Ardan. said. He was angry at the exorbitant amount but didn't say anything. They would just have a lean winter.

"Could we pay in vegetables? Or I can include some of my medicinal plants for you Romans. Maybe thirty baskets full? And drop the wheat to nine bushels." Bebhinn said.

Gnaeus Hortensius Aquila cocked his head sideways making his double chins triple and nodded. "If you include some of your medicinal plants in the thirty baskets we can do that." The publicani grinned broadly thinking of how primitive the Celts were and that they couldn't possibly have any medicinal plants Rome would want. But he said: "You will have to teach my men the medical properties so they can write down the efficacies of each plant and what it cures."

"Done then. We will do that for our taxes." Ardan finally smiled. He put his arm around Bebhinn and walked out with her. "You saved us from a lean winter with your quick thinking back there. I didn't know he would be interested in vegetables and you pharmacopoeia of medicinal plants."

Bebhinn smiled and blushed at his praise. "I didn't either. But Niamh told me to barter when he got to the amount of the taxes and it worked. We'll need to pay her back with a party or something."

Ardan smiled in anticipation. "That sounds good. We have been working so hard these past weeks that taking time out for a celebration would be diverting."

They walked out and ran into Niamh and Galahaut who were outside talking to some of the smaller farm owners that were unsettled because they couldn't afford their tax bills. Their winters would be lean indeed and they were all worried. There were also those smaller farmers from that just lost their farms. They were all in shock, their wives crying on their husbands shoulders. One of the smaller farmers that were worried about payments of the taxes and how it would affect their winter was Tierney and his wife Liadan. She was carrying her new infant daughter Einin in her arms. "We will probably need to get rid of our cows. We are required to pay nine bushels of wheat but that will take away our fodder for the cows in the winter. We will have a very lean winter season." Tierney said. Liadan shook her head and bounced her new babe. Einin was beginning to root around for her midday meal so Liadan went over to the side and sat down on the ground. She began to breast feed Einin, talking soothingly to her new daughter.

Another small farmer Lachlan and his wife Neala came over to their group. "We were taxed twelve bushels. But we negotiated fifteen baskets of vegetables and three of our cows to take the number of bushels of wheat down to six. It will still be a lean winter and tough spring for us. We thought about getting a loan from Gnaeus Hortensius Aquila but the terms were so exorbitant."

"What were the terms?" Niamh asked curious to see what they were.

"Payment due the next season at twenty bushels. There is no way we could possibly handle that." Neala said with a shudder. There were cries of disbelief from the farmers standing around listening.

"Gnaeus Hortensius Aquila is a greedy pig. He treats Celts like sheep, herding them this way and that to get his taxes for Rome. Never get a loan from him. If you need assistance come to me before you go to him. I'll offer you much better terms. There are other more prosperous farmers that can help out too. You can also go to Declan or Ronan for loans of coin. We'll help you out. Don't go to that Roman publican." Niamh said with a huff. There were several members of the crowd that started to step forward and ask her for help. "One at a time, please!" Niamh said.

Tierney stepped forward. "Please help us Niamh. We need help. I can probably provide Rome six bushels wheat but not the fifteen baskets of vegetables. Losing the three cows will be enough of hardship."

Bebhinn patted his arm. "I can help you with the fifteen baskets of vegetables Tierney. It would be my pleasure. Just come over to my garden when the harvest time comes around. I'll help you to harvest the vegetables."

Tierney looked surprised. "Thank you Bebhinn. You helped in the birthing of our precious Einin and now you're helping us with our taxes. May the gods bless you and your family."

Lachlan and Neala stepped forward. Neala asked: "Niamh, could you help us with the twelve bushels of wheat? Or do you advise we harvest some of our lumber on our farm and give it to the Romans in place of some of the payments?"

Niamh considered a moment before she answered. "That's a good idea. But you might want to go back inside and clear it with the publican first. He wants to keep tabs on all the produce, lumber and farm animals going to him. I know you have a lot of pigs, why don't you give him some of them. Maybe six or ten. Romans love to eat pork."

Lachlan smiled. "Thank you Niamh! I did not know the Romans love to eat pork. My sows just had two litters apiece and I can take the twelve from one of them to pay for taxes. I'll go in right now and offer them up." He took Neala's hand and they disappeared into the tavern.

"What is to become of us?" Asked Tyree, one of the young farmers who couldn't pay his taxes and lost his farm to the publican. He was wringing his hands and tears were coming out of his eyes he was so upset. "We don't even have a place to live anymore. My wife Brigid and I have two small children. She doesn't even know the bad news I have yet."

Ferdia and Aideen had wandered over to listen to the news. Ferdia stepped forward. "Tyree, you and your family can come stay at our farm. They aren't far from each other and we have plenty of room. I could use the extra help on the farm."

Tyree was so thankful. He was emotional about losing his farm and dreaded going home to tell his wife and kids. "Thank you

Ferdia and Aideen. I will gladly take your offer of staying at your farm. I will help on your farm and my son who is twelve summers old will help as well. We'll do all we can to help you out on your farm."

"Good, we will enjoy the company. Aideen will enjoy the company and help that Brigid will give her in the farmhouse. We have three sons all under the age of seven seasons. She'll enjoy the companionship." Ferdia said kindly. He put a consoling hand on Tyree's shoulder while Tyree broke down sobbing. "Take as much time as you need to transfer all of your things over to my farm. I have plenty of space, in the barn and even in the farm house."

"It won't be much. Just our clothes and some cooking implements. The publican took everything else. Even all my farming equipment." Tyree choked out. "I hate that toad."

"We all do Tyree." Niamh said and she gave him a soothing hug. "Cheer up. Eventually you'll get back on your feet and buy another farm. And when it does great you'll be able to deal with Gnaeus Hortensius Aquila again but on a more equal level than before."

Tyree let out a little bark of laughter, spraying spittle out of his mouth when he did so. "Wouldn't that be a lark. Thank you everyone for helping out. Brigid and I don't have any family to go back to so we had no place to go."

"That's what we do here in Gosbecks. Look after each other." Niamh said kindly.

Bebhinn reached out to rub Tyree's back in a reassuring way. "I birthed your children and would like to birth more. Keep believing in yourself and work hard. May the gods will grant you luck in the future seasons."

◻◻◻◻

Gnaeus Hortensius Aquila stayed for several days tallying up the taxes due to Rome from the people of Gosbecks. Some of the populous found they had to ask for loans from the publican and found it to be at exorbitant rates. The next season will tell the tell if they would be able to pay back the loans. Others were smart enough to go to the richer farmers in Gosbecks to get relief on their taxes. Cathmore was happy to find that he was able to house another family that lost their farm due to non-payment of taxes. Cathmore, with his withered left arm, couldn't do a lot of the jobs on his rather large farm. He also had only two daughters so a lot of the jobs weren't getting done. Cathmore was able to get a family with two sons that could do the work that had been left undone for several weeks. But the atmosphere of distrust and hatred was simmering just below the surface in Gosbecks toward the Roman government.

The publican made a great deal of money this trip to Gosbecks. He was very happy and when he paid Oisin he tipped the sycophant an enormous amount. Oisin was over the moon at his windfall. He quickly ran to Grania and showed her all of the sestertii he was paid for the food and drink. He swiftly placed another large order for Falernian wine and olives from his Roman seller. "I hate the publicani but I love his money." He told Grania. She nodded her little bird like head.

回回回回

Word came down that there was discontent among the tribes. The Iceni[74] were fomenting and talking to all of the tribes in the area. It seemed like more problems with the Romans was the cause this time. The people of Gosbecks were sympathetic. They were having the same problems with the Roman tax authorities. They were being squeezed because of their poor payments of taxes from last years bad harvest due to the rainy weather.

---

[74] https://www.britannica.com/topic/Iceni
http://www.britainexpress.com/History/roman/iceni.htm

"Well hail Miach! Good to see you this morning. I've been hearing from some of the patrons that the Iceni are fomenting against the Romans. What's up with the Iceni? Do you think they are having the same problems that we are Miach?" Asked Oisin in the morning when Miach came to break his fast at the tavern.

Miach walked into the tavern and took a seat. He sat down and stroked his beard thinking of his response. "There are rumors that the Romans do not recognize Queen Boudicca[75] as the next Queen of the Iceni. You see her husband King Prasutagus has died and Rome has not recognized Boudicca as the queen of the Iceni. Prasutagus was considered a client king and the treaty is void upon his death. Rome does not recognize Queen Boudica because they only recognize client kings not client queens in their treaties. In fact the Romans have tried to take over the goods and lands of the Iceni. Even her daughters aren't recognized as princesses. It seems the Romans don't recognize women as queens and singular holders of power."

"Will they do that to us?" Oisin asked worriedly, smoothing his lank straight hair behind his ears. His rat-like face showing his anxiety.

"It's possible. The Romans only want to own the lands that we currently have. Any means of acquiring them is good cause to take our lands with the Romans. If that means taking over the farms because of non-payment of taxes then they she will do it. We must be vigilant to help our neighbors keep their farms and prevent this from happening." Miach shook his head in exasperation. "We need to work together as a people, as Trinovantes[76]." He looked tired. He had been up all night long deliberating this problem, trying to see ways around it. It was difficult. The first thing the tribes wanted to do was act as a separate unit, unified by their own peoples. They

---

[75] http://www.historynet.com/boudica-celtic-war-queen-who-challenged-rome.htm

[76] http://www.historyfiles.co.uk/KingListsBritain/BritainTrinovantes.htm

didn't have any experience otherwise. The future would depend on something new to them and it was up to the druids to help get the tribe through this difficult time.

Cathmore and his wife Meara walked into the tavern at this point. Cathmore saw Miach and made his way over to him. "Well hail Miach. What brings you into the tavern?"

Miach stroked his beard with his hand in contemplation. "I was just telling Oisin that there is word the Iceni are unsettled because the Romans do not see Queen Boudicca as a legitimate leader of the tribe. They consider their treaty with King Prasutagus is over because he died without a male heir. Boudicca and Prasutagus only had daughters. I'm told their laws do not recognize the female line of authority." Miach told Cathmore. "I am worried that they will now turn their attention to some of our farms looking to take over them as well."

Cathmore and Meara looked at each other in surprise. Cathmore said: "What do you think they'll do?"

"The Romans will use whatever excuse they can in order to take what they want, land, farms, extra crops, cattle, other livestock. We are not safe. No one is." Miach answered gravely.

〓〓〓〓

The next day they had a assemblage of envoys from the Iceni came to Gosbecks. The group asked to speak to the leaders of Gosbecks including Miach. Word went out that there was to be an emergency meeting at the neighborhood tavern. The leaders of Gosbecks all assembled in the tavern . Leaders such as owners of large farmsteads, the smith, leading commercial holders, and the local druid Miach were all included. There was a great deal of interest as to what the meeting would entail.

As they gathered the envoys stepped forward. "I am called Cian, and I have come to ask you to join Queen Boudicca in a rebellion against the Romans. She is gathering many tribes together to fight against the tyranny that the Romans have been levying upon us. The Queen has been wronged and will seek recompense for the brutal assault the Romans did to her person And to her daughters.. She seeks justice."

The other envoy stepped forward. "I am Enda and I want to talk to you about joining this glorious enterprise. We all know that the Romans are greedy and looking to take over as much land as possible. They are crushing us with taxes. They are forcing us to give more and more in repayment of loans made at outrageous terms. They are even enslaving our people in record numbers." Here the envoy wiped his impassioned brow with a handkerchief. His forehead beading up with sweat as he got himself worked up "We all know that the Romans want our land. Let's not give them the excuse to take it!" Enda struck his hand on his other with force to make a loud slapping sound. The listeners were nodding their heads and agreeing with Enda and Cian. They had all experienced these indignities to varying degrees.

"What can you do to allay these problems?" Miach the druid asked. He stood tall and dignified in the midst of the crowd. His robes a distinguished gray with an embroidered edging in woad blue dyed spirals. Likewise his cloak was embroidered with Celtic whorls. His long gray hair and beard lent him an air of formality.

Cian stepped forward. "We would like for you to join in this rebellion. We are tired of working for the Romans. They are bleeding us of all of our goods and services. They have just about bled our men working on the temple for their emperor Claudius that has just died. They declared him a deity and our men are spending all their time building the massive temple. Time and money is spent building the garish edifice. It is faced with marble and inlaid with gold!" He tossed his black braids back from his face. His hands going to move the braids behind his ears. He had a pleasing face with his dark eyes and strong features.

"We don't need any more deities like the god emperor Claudius. It is just another way to raise more taxation on the Celtic people.

They will be asking for more tribute soon," Enda said with a disgusted look on his rather homey face. He pushed his rather drab dirty brown hair back behind his ears and smoothed his scrawny beard.

"So you would like us to join your army? What have the leaders of Camulodunum said? Will they be joining you?" asked Declan, Gosbecks smith. He stood with the leaders despite having to turn over his smithy to his son because he had lost his right arm in a battle with the Romans not six months prior. It was a big blow to Declan but he was well respected in Gosbecks and retained his leader designation according to to people of Gosbecks. He stood there with his large bulky frame and light colored hair smoothed back in a ponytail.

Cian stepped forward and said: "The Camulodunum Trinovantes will fight with Queen Boudicca. So will the Trinovantes around Londinium. Everyone is turning to follow the Iceni queen." He smiled and wiped his forehead again with his handkerchief.

Ardan stepped forward to offer his opinion. "I have seen the injustices perpetrated on the Celtic people in particular the people of Gosbecks. It is unforgivable. I think we should move to take up this call to arms." His handsome face looked determined. He moved his graying wavey hair behind his ears in an unconscious mannerism. He stood tall and proud. Bebhinn started. She looked worried at his pronouncement.

"Wait a minute, why are you so willing to join this enterprise," a matronly woman at the back stepped forward. She had a determined face with long gray hair braided and wrapped around her head. Her well endowed body was dressed beautifully with a long tartan dress trimmed with furs showing her wealth[77]. Her matronly face was wrinkled with suspicion and not happy about it.

---

[77] http://theceltsat.blogspot.com/2010/08/ancient-celtic-clothing-french-celtic.html

"Now Niamh, not everyone has successful farms like ours. We have the largest farm in Gosbecks and we work hard to keep it. Let the others make their own decisions. I am in agreement with Ardan. I am inclined to join the fight as well," her husband Galahaut said. "I am even willing to have Adair come with me in this heroic endeavor." Galahaut stood there with his ample girth and a big grin on his jovial face. He was an easy going man and left his wife to handle the business side of running the farm and making th harsher decisions needed on farms. His clothes were well apportioned and nice. His robes lined with fur and looked rich.

Niamh snickered. "You think to fight with Adair in Boudicca's army? As what? You haven't wielded a sword in many years. You would be better off acting as their purchasing agent for food stuffs. You and Adair don't have what it takes to fight."

Galahaut smiled good naturedly, showing that he was a long suffering husband to Niamh but he enjoyed her sniping. His pleasing round face smiled. "I am perfectly aware of my shortcomings on the field of battle. I will take a position at the back of the battle with Adair. We'll take the road of least resistance but I want to lend our help if we can."

"I don't think you'll be able to help but I applaud your enthusiasm." Niamh smiled.

The towns' tavern keeper Oisin stepped forward. "What do the Iceni hope to accomplish? Are they going to knit together a lot of the tribes to fight the Romans?" He was a small man with quick hands and couldn't seem to stand still very long. As soon as he asked his question he motioned to his wife Grania to take more orders for ale from those present. His wife was also small like Oisin and birdlike in her movements as she scurried off to take more orders for ale from those near her.

Enda stepped forward. "Queen Boudicca is talking with all of the tribes, even those that she hasn't got good relations with. She is trying to knit together a vast quilt of tribes to be including their contributions to her army. So far we have the Trinovantes. The next we will have the Cantulauvani[78] and Atrebates[79], the Regnenses[80] and the Cantiaci[81]."

"That's quite a lot of mixing of the tribes. How is Queen Boudicca going to forge the alliance?" asked Miach.

"With a lot of negotiating between the heads of the tribes. The kings will require a lot of discussions to find the correct and agreeable end." Cian motioned with his hand to show that the negotiations will be arduous. The people in the crowd all nodded their heads in agreement.

Enda said: "There is currently a lot of bad blood between some of the peoples in the different tribes but to make this endeavor work we must all work past the differences and work together against the Romans. The Romans are the foe, not the different Celts."

"How will this affect the markets?" asked Ronan, a prominent merchant. He was small and dark headed. He was well respected for his woven wares. He wore a fine tartan[82] of interesting design.

Cian glanced at Enda. He looked nonplussed but then said: "We are talking about shedding the skin of the snake that is Rome. I don't know what the repercussions would be for the markets other than that they will be free of the money lenders and taxes that the Romans levy on all of us."

"I'm asking because if everyone leaves to go fight the Romans there will be a great absence of men, women and older boys and girls that will all flock to fight in the rebellion. That will affect those of us who do not go fight. We will be left here with those who must stay and bring in the crops from the fields." Ronan smiled but under his smile was the worry that many were beginning to feel, those of

---

[78] http://www.bbc.co.uk/history/ancient/british_prehistory/iron_01.shtml
[79] https://www.britannica.com/topic/Atrebates
http://www.historyfiles.co.uk/KingListsBritain/BritainAtrebates.htm
[80] https://simple.wikipedia.org/wiki/Regnenses
[81] http://www.bbc.co.uk/history/ancient/british_prehistory/iron_01.shtml
http://www.historyfiles.co.uk/KingListsBritain/BritainCantii.htm
[82] https://en.wikipedia.org/wiki/Tartan

the crowd that were not that keen on kicking out the Romans such as those in commerce.

Enda smiled. "We should all look forward to the day when the Romans are no longer in Britannia. The land should go back to how it was before the Romans came and imposed their rule on us." At that several people clapped their approval. Then more people clapped and some ventured to say they were going to join the army for Queen Boudicca.

Cian then stepped forward. "I want everyone to know that this endeavor will be sung about from all the fireplaces from now to time immemorial. We need to show the despicable Romans that we want to kick them out of Britannia. They murdered our druids on the Isle of Mona and now we need to show them that it is not allowed for them to keep in power here." He gesticulated with his arms and hands the entire time he spoke. The people around him started to agree with the envoy saying "Yes!" and "We approve!"

"So how many men and women should we send to Queen Boudicca?" asked Miach getting to the heart of the matter immediately as he usually did.

"We would like to take as many as you can afford to let go. Of course there will be a need to keep some of the men and women here to reap the fields when harvest time comes which will be shortly. The rest can come with us to join Queen Boudicca's army," Enda said, he mopped his forehead again as he got excited about adding the advent of the army from Gosbecks.

"That is an open ended amount of people. It sounds like you are asking for all of the able bodied men and women to come and fight. I think this is very scary," Ronan said, his anxiety showing on his face. His wife stood next to him and clutched his arm in solidarity. Her pretty older face showing her worry.

"We are needing enough to fight the Romans. They have the armies but we have the numbers." Cian stated with alacrity. He felt strongly confident about their impending victory. There was stronger smattering of applause. More people saying "Yes!" and "We need to go now!" and "More people need to join!"

Miach stood there with a pensive look on his face. He was picturing the amount of people that would follow the envoys to Queen Boudicca's army. That left a small amount of people left in Gosbecks. Barely half of the population would be left. That was alarming. "When do you want the people to assemble for the army?" he asked.

"We anticipate leaving shortly before the harvest. That gives us plenty of time to fight then come back and finish the harvest." Enda said. His homely face creased in a huge smile. He smoothed his lank greasy hair behind his ears. There was a great swelling of applause from the people in the tavern. If it was because of the drinks that had been served to the patrons or the information from the envoys it was not determined. Probably a little of both. They decided to get those who would like to go volunteer later in the week so the envoys could get a grip on the numbers coming from Gosbecks. They were very happy with the way their morning went. The tavern began to break up as the people started to head back to their homes. Ardan and Bebhinn started back to their own farm and caught up with Niamh and Galahaut who had their farm closest to theirs.

"So what do you think about the meeting?" Niamh asked Bebhinn. "I'm not sure I like the fact that so many people will be leaving Gosbecks to fight." She moved an errant strand of hair from her mouth as she walked forward.

Bebhinn glanced at Ardan who was deep in conversation with Galahaut. She looked very pensive and bit her lip. "I don't know what to think about this whole endeavor. There are legitimate issues to fight for but there is also the fact that the whole Roman army vastly out did our Druids on the Isle of Mona. They have a really fine and terrifyingly able army. Nothing seems beyond their army to vanquish."

"I agree with you. I am afraid for Galahaut. He is not a soldier.

Adair is just like his father. Both of them will not make it in a pitched battle. Galahaut has never really fought." Niamh pursed her lips. "I just wish I can talk him out of going."

"I need to talk Ardan out of going as well," Bebhinn assured Niamh. She looked worriedly at Ardan again. They continued walking along the dirt road to their farms. The dirt road was edged by beautiful oaks and elders arching gracefully. There were blackberry thickets growing under the trees, this was a favorite spot for Bebhinn to pick blackberries in the late summer and fall. Bebhinn got her fill of the ripe, deep black, lovely berries at that time. She was able to pick enough to flavor some of her elixirs she used for her healing. She was trained by the Iceni druids to be a full-fledged healer. She fell in love with Ardan one Beltane festival and came to live with him. She got Edana her eldest child out of that happy coincidence.

She loved Ardan but his single-minded purpose chilled her. He was always like this. He'd get an idea and would follow it to fruition. He was like that on their farm. He got the idea to raise goats despite it being different from the other farmers. Most of the other farmers raised sheep. Now they had a herd of fifteen goats. Bebhinn was able to use the goat milk for some of her elixirs when healing. Plus they also loved the cheese they got from the goat milk. Their farm was successful but it was also a lot of work. It took all of Ardan and their son Carrick's time to bring in the harvest. That was with the help of Bebhinn and Edana their eldest daughter. Bebhinn shook her beautiful head, her red hair bound up in braids shook. She was tall and willowy, and moved with the natural grace of a deer. Ardan loved her very much. He loved the prestige he gained by having her, the village healer, as his wife. He also gained prestige with the druidic world since Bebhinn was considered a druid in her own right. This made visiting druids stop by to talk with her. Miach was a regular visitor to their farm. Especially now since their youngest son Ailbe was showing signs of druidic ability of foreseeing the future in his dreams. It was often disconcerting to have the youngest know exactly what was going on in the adult world but seen through the lens of a seven year old. He often got scared because the dreams didn't make sense to him or even to Bebhinn or Ardan. It took the interpretation of Miach to bring them into focus. Miach said Ailbe was quickly becoming a first class prognosticator of future events. Ardan felt so proud to have Fabered a druid.

"We'll need to work together to turn the men's heads regarding going to war. War is always a bad thing. There is always unintended consequences. Ronan is right there will be a disruption of the commerce around here. There will be shortages for some of the staples such as salt and certain foodstuffs such as milk products. Bebhinn you might see an uptick of sales of your goats milk and cheeses. You know how much your people love milk products," Niamh said with a frown.

"I don't think I have enough goats to keep up with the uptick of orders. We barely keep up with the orders now as it is. I'll need to buy some more goats at the next market day," Bebhinn worried. The sun dappled the road as they continued to walk on. A thrush twittered in the undergrowth being startled by the people coming by.

Ardan and Galahaut kept their heads together as they discussed their plans to join Queen Boudicca's army. Both had let the romance of a big endeavor, a great event to anticipate get the better of them. They discussed how they would get to lead in the army. Each assuming they would be a general over someone. Galahaut assumed he'd be the quartermaster and order goods and foodstuffs for the army. Ardan assumed he would be the high level officer in the tactical wing of the army. He'd be involved with the orders to fight, the tactical arrays to be tried. Both felt they could contribute greatly to this great struggle. Both saw the inevitable victory of the Celts. After all they outnumbered the Romans a hundred to one. It was assumed that a Celt was worth fifty Roman soldiers.

They parted ways at a fork in the road, one way went to Niamh and Galahaut's farm and one to Bebhinn and Ardan's. The fork in the road was beautiful. The lanes were surrounded by hawthorns that were heavy with attractive foliage. Lining the way was wild roses that were blooming with profusion, their red heads nodding in the afternoon sunshine and slight breeze. "Let me know how your endeavor goes," Niamh told Bebhinn.

"And yours as well," Bebhinn told Niamh. Galahaut and Ardan just clasped each others hands and moved onto their prospective farms.

回回回回

Back at the farm Bebhinn and Ardan went into the main farm house.. Instead of going into the farmhouse Ardan turned and went to go gather the goats from the upper pasture lush pasture. The farm had many pastures, the closest one had the oxen and horses in it. They separated the goats frequently from the oxen and horses because the goats ate so much. The closest pasture was a rolling green field filled with summer flowers. The edges had oak and elder bordering the pasture with hawthorn growing between the trees. It was very beautiful. Bebhinn turned and went inside the farmhouse. She wanted to talk with Edana.

"How was the meeting mother?" asked Edana, the eldest of Ardan and Bebhinn's children. At eighteen she was the image of Bebhinn. Tall and willowy like her mother but where Bebhinn had red, curly hair, Edana had blond curly hair. Edana had clear gray eyes that looked through to the soul of the matter when she looked at anyone. Many thought her clear gray eyes were unnerving. Others thought they were lovely.

"The meeting was interesting. The Iceni Queen Boudicca is sending envoys out to get the different tribes to pledge soldiers for her army to wage war against the Romans. So far a lot of the Trinovantes have turned to her cause, m ost from Camulodunum and Londinium," Bebhinn told her.

"So there is to be a fight against the Romans? How bad will that be for those of us who do not fight?" Edana asked.

Bebhinn shook her head and frowned. "It looks to be a big endeavor. There is a lot of people not happy with Roman rule. There are a lot of people crushed under the yoke of Roman taxation and moneylenders. They see this as a way to get out from under the yoke of the Romans."

"But they will be waging war! War is never a good or reliable way to deal with issues." Edana looked worried as she thought about the repercussions of a possible war with the Romans.

"Yes, you see the problems clearly. But there are many who look forward to fighting the Romans to get them to leave Britannia." Bebhinn looked anxious. "Your Faber wants to go to war and will take Carrick with him."

"Faber and Carrick! We can't have that happen, they need to stay here and harvest the fields. When are they to go to war?" Edana looked really worried. She ran her hands distractedly through her hair.

"They are to go to war shortly before harvest time. The thought is that the Romans will lose and everyone will return in time to harvest the grains."

"They'll be back for harvest? What if they don't come back? How are we to bring in the harvest? That means we'll probably have to leave some of the wheat or barley in the fields!" Edana threw her hands out in exasperation.

"Yes, that is exactly what that means. However we outnumber the Romans one hundred to one. That means they won't win. We will be able to vanquish them." Bebhinn said but didn't sound to sure.

"We outnumber the Romans by that much? Maybe it will be a good war than." Edana looked a little more confident.

Ailbe ran into the kitchen to find his mother and Edana talking and rushed into Bebhinn's arms. "Where did you and Faber go this morning Mother?" he asked.

"There are envoys from the Iceni that have come to Gosbecks.

We wanted to hear what they had to say." Bebhinn hugged Ailbe as he crushed her with his arms.

"What do they have to say?" Ailbe seemed to be interested in what the Iceni wanted to discuss. "Are they your relatives? You come from the Iceni tribe after all."

"No they aren't my relatives. I don't know them. They came to ask for volunteers from Gosbecks to go fight with them in the Iceni Queen Boudicca's army." Bebhinn looked at Ailbe with worry. She hoped he had not dreamt of the war yet. She did not want to know what he would have to say. She was in fact fearful of what he would have to say.

"An army? Who will they be fighting Mother?" was all Ailbe asked.

"They will be fighting the Romans," Bebhinn said looking at Ailbe closely.

Ailbe looked at Bebhinn with a quizzical look on his small boys face. "But we are not at war with the Romans, are we?"

"The Romans are doing a lot of things that we do not like. Taxation is getting more and more as time goes on so a lot of the people are angry about that. Then there are the money lenders. Those Romans lend money at exorbitant rates and make it hard to repay. They seem to be doing it on purpose so they can collect on the farms from those that can no longer pay back their terms. They do this this so they could get the land or piece of equipment or whatever the money was lent for." Bebhinn smiled sadly at Ailbe. "Just be glad that your Faber and I have not had to borrow money from the money lenders."

Ailbe looked troubled. "So if the Romans are doing these things a war with them will be a good thing?"

Bebhinn shrugged her shoulders. "They said that if the Celts go to war with the Romans the Celts outnumber the Romans a hundred to one. With those odds it seems like a good reason to go to war. Winning seems likely."

That evening at dinner there was more talk about the upcoming war. Carrick had been filled in on the call to arms by the envoys. "I am looking forward to going to war!" he enthused. "I'll be the first to kill several Roman soldiers. I've been practicing all summer with my friends. I'm quite good. I'm quick. And I'm deadly."

"We need to do more practicing. We'll get going late summer, and be back in time to harvest the wheat and barley. After last year's bad harvest this will certainly be a boon." Ardan looked happy. He was feeling good about this endeavor.

"I'll practice with you as well!" shouted Ailbe. "I need to be able to fight for Mother and Edana while you are gone."

"And so you shall. You need to be able to defend your Mother and sister against the hordes of Romans who might come after we are gone." Ardan beamed. Ailbe let out a whoop of triumph. He and Carrick started to wrestle on the floor of the dining area. There was a lot of laughing between Ardan, Carrick and Ailbe. Edana and Bebhinn shook their heads and bent to cleaning up their dinner scraps. They tidied up the remains of their dinner of goose and wild onions with greens and set them aside for a nourishing morning meal. The dandelion salad was also scraped into the pigs slop bucket along with the remains from everyone's wooden bowls. They then cleaned the bowls and eating spoons and knives.

"Why is Faber so happy? Doesn't he know they could be killed?" Edana whispered to Bebhinn.

Bebhinn kept her head bent to her task. "Maybe he knows something we don't. The odds are in his favor they will win."

"But the Romans decimated our druids on the Isle of Mona. That was with an assemblage of the best druids that we had. The head druids The O'Shea, The O'Connor and The O'Reilly and the O'Nialle were all killed. We have no more top hierarchy in the druidic counsel left. They were all killed by the Romans. Do you think they will fight better than we think?" Edana asked.

"Let us hope they don't. We need to pray to Badb Catha[83] to ensure their victory in battle." Bebhinn looked up and it was then that Edana saw the tears in her mother's eyes. She realized at that moment that her mother was frightened for her Faber and brother.

〄〄〄〄

For the rest of the summer they all prepared for the impending harvest. Bebhinn and Niamh were unable to change the direction of Ardan and Galahaut's decision to go to war. The men planned on going to war and didn't deviate from the decision. In the meantime all of Gosbecks was in a frenzy to prepare for the oncoming midsummer exit to war. The men and women who planned on going were all ready. The smithy was in overtime to prepare for war. New swords were smelted, taking the place of the regular items such as plows normally done at this time of year in preparation for harvest time. They also made up caps for the water canteens, knives, and dirks for their mess kits. The smithy was really busy especially since they were down the premier smith Declan. Declan, despite his amputated arm, still leant support for his son Addis. He offered advice and helped out around the smith.

The farms were all preparing for the early advent of the men and women leaving for the battle. Each one feverishly prepared for the summer harvest. At Ardan and Bebhinn's farm they were tirelessly preparing for the upcoming harvest. They got their one oxen off to the side to prepare him for the harvest. They took turns training him in their ways to lead him since he was new to them. The fact that they got him last year showed that they were one of the more prosperous farms. The oxen lowed and shook his mighty head as they led him over to the shoulder harnesses and tacked him up. He stood by patiently and chewed his cud as they finished

[83] http://megaten.sesshou.com/wiki/index.php/Badb_Catha
http://paganroots.com/information/gods/celtic-gods-goddesses/badb/

up on getting the large bovine tacked. Ardan took him first and led him through the commands of left and right, go forward and stopping or hoing. Then Carrick took the reins and did the same. Next came Edana and Bebhinn. All of them took turns getting the ox to go through his paces which he patiently did. He was a good and docile animal with a red soral hide.

They were getting closer to the departure date. The last night Bebhinn spent it making a special dinner for Carrick and Ardan. A dinner of deer with turnips, carrots, and parsnips. A dandelion salad provided the greens. Then she made a blackberry cobbler for them complete with clotted cream. She tried to keep from sniffling during the meal but couldn't. "I'm sorry," she said as she wiped her face. "I am trying to be happy but I am afraid of what might happen."

"Don't be worried my love. We will return with accolades to regale you with. You will be entertained by our stories of victory." Ardan hugged her as they were finishing up with dinner.

"I hope so." Bebhinn smiled through her tears.

Edana also came over to offer her support to her father and brother. You two will be fine and do well," she enthused. Ailbe came over to them and also smiled. "Ailbe have you dreamt of anything?" Edana asked her little brother.

"No, I have not had any dreams yet. It could mean that the battle will be so small that the gods are not even thinking about it." Ailbe grinned. Bebhinn wiped her face and smiled. She smoothed Ailbe's blond tow hair out of his face.

That night Ardan and Bebhinn had a passionate night. Bebhinn still cried but Ardan tried his best to sooth his wife. "I wish you won't go," Bebhinn breathed.

"I must go sweetheart. After all Boudicca is your Queen." Ardan kissed her hard and they made love again. They drifted off to sleep in the wee hours of the morning.

The next morning Ardan and Bebhinn were getting ready for the impending time to leave. "You know I would answer the call to arms with Boudicca's army. I have no other way of going about the order." Ardan said with patient understanding as he sat on their horse waiting for his son Carrick to mount their other horse. The Iceni were known for the quality of their horses and they traded with the Trinovantes for grain and goods. Bebhinn had traded for these fine steeds just last month. The sun shone in earnest on the bright morning. Bebhinn stood by Ardan's horse and extended her hands to his. They were loading up the horses for the trip. The horses stood good-naturedly in the early morning sunshine enjoying the attention..

Bebhinn brushed her red hair out of her eyes as the wind blew it. Her beautiful eyes looked tired and puffy from crying, the gray eyes sad. She had stayed up most of the night trying to talk Ardan out of answering the call to arms by Boudicca. Her Queen as Bebhinn was Iceni too just like Boudicca. Bebhinn had married Ardan in the neighboring tribe of the Trinovantes. The two tribes were quite good neighbors and often did things together. Like share in soldiers.

CHAPTER 5
THE REBELLION

"**P**iss and pestilence, does it ever stop raining in this gods-forsaken land?"* Quintus Agricolanus looked up at the cold, weeping, blustery sky and sighed in his cloak. He'd been in this green, verdant but very wet land for eleven months now and was following this inexhaustible trail through lush woodland that seemed like a new kind of Hades to him. The forests seemed to run on forever without breaks. Ancient oak and elm bowed under their heavy weight with the tracks between them dark, dank and muddy. Even the sounds of the horses and carts seemed muffled in the loamy soft ground, years of leaves still sitting on the forest floor. Settlements were few and far between in this lush verdant land and tended to be small affairs with only a few houses and small market squares. The houses themselves were strange affairs, round in shape made of stone with wattle and daub walls, drab gray colored thatched roofs, no windows to be seen except for the large front doors. They were quite different from the Roman style buildings[84], no solid square stone structures with windows and large airy atriums and peristyle gardens only seen in the Roman settlements like Londinium and Camulodunum. Quintus grunted and shook his grizzled wet head, his dark brown hair losing its normal curl in the rain making him appear like a wet dog.

His assigned century had been selected to provide protection to the baggage resupply train for his legion on their way to Londinium. He was ordered to reconnect with Britannia's Governor Gaius Suetonius Paulinus and his army which was coming back from the attack on the druids at their stronghold in the island of Mona. The campaign had been brutal but effective as the druids' island home base had been annihilated. This assignment, however, was the only thanks he got for saving the Tribunis Laticlavius Gaius Catullus from a yowling group of barbarian Celts Now he got this thankless job, not up to his level of expertise as a capable centurion of the Tenth Legion. It was just a baggage mover's job, slave labor not fit for a centurion and his century to guard. "This is what I get for proving my ability to the governor by saving the Tribune Gaius Catullus, the extra effort to get the angry hoard of Celts away from his horse and save his pasty hide!" Quintus grumbled. Tribune Gaius Catullus had been appreciative in his snobby, patrician way, his smooth handsome face smiling at the end of the day in gratitude. "Your quick action to save me from meeting Hades so soon was heroic; I am far too young and important for such an ignoble end," he had said in a roundabout way of showing gratitude. The backhanded compliment of not even having the Tribune come along on this mission because he was incapacitated by his injury. It proved to Quintus that this mission was truly a just baggage movers operation far beneath his talents.

---

[84] http://someinterestingfacts.net/facts-about-roman-villas/ https://images. search.yahoo.com/yhs/search?p=Roman+Villas&hspart=att&hsimp=yhs-att_001

Once more he looked around at the surroundings, the drenched wet close set trees, boggy bottoms, and a sodden wide trail. The large trees bowed under their weight of heavy branches, dripping wetly on the baggage train as if in retaliation for the Romans' intrusion into the forest. Despite it being almost October the wind blew blustery and cold, seeping into the bones as it howled. Surely the fall would last longer before winter lashed out with its icy grip, . Didn't the new growth of plants need the sun? It had been cold since he arrived in Britannia; the summer was pleasant but far too short and not warm enough. When he first landed here with the troops for General Gaius Suetonius Paulinus to supplement his legions, rumor had it the governor had the blessings of Emperor Nero to clean out the island nation of Britannia of disgruntled, warlike Celts. The previous emperor Claudius[85] had the misfortune of dying before shoring up this new Roman province. Plenty stories abounded of the resentful Celts not bowing down as they should in accepting the civilizing new way of Roman life. The general went straight to the perceived problem of the fomenting Celts which is their religious priestly caste of Druids and hence the brutal undertaking at their most sacred island of Mona. Through the exemplary discipline the Roman legions extinguished the barbarians with their well drilled tactics; the final deciding factor was the classic pincer move by the cavalry from the right which shut the Celts down in a final decisive operation. Afterwards the General Gaius Suetonius Paulinus had the sacred grove razed and burned. The surprisingly few remaining Celts were then enslaved, their ears cut in the traditional manner that signified they were now slaves[86].

Fullo rode up next to Quintus, his light brown hair sodden and lying flat to his head making him look like a seal. They rode awhile in companionable silence studying the terrain. Fullo as Quintus' oldest companion rode together when they went on patrols. Fullo

---

[85] https://www.britannica.com/biography/Claudius-Roman-emperor
[86] http://www.bbc.co.uk/history/ancient/romans/slavery_01.shtml

and Quintus had had quite a few battles where each saved the other from the fighting barbarian hordes. Fullo turned his disgruntled and wet, handsome face to Quintus, "What is the matter with this bleeding place, I've not seen the sun in three days, it has rained every day and my feet are cold and wet all the time, my leggings and sandals will need another dose of oiling if it does not stop!" Quintus looked at Fullo who did indeed look like a drowned rat as did everyone else in the baggage train.

"We just need to get to Londinium to resupply and reconnect with the rest of the legions west of that, you know the drill." Quintus grumbled.

"I know but I need to complain first. Speaking of complaints, I need to find a warm woman to share my bed when we resupply in Londinium, I've been without that comfort since before Mona. I'm getting restless and have a lot of unused energy to burn off." Fullo smirked.

"You should see the medic for that, I told you to watch out for fleas." Quintus laughed

Fullo smiled: "I just need a bit of womanly loving and I'll be right as the gods have foretold. The Celtic women are a handful in just the right places." Quintus just grunted an affirmative. He turned his attention to the discussion in front of him between the two resident experts on Roman military might, Faber and Coriaro.

Faber and Coriaro were discussing the lack of war machines on this resupply mission. Faber, the smith, bulky and dark was the undisputed expert on Roman military might. He began the discussion by extolling the best points of his favorite ballista[87]. "I prefer using stones bolts; you get a wider area of coverage with the same deadly accuracy. Plus you can always find replacements every time you cross a stream or river."

---

[87] https://www.pinterest.com/VanDiemensLand/roman-war-machines/
https://images.search.yahoo.com/yhs/search?p=Roman+War+Machine+
Ballista+Catapult&hspart=att&hsimp=yhs-att_001

"True, but you lose the ability to kill if you don't use the Scorpius. The bolts pierce all manner of shields and any armor. Give me a Scorpius any day over a ballista." Coriaro retorted. Coriaro always felt outclassed when discussing the war machines with Faber. Faber had served with the Ballistarii, or the engineering division, in Gaul and had the better training on war machines than he did. "What about the bigger onager[88]? It is not as small as the ballista and has a longer range for the rocks it sends, much better if you want to down forts or ramparts of the enemy."

"Yes, the onager is larger but you lose the torsion faster needing to rebuild that part of the machinery. You also lose accuracy with the added distance," replied Faber in a patient tone. "Like the name implies, a kicking donkey, the onager is best for long range shots, the ballista is smaller and easier to repair on the battlefield. That is why you have more with any army."

"Well yes they are larger but better for fighting large sieges against the big forts. But I don't know why we are even discussing this since we don't have the Scorpius, ballista or an onager on this mission. We are just providing support for this baggage resupply mission," Coriaro retorted disgustedly. Coriaro shook his light brown hair and wiped his face with his hand, his crooked nose standing out starkly in the cold sending out puffs of fog.

"You still nattering about which siege engine is best? Look no further than my sword! A gladius, the Roman short sword, is all a Roman legionary needs, that and his shield and spear. You can get into formation and perform all the military drills needed, from pincer movements, saw movements to the best iron turtle or testudo[89] there is," said Bundarus coming up from behind them on the left. Bundarus nodded his bald pate and rolled his strong shoulders.

"Of course you'd say that as that is all you know, the proscribed

---

[88] https://www.pinterest.com/VanDiemensLand/roman-war-machines/
https://en.wikipedia.org/wiki/Onager_(weapon)
[89] http://quatr.us/romans/war/romanarmy.htm

legionary drills," ground out Coriaro. "We are discussing the finer parts of war machines, not just the legionary movements. Together all are important but the siege engines such as the ballista, onager and Scorpius can put an end to any conflict much faster than the soldiers in a legion alone can do."

"Oh tell that to Gaius Suetonius Paulinus, he got us all working in legion formations to overthrow the druids at Mona not too long ago, or maybe you've forgotten your part in that fortaign we just went on?" Bundarus rejoined.

"Exactly, and we used the war machinery then too," interjected Faber gaining him an appreciative glance from Coriaro. "Yes, we spent our time digging post holes for sharp stakes with the best of them but it was ballista that got us onto the island of Mona."

"Not much of a trial getting to the island, we had no problem crossing the jetty to it," interjected a new speaker from the right. Grex the wiry, merry little Sicilian who never wasted time joined in the discussion. "We could have walked across the jetty and not faced any retaliation!" Grex laughed.

The men continued their discussion about fighting in Gaul but Quintus stopped paying attention. Boreas was unnerved by something. He kept sidling around and shying at noises. Quintus was remembering his grandfather's admonition to pay attention to his mount because horses can see, smell and hear problems before his rider could. Something continued to prickle at the back of Quintus' neck in the unnatural quiet of the surrounding woodland. It was as if he had someone's eyes on his back. Fullo moved his mount up alongside Quintus' horse. "You feel it too, the unnatural calm." He grunted looking around uneasily. "There is something brewing but I do not know what it is, sort of like the time we were in Gaul last year, with the Nervii[90]. I'm getting that same unsettled feeling as I did then." Quintus agreed with Fullo.

"Let the others know something might be up and begin to

---

[90] http://wiki.totalwar.com/w/Total_War:_Rome_II_-_Nervii_Faction

prepare for any possible assault, but do it quietly so as not to let whoever is watching us know." Quintus murmured quietly. Fullo nodded and turned his horse forward. He rode off quickly but with purpose and spoke quietly to everyone.

They continued moving forward, trudging along in the wet trail. Quintus saw Fullo notifying all the legionaries and in doing so they all made their way to the front in a loose wedge shape, Bundarus, his best swordsman, Faber and Coriaro his two best mechanics and war machine makers, and Grex, the fun-loving little Sicilian who had retrieved his bow in which he was a dead shot. They sidled into position looking relaxed but their eyes tracking everything in the undergrowth. The wagon train moved forward slowly but inexorably on toward Londinium. After a few hours they came to a meadow which opened into a bowl shape in the distance, the sky abruptly made visible. Suddenly there was a guttural war cry on all sides, Celts jumped up from their hiding places behind trees and in the high grasses, their clothes all brown and gray to camouflage them. The front wedge of Romans jumped into action, Bundarus catching a Celts swing of broadsword with his shield and returned with a ruthless jab of his short sword. The Celt's face showed surprise as he had not felt the short gladius slice into his belly until he looked down. Coriaro and Faber, his two top war machine makers went smoothly out into the howling Celt mass, each had their shield positioned to fend off the barbarians' long slashing swords. Coriaro used his shield to bash an unsuspecting Celt in the neck, the foes eyes widening in disbelief as he lost the ability to breathe. Faber used his throwing spear to pin another Celt to the ground sticking up from his chest like a tree branch that impaled him in a high storm. Grex came out like an archer fiend and smoothly took out at least four Celts as they jumped up from the tufts of grass and behind trees, every time he shot the arrows finding their target in the Celts torsos, the fourth Celt found the arrow in his throat.

Seeing the melee commence Quintus joined the fray jumping

from Boreas to engage the Celts one on one, his shield held defensively in front, and his spear ready to jab at the oncoming mass of howling barbarians. Once engaged the battle fever took over as he thrust and countered their wildly swinging long swords, instinctively parrying without pause. Surprised at the onslaught of the Roman defensive expertise the Celts surrounding him backed up and gave him room. One tall older Celt with white-blond hair lunged at him with his long sword. Quintus easily blocked the wild swing and used his shield to push it aside and knock the older Celt off balance. This gave Quintus the ability to thrust his spear into the Celt's side, catching the space between his ribs smoothly. The barbarian recoiled but did not go down. He hefted his long sword and gave a great wild swing at Quintus' head causing Quintus to be knocked to the ground. Quintus hit the ground but rolled into a crouch. He ducked the older man's oncoming swing. On their feet they fought back and forth, each judging the other's ability at hand to hand combat and sought an advantage. Circling each other in grim determination they parried. Quintus moved in and slashed the Celts smaller wicker shield quickly destroying it. Warily they circled each looking for an opening.

Suddenly from the left came a smaller, boy barbarian with an oversized sword. Obviously the new contender was young and out of his element but his furious gaze showed steely determination to defend the larger, older white headed Celt. From the quick glance at both of them Quintus saw the similar facial structures. Must be related, quickly surmised Quintus. The younger Celt lunged forward and swung his sword at Quintus who easily parried the blow. He moved forward to pin the sword to the ground with his and used the shield to knock the boy back. The boy fell hard on the ground and lost his grip on his sword.

At this point the older Celt yelled a bloodcurdling war cry and sprang into the fray. He moved to the opposite side of Quintus on the right and slashed his sword which was closest to the young Celt. *Keeping me divided, I see where this is going, separate and get the young one free to attack me from behind*, thought Quintus. He moved warily back giving space to the young one still on the ground but keeping his eyes on the older one. Exactly on the mark the older Celt moved forward slashing his sword again towards Quintus's right side maneuvering him away from the younger boy. *Not so fast*, thought Quintus as he lunged forward using his shield to block any further parries and started jabbing with his sword at the older man. Back and forth they furiously fought, the Celt beginning to falter from fatigue and loss of blood, loud gulps of air being sucked into his lungs. His blows becoming more erratic as they continued. Out of the corner of his eyes he saw the young boy get back onto his feet and grab his sword from the ground. He then looked at Quintus with determination and sprang forward raising his sword in a wild overhand swing. Quintus couldn't stop his parries with the older Celt who was raining wild blows from his sword to take on the younger boy. Despite the older mans' fatigue and blood loss he was too determined to let Quintus divide his attention. The younger boy yelled and lifted his sword but stopped midway with a look of disbelief as an arrow buried itself in his chest. Glancing up at Grex, the shooter, he toppled backward with a gaping mouth opening and closing in surprise, his eyes looking in disbelief at the arrow buried in his own chest. The older Celt cried out and wildly swung at Quintus, who easily blocked it with his shield then moved forward with a killing thrust of his own sword.

In the sudden stillness the Romans look at each other. "My thanks to you Grex, you saved my life from these two," Quintus panted. "I could not have taken them down on my own." Quintus looked again at the two dead Celts laying on the wet ground with blood pooling around them.

"Didn't they teach us back when we joined the military never to take on two determined foes at once, especially when they are working in concert to take you out?' Grex grinned, "I saw the need to step in and help."

They looked around at the lessening of commotion going on

around them. "This was all planned by the looks of it but not well planned, we were able to stop it quickly. If it was a more coordinated attack they would have done more damage. The fight was winding down but these barbarians are way too determined to win despite taking heavy losses," observed Quintus, "I don't like this. Get me any survivors for questioning. Something tells me there is more to this than just a chance skirmish."

"Yes centurion," Grex saluted and darted off.

Quintus looked down at the two Celts that he'd just fought. They must be Faber and son he thought; they both have the same light colored hair and features. Glancing up he saw Bundarus and Fullo coming towards him, both liberally covered in blood and gore. He could see by the way they moved that it wasn't theirs. "Give me your report."

"The battle was hastily put together, probably because they had word of our baggage train. There was about fifty or sixty Celts involved but they were not well organized, simply jumping out of their hiding places and fighting. No front line just oncoming Celts." Fullo said disgustedly.

Bundarus offered "Their long swords are made for wide swings, not disciplined jabs like our shorter Roman swords. They need space to wield them so the best way to combat is to get close and crowd them out. Fighting in close quarter formation is the best defense."

"Possibly a precursor to a larger fighting group but we need verification from any barbarian captured," looking around he pointed to a group of ten wounded Celts to the side, all wounded, the worse laid on the ground which showed the Celts determination not to surrender. "We can start there."

Quintus waved at his men to follow and went to the group. The sullen looks he received were expected, the murderous expressions where a surprise. In accented Celt Quintus asked: "Who speaks Latin here? I speak Gaulic Celt but it is not exactly the same as your dialect."

Furtive looks between the Celts passed until the most grievously wounded Celt lying down on the ground, holding his stomach said "I do" in heavily imperfect Latin.

"Why did you attack this supply train?" Quintus ground out.

"We received word there was a supply train coming to Londinium and were sent to attack."

"Who sent you?"

"We were sent by our Queen Boudicca, just after we razed Londinium!" the Celts' face showed pride at the words despite his obvious pain.

Surprise and anger showed on Quintus' face. "Who is Boudicca? Why did she raze Londinium?"

The Celt just smiled haughtily "She is the Queen of the Iceni and is leading a group of confederate tribes to combat you Roman scum. We are tired of your taxes and the indiscriminate taking of lands. You are nothing but thieving criminals who take everything! We have already razed Camulodunum[91] with your putrid temple to Claudius paid for by all the taxes you've leveled on us. We do not bow down to you Romans anymore!" he laughed and started to choke as the wound opened further on his belly.

"Londinium and Camulodunum razed? The two largest towns settled by Romans? What of the Romans in these settlements, what happened to them?" disbelief sounded in Quintus' voice.

"Killed in both places, I personally helped in burning down the so called temple to Claudius[92] complete with Romans inside. Their howls were music to our death goddess Morrigan," the Celt ground out his eyes alight with hatred.

Quintus swore, took his sword and stabbed the Celt, ending the conversation. The other Celts murmured low and ominously,

[91] http://www.bbc.co.uk/history/ancient/romans/colchester_01.shtml

[92] https://en.wikipedia.org/wiki/Camulodunum#Iceni_Revolt https://images.search.yahoo.com/yhs/search?p=Temple+To+Claudius+In+Camulodunum&hspart=att&hsimp=yhs-att_001

talking amongst themselves in their own language that sounded like curses.

"Bloody hell, both Camulodunum and Londinium razed! There were hundreds of Romans in each place, taxation courts with their prefects and secretaries, traders, new land magnates not to mention the large colonia and civic center at Camulodunum, the governor's palace! All of the wine and olives and goods from the Empire comes through Londinium. The swill they call ale here is horse piss compared to good Roman wine." Fullo swore some more under his breath.

"We'll need to notify the general immediately of this Quintus." Bundarus urgently said.

Grex returned with Faber and Coriaro. They had another Celt between them. "I've found this barbarian who speaks Latin; he tells me this is the forward advance scouts of a group from Londinium. What happened there? Are we fighting a rebellion?"

"Yes, it seems we are. Another Celt just said they've razed both Londinium and Camulodunum and killed all the Romans in both places." Quintus disgustedly said. The thought of both those key settlements being gone was a severe blow to the Romans in Britannia. All commerce and governance would be stopped if it was so. Londinium was where the governor would hold all of the trade meetings needed to run this outpost of Rome. Camulodunum was the civic center; all governance was done from there and would eventually be the governments' capital. It had the larger population including a colonia, a settlement of discharged Roman soldiers. Both would take a long time to recover. "Word will need to be sent without delay to General Gaius Suetonius Paulinus once we gather all the information we can. Make it happen and report back to me as soon as you can."

"I'll gather the report together of this atrocity," Grex said. He turned and took off.

Turning to the little prisoner between Faber and Coriaro Quintus asked: "What is happening south, did attacks occur in

Londinium and Camulodunum? Who is Queen Boudicca?" Quintus wanted to get independent verification from another subject.

The Celt wiped his bloody face before answering, "Yes we attacked all places Rome has settlements including Verulamium[93]. Queen Boudicca is leading a massive army to engage the Roman army under the governor because of all the injustices you've been heaping on us. My own farm was taken from my family and given to your tax collector since it was determined I could not pay the levy. They took my sons and daughter, cut their ears and turned them into slaves! You Roman scum!" Another bitter Celt, Quintus wearily thought. Are they all going to tell me this same story?

As the intelligence trickled in the story was verified that Queen Boudicca was in fact leading a large army to fight the general's army and expel all Romans from Britannia. There were the same complaints about exorbitant taxation, the taking of land by the tax assessors and turning Celts into slaves to pay for taxes in arrears. The army's numbers were sketchy but thought to be upward to an astounding one hundred thousand strong including war chariots since several tribes had joined in the attack. The fact that the tribes were working together was the biggest surprise since they usually fought each over any perceived fault. Quintus sent a courier post haste to the governor with the horrific information.

Now why do I keep thinking about the two blond haired Celts now that all this has come to past, I've more important things to do than to consider them. In the back of his mind he knew the gods are letting him know their death would determine his future here in Britannia.

"Now if we can do something about this weather," mumbled Quintus, "Piss and pestilence!"

回回回回

---

[93] https://www.britannica.com/place/Verulamium https://images.search.yahoo.com/yhs/search?p=Verulamium&hspart=att&hsimp=yhs-att_001

That spring Boudicca's rebellion was swiftly put down by Roman's superior military tactics. The Celtic horde was indeed large, almost one hundred thousand Celts plus war chariots. Boudicca herself gave a rousing speech from her war chariot[94] with her daughters claiming to be not a Queen of the Iceni but an ordinary person, avenging her lost freedom and lands, her battered body, and the abused chastity of her daughters done to her family at the order of the Roman army. She said their cause was just, and the deities were on their side, the one legion in Londinium that had dared to face them had been destroyed. She, a woman and a Celt, was resolved to win or die.

However the lack of on the field generalship from the Celts became glaringly apparent when General Gaius Suetonius Paulinus held his Roman legions in check at first and waited for the Celts to come. He performed a classic wedge and saw maneuver[95] to combat the large mass of Celts. He positioned the Roman army in a defile with woods behind them. He then allowed the formation to take care of the oncoming swarm of Celts who in such close quarters quickly lost the ability to swing their long swords. At the right he positioned his cavalry to wait for the appropriate signal to charge. The Romans, using their shields to push inexorably forward and their spears, or pila to take out more Celts as they moved forward, decimating their foes. The Romans continued to move forward slowly and as the Celts rushed the Roman troops those caught at the front were quickly killed. The Celts that realized what was happening tried to turn back but the oncoming mass of Celts moving forward from behind made it impossible to stop the forward momentum causing the Celts in the middle to be exterminated. On the right the Roman cavalry received the signal to attack. The Celts in the backsaw what was happening they began to turn as well and retreat and were met by the charging Roman cavalry.

---

[94] http://www.bbc.co.uk/history/historic_figures/boudicca.shtml
[95] http://www.roman-empire.net/army/tactics.html

The Celts had nowhere to turn, in front was Roman army coming forward like a bristling, implacable death-dealing giant and behind them were their own Celts coming forward still wanting to be part of the fray. The very back of the fields there were the Celtic families who had pulled up to see the glorious win with their carriages ringing the battlefield. These laden wagons prevented further retreat by the Celts who found themselves trapped. The ensuing slaughter was inevitable and massive. Despite being outnumbered ten to one the Romans defeated the Celts in one decisive blow. The ensuing confusion made it easy for the Romans to move in and finish, mopping up the small pockets of resistance.

In one of the pockets of resistance, Quintus with the remaining members of his *Contubernium* Fullo, Bundarus, Faber, Coriaro, Grex, Titus and Rufus fought together. The fighting was fierce but with Roman discipline it was turning the tide inevitably in their favor. The Celts continued to come in with increasingly tired and wild swings of their swords, each yelling bloodcurdling howls but not landing effective blows. The Romans stayed in a tight formation with their interlocked shields up combating the onslaught, letting the Celts tire themselves out first before moving forward as one to take care of the stragglers. Their gladius and pila flashing from between their shields in lightning strikes taking out the most bold of the Celts.

"Let's finish this, I'm done with this gods-forsaken battle," Fullo growled from behind his shield, fatigue beginning to tell on his face.

Next to him Faber agreed, "They are at the end of their rebellion and flagging, we should take this last group and make examples of them!"

"They are failing but best to keep with Roman military tactics so we can all survive this day. Let us continue with the iron turtle and win without getting wounded." Bundarus cautioned restraint. Titus and Rufus agreed with him. The iron turtle or testudo was devastating in close quarters, a small squad or *Contubernium* of eight soldiers would hold in tight formation, interlocking their shields and move forward as one, just using their short swords and spears to jab at their opponents without giving opening up, hence the term iron turtle.

Listening to their grumbling Quintus was feeling also tired of the incessant rebellion, he wanted to destroy these barbarians but realized Bundarus had the correct assessment of the situation. They were all exhausted and at the end of their surge of battle energy, at this time unwise decisions could cost lives. "We stay in formation until this last group is taken care of, no time for short cuts that makes us sloppy." He continued with the forward press and thrusts of his sword and spear. The others groaned but followed.

Soon the skirmish was dwindling now with only four exhausted and bloody Celts left to fight the battle. They still yelled out curses but their swords were not swung with as much vigor. After two were dispatched, thanks to Bundarus and Grex's spears the last two threw their swords done in surrender. The pocket of resistance was over.

In the end the Romans had dealt a massive blow to the Celts, further thoughts of rebellion were no longer entertained. The confederation of Celtic tribes Queen Boudicca had managed to fuse melted way, their lands, goods, and peoples enslaved. The end of the Celtic resistance as well as the end of their Druid priests ensured their resulting compliance to Roman rule. Now all that remained was the slow but methodical Roman nation building. The Romans had to reestablish trading lines and entice more traders to come fill the void left in Londinium, Camulodunum, and Vernonia and more was needed to fill out other centers of Roman civilization.

In the ensuing months more traders and land magnates made their way to Britannia to exploit the war ravaged land. Rich businessmen called knights made their way from Rome to Britannia with their coffers open to ease away the large Celtic farms. Londinium was infused with needed capital again as traders and their agents once again offered Roman luxury items. Wine and olives, damascene silks, glass ware vases and bottles, jewelry and of course all of the confiscated Celtic torques once again were found at the market.

In winter the decision was made by Gaius Suetonius Paulinus to gift the most deserving legionaries with their own farms from the lands confiscated from the rebellious tribes to replace the large colonia at Camulodunum and to establish additional smaller ones further into Britannia. The best way to subdue Britannia was through colonization with integration into local society made up of retiring military members intermarrying with the local peoples. One of the many deserving military men was Quintus Agricolanus, he along with the with the rest of his *Contubernium* Fullo, Bundarus, Faber, Coriaro, Grex, Titus and Rufus received notice that they would all get land from the Trinovantes tribe, who joined the rebellion with Boudicca and the Iceni. Putting this small fighting group together to colonize and Romanize the area was considered a good move by the Governor to shore up the unsettled area and pay off his troops after their years of service. Gaius Suetonius Paulinus called them up to receive the announcement of their official retirement parcels.

"I am granting you farms confiscated from the Trinovantes in the village of Gosbecks, about one day's march from Camulodunum. There are several farms you and your men will be granted. It is a very prosperous area with lush farmland and you should do well settling there." Gaius Suetonius Paulinus smiled as he told Quintus and his soldiers. "The area had a lot of members who fought in the rebellion but are no longer returning to their farms. The land is now yours. My Legate Marcus Flaccus Antoninus," the governor turned to the haughty patrician standing next to him, "Will be in charge of assigning the farms to you. There will be resistance but I am confident you will be able to overcome it and settle into this new life. Just make sure the flow of taxation goods flows without disruption. You have the authority to implement any means necessary to do so."

The Legate Marcus Flaccus Antoninus stepped forward to

speak next, his arrogant patrician face looking at the soldiers, "We will divide the farms according to rank. Quintus Agricolanus as a retiring Centurion and Princeps Pila, you will get the largest land holding but the others will be doled out based on quality and years of service. Titus and Rufus will get the smallest land plots as they only have the minimum of fifteen years. The other members of the cContubernium Fullo, Bundarus, Faber, Coriaro and Grex have all served seventeen plus years with distinction and will receive bigger farms. I will personally help in portioning out the land plots since this is my job," he added with a bored smile. The men looked at each other knowing the legate was more interested in determining how much the Trinovantes land would bring the empire in taxation, trade deals and new land sales.

The Governor continued: "You will be released from the military in the spring to take over your lands in time for the seasonal planting and the management needed for your new farms. Get together with your officers to make the transition seamless, I expect more soldiers will be retiring at the same time so the turnover will be easy. The Roman military is a well-oiled machine after all so I expect this turnover to go smoothly. I'll be by the new colonia when you have moved down to it. I expect to see a successful new Romanized village. I foresee a very prosperous enclave of Roman civilization," with that he abruptly finished the meeting. Turning with the legate the two departed the meeting for the command tent.

"Well now that the formalities are over we can get the actual celebrations going forward," Fullo beamed and rubbed his hands. "I've got several ladies waiting for me and whoever wants to join me!"

"I'll take you up on the offer," Rufus said. "Now that I've earned my retirement I've got the wealth to back up my fun." Rufus and Titus were the newest members of the *Contubernium*, they joined them in fighting the Nervii in Gaul to shore up the six to the more traditional number of eight as required by military regulations.

Whilst they hadn't fought as long together as the original six they proved themselves on the battlefield time and again, Titus and Rufus were like Bundarus in their ability with the sword and spear. Their understanding of military formation drills made them solid Roman legionaries They'd proven themselves to the general at the battle on Mona with their quick work of the battling barbarian Celts without letting the unnerving atmosphere of the island spook them. They laid waste to the grounds without questioning their orders.

"Good, we'll go enjoy the wonders of rounded Celtic women, any other takers?" Fullo looked to the others. The Bundarus, Faber and Coriaro looked at each other than agreed to come. "A party it is, what about you Quintus and Grex? Any way we can entice you two?"

"I already have a raven haired Celtic woman waiting for me outside of fort, I've already made the arrangements," Grex grinned.

"I have paperwork to finish with the legate; all the plots need to be laid out contiguously so we may have a defensible colonia. I'll catch up later and join the party." The grim faced Quintus turned and moved to follow the governor and legate.

"Sad that, he does all the work and doesn't have the chance to enjoy himself," muttered Fullo and turned to join the others already leaving for their night of merriment.

回回回回

Inside the well-appointed governor's tent Quintus was led by a slave to a table where maps of Britannia littered the surface. Both Gaius Suetonius Paulinus and the legate Marcus Flaccus Antoninus were perusing their surface. The furnishing was lavish in its' simplicity with wooden tables made from cedar and sandalwood, the air redolent with incense smoking from braziers spaced around the tent in strategic places. On the tables were brass bowls filled with fruits and nuts, brass chalices and beakers filled with ruby colored wine sat near the maps. Interspersed throughout the tent were expensive lamps, their light spilling out in golden circles with the largest hanging over the table with the maps.

"Come on in Quintus Agricolanus, I have several items to discuss with you regarding the land to be parceled out in Gosbecks," the Governor said not even looking up, his striking aristocratic face concentrating on the map, "This village is one of the Trinovantes strongholds that pledged a full century of people to Boudicca's rebellion. Most did not return alive and as such the land has suffered. The farms lay fallow for the most part; those that are still being worked have half a labor force. Now as a Roman coming in to establish a colonia prepare for resistance. The Celts are notorious for not being forthright on information and staying closemouthed. Treat all of them as hostiles. But you will need tread a fine line. It is vital that Rome gets her taxes." He looked up at Quintus, his hazel eyes squinting as he smiled, wrinkles around his eyes and mouth standing out, his dark hair gray at the temples.

The legate Marcus Flaccus Antoninus stepped forward and began speaking: "The land lends itself to an ideal colonia, as it is located in a valley surrounded by lakes and rivers that help transport the goods and crops. The Trinovantes already have a good system of roads and trails that connect to the surrounding villages and ultimately to Camulodunum which is approximately a day and a half away. As the governor noted this was a hotbed of rebellion, it is estimated half of the labor force is no longer alive to work the farms," he paused and took up an apple to take a bored, desultory bite and chewed slowly, he turned and his patrician face looked bored intentionally as if the meeting was a beneath him, "This is a major problem because taxes will still need to be paid. When we first get there I will need your assistance in gathering the remaining farmers to determine how Rome will be paid. Your job will be as the muscle to arbitrate in any quarrelsome situations. Along with your *Contubernium* who will stay, we will be bringing additional soldiers in this interim period, about thirty should be plenty, to get the colonia up and running. Some of those soldiers coming with us may even choose to stay and will apply for their retirement parcels of land which would be ideal, the larger the colonia the more settled the area will become."

The general added: "You will have the interim soldiers for as long as needed, I expect at least half of the year to settle any potential unrest that may occur. Should they be needed longer you must write a request for additional military soldiers to help quell any problems. Remember this is an area that supported Boudicca. There may be times when conflict may erupt. It is your job to see that it does not foment into another uprising."

"Do you think it will come to that?" Quintus asked with no little amount of worry.

The general looked at him with an intent, serious expression, : "Make sure it does not get to that point. You have the authority to do what it takes to settle this area, if you see the need to annex more farms, do it. If the people do not like it, use the soldiers to influence them otherwise. You also have the authority to enslave the most problematic of the villagers. Do this and you will make sure the populous bows to Roman civilizing."

Quintus realized at that moment that this assignment of land will be a proverbial viper pit to oversee. The people still smarting at losing the rebellion was to be expected but the emphasis on possible future problems let him see this was a far from a stable area. This might be one of the areas that had the largest amount of fighters. If so the fact that a full half did not return meant that the remaining Celts and certainly their families would be indulging further potential revolt notions. *Great*, Quintus mused to himself, *I am getting a farm where they do not want any Roman soldiers and have reason to hate me. This will make retirement so much easier.* Quintus gave an exasperated sigh turned to the Governor and Legate and said: "When do we go?"

"As I said earlier in the meeting spring should be when you go officially, but you might want to send a small group to scout

out the situation before then. An advance reconnaissance mission if you will," replied the governor. "You should leave in the early winter, early spring, or whatever they call the warmer weather in this wretched land. Personally I cannot wait to return to Rome and the warmer weather, even the summers in this land are cold," he shivered on cue.

Quintus had to agree, the weather even in summer was either raining or foggy, the sun never seemed to shine enough here. However the land was fertile and lush. Perhaps farming would be more agreeable than going through the seasons on marches, settling down sounded good to him since he had not been in one place for many years. His time in Gaul was memorable only by the few times they were able to stop and stay in the forts they built. It seemed once they stayed more than six months they needed to move on to the area to deal with further problems. The Gauls seemed to forever be in a flux until the governor subdued them all, Quintus just hoped the Celts in Britannia were different and would not be encouraged to fight again. He had seen enough of war and blood to last a lifetime, now was the time for building a farm and home and settling down.

Seeing the meeting was ended he thanked the governor and legate and left to find his mates. He'd have to figure out when to go on the short reconnaissance mission, he already decided to bring his Contubernium. For now they needed to enjoy themselves for a while, and so did he.

Quintus left the generals tent to look for his *Contubernium*, who if he knew Fullo, was already in with the ladies at the local tavern located in the back of their fort. He made his way there going through the evening gloom which was still light despite the late hour. Out in the fort the legionaries were settling down for the night and conversations were muted. Wearily he made his way to the tavern, thinking of additional items he'd have to get taken care of before they left for Gosbecks on their reconnaissance mission and eventually relocating for good there. He would need to have enough military equipment to support the additional thirty soldiers beyond his *Contubernium*. He'd also need to wrap up with the new Centurion all the day to day managerial items here at the governor's fort. His current duties also included discipline of unruly soldiers and there were about four problem men in the brig. They had been out carousing and destroyed several Celtic barges filled with grain coming into fort as expected. They were due to get out tomorrow but their disciplinary punishment needed to extend to the Celtic barge owners. It would be a sticky situation.

Brushing the thoughts aside he came upon the tavern which was full and had a lot of boisterous patrons both Roman and hanger-on Celts. A lot of the daily business in forts attracted these hangers-on whether it is the business men providing foodstuffs, fuel for fires, and clothing for the women who service the soldiers. Quintus entered the tavern and looked around for his *Contubernium* members. In the corner were Bundarus, Titus and Rufus surrounded by women. Further to the back he spied Faber and Coriaro's big bodies by three scantily clad women who were draped around the two. Fullo was nowhere to be seen obviously already having found his woman.

Apparently the word had already gotten out that the members of the *Contubernium* were newly to be let go from service. It is at this point that men either paired up with the women or the hangers-on tried to tie themselves to the men. Most soldiers were fine with this situation, having usually found a particular woman who comforted them when they got finished with their soldiering duties. Once word got out that certain soldiers were granted their land there was a surge of women who wanted to get out of the life whoring. If the soldier liked the woman enough to overlook the possibility that a child already in her belly not being his own then it was an agreeable arrangement.

Quintus walked in and was immediately surrounded by women. *Word had indeed gotten out*, he thought. "What's the need today handsome Centurion?" one voluptuous hooker said. "You need some soothing tonight?" another skimpily clad one said. Another simply grabbed his arm and pressed her breasts against him in a suggestive way.

"Ladies I need to find my mates first, let us go over to the table over there," Quintus steered his new entourage toward Bundarus, Titus and Rufus's table. "How goes it this evening men?" Bundarus laughed and Titus grinned. Rufus was busy kissing a woman to his right who had her hand on his chest, drawing a circle which was getting lower to his crotch. "No need to answer I see exactly how it going. Do you know where Fullo is or Grex?"

"Fullo is engaged and has been since we got here," Bundarus smirked, "He was the first to leave the table with a rather well-endowed Celtic wench. Grex had a previous engagement with his significant other; you know the one he has had for the past six months. Faber and Coriaro are over by the wine and look to be leaving soon," Bundarus crooked a thumb in their direction just in time to see both leave. Both the men and ladies had already engaged in negotiating the price then left shortly afterwards.

"Ah well, then I'll be next to go out, which one of you lovely ladies wish to join me?" All three of them indicated their willingness but Quintus took the one already latched onto his arm and left. Because she didn't talk, she'll probably just ride me and be done with it he told himself. In the back of the tavern he led her to the small alcoves used by the hookers to take their men and turn tricks. Turns out he chose correctly because she didn't talk just fondled his cock, took it into her mouth and gave him a good start with her mouth. Then when he thought she would take him all the way she stopped and lay down on the pallet, she lifted her tunic and presented him with a view of heaven. Quintus lay down on her and took her quickly, not wanting to lose the moment she began with her mouth. She lifted her legs and crossed them over his buttocks giving him a deeper penetration. Roughly he slammed into her and set a hard rhythm seeking fulfillment. All that could be heard was his grunts and her moans. He came quickly with a loud groan and jerky movements. "Was that good for you my Centurion," asked his partner, "Do you want to do it again only this time I'll ride you or if you prefer you can take me like a bull does a cow?"

"I'll take you has a dog does a bitch in heat, but first you need to get me up and ready for it with your mouth," grunted Quintus after he had rolled from her. It felt good to let her take him in her mouth again. Fortunately he wasn't quite soft yet from his previous bout. She was quite talented with her tongue and ran it up and around his cock from the head up the staff. Her hands found his balls and gently rolled them, occasionally pulling but not too hard. Once he was erect he moved her mouth away and turned her over, settling behind her buttocks. She was nicely rounded and had good curves to hold onto. He took her from behind quickly and settled into a good fast pace, the sound of their bodies making a slapping loud in the small room. Her moans quickly became loud as he increased the pace. "Not too loud!" he said and smacked her butt. The swat was followed by another as she continued to mewl out loudly. He grunted and grabbed her hips hard as he started increasing his speed; the slapping became lurid in its intensity. Their breathing became grunts, and she started to whimper as the speed and intensity no longer was pleasurable but bordered on pain. Grunting out his climax at the zenith of his effort he ended with jerky movements. Panting he moved to the side taking the woman with him. "You've earned your pay tonight my girl." He reached into his tunic and retrieved his pouch for coins.

"It could be for free if you take me with you to your new farm," she said from beneath her lashes as she turned to look at him. "I know you will get a big farm, I have experience running a farm, my own was razed but I hold no grudge, I just want to help you run yours."

"Not interested, I needed the solace tonight but it is only for a one time deal. My farm will be taken care of later with local help, not a transplant from another tribe. I need the help I'm sure but since I am not there yet I will not make plans now." Quintus removed the coins from his purse and gave them to her, stood and left the alcove.

Back in the tavern Quintus mumbled to himself "Greedy bitch, I knew that was coming." He returned to the table no longer full with Bundarus, Titus and Rufus. They'd obviously found their wenches to their liking. From across the room he spied Fullo making his way to the table.

"I heard from Bundarus that you were looking for me," Fullo looked at him over his cup of wine. Fullo looked much more relaxed than he did earlier, apparently he'd already relieved himself the same way Quintus had.

"Yes, I am glad you're finished with your whore because I need your help. The general and legate talked about taking over the farms in Gosbecks. Apparently they are located in a hotbed of rebellion .We need to go early for a quick reconnaissance mission before we move there. We need to determine if the area is fomenting another revolt." Quintus quietly said, looking around the room as he did.

"Fuck me! No wonder they were so generous with our retirements. We'll be working hard for the next twenty years to make sure Britannia will be settled! No wonder that fucking Legate Marcus Flaccus Antoninus is coming with us in the fall. I thought it was just primo land but it is much more." Fullo cursed again.

"Exactly Fullo," Quintus said wearily. "We also need to figure when we leave for this clandestine trip to get the lay of the land. I'm thinking just our Contubernium but if it is such a hotbed of insurgents maybe more is needed."

"Agreed, but just the *Contubernium*, I do not think bringing more soldiers will be worth it if we are just going to see the lay of the social setup, more would be seen as aggressive. We are used to working as a unit and can get in and out with no problem, not causing alarm. We might want to leave our shields back at fort and just be lightly armored, gladius only," Fullo replied. He wiped his face, "I guess this night of merriment is over, I'll return and get my pack ready. Are we leaving in the morning or waiting until early spring?"

"We can leave soon for a quick look-see. Spring will come soon enough and it is already fall now. What is the name of that weird Celtic celebration … Samhain[96] is it? We should leave at that time using it as an excuse to peruse the roads. Perhaps we could pass as bystanders in their celebration," Quintus replied, "Samhain should come in the next two weeks, plenty of time to see if the Celts in Gosbecks are fomenting."

Fullo grinned, "If that is what we are planning then I'm up for round two of the merriment, care to join me for another cup of wine, maybe catch up with the others?"

"Of course, I can always do with another cup with my mates." Quintus got up to get a cup and get a refill for Fullo. "Tomorrow is soon enough for me to finish all the preparation for our trip."

囗囗囗囗

Several weeks had passed and Quintus had gotten his *Contubernium* ready for their reconnaissance mission to Gosbecks. The plan was to travel light with just the eight members, all riding horses and lightly armored with just their cuirasses, gladius and light cavalry shields. Pila or spears were deemed not needed. They were to leave one week before Samhain, the only information they had on Samhain called it an end to the harvesting season and celebration of the beginning of winter. *As if you need to celebrate the long cold, dark, and damp winter just like the one he'd experienced last year,* mused Quintus, *the Celts would need anything excuse to celebrate in this gods-forsaken land.*

Their plan was to follow the main route to Gosbecks which would take them through Londinium. He was curious to see how reparations from the rebellion were proceeding. The news had been horrific as to what havoc Boudicca's rebellion had wrought. All of the Romans including the women had been put to death. The

---

[96] https://en.wikipedia.org/wiki/Samhain

stories were even more gruesome regarding Camulodunum. The Roman women there were impaled on spikes, their breasts cut off and stuffed into their own mouths. The raw rage directed at the Romans was undeniable. No wonder this colonia in Gosbecks was going to be a challenge. Once they got to Gosbecks they would try to quietly infiltrate into the village to see just how many farms were fallow and how smoothly the inner workings of village life was running, such as do they have a working smithy, is trade being conducted in their market on a regular basis. If they were able to levy that many fighters for the rebellion what percentage of them returned and if they did return are they able bodied and can labor on the farms.

As they got assembled to leave the legate Marcus Flaccus Antoninus met them to give departing instructions. "The level of unease may be great but the most important thing is Rome will want to get its money back from the cost of the recent insurrection. See just how much land we can incorporate into the colonia. The more acreage we can take the more retiring soldiers Rome can sent your way. A thriving community of ex-Roman soldiers will be the best at civilizing Britannia. The Celts and Romans will integrate and create a stable province for the empire." He then waved them on and as they left he turned to his secretary. "Note in your papers that the colonia at Gosbecks is going to be problematic. The natives are unruly and untrustworthy. We will need to keep a close eye out for possible druidic meddling in this area."

Quintus and his men pulled out of fort and headed for Londinium at a good clip knowing it should take them the full week to get to Gosbecks. After several days of uneventful travel they came upon the outskirts of Londinium. The rebellion left a lot of burnt scars upon the landscape that had yet to be cleared up. Small hamlets were still cleaning up in earnest now that harvesting was almost upon them. On the outskirts were more fields that still needed to be threshed and crops gathered proof that the farmers had joined the rebellion. The sheer amount of crops still in the fields gave Quintus an uneasy feeling. If the Celts here have not gathered their crops in as yet then the winter would be bleak indeed, starvation would be knocking at the door. Closer in were the still smoldering evidence of the pyres left from burning the bodies. Despite the rebellion having happened two months prior, the acrid oily smell of burnt bodies was still evident.

Further into the area around Londinium were the larger out-buildings and homes of the upper class. All were burnt husks of their former glory prior to the rebellion, even their gardens were destroyed. The larger villas had not been rebuilt or even cleared of debris; even their quays that thrust out into the Thames to supply the rich were burnt and destroyed. Clogging the Thames were burnt wreckage of pleasure ships[97] for the once rich owners, nothing was salvageable. Looking in one of the villas revealed the barbarity of the attack, blood still painted the atrium[98], the impluvium pool[99] was littered with debris, the water turned brown from the refuse. Further in the villa the statuary around the peristylium[100] were toppled, all the vases smashed, all plants burnt. The beautiful murals on the walls showed brown smears of long dried blood. There were no workers or slaves doing anything in the ghostly piles of stone. When they pulled aside a man from the road they were told there were no longer Roman overseers to get the work parties to start clearing the rubble. The whole picture was very disturbing.

Previous trading businesses on the Thames run by Romans were burnt rubble. The warehouses destroyed and scorched to the ground. Out by the wharves of these establishments were destroyed lifting cranes used to haul the goods from ships, their great lifting arms looked like desiccated limbs being charred and rendered

---

[97] https://images.search.yahoo.com/yhs/search?p=Roman+Pleasure+Ships&hspart=att&hsimp=yhs-att_001

[98] http://www.roman-empire.net/society/soc-house.html

[99] https://images.search.yahoo.com/yhs/search?p=Impluvium+In+An+Ancient+Roman+Home&hspart=att&hsimp=yhs-att_001

[100] http://www.merriam-webster.com/dictionary/peristylium

unusable. The stores at the front were cleaned out of any goods, what was left were only the broken shelves and tables. Taverns and inns that catered to the Romans were likewise destroyed, the small kitchens charred, the tables and seating gone, any rooms that were rented out to customers burnt to the ground.

Further from the Roman businesses the only good thing they saw was the docks were bustling with new loads pulling up to the quays. The shipments of lumber, hemp for ropes, and masonry being unloaded by slaves for the military engineering corps set to rebuild the infrastructure of Londinium. The Roman military machine was ever efficient with their soldiers on hand to rebuild; engineers had set up their tents to help, their officers and secretaries bustling with scrolls with designs for the rebuild. Within the group were Lucius Silo and Gnaeus Domitius, upon hailing them they wearily came over to talk.

"Glad to see you are alive and made it through the rebellion!" Quintus hailed.

Lucius wiped his face with a grubby linen towel and nodded. "Thank the gods we were not overwhelmed by the Celtic throng like most of the Romans here. They divided up and the group set upon the fort was large but not as disciplined as we were. They came at us in waves, fought well but the walls and ramparts were beyond their ability to assail. They had no siege machines, just hordes of yelling barbarians. The initial assault took out our guards and the first responders. We were able to regroup and fought against the rabble because they acted more like a mob than a true fighting group. Lepidus Piso and all the centurions were able to organize the resistance. I am very grateful for that old war horse; he was everywhere when we needed him."

"Should we stop and see him. Is he available for meetings?" asked Quintus, Faber who was beside him nodded.

"I don't think so." Gnaeus shook his head, "He was injured in the final assault and is recovering from a leg wound. He is cranky normally but now he is unbearable. He is holed up in the infirmary and driving the surgeons batty with his demands. If you are on a schedule I wouldn't advise it."

"He is driving us all very hard with his demands. He sends runners every meal time and sometimes in between with new orders to get the repairs finished," Lucius shrugged. "I am exhausted and would like to take a break."

"The only tavern that is open now is 'The Sailor'. All the others were so badly destroyed that they need to be rebuilt from the ground up," Gnaeus said sadly. "We could all do with a good round of that piss they serve for ale."

"How many soldiers were lost?" Quintus was almost afraid to ask.

"We lost almost six centuries in the rebellion, just shy of a full cohort[101]," Lucius said quietly.

Quintus and the rest of his *Contubernium* gasped at the number. "What are they going to do to replenish the troops here?" asked Bundarus.

"They say they're being sent from Gaul as we speak. The biggest number will go to Camulodunum to help them replenish their numbers at the fort. They lost more than we did. We'll get the larger number for engineers so we can get the docks back to it where it was before this mess. In the meantime it is double-time work for all the engineers until they get here," Gnaeus said and wearily rubbed his forehead.

The men just stood there for a moment letting the enormity of the situation hit them. Boudicca's rebellion was bigger than they thought originally, after hearing the bald numbers from Lucius and Gnaeus they almost couldn't get their heads around the problem.

Quintus said: "We are on a mission ourselves to Gosbecks, about a day and a half's ride from Camulodunum. I think our mission

---

[101] http://www.roman-empire.net/army/army.html https://images.search.yahoo.com/yhs/search?p=Cohort+In+the+Roman+Army+Organization& hspart=att&hsimp=yhs-att_001

just got harder after hearing what went on here in Londinium and Camulodunum . We'll get going and let you get back to you work." He shook their hands. The rest followed him and they all got back on their horses. They turned and looked out at the bustling engineers getting their fort back to rights. "Gods be thanked that you and the fort survived." Many more people were swirling around ships bringing in goods and fresh produce for the remaining populous. The normal daily routines had reconstituted after the rebellion. Regular life must continue even after such a disruption.

As they traveled beyond Londinium the ravages to the countryside were more pronounced. There were many more fields lying fallow, the crops just left to rot in the fields. Fire hollowed buildings lined the road, their hulls standing out like rotting carcasses. There were people on the road but not much news, most of them fleeing to or leaving Londinium. Many were hauling all their household goods in overburdened carts. One passerby they were able to stop said they were going to find work on the docks or seek work to rebuild Londinium. Another simply grunted that he was quitting a dead city for their own tribal lands south east of the city. If the fallow lands were any indication Quintus was sure they would be able to find empty farms to take over without a problem.

They turned off toward Gosbecks deciding not to travel through Camulodunum since it would add several days to go up to the city and then back down to the southwest. It was just as well since on the road they heard even more gruesome stories about the havoc wreaked there. Especially when they were told how the Celts had burned half the Roman citizens trapped in the unfinished temple dedicated to the newly deified emperor Claudius. It seemed the local Romans fled to the temple in supplication to the god Claudius, their cries for mercy were not heeded by the by the marauding Celts. They were all trapped as it burned to the ground with the temple.

On the trail Fullo rode beside Quintus in his accustomed

position. "Have you figured out how we're going to infiltrate Gosbecks?" he queried.

"The information on Samhain has been little and I have the direct impression it is incomplete if not outright incorrect. When I've asked our guides they just consider it as an end of season celebration but I also get the impression there is something they are not telling us. Do you think the druids will be involved in anyway? I thought they were all annihilated at Mona." Quintus replied with exasperation.

". It might be each of these small hamlets have their own druid but now without the governing main governing body that we decapitated in Mona. They might not be in contact with anyone in authority from their religion, sort of like suddenly not having the priestly colleges surrounding Jupiter Optimus Maximus. All their auguries are no longer being taken for optimum godly pleasure and need." Fullo replied.

Quintus looked at him with surprise: "Are they that civilized? I thought they just gave the druids their votive offerings and let them do as they wanted. The island Mona had no structures, just those gods-forsaken trees and main clearing. Other than the bonfire pit that looked well used there was nothing else."

"I have heard talk of standing stones on a plane in the center of Britannia. No temple but it is supposed to be impressive. I think their religion is more nature based, sort of like the rights of Pan, more tied to forests and such. But to tell you the truth I am not the one to ask, you need to talk to Grex. Since he is our resident herder from Sicily he would know about these things. His little Celtic woman I hear might be coming along to Gosbecks with him. He has a way with the locals and can get this type of intelligence that you need. I'll go get him." Fullo turned his horse to the rear to go get Grex who usually brought up the rear.

Presently Grex moved up to ride by Quintus: "I hear you need some information about Samhain, what you want to know?"

"What is Samhain exactly and is it just the end of harvest season or is it something else, something that has to do with druids?"

Grex eyed him: "I don't know everything but what I do know my young Celtic woman has told me. What the locals tell Romans is it is a celebration of the end of the harvest and beginning of winter but it is also the time of the year that coincides with equal times of light and dark during the day. This makes it so much more of a religious time for the Celts. She called it the time when both the spiritual realm and the human realm are closest together at this time of year. There can be a mixing of the two realms but it is also very hazardous if there is a mixing. Good and bad spirits abound and you might have the misfortune of communicating with the bad sort."

"What has this to do with Samhain?" Quintus asked tiredly.

"Because the Celts have celebrations for both the good and bad spirits, I couldn't get my girl Cai to tell me exactly what the rituals are but she let me know they are bad and can be bloody. There is always dancing and singing but it can devolve into something worse as the night goes on." Grex said uneasily, "Cai was really dodgy about telling me everything, sorry but that is all I know."

"Well that is more than I knew before; once again the damned druids are rearing their ugly beards. Thank you Grex." Quintus said. They had just half a day's ride and Samhain would be upon them. At their current speed they should make it with no problem. They continued on with their journey to Gosbecks.

CHAPTER 6
WHAT IS LOST IS FOUND

Preparations for Samhain[102] took place in a flurry between harvesting the crops and setting the needed arrangements for the festivity. The end of the growing season was always met with long days in the field reaping the wheat and barley, the last minute crops to be gathered and set aside for the long winter season, preparing flax and nettles for clothing, searching for herbs in the meadows and forests for cooking and medicine, hunting and smoking meats for the long winter. The time went by very fast.

Normally preparations were joyful. The end of the season coming to pass and all the hard work of the previous season coming to fruition but this year was different. A full quarter of Gosbecks were gone and the absent hands were sorely missed. The remaining laborers were mainly older or wounded men, older women or women with young children, and very few young people. The pall of missing family fell heavily on the residents as they went

---

[102] http://paganwiccan.about.com/od/samhainoctober31/p/Samhain_History.htm

through the traditional steps for Samhain, setting aside goods for the mummers to throw into the bonfires to lure away the wicked spirits and malicious beings. Arranging the wood for the bonfire that evening was the only happy event mainly because it signified the true end of the season, many hands were surrounding the site for the first time in weeks to mound the wood and tinder, beacons to the spirits and the living combined.

Edana, Eilis, Sadhbh and Meadghbh were preparing their mummers disguise together at Meadghbh's home, burdock leaves woven together into tunics and wheat sheaf headdresses that sprang from their heads in a flat star pattern. Edana added some late autumn flowers into their hair from the forests to their disguises. The night was cool but promised to be much colder as the sun when down so they made sure to wear fur under their burdock tunics for warmth which added a measure of wildness to their disguises. It gave them the appearance of rounded woodland creatures instead of young ladies. In the end all of the girls were much different than they normally looked. Bebhinn gave each of the ladies mistletoe to wear in the wheat headdresses for additional safekeeping. "You never know what sprites and spirits you'll encounter on Samhain. Most will appear as human but no one you are familiar with. They will try to lure you away with words of fair encouragements or treasure. Others will berate and scorn you, trying to convince you to follow them or else your loved ones will suffer their wrath."

"What will they look like?" asked Eilis who out of the four of them was the most timid.

Bebhinn answered "Not like anything you've ever seen. If you glance at their faces they will try to beguile you. They covet what we have which is life and love. Remember to go in pairs and not be alone even for one minute. Mummers have to go from home to home begging for foodstuffs and goods to return and throw into the bonfires. All the year's desires and hopes for safekeeping will go up in the smoke of the bonfires and return to the other world."

"How many homes must we go to?" asked Sadhbh

"All must be visited tonight. Divide up the homesteads between you four and mark out in your heads which ones you'll go to. We are lucky that Gosbecks is small, there should be no problems. Remember to visit each one as soon as possible. Each homestead you visit will give you an offering, it is your job to make sure they are thrown into the bonfires. Our home is the furthest, you might want to pick up my offering first and then work your way into the closest ones to the bonfires for safety sake."

"Meadghbh and I will pick up the offering Mother as soon as we finish our plans for tonight with everyone. Will you follow us back to the bonfire after we do?" Edana said.

"No, you should never have a family follow you back to the bonfire They may be lured away as well by the malevolent other worldly spirits. Remember Samhain is when the veil between the worlds is at its thinnest, more than just spirits may cross. Ailbe and I will wait until you've departed for at least an hour before we go join the festivities," Bebhinn replied.

She gathered her skirts and left to go home, grabbing Ailbe on the way out who was playing with Eimear, Meadghbh's mother. "I'll see you later Edana, you look beautiful!" Ailbe snickered as he was dragged out by his mother "She looks like a beautiful woodland troll."

"I'm supposed to be imposing not a beautiful troll you silly boy!" laughed Edana. She watched her mother and brother leave Meadghbh's home. She turned to her friends: "I propose we half the village, Eilis and Sadhbh take the eastern half and Meadghbh and I will take the western."

"But that makes you go to the most far flung farms," said Eilis, "You two will be far out and subject to more unrestful spirits." she chewed her lip, worry making her face pinched,.

"We can do it because both of our farms are on the west side. We know the short cuts to each farm and can get there in record time. We'll get the furthest first and work our way back into the bonfire. Meadghbh and I have been talking about this ever since we've been collecting burdock for our mummers' disguises. We'll start with my home and work our way in. Niamh's farm will be the tricky one as it is on the outskirts on the high ridge bordering our farms. But we'll go there directly after mine." Edana said.

Eilis looked stricken: "That's so far! I think maybe we should all stick together and do all of the homes as one big group, more to keep away the spiteful spirits."

"We're better if we split up Eilis, you and I will get the inner homes quickly and we'll be able to spend Samhain with people, not spirits," laughed Sadhbh who was much more optimistic than Eilis and not at all worried about their mummer duties. "Plus with only half the village and less people to do Edana and Meadghbh will also finish early too. Let's go and get this done," And as if to end the discussion she grabbed Eilis' hand and pulled her to the door.

"We'll all get going now," said Edana and she grabbed Meadghbh's hand too, all four of the girls left at the same time. "Happy Samhain!" Outside the girls split up with one group going east and the other west.

Edana and Meadghbh headed for Edana's home on the far west side. The night was crisp with just a hint of mist swirling around the trunks of the trees in the woods. The eerie picture was not lost on the girls but they bravely pressed ahead, moving silently forward into the fog, the scenery disappearing into the mist. "We must keep together and not get out of each other's sight, it looks like the spirits will be active tonight," Meadghbh said under her breath as they trudged through the woods and still had a ways to go so they kept at a good clip.

"Since we passed the forked road we'll get to my house soon, from there to Niamh's farm and back to the bonfire to throw the offerings in. Then we should go next to Cathmore's farm. With those out of the way we'll be able to circle back into Gosbecks without mishap." Edana tried to sound confident but even her worry was sneaking through on this Samhain night. There seemed to be a preternatural stillness to this Samhain night.

Worriedly the girls trudged through the night without misfortune and made it to Edana's home. Per the rehearsed saying they came to the front and demanded to be appeased by those within: "We claim the right to be appeased from the inhabitants of this home!" they chorused in loud keening voices. From within Bebhinn opened the door and gave them the package of bound wheat and barley from their own fields proving to the spirits they were willing to share in goodwill.

"Be safe, tonight is unsettled in the weather and in the heavens. The meeting of our world and the other world is strong tonight," she murmured. The girls glanced uneasily at each other but thanked her for the package as expected for the spirits. With that Bebhinn backed away and closed the door. Inside she said a quick fervent prayer to Manannán mac Lir for the safe deliverance of the girls. Ailbe sitting in the corner watched her and said nothing, not even a question which was unusual for the little boy. "What do you see for the girls Ailbe?" Bebhinn asked not really expecting an answer from him.

In a strangely hollow sounding voice he replied: "They will be spared from the spirits meddling tonight but will meet some that are not of this world." Bebhinn was startled and looked stricken, however she took comfort from this pronunciation that they would at least be spared. Ailbe had said nothing of them returning to their homes. Bebhinn missed that fine point.

Outside Edana and Meadghbh clasped hands and continued to Niamh's home up on the high ridge. The moon was obscured by the clouds but occasionally they got a watery glimpse of the moon as they scudded across the face. The night was bizarrely quiet with the heavy feeling of something watching, waiting for the opportunity to come out at them at any moment, their breaths puffing in unison in white before disappearing as they continued on to the high ridge. The girls were getting increasingly worried as they continued, expecting something to jump out at them. The girls had never felt so far away from the comforts of their hearths and homes then at this moment.

They had chosen to go through the woods at this time, a short cut to take off at least a half a league off their route. Inside the tree canopy the fog was even thicker, swirling in tendrils that seemed to grasp at their legs and slow them down further. They increased their pace, walking silently only their breathing making any sounds as they gulped at the thick air. Ahead was the beginning of a slight rise in the terrain, the top of the ridge that was their destination to their left. There wasn't a clearing per se, just a lessening of the dense woods, a natural break in the foliage. Ahead they heard stamping from hooves and deep rumbling of hushed voices. The girls tensed and stopped, looking forward but not truly seeing anything, just large moving shapes in the gloom. The voices continued but they couldn't understand what was said, just a litany of syllables that flowed over a quick tongue in a low, deep voices. Expecting to see spirits form another world the girls crouched down low, hoping their disguises would melt them into the foliage, into their woodland surroundings. Hearts in their throats they looked at each other.

"I think these are spirits here to lure us away, I cannot understand their talk and the voices are deep like a dark cave, rumbling like gravel. It must be some sort of underground spirits!" Meadghbh breathed as low as she could, her eyes wide with fear.

"I do not understand them either; perhaps they are the fey and have come to take us away to their realm. I think we should just stay low and wait for them to pass. We must get further back into the undergrowth to hide. I do not think they can see us up there on the higher ground." Edana answered urgently, pulling Meadghbh's arm. "Quite now, we'll be able to let them past us." Backing up the girls moved into the denser undergrowth. Edana stepped back, her foot landing on a dry branch that cracked loudly in the gloom. The low speaking stopped immediately; they then heard one set of hooves move off toward them. Out of the gloom a rider appeared on a large dark horse, the face still obscured but the body unnaturally large with great hulking shoulders. The girls were not deep into the foliage and could be seen. A deep voice rumbled at the girls, but they could not understand the language. Seeing no way out they looked up silently and anxiously. The other riders appeared out of the fog, each talking to the others. There were eight horses now facing the girls.

The first hulking rider rumbled out more, talking to his comrades, gestured to the girls. One at the back signaled to a smaller rider on a gray horse who disengaged from the others. In heavily accented Celt he said: "Who are you and why are you out on this night?"

Terrified the girls looked at each other, Meadghbh gestured to Edana to talk to the spirits. "I am Edana and this is Meadghbh. We mean you no harm and wish to be on our way." She said as bravely as she could.

The being in the shadows shook his head, "I think not, you have seen us. You will be coming with us."

"We have a lot of duties for this Samhain night and must visit several places. We must continue on our mission," Edana croaked, "We cannot go with you to whence you came from."

The man in shadows turned and spoke in the fluid language to his comrades. There were several rumbles of laughter from the other riders. Edana looked at Meadghbh with worry, thinking they are in trouble. They exchanged a look and then took off running the opposite way from the riders. Their feet taking flight, running as they never had before. Behind them the large hulking rider followed with the smaller one who shouted: "Why are you running, we only want to talk with you!"

As one the girls turned from the path into a deer run, smaller and harder for the horses to follow. Behind them the larger rider yelled something since he could not follow them. They heard him jump off his horse and the pounding of his legs as he followed them. They redoubled their efforts but his longer legs quickly overtook their shorter ones. He grabbed Meadghbh first then Edana who cried out in the fear. His hands were big and rough, he held them securely but not harshly as if he didn't wish to harm them. He dragged them back to the small clearing where the other riders were still waiting. The one on the gray horse said: "Are you trying to alert your people to our appearance here in Gosbecks?"

"No, we are not going to tell anyone you are here," Edana fearfully said.

"Where were you going? Why did you run?"

"No, no one would believe us if we told them that you are in Gosbecks," Edana truthfully said, "We are only mummers that are performing the propitiation rites for Samhain, so spirits will leave and return to their realm."

"You think us spirits? Does Faber holding you fill solid?" he gestured to the man holding them. He turned and said something to the others which got another round of laughter. The one called Faber shook their arms a little in response. Meadghbh cried out in dismay at the action.

They were well and truly caught and each girl trembled, knowing they will be dragged back to the fey world by their captors. There was no light to see their faces but their bodies seemed unnaturally large, especially through their chests. Their horses were restive and danced but the riders kept them in check with no problem. One of them on the end rode forward, his big bay horse chomping at the bit and prancing as if impatient to get moving. "Do you know the people here? On the next rise is a farm, is it yours?" The man's voice was heavily accented but understandable, his voice smooth and deep, oddly compelling.

"We know the owners of the next farm but it is not ours," answered Edana, "It is owned by Niamh who is expecting us."

"Do you have a meeting set up? I'd like to attend if you do," the unknown man answered, his face obscured by shadows.

"No meeting just another propitiation rite for Samhain."

"What is this rite, is it religious? Is it done as a supplication for services rendered and what are the services?" he rapid fired the questions, sounding gruff in his interest to be answered.

"It is religious, do you not celebrate Samhain? Is it not the same for the fey[103]?" Edana was getting confused at this roundabout discussion as if they were discussing something else entirely.

"Fey? I am not familiar with this word, what is the meaning?" He asked quizzically, he then turned to the others and asked them a question in their lilting, fast language. They seemed to discuss the matter but they shook their heads as well.

"Fey is what you are, you are from another realm, from beyond our world. Are you not from another realm?" she asked worriedly.

He laughed, "Yes we are from another realm, not this one, a place far away and much warmer, a place that is *much more civilized*." In the background several riders guffawed at what was said.

The girls looked at each other; they caught the derisive tone in his words, and did not like what they heard. "This is a very civilized land, for generations we've been following the correct path given to us by our gods, we follow our laws and have a bustling trade amongst our villages. I do not understand why you say we are not civilized." Edana retorted.

"Because you are a small nation and not a vast expanse of nations which we have under our sway. We have lands in the far south where it rarely rains and in the east where civilization began. We transvers the seas and have marched across plains that are vast and seemingly without end. We hold control over lands where there are massive mountains, the snow is deep in winter and meadows are green in the summer," the dark man said proudly.

Not understanding what he meant Edana held her tongue for a moment and thought furiously. If he was indeed fey than it must be a larger realm than she thought, she needed more information from him and the more she got him to speak the more likely she would be able to get away from them. "Where is your realm located?"

"We are located here and to the south across the sea in Gaul,

---

[103] http://www.thefreedictionary.com/fey

further south than Spain, to the west of Greece and north of the vast Africa."

"I've never heard of these places, are they further than Londinium?" Edana asked

Laughter met her question from the other riders. "Yes it is much further little one, much further. It would take us many months to transverse our realm, maybe even many years."

Silence met that declaration. Edana and Meadghbh looked at one another nervously. Meadghbh said: "What do you want from us then, are you going to take us to your realm?"

"No, we just want to go to the next farm up over the ridge from here. We do not wish to take you back to our realm," the dark man said resignedly as if she bored him. She wanted to hear more from him, his voice was so enthralling. Maybe because he was fey and casting a spell over her, she thought worriedly.

"What will you do to the people there?" Edana asked curious at this turn of the situation. They only wanted to talk to Niamh's family, maybe take the whole family to their realm? Enslave them all with enchantments?

"I want to talk to them about the future," the dark man said in his heavily accented deep voice. "Come ride with me, your friend can ride with Faber. We'll go to the farm on the ridge."

With that Faber walked her over to the dark man and hoisted Edana up in front of him on his dark horse. He then walked over to his big horse and put Meadghbh onto his own horse. Meadghbh's face was a mask of fear but she did not cry, just held onto the horse's mane as the large man got onto the horse behind her. He systematically took off her wheaten headdress because it was in his face and pitched it into the darkness. The dark man laughed and did the same to Edana's headdress. "I cannot ride with this in my face." He said as took off her headdress and carelessly pitched it away, the he reached around her to grab the reins and moved the horse into line with the others who had already moved off.

Edana trembled as she rode in silence with the dark man.

Cathmore said burdock and wheat would be noxious to spirits but this fey just touched her crown and he is also pressed into her with her burdock tunic with no reactions. She found to her dismay that she liked having him hold her, touch her. I need more information from him. Is it possible they are not fey at all but something else, something even more dangerous, she thought? Thinking back on his answers she was even more confuses that he never denied being fey and talked about being in charge a much larger realm than hers. Then cold understanding dawned. "You are not fey but Roman?" she asked in a breathless voice, fear resurfacing as she remembered her conversation with Cathmore.

The dark man chuckled: "It took you awhile but you figured it out on your own, yes we are Roman. It is most propitious that we met tonight. I want you to take me on all of your stops tonight so that we can meet those that live in Gosbecks. We would like to talk to your people about a few matters that have come to our attention. Don't misunderstand me I'm not here to cause problems, on the contrary we are here to meet those who are in charge and let them know we mean to cause no difficulties. By the way you may call me Quintus Agricolanus that is my name."

Presently they gained the ridge and could see Niamh's farm in the distance. Edana's head swam with the events of this night. Yes, they did not run into spirits or the fey but they did run something much more dangerous, Romans! And they wanted her to take them to meet with everyone in Gosbecks which meant she'd be tainted as a Roman collaborator, a traitor to her people. She had to figure a way out of this situation, to get out of helping the Romans. She hoped Meadghbh was faring better than she was.

Meadghbh was faring no better than Edana. Where Faber was not talkative his hands were roaming all over of her body. She was so scared it never occurred to her to ask questions of the hulking man behind her. Faber for his part was enjoying the feeling of the woman in his arms. At first look he thought she was a fat child but his arms were able to feel she had breasts and soft hips under her outrageous outfit. The costume made her hips and breasts disappear under the strange leafy tunic. Adding the fur underneath made both girls looked like round children but on closer inspection of his hands and arms Faber was pleased to find it was in fact a trim woman in his arms. His voice rumbled as he asked in heavily accented Celt: "Are you comfortable? If you are scared you'll fall from my horse you can hold my arms or legs. I won't let you fall off." His Celtic was so heavily accented she almost didn't understand him at first.

"I've ridden before and I'm not worried that I'll fall," she answered in a soft, unsteady voice.

"Then you are afraid of me I take it," Faber said with a sigh. She merely nodded her head in the affirmative. "What can I do to let you know you needn't fear me?" His hands continued to roam around the upper portion of her torso, dangerously close to her breasts.

"Let Edana and I go," she sniffed, tears pricking her eyes as his hands continued their exploration of her upper body. Meadghbh hoped the Edana wasn't also getting mauled by her fey captor.

"Alas that I cannot do, you and your friend are our guests until we are done," was his dark reply. They continued in silence for a few minutes, his hands and arms continuing their exploration of her body. One of his hands got so bold as to brush the outside of her breast and moved inward to touch her nipple. Meadghbh let out a squeak.

"Please don't touch me," she implored, tears beginning to run down her cheeks.

"I am just determining if you are cold, which I think you might be," his hand continued to brush her nipple then plucked it which caused her to squirm.

"Please stop! I don't want this," she begged, tears coming down in earnest now.

Ahead Coriaro heard the exchange. In Latin he said: "Faber she is crying, what are you doing mauling her? She's just a child."

"No, she's not a child but a full grown woman, this ridiculous outfit hides everything, I feel nice sized breasts and rounded hips. I am placing a claim on this one for sure." Faber rumbled.

"You might have to ask Quintus first, we have only now just arrived in Gosbecks, getting involved with the locals is not such a great idea. Wait and see then place your claim," Coriaro replied a little put out at the way Faber had already laid claim to the woman.

Also hearing the exchange Fullo put in his opinion: "What if I take a turn at the woman, she won't be crying if I'm feeling her titties. She'll be cooing and showing me all the respect a good Roman soldier deserves."

"I'll stop when we get to the farm, not before. She feels and smells good, like the wild foliage around here, sweet and earthy," Faber growled beginning to bury his face into Meadghbh's hair.

"Keep you cock in your trousers, we have work to do, the farm is just right there and we'll have work to do keeping the residents under surveillance," Bundarus joined in the discussion. As usual he was focused on the work at hand and not playing around with the captives. The others started laughing but the discussion was curtailed.

Meadghbh squirmed trying to get away from Faber's hands and nose, not understanding she was the subject of the discussion, just becoming even more uncomfortable with the increasingly aggressive hands that were roaming her body. Looking up she saw the Niamh's farm coming into view and prayed to the gods that nothing bad will happen. Not realizing who the groups of riders were she was still under the misconception they were fey and not human. She hoped Edana had a better idea of how to get them out of this situation.

Meanwhile Edana was formulating a plan but a lot would have to rely on how Niamh would respond to a group of eight Roman riders, there are a lot of moving parts. . Niamh was notorious for her suspicious nature and strong will. She lost her husband and sons in Boudicca's rebellion but managed to keep her large farm running relatively smoothly by keeping her extended family in one place. Her mother, father and four daughters ran their farm as well as could be expected; her daughters were just as strong-willed as Niamh and did all the plowing and threshing. Edana needed to get alone with Niamh to explain why she showed up with the riders and needed to get her help to distract Quintus Agricolanus and his men long enough for Meadghbh and herself to escape. Getting the opportunity to be alone was the problem

The riders arrived at Niamh's farm and four dismounted including Quintus and Faber with their captives. They went up to the front door to ask for admittance. Niamh being alerted by the sounds me them with no little amount of surprise to see Edana and Meadghbh accompanied by strangers.

"Here now what is the meaning of this?" Niamh asked sharply, "Why are you with these men Edana?"

Quintus answered the woman at the door in his heavily accented Celt: "My men and I came into contact with these girls on their way to offer you Samhain propitiation rites and I offered them the chance to ride in safety with us. I would like a moment of your time?"

At the door Niamh's father Drust appeared and pulled her to the side, "Why do we discourse with strangers on this Samhain night? Don't you know it could be a ploy to get us to open our home to unnatural beings?"

"Or I could just ask Edana and Meadghbh who are standing right there in their mummers outfits. These so called spirits don't seem uncomfortable by their burdock tunics since they are standing right next to them, anyone could see they are not spirits but men," Niamh snapped. Turning to Edana and Meadghbh she asked again: "What are you doing with these men?"

"We were on our way to your farm when we came across these men and they convinced us to ride with them," Edana looked at Quintus quickly, "We need to do the propitiation rites for Samhain and be on our way, we need to do the *dance* required." She looked at Niamh meaningfully, willing her to understand since there is no dance involved for the propitiation rite.

Niamh seemed to consider what she said for a moment, and then understanding dawned on her. "Then you best start the rite in our back paddock next to where we have our own bonfire." She waved them to go around the building to the back paddock.

"But that is not needed, there is no dance …," sputtered Drust until he was hit by Niamh elbow.

"Of course they are going to dance, this Samhain is very significant because of all those that we lost during the rebellion. There are many unsettled spirits around and we must offer dances in *appeasement*." Niamh looked at Edana and nodded.

Thank the gods Niamh got her unspoken message, thought Edana gratefully; *we just might be able to escape the Romans.* Niamh ushered Edana and Meadghbh around to the back paddock, unfortunately Quintus also followed with Faber, Fullo and Grex in tow. The back paddock was closest to their small herd of lowing cattle, all bunched up near the fence of the back paddock. Their horses and goats were also in the same field giving the impression of a bustling and profitable farm. In the back paddock there was a large bonfire with a cleared space around it, already standing out there was Niamh's daughters and her mother. At the appearance of the unknown men all the women let out startled cries of dismay, until Niamh shushed them and quickly explained: "These are guests of ours tonight to help with the Samhain propitiation rituals. They escorted Edana and Meadghbh here and will be joining in in the ceremony." Looking at the men she gestured for them to move to the side and stand. They reluctantly allowed her to usher them into specific places away from Edana and Meadghbh, saying: "Now Edana and Meadghbh will need plenty of space for the dance they must perform tonight." Faber looked disgruntled at being separated from Meadghbh whom he had kept near the entire time. The other three just did as bidden regarding the situation with suspicion, looking around at the faces of the women with varying degrees of distrust.

Edana and Meadghbh went to the center nearer the bonfire: "We claim the right to be appeased from the inhabitants of this home!" they chorused in loud keening voices. Then looking at each other they began a wild gyrating dance that careened them around the bonfire in wide circles. Niamh's daughters at first not sure what was occurring looked at their mother for explanation but Niamh only clapped and encouraged the wild dance. The daughters looked at each other then followed Edana and Meadghbh's lead, clapping and encouraging in their actions. Then Niamh and her mother went further and joined in the dance.

Soon all six women were dancing around the bonfire with Edana and Meadghbh with loud, keening shouts of joy. The dance became more frenzied, the dancers twirling wildly in no logical order. While there was no music the women's feet beat out a rhythm. Back and forth the dancers spun around the bonfire, desperate movements spiraling into madness. The Romans were taken aback by this bacchanalian[104] turn of events; they were used to the measured steps of their priests in their religious ceremonies. This seemed to be a spontaneous celebration of turmoil, the wildly dancing women with sightless eyes making the men uneasy, their bodies seemingly disregarding the flames around which they danced. As the dance seemed to reach a wild crescendo it took a while to notice that within the dancing women Edana and Meadghbh were no longer in their midst.

Faber was the first to cry out in alarm at their absence. "Where are the girls that we brought here?" Faber asked uncertainly in Latin, "They were dancing a moment ago around the bonfire." Then the others stepped forward with indecision looking at one another.

"They've managed to get out the back. Grex and Fullo see if

---

[104] http://www.dictionary.com/browse/bacchanalian
https://en.wikipedia.org/wiki/Bacchanalia

you can't track them down," snapped out Quintus. Grex and Fullo leapt to comply moving fast.

"What about me?" asked Faber.

"You stay here with me to unravel this dilemma; they were well and truly enabled in this situation by the owner of this farm, we'll need to ascertain what their grounds for doing it are," Quintus ground out, irritation laced his voice.

The women continued to dance around the bonfire with abandon, passing in front of the Roman soldiers then darting away just as quickly as if they knew Quintus wanted to stop them to ask questions about the girls' disappearance. Niamh made sure to keep the celebration going a least long enough to buy time for Edana and Meadghbh to get away, she kept yelling her joyous incantations to Cernunnos and Mannon. For their deliverance from the Romans. She realized who they were from the beginning especially when Edana made the odd request to hold a dance for the propitiation rites and saw it as a way to escape them. They continued to whirl around, stamp out a rhythm with their feet and yell out until Quintus and Faber stepped in their midst to stop them.

Quintus put his hands out to grab Niamh, "Where are Edana and Meadghbh? They are missing and have been for several moments. Where have they gone?"

Niamh shook her head disdainfully, "Don't you Romans know anything? They are performing their mummer's rites for Samhain. You need to let them continue to do their duty to our village and visit other farms to get their propitiation offerings. This is what we do on Samhain, we hold this very seriously."

Shortly after Niamh's courageous remark Fullo and Grex returned empty handed, "There are too many confusing tracks left by the cattle, horses and goats. They have disappeared into the surrounding forest like woodland sprites. They know shortcuts through the area and it is too dark to follow them," Fullo said

Grex nodded and added "We have no way of tracking them in the forest tonight, they are gone."

Quintus turned to Niamh: "Then you will take us to Gosbecks in their stead. I will need you to lead me there now."

"I can't leave my family on this night of all nights! There are malign spirits about, I must keep my family safe here," She replied aggressively as she pulled away her arm from Quintus's hold.

"You will tonight, Samhain or not. It is your actions that allowed the young ladies to escape," Quintus ground out.

Drust stepped forward at this moment, "I'll take you into Gosbecks."

Quintus looked at the old man seeing the resignation in his face. "Let us go now before word gets back to everyone that we are in the area." He had to admire these people for quickly understanding the predicament the girls were in and doing something to aid them albeit clandestinely but so rapidly. He wondered that if the girls did get to the next farm they could raise an alarm. And if it was raised it would to keep him from doing anything in Gosbecks at all, which would seriously jeopardize his whole undercover mission. He shook his head; no they could not let that happen. He signaled to Fullo, Faber and Grex to get ready to leave. They followed Drust around to the front and the rest of the men. Quintus said for the benefit of those soldiers still waiting in the front "Go get your horse and we'll follow you to Gosbecks. Be quick we need to leave as soon as possible." Then he and the others mounted up on their horses. Presently Drust came around the corner on a small horse ready to take them on to Gosbecks. They all took off at a fast trot allowing Drust to lead the way.

Niamh, her mother and daughters came out after the soldiers left with Drust. Niamh quickly dispatched two of her daughters to tell Bebhinn what had transpired. The Niamh and her oldest daughter took off to their nearest neighbor which was Cathmore's farm, hoping that was where the girls went first. They hoped to meet up with them to get more information from this troubling turn of events on this particular Samhain.

⌐⌐⌐⌐

From Niamh's farm Cliona, Nola and Niamh's mother Ealga had gone to Edana' farm to pick up both Bebhinn and Ailbe and to relate what happened to Edana and Meadghbh. "Don't worry about the girls, they escaped and went off to complete their propitiation rites for Samhain. Mother and Aibhlinn are going to tell the other half of Gosbecks what occurred and we'll all meet up at the bonfire in Gosbecks." Cliona told her.

"I had a feeling something was going to happen, if not from the restive spirits it would be something else and it was definitely something else." Bebhinn looked more worried.

Ealga smiled, wrinkles around her eyes and mouth showed prominently. "With all that went on around the land this past year it could have been worse. Edana and Meadghbh escaped and can now finish their mummer duties. Come with us to the Samhain ceremony in Gosbecks. We are set to meet up with everyone at the bonfire."

"Yes come and bring Ailbe, this is a momentous Samhain," Nola added.

"Alright we'll come, let me get my medicine satchel in case a healer is needed," Bebhinn said. She turned and gathered her medicines, tonics and bag. "Come to me Ailbe, let me make sure you are dressed warmly enough, it will get colder as the night wears on." Once she had everything and Ailbe was dressed they left.

As they got closer to Gosbecks the roads became more thronged with revelers, all going to attend the Samhain propitiation ceremony. On the way they ran into some of Gosbecks musicians Iollan the drummer and Lorcan the piper. "I see the healer is here to mend any mishaps tonight," joked Iollan.

"Probably from your fierce drumming and my mad piping, we can set people into frenzy easily!" laughed Lorcan. That caused a lot of the people surrounding them to applaud at the conversation. "We want a frenzy tonight, It is Samhain after all!" one man cried out. Another chortled: "Bebhinn will patch up anyone who needs it!"

"I'd prefer not to have to patch anyone up and just enjoy the celebration," answered Bebhinn but she smiled anyway. Ailbe danced along at her side and giggled.

They continued along the road as more people joined the crowd. Cliona, Nola, and Ealga walking with Bebhinn and Ailbe, moved to the side and kept their counsel. "For the later ceremony we'll take Ailbe back with us to our farm, he cannot stay up that late, plus the rites might be a little frightening for such a young child. Cathmore was telling us about his connection to Cernuous for hunting, it would be most important that he is not there for the darker rites of the ceremony. The spirits might see him as a willing vessel to take over," Ealga said in a quiet undertone to Bebhinn making sure Ailbe didn't hear as he continued to dance in the festive throng.

"My thanks Ealga, I was worried about that as well, he does exhibit the connection with the gods at the most amazing moments. After Edana and Meadghbh left to perform the mummer rites tonight he told me not to worry that they will be meeting someone important that will affect Gosbecks for the future. Who could have foreseen the Romans were what the gods were whispering to him," Bebhinn replied anxiously.

"But did the gods say they would harmed?" asked Ealga.

Bebhinn looked over at Ailbe as he walked with seemingly no care in the world. "No he did not but he was not anxious or worried when they left. Just that serene look like he has now so maybe the Romans won't be as bad as we feared," she said hopefully.

"Yes possibly, but in dealing with the Romans it is always best to go into any meeting with them with caution. They never do anything without a cost benefit to them, which means we will be the ones paying for it," Ealga said.

They entered Gosbecks and continued on to the main meeting area around the bonfire. The crowd had swelled to more people than a regular market day showing that the Samhain ceremonies were well under way. They gathered at the front of the bonfire hoping to run into the mummers. Eilis and Sadhbh were already there putting their propitiation gifts down by the bonfire. The crowd was getting restive and several impromptu singing and dancing sessions were beginning. Presently Edana and Meadghbh joined them with their gifts and the music began to play. Bebhinn wanted to ask Edana about the Romans but the press of the crowd was too great so she kept to her place. The drummers and pipers started the Samhain music and singing began in earnest. As soon as the celebration dance began Bebhinn, Ailbe, Ealga, Cliona and Nola joined in. Ailbe was very happy and kept up with the dancers even though his short legs made him stumble a lot. Bebhinn and Ealga's hands held him up and prevented him from falling. At the zenith of the good harvest song all the propitiation gifts were thrown into the bonfire and ended the dance. The next song gave thanks to the gods reverently, fading into a blissful end. The end of the first part of Samhain was over.

As the crowds started to thin and leave Ealga then took Ailbe from Bebhinn. Bebhinn began to explain to Ailbe that he'd be leaving with Ealga but he stopped her: "I know and I'll go willingly with Ealga and her granddaughters. We will find Drust and go back to their farm for the night. You have duties to do tonight."

Ealga and Bebhinn looked at him in surprise but nodded to each other. "I see what you mean Bebhinn, he does know things beyond this world," Ealga said. Then she and Cliona and Nola, went off to find Drust who would be staying with Niamh, Aibhlinn for Samhain. They then took Ailbe back to their farm for the night.

Bebhinn went in search of Edana and the other mummers. She found them talking to Niamh, Cathmore and the druid Miach. Bebhinn ran up and hugged Edana. "I was so terrified when Ealga told me what happened at Niamh's farm. I am so thankful to the gods for your escape from the Romans."

"Niamh is the heroine here, she figured out exactly what was going on and followed my lead about a "special" dance. You should have seen how wild the dance was, it was because of our neighbors that we were able to escape.," Edana hugged Bebhinn back.

"The Romans didn't know what to think. They just stood there and then yelled when they realized the girls duped them," laughed Niamh, "I for one, think they are not that smart."

"Be careful with that complacent talk Niamh. The Romans are calculating. just remember how Quintus Agricolanus spoke to the crowd about the mill and roads. They plan everything and see that is done," Miach snapped his large gray eyes flashing.

"And you nearly revealed that you are a druid, Miach. You must be more careful when we talk to them in the future," Cathmore retorted.

"I missed this discussion, what about a mill?" Bebhinn asked.

"The Romans are dangling a mill being built in Gosbecks. *It will only mean more intrusion of Roman government and money lenders here.*" Miach expounded. "We ended their talk about all the things Romans can do for us here by telling them we'll meet to discuss their proposals. I think the whole idea of having them here in the first place is a problem but it sounds *like Rome has already deemed Gosbecks a fertile area and ripe for the taking,*" Miach said disgustedly.

"Can they?" anxiously Bebhinn asked.

"Romans can and will do what they want now. They defeated us and will take advantage of everything they can, they are the victors," Cathmore said worriedly and unconsciously rubbed his crippled arm.

"What about the Samhain ceremony later, should we still hold it?" Edana asked

"We must hold it, but we'll do it much later and wait until the Romans have gone to their fort. The oak, elder and yew have eyes and ears, but not for the Romans, our gods do not want them involved." Miach said invoking the traditional saying about the forest that lent seriousness to his declaration. It meant the gods were present. "Have you brought Ailbe?"

"Ailbe is too young for this meeting Miach, he willingly went with Ealga and Drust back to Niamh's farm, *he told me he understood that tonight I had duties to perform*," Bebhinn told him with meaning.

"Huh, that is interesting. It would have made for a great Samhain ceremony but if the gods directed him to leave then so be it," Miach shook his long gray hair and let the matter drop.

"Should we begin to gather in the forest? Many have already made their way there. Is the Roman fort far enough away?" Cathmore asked.

"They are far enough away. We've put them by the old fishing stream. The sound of the water rushing over the rocks will help to mask our noise and prove lethargic for them. However if they do hear something it might put the fear of the gods into them, better if it does. I am sure we will get guidance from the gods tonight" Miach said.

At these stark words the group grew quiet. Miach had never before admitted that the gods will be present so forcefully at the Samhain ceremony. They began to uneasily sidle away toward the forest clearing where Samhain would continue and take place, each with their own thoughts. Bebhinn walked next to Edana and Meadghbh and asked quietly: "Are you alright? Nothing happened except meeting up with the Romans right?"

"I was able to talk with Quintus Agricolanus, Meadghbh was not so lucky, she had a randy soldier holding her who spent much of his time feeling her curves. Quintus was actually quite the gentleman in comparison," Edana replied.

"The one who held me, Faber, was more interested in what was between his legs. I was so frightened that I continued to believe they were fey and not men," Meadghbh said.

"How did you figure out that they were men and not fey?" Bebhinn asked Edana

"What Quintus told me gave me the clues. He patiently answered my questions and only chided me that it took me long enough to figure out they were Romans. I did not have time to ask more because we arrived at Niamh's." Edana told her.

"Did you hear the discussion about a mill?"

"No, we were too far away standing at the bonfire to hear," answered Meadghbh. They trudged through the woods a little more in silence. Sounds from the crowd ahead began to filter back including the sounds of piping and drumming, snippets of song and laughter. The girls increased their stride; Bebhinn had to trot to keep up with them.

"There is another thing you need to know Mother; Quintus Agricolanus is the Roman who killed Father and Carrick. Cathmore confirmed that and told me earlier tonight." Edana said sadly.

"Now I know tonight was preordained, Ailbe told me when you left that you meet someone that will have a big consequence on Gosbecks but I did not think we would be this privately involved," Bebhinn said, "My heart is sad at this news."

"As is my heart Mother." Each continued in silence with their own thoughts, Bebhinn about her husband and son, Edana with thoughts of Quintus and how good he felt when she was riding with him. She wanted to get back to him again to talk more.

CHAPTER 7
GREEN MAN'S CLEARING

Preparations for Samhain[105] took place in a flurry between harvesting the crops and setting the needed arrangements for the festivity. The end of the growing season was always met with long days in the field. They needed to reap the wheat and barley, the last minute crops to be gathered and set aside for the long winter season, prepare flax and nettles for clothing, search for herbs in the meadows and forests for cooking and medicine, hunt and smoke meats for the long winter. The time went by very fast.

Normally preparations were joyful for the Samhain festival, the end of the season coming to pass and all the hard work of the previous season coming to fruition but this year was different. A full quarter of Gosbecks were gone and the absent hands were sorely missed. The pall of missing family fell heavily on the residents as they went through the traditional steps for Samhain. They set aside goods for the mummers to throw into the bonfires to lure away the

---

[105] http://paganwiccan.about.com/od/samhainoctober31/p/Samhain_History.htm

wicked spirits and beings. Arranging the wood for the bonfire that evening was the only happy event mainly because it signified the true end of the season. Many hands were surrounding the site for the first time in weeks to mound the wood and tinder, enough to last the entire night, beacons to the spirits and the living combined.

From Niamh's farm Cliona, Nola and Niamh's mother Ealga had gone to Bebhinn's farm to pick up both Bebhinn and Ailbe and to relate what happened to Edana and Meadghbh. "Don't worry about the girls, they escaped and went off to complete their propitiation rites for Samhain. Mother and Aibhlinn are going to tell the other half of Gosbecks what occurred and we'll all meet up at the bonfire in Gosbecks." Cliona told her.

"I had a feeling something was going to happen, if not from the restive spirits it would be something else and it was definitely something else." Bebhinn looked more worried.

Ealga smiled, wrinkles around her eyes and mouth showed prominently. "With all that went on around the land this past year it could have been worse. Edana and Meadghbh escaped and can now finish their mummer duties. Come with us to the Samhain ceremony in Gosbecks. We are set to meet up with everyone at the bonfire."

"Yes come and bring Ailbe, this is a momentous Samhain," Nola added.

"Alright we'll come, let me get my medicine satchel in case a healer is needed," Bebhinn said. She turned and gathered her medicines, tonics and bag. "Come to me Ailbe, let me make sure you are dressed warmly enough, it will get colder as the night wears on." Once she had everything and Ailbe was dressed they left.

As they got closer to Gosbecks the roads became more thronged with revelers, all going to attend the Samhain propitiation ceremony. On the way they ran into some of Gosbecks musicians Iollan the drummer and Lorcan the piper. "I see the healer is here to mend any mishaps tonight," joked Iollan.

"Probably from your fierce drumming and my mad piping, we

can set people into frenzies easily!" laughed Lorcan. That caused a lot of the people surrounding them to applaud at the conversation. "We want a frenzy tonight, It is Samhain after all!" one man cried out. Another chortled: "Bebhinn will patch up anyone who needs it!"

"I'd prefer not to have to patch anyone up and just enjoy the celebration," answered Bebhinn but she smiled anyway. Ailbe danced along at her side and giggled.

They continued along the road as more people joined the crowd. Cliona, Nola, and Ealga walking with Bebhinn and Ailbe, moved to the side and kept their counsel. "For the later ceremony we'll take Ailbe back with us to our farm, he cannot stay up that late. Plus the rites might be a little frightening for such a young child. Cathmore was telling us about his connection to Cernuous for hunting, it would be most important that he is not there for the darker rites of the ceremony. The spirits might see him as a willing vessel to take over," Ealga said in a quiet undertone to Bebhinn making sure Ailbe didn't hear as he continued to dance in the festive throng.

"My thanks Ealga, I was worried about that as well, he does exhibit the connection with the gods at the most amazing moments. After Edana and Meadghbh left to perform the mummer rites tonight he told me not to worry that they will be meeting someone important that will affect Gosbecks for the future. Who could have foreseen the Romans were what the gods were whispering to him," Bebhinn replied anxiously.

"But did the gods say they would be harmed?" asked Ealga.

Bebhinn looked over at Ailbe as he walked with seemingly no care in the world. "No he did not, but he was not anxious or worried when they left. Just that serene look like he has now so maybe the Romans won't be as bad as we feared," she said hopefully.

"Yes possibly but in dealing with the Romans it is always best to go into any meeting with them with caution. They never do anything without a cost benefit to them, which means we will be the ones paying for it," Ealga in her wisdom said.

They entered Gosbecks and continued on to the main meeting area around the bonfire. The crowd had swelled to more people than a regular market day showing that the Samhain ceremonies were well under way. They gathered at the front of the bonfire hoping to run into the mummers. Eilis and Sadhbh were already there putting their propitiation gifts down by the bonfire. The crowd was getting restive and several impromptu singing and dancing sessions were beginning. Presently Edana and Meadghbh joined them with their gifts and the music began to play. Bebhinn wanted to ask Edana about the Romans but the press of the crowd was too great to she kept to her place. The drummers and pipers started the Samhain music and singing began in earnest. As soon as the celebration dance began Bebhinn, Ailbe, Ealga, Cliona and Nola joined in. Ailbe was very happy and kept up with the dancers even though his short legs made him stumble a lot, Bebhinn and Ealga's hands held him up and prevented him from falling. At the zenith of the good harvest song all the propitiation gifts were thrown into the bonfire which ended the dance. The next song gave thanks to the gods reverently, fading into a blissful end. The end of the first part of Samhain was over.

As the crowds started to thin and leave Ealga then took Ailbe from Bebhinn. Bebhinn began to explain to Ailbe that he'd be leaving with Ealga but he stopped her: "I know and I'll go willingly with Ealga and her granddaughters. We will find Drust and go back to their farm for the night. You have duties to do tonight." Ealga and Bebhinn looked at him in surprise but nodded to each other.

"I see what you mean Bebhinn, he does know things beyond this world," Ealga said. She and Cliona and Nola, went off to find Drust would be staying with Niamh and Aibhlinn for Samhain. They then took Ailbe back to their farm for the night. Bebhinn went in search of Edana and the other mummers.

She found them talking to Niamh, Cathmore and the druid Miach. Bebhinn ran up and hugged Edana. "I was so terrified when Ealga told me what happened at Niamh's farm. I am so thankful to the gods for your escape from the Romans."

"Niamh is the heroine here, she figured out exactly what was going on and followed my lead about a "special" dance. You should have seen how wild the dance was. It was because of our neighbors that we were able to escape.," Edana hugged Bebhinn back.

"The Romans didn't know what to think. They just stood there and then yelled when they realized the girls duped them," laughed Niamh, "I for one think they are not that smart."

"Be careful with that complacent talk Niamh. The Romans are calculating, just remember how Quintus Agricolanus spoke to the crowd about the mill and roads. They plan everything and see that it is done," Miach snapped, his large gray eyes flashing.

"And you nearly revealed that you are a druid, Miach. You must be more careful when we talk to them in the future," Cathmore retorted.

"I missed this discussion. What about a mill?" Bebhinn asked.

"The Romans are dangling a mill being built in Gosbecks. *It will only mean more intrusion of Roman government and money lenders here." Miach said with emphasis.* "We ended their talk about all the things Romans can do for us here by telling them we'll meet to discuss their proposals. I think the whole idea of having them here in the first place is a problem but it sounds *like Rome has already deemed Gosbecks a fertile area and ripe for the taking,"* Miach said disgustedly.

"Can they?" anxiously Bebhinn asked.

"Romans can and will do what they want now, they defeated us and will take advantage of everything they can. They are the victors," Cathmore said worriedly and unconsciously rubbed his crippled arm.

"What about the Samhain ceremony later, should we still hold it?" Edana asked

"We must hold it. We'll do it much later and wait until the Romans have gone to their fort. The oak, elder and yew have eyes and ears, but not for the Romans, our gods do not want them involved." Miach said invoking the traditional saying about the forest, lending seriousness to his declaration. It meant the gods were present. "Have you brought Ailbe?"

"Ailbe is too young for this meeting Miach, he willingly went with Ealga and Drust back to Niamh's farm, *he told me he understood that tonight I had duties to perform,*" Bebhinn told him with meaning.

"Huh, that is interesting. It would have made for a great Samhain ceremony but if the gods directed him to leave then so be it," Miach shook his long gray hair and let the matter drop.

"Should we begin to gather in the forest? Many have already made their way there. Is the Roman fort far enough away?" Cathmore asked.

"They are far enough away; we've put them by the old fishing stream. The sound of the water rushing over the rocks will help to mask our noise and prove restive for them. However if they do hear something it might put the fear of the gods into them, better if it does. I am sure we will get guidance from the gods tonight," Miach said.

At these stark words the group grew quiet. Miach had never before admitted that the gods will be present so forcefully at the Samhain ceremony. They began to uneasily sidle away toward to the forest clearing where Samhain would continue and take place, each with their own thoughts. Bebhinn walked next to Edana and Meadghbh and asked quietly: "Are you alright? Nothing happened except meeting up with the Romans right?"

"I was able to talk with Quintus Agricolanus. Meadghbh was not so lucky, she had a randy soldier holding her who spent much of his time feeling her curves. Quintus was actually quite the gentleman in comparison," Edana replied.

"The one who held me, Faber, was more interested in what was between his legs. I was so frightened that I continued to believe they were fey and not men," Meadghbh said.

"How did you figure out that they were men and not fey?" Bebhinn asked Edana

"Quintus gave me the clues. He patiently answered my questions and only chided me that it took me long enough to figure out they were Romans. I did not have time to ask more because we arrived at Niamh's." Edana told her.

"Did you hear the discussion about a mill?"

"No, we were too far away standing at the bonfire to hear," answered Meadghbh. They trudged through the woods a little more in silence. Sounds from the crowd ahead began to filter back including the sounds of piping and drumming, snippets of song and laughter. The girls increased their stride. Bebhinn had to trot to keep up with them.

"There is another thing you need to know Mother; Quintus Agricolanus is the Roman who killed Father and Carrick. Cathmore confirmed that to me earlier tonight." Edana said sadly.

"Now I know tonight was preordained. Ailbe told me when you left that you meet someone that will have a big consequence on Gosbecks but I did not think we would be this privately involved," Bebhinn said. "My heart is sad at this news."

"As is my heart Mother." Each continued in silence with their own thoughts, Bebhinn about her husband and son, Edana with thoughts of Quintus and how good he felt when she was riding with him. She felt compelled to get back to him again to talk more.

The crowd continued to walk through the forest, the trees bending in the wind. They arrived at the clearing in the forest where the Samhain celebration would continue, the clearing large circled by ancient elms and oak. Another bonfire was lit and burning brightly in the center of the clearing, a crowd was gathering around it. The musicians were gathered off to the side and had arranged themselves to provide the best area for dancing. As Miach entered the clearing the crowd welcomed him with a great happy cry of: "The Green Man[106] has entered! Now the festivities can begin." His gray and brown cloak swirling around him, he moved forward with his hand on his staff with purpose. Music swelled up and singers started their song of Samhain. The beat and pipes started a shadowy swirling sound reminiscent of unknown dark

---

[106] https://en.wikipedia.org/wiki/Green_Man
http://www.spiritofthegreenman.co.uk/green-man-mythology.htm

things, the singers' voices low and ominous like a thunderstorm. The dancers started swaying and twirling, twisting into frightening shapes, their shadows leaping around them as it they were secondary dancers. The most important part of Samhain began in earnest.

Miach stepped into the center of the dancers, and held up his arms to the night. "Come to me spirits of the world, come tell us what is to happen, what is to be, come into me!" he yelled, intoning the prayer. The wind began to pick up, its' harsh bite only intensified the eager dancers to reach the culmination of the ceremony. All those around had joined in the dance, shedding extra clothes in the process. They danced around almost naked in the harsh light of the bonfire on Samhain night. Miach stripped off his robes and stood naked, proud and still, his bony body held taut in the wind, the only one of the group not moving. On his body were tattoos painted in woad, leaves and twining branches circled his arms and legs. Circular symbols were on his torso and back, coiling together and splitting into new fantastic designs leaving little of his skin unadorned.

The wind began to howl with an unearthly growl. The dancers continued in their gyrations around Miach and the musicians redouble their efforts at playing the unearthly music. The wind picked up its howling and moaning. Suddenly one by one random dancers went prostrate on the ground, not all but one out of every five of the crowd. They writhed on the ground, mouths open and growling sounds came out. Never before have so many been struck down like this during a Samhain ceremony, testament to the number of impatient spirits around the world that night. Miach held his arms outstretched, his staff held out in front of him as if addressing a vast crowd, his voice boomed out: "It has begun, the crossover of spirits into our world, those who wish to impart their final wishes to those remaining with us! Heed their words for times to come in the next seasons!"

Meadghbh was one of those stricken first, her face contorted as if in pain, growls coming forth from her mouth. Eimear dropped to the ground to hear any message from those who passed beyond this world, hoping it was her husband or sons coming through, her sister Brenna also stopped dancing to hear the message. Meadghbh's growls began to lessen then a man's voice emitted from her: "Eimear my mother, be at peace, Father and Caolin are here with me. We must warn you, the coming seasons will be full of sorrow and pain, what is yours will be taken away and what is most precious will be stripped. Take heed and be strong." The voice faded and was gone. Eimear and Brenna called out their worry and sorrow. No message of happiness on the other side just an ominous message of upcoming dread.

Over by Niamh, her daughter Aibhlinn fell to the ground and laid lifeless, her mouth open in a silent scream. Niamh, Drust and Cliona sank to the ground by her, their breaths harsh in the howling wind and dropping temperature. Aibhlinn began to moan and suddenly a man's voice came through: "Niamh I am here, your husband Galahaut, Adair is with me. I am very proud of your work on the farm; you will continue to prosper in the coming seasons. But your help will be needed on many fronts, from those close to you and those not known to you at this time. Be open to new ideas, it will work to your benefit. But be careful and not too open to new gods and their ways, they can be a downfall with unforeseen consequences. Keep the farm and you will prosper," with that last bit of information Galahaut stopped talking. Niamh felt better, she was afraid the message would be more dire but it was also confusing. Typical of Galahaut he omitted any soft feelings for her even though she knew he loved her and the family. If only he could have told me he loved me, she mused, it would have made the long hours of the lonely nights easier. Tears fell from her eyes.

Next to Bebhinn the dancing Edana fell to the ground and started writhing on the ground, her face in a rictus of horror, growls coming from her too. Presently the growls resolved into a man's voice: "Bebhinn my love it is I. Ardan, Carrick is here with me in the next realm. I have sorrow to impart on you, the next seasons will be hard, full of sorrow but also there will be joy. Tell Edana to be strong and keep her faith in the old ways, they will get her through the next several seasons. It will be hard but if you and Edana keep to the old ways you will flourish. I give you my leave to seek another partner in the future," and with that the voice faded away. *Too soon, the message was over too soon and not enough. I need more information!* Thought Bebhinn. *I do not understand what my husband Ardan said. I need his arms around me again!* She dissolved into tears as she helped Edana come to after the possession of her father. "I need more time with him," she gulped her sorrow back down.

Throughout Miach stood with his arms outstretched not moving despite the cold wind howling, his long gray hair swirling around him. His eyes took on a distant stare looking into the sky as if he was the conduit of all the spirits inhabiting the fallen dancers. All around the messages from departed ones were coming through to their loved ones. Most had dire predictions, some were less horrific but nonetheless sad. The populous of Gosbecks had a clear message from loved ones in the other realm that the upcoming seasons would be full of change, some good but most bad. Great care would need to be had on any upcoming decisions regarding dealings with the Romans.

As the spirit possessions ended the people began to look at Miach for guidance, all turning as if on cue to look at him. What would become of the people now, who will look after them? Miach looked back at them with the empty stare and said in a hollow voice not of this world: "A sacrifice must be made to propitiate the gods, a man of substance and will, a leader must be given," he intoned. The crowd uneasily looked around. Cathmore stepped forward and said: "I am willing to give my life for the people." Meara and Bebhinn stepped forward to say no but he waved them away. "I am a leader and have the substance and will to do this."

Iollan stepped forward and said: "I am a leader in the village and will willingly give my life for the people." The people looked at him sadly and shook their heads, he was young and fit and the only thing he led was the musicians. He did not fit the request made by the gods.

Four other men stepped forward with their exaltations of being leaders and the one needed for the willing sacrifice but Miach said nothing. Then Declan the smith moved to the front: "I am a leader and have the will to give my life for my people."

Etain his wife shook her head in negation, "NO, not you too, isn't our son enough to lose for the gods?" Sadhbh and Lavena stepped forward in horror to see their father volunteer on this difficult night of all nights.

Miach simply turned and pointed to Declan and said in the otherworldly voice: "The decision is made, he will be the sacrifice!" Miach pointed with his staff at Declan and looked at him with a fathomless stare.

Declan turned to Etain and held her, his one arm going around her: "Etain my love it is best this way. The Romans robbed me, smith of Gosbecks, of my right arm during a paltry skirmish. Now I have purpose again, probably a better purpose even than being the village smith. See my right arms it is chopped off at the elbow, it is worth nothing. I cannot make the shovels, plows, and swords anymore for a living. I cannot do what the people of Gosbecks need." He raised his stump and looked at it: "Can you see my right hand anymore, no of course not, but I do. I still feel it. I'll go to the other realm and see Addis again," he dropped his stump and looked at her sadly. He then kissed Etain passionately. "You are my given, my twin in this harsh land, I wish the best for you and my girls. Please let me do this for everyone in Gosbecks. It is the best that I can do for everyone."

He then turned to Sadhbh. "My little helper, so happy in everything and the perfect mummer for this momentous Samhain. Be at peace and watch after your mother and your little sister Lavena. They will need your strength in the coming seasons, they will look to you for help and guidance," he then kissed her. Lavena was standing next to him and grabbed his arm, "And my little Lavena, you are so beautiful and full of life, keep the old ways for your mother and sister. You will need to lean on them from now on." He kissed Lavena as well. Then he turned to Miach and said: "I am ready." Looking at Declan Etain could have sworn she saw his right hand mysteriously appear for a moment then fade into invisibility.

Hands grabbed Declan and wrenched him from Etain's tear stained grasp. They set a noose reserved for this type of sacrifice and tied it around his neck, tightening it beginning to choke him. Declan started to choke and gagged. One of the men behind Declan and rapped his head with a sharp blow sending Declan falling forward. Then another man took out a knife, pulled back his head and slit his throat. Declan was given the thrice killed death[107], the most honorific way for a willing man to give up his life for the people. The killing was brutal but swift. The only sounds left were the sobbing from Etain, Sadhbh and Lavena, and the bonfire. All the others had silently looked on. The willing sacrifice was needed in this most sad of Samhain ceremonies, seen only in times of great distress. As Declan finally expired his body was picked up and thrown into the bonfire, landing in the middle on top. The crowd silently watched as it slowly singed, then caught fire and began to burn, the hideous smell and crackling of the body as it slowly went up in flames.

The otherworldly wind continued to howl and blow, the spirits crying out in joy at the ceremony. The cold and tired Celts began to sluggishly start getting back in their clothes, world weary at the sad end of the Samhain ceremony. Normally it was a happy festival but this year the rebellion and loss to the Romans took any joy out of the season. The messages they received from their loved ones from beyond this world made the onlookers feel dejected, gloomy and downtrodden. There was some that sobbed for Declan but also for

---

[107] http://articles.latimes.com/1990-06-24/books/bk-715_1_druid-prince
https://en.wikipedia.org/wiki/Threefold_death
http://www.irishcentral.com/news/bog-bodies-are-kings-sacrificed-by-celts-says-expert-129289548-237410131.html

themselves. Others moved slowly like in a trance as they began to gather their clothing and get dressed to make their weary way back home. Bebhinn sidled up to Miach and asked: "What do we do for the coming seasons; everyone seems to have received bad tidings?"

"We turn to the old ways, this years' sacrifice should appease the gods for a while but it is only temporary. The Romans are coming and will change our way of life. They will come in promising a better way to live, to mill our grain, to sow and reap our fields but they have a hidden plan that only benefits Rome, not the Trinovantes, not the people of Gosbecks." He murmured, sounding tired and dejected but still looking formidable. He slowly got back into his clothing and cloak, the browns and grays of his cloak oddly appropriate for this sad ceremony.

"Is there anything we should guard against? Any deals we should shy away from?" she asked.

"As the issues come up we must deal with them on a day by day basis, starting with the benighted mill," Miach said sorrowfully, "It will be a black well hole of debt for those who agree. The Romans will use it to get a toehold in Gosbecks, the next thing will be the large land owners coming, they will take our farms under the guise of taxes being unpaid. I fear the people will lose their freedom; I have seen it in my dreams." He wiped his leaking eyes with the corner of his cloak smearing dirt across his cheeks.

"Is there no way around this, are we to lie down and let it happen without fighting?" Bebhinn was getting more anxious. As they talked more of the crowd was gathering around them, listening to their conversation. There were uneasy murmurs, sounds of despair coming from some of the women, the men grumbling and talking under their breath to each other.

"What can be done, Miach? Are we to fade away as a people? Or do we take up arms against the Romans?" Cathmore barked.

"No more fighting, we do not have the people for it; they all died with Boudicca's rebellion. We need to work together as Trinovantes, as the people of Gosbecks and the surrounding areas.

Do not take what the Romans give without looking at the proffered gifts from all angles and their consequences. They will come with money lenders to extoll buying on credit or on time. Steer clear of these schemes; they will only take your farms. And should you lose your freedom because you can no longer pay your taxes, go into slavery willingly, but keep your dignity, it will not be forever. The Romans want to gain the upper hand, come out on top, do not let them. Do your work willingly but keep your faith in the old ways. The gods have been appeased for now; maybe in the future we will need to offer up another willing sacrifice to ensure ongoing good weather, hunting, and business opportunities. Offer up sacrifices to Mananan Mac Lir[108], Cernunnous[109], Taranis [110], and Epona[111] even to dark Morrigan and angry Belatucadros[112]."

"Miach you are telling us to submit," Lorcan said disgustedly.

"No, I am telling you to live, leave the fighting for another day. We are just not strong enough now, and we need to heal from the past brutal seasons. We need to concentrate on life and rebuild our numbers," Miach retorted, his voice becoming great and loud with the emotion of his words.

"But we do not have enough men even to find a mate," Aibhlinn said, "All of the single men are gone to the next realm."

Miach nodded wearily: "Yes but more will come, from other tribes, from other villages and even from the Romans. We need to rebuild our numbers from all of these groups; the Trinovantes will endure as long as the women endure to teach the young our ways. This makes you even more vital for the future."

"Are you saying our women should lay with the Romans? They are the swine that put us into this mess!" Iollan yelled.

---

108 https://en.wikipedia.org/wiki/Manann%C3%A1n_mac_Lir

109 http://paganwiccan.about.com/od/godsandgoddesses/p/Cernunnos.htm

110 https://en.wikipedia.org/wiki/Taranis

111 https://en.wikipedia.org/wiki/Epona

112 https://en.wikipedia.org/wiki/Belatucadros

"Yes even the Romans can be used as sires for our young; they will mix well with the Trinovantes. Their blood is hardy enough to expand to our shores from way down south from whence they came. I do not know where their stock is from but it is hardy enough to come and vanquish us with little numbers. We must learn as much as possible from them, learn their war tactics since their smaller army was able to so easily take our greater numbers. We need to learn, I need to learn. Is there anyone here that understands their language?" Miach earnestly said.

A younger man, Aedan, stepped forward: "I speak their language after a fashion, they needed an interpreter after the rebellion and since I was injured but not gravely during the battle I was pressed into that service. I don't speak Latin well but can be understood. I can teach anyone their language."

Miach nodded happy to hear they had their own interpreter: "You will teach as many as possible how to speak their language, starting with me. I will need you to come with me after this night and start as soon as possible. We need to know them and their language is the place to start." Aedan nodded and eagerly said: "I will do it gladly."

The crowd seemed to relax a little more until another voice rose up from the back, one of the musicians, the piper Kearney, stepped forward: "I don't want the Romans welcomed in Gosbecks, why do we even entertain the idea? They should go back to Camulodunum and stay there."

"They are here now for a reason and we will not be able to get them to leave. They have already determined that Gosbecks is ripe for the taking. There are too many fertile farms in our area. The ones we need to take care for are the farmers that have let their taxes go for this season. They will be the ones under the Roman yoke whether by the money lenders or the Roman military. We will need to gather around these families and make sure they are not penalized. Some will be allowed to continue some will not and be enslaved," Miach said.

"If we are enslaved, we'll just run away from them. Get out from under their boot!" Kearney retorted hotly, his face becoming as red as his hair as he got madder the more the discussion went on.

Miach sighed and shook his head: "It will not be that easy; they might cart off the newly enslaved and ship them elsewhere. We might get lucky that they keep them here to work the farms but there is no guarantee they will. We do not need to run away from this loss of freedom, we can endure here. We must endure here in Gosbecks." Miach looked earnestly at Kearney hoping he understood what was being said, the importance of it.

Kearney angrily snorted: "It sounds like full capitulation to what they want!"

"Don't you understand? They are the victors here, we are the losers. If it were the hated Catuvellauni tribe they would just take our land and leave us to roam without a home. The Romans are doing the same!" Miach said angrily, his voice swelling with emotion.

"Then we should fight back!" Kearney yelled.

"*We have no army; our best went to Boudicca's rebellion and few returned.* If we did fight they would take all our lands and enslave everyone, leaving no one to benefit but the Romans. *We need to be smarter than that, to agree to live with them, to capitulate and bide our time,*" Miach said with heat. "Going to war would do nothing but bring grief to us all."

"I don't have to capitulate; I just need to stay under the Roman yoke? That is something I'm not able to do!" Kearney said furiously, stamping his feet for emphasis. Those standing by him moved away, shaking their heads thinking he acted like a small child.

"Then you should leave and take your dangerous ideas with you," Miach said wearily. "There is no place for you in Gosbecks."

Kearney looked at him with astonishment; he turned to the others in the crowd: "What about you Lorcan? Are you going to stay and take it, take being enslaved like good little Trinovantes? What about you Iollan? Are you going to lose your farm to greedy Roman tax men? Are all you sheep to Miach' shepherding," Kearney said in exasperation as he kept looking at the group of bystanders. "Anyone?!" Turning he looked at Cathmore: "Cathmore what about you, you've got a lot of fallow fields on your farm, you'd be ripe for enslavement!"

Cathmore shook his head: "I agree with what Miach is saying, we need to deal with the Romans but it will be their terms as victors, not as equals. . My daughters Aine and Flann will still be free if I willingly give up my farm. There is a chance that I might lose my freedom but I will still be Trinovantes." He stood looking hurt but resigned.

Kearney looked at him in astonishment: "You'd give up your farm to the Roman wolves?"

"I would keep it if I could but if that is not possible then yes I would," Cathmore said forcefully. "I would lose my farm before my freedom but if the gods have something else in my future then so be it."

Kearney spat on the ground, the ultimate sign of extreme disgust, the turned and walked away. Under his breath he muttered: "Spineless cowards, letting the Roman wolves eat up their farms with no fighting. They might as well offer them to take the farms and be done with it." The crowd turned and watched him go. "Do you think he'll leave?" Lorcan asked Iollan. "I hope not but if he continues in this way of thinking it might be best if he does," Iollan answered watching the retreating back of his friend, sadness in his voice.

The crowd started to disburse slowly, many going up to Etain, Sadhbh, and Lavena to share their condolences at the loss of their husband and Faber, many hugging the family and giving them assurances that they will be looked after. One of the last to talk to the family was Bebhinn and Edana. Edana held onto Sadhbh: "We will help when you need anything, you've only to ask. I don't know how to thank you for your Fabers' willing sacrifice."

Bebhinn looked at Etain: "When the winter gets cold I will be here to offer you warmth by our fire. Keep your head held high,

Declan's sacrifice was for the benefit of us all. I too have lost my husband and son. We will get through the coming seasons together somehow."

Etain had had enough of the platitudes: "We will endure because we have no choice. We have no lands except for the small one for our use alone, just a garden and small stand of wheat and barley. The girls and I cannot live on freely given goods from others that also need their crops to pay for taxes. Where is the honor in that"

Bebhinn nodded and said: "I am in arrears as well but I would gladly give part of our wheat and barley that we managed to reap. And of course my garden is always open to you for anything you need. Maybe we'll be able to pool our resources from among the willing and get your taxes paid. Freedom is the most precious thing we Trinovantes own, we will do what is needed to help you keep yours."

"Thank you but the same should be said of you, Edana and Ailbe. What would we do if the healer for Gosbecks is sold into slavery? Those with any extra to give will pool for you and not for us." Etain started to cry again in earnest. Presently Miach walked over to them and laid a hand on her shoulder.

"I have seen that you will not be sold into slavery, that there is one coming that will be able to get you and the smith going for Gosbecks again. I just do not see his face, nor have the gods let me know when or where he is coming from. Stay strong and know that help is coming. The gods will not let you suffer for his willing sacrifice." Etain nodded, turned to Sadhbh and Lavena and sadly murmured: "It is time to return to our home." She gathered the sobbing girls up and slowly left the clearing without a backward glance at the bonfire.

"Do you know if we are going to lose our freedom?" asked Bebhinn.

"The way will be difficult for you, I do not know if you'll be enslaved but I do know you will not leave Gosbecks. For now you, Edana and Ailbe are safe." Miach said. He moved slowly as if the night had taken a lot from his body and mind, and it probably did. Turning he told Bebhinn: "Gather up Edana and head back to Niamh's farm. You should spend the remainder of the night with them and then return to your home. Keep to your farm and only venture into Gosbecks if you have no choice. Keep Edana and Ailbe safe on the farm. I will stay to make sure the bonfire consumes Declan's body and no trace can be found per our custom. I will ritually process his head to make a blessed drinking vessel. Go now and take care of your loved ones."

Bebhinn and Edana left to catch up with Niamh and her group. They moved stiffly but with purpose knowing they would not be leaving Gosbecks and that Etain, Sadhbh and Lavena will be looked after. Soon they caught up with Niamh, Drust, and Aibhlinn, and fell into line with them. All moved slowly and stiffly in the wailing wind which did not let up, the trees bending as if in sorrow.

"Come to our farm and spend the remainder of this night with us. This storm does not look like it will stop howling like a chastised child for a while. Catch your breath with us at the farm. Eat a good meal in the morning and then go back to your farm." Niamh offered kindly.

"That is exactly what Miach said to do so thank you. I do not think I've got the energy to leave for our farm after we get to your home. There were too many sad things Ardan told me tonight. Looks like Edana, Ailbe and I will have some difficult seasons ahead of us," Bebhinn replied.

"Good then it's settled, we will get home and you'll remain with us on this sad Samhain night." Niamh patted her arm. They all trudged wearily back to her farm.

The night continued to whine around them, the wind still blowing a blustery gale, the spirits continued to be unsettled as they cried out with unearthly moaning as if in a rage and pain. Finally they reached the farm and lumbered into the farmhouse. Drust went off to check on the horse that he had rode on with the Romans. Inside they found Ealga, Cliona, Nola and Ailbe still awake. Surprised Bebhinn said: "Why aren't you asleep ? It is late and you are tired."

Ealga said: "He has been visited by Ardan tonight. He let us know what was going on at the Samhain ceremony. Is it true that Declan was a willing sacrifice?"

"Yes, Declan was chosen by the spirits to be a thrice killed willing sacrifice for the sake of everyone in Gosbecks. His was a superior sacrifice," Niamh answered.

"What did Ardan say? Did he talk about the upcoming seasons?" questioned Bebhinn.

"Yes that it will be tough for Edana and you but that you will survive." Ealga said. Bebhinn nodded. "Now time for all of us to get to bed, we are tired from this long stressful Samhain."

"It is a long Samhain but also a good one Mother. Father said to me that Edana, you and I will all be looked after by a kind man. The future looks dark at first but if we keep to the old ways it will be good," Ailbe said and yawned, "I want to go to bed now."

"Then we are off to sleep what is left of this night," Edana said and grabbed him to lay him on the soft pallet already prepared for them. "Thank you Niamh for the pallet and the roof over our heads, it sounds like the storm will rage all night."

"Off to bed the lot of you, I am swaying on my feet from fatigue. Tomorrow will be here faster than you think." Niamh said and she gathered her daughters up to go to bed in their sleeping alcoves. Presently Drust came in and he went to bed as well. Ealga was the last to go as she banked the fire and snuffed out the candles. "It was eerie having Ailbe speak as Ardan but I'm glad he did, we were very worried about everyone," and then she too went to the sleeping nooks.

Alone Bebhinn thought of the last bit of Ardan's' message. They will have dark days coming but they will be able to stay in Gosbecks. She found comfort in that and took her candle. "I can get through the next seasons knowing we will come out fine. But I miss my husband and Carrick. How are we going to make up the amount of taxes we are in arrears for?" She thought: "We might be able to eke out subsistence for the winter but what of all of Gosbecks. If they come to me for medicinal plants I didn't get the opportunity to plant more, I am short on feverfew already."

"Come to bed mother, you need to rest too after this long night," whispered Ailbe. She looked down to see Ailbe standing by her side. He reached up and grabbed her hand, "Even you must know that the gods will see us through the coming dark seasons. You must keep to our faith and trust in the old ways." Together they went to their pallet where Edana lay already sleeping. They arranged the pelts and snuggled together. "I love you mother."

"I love you too, my little Beltane boy," she drowsily said, hugging him. But for Bebhinn the night was far from over, she continued to replay the events of this Samhain over and over, the willing sacrifice of Declan, the message from Ardan beyond in the next realm, and the discussions of how to deal with the Romans by Miach and Kearney, even the affirmation of Cathmore in support of Miach's' teaching on how to deal with the upcoming changes from the Romans. I hope the next seasons aren't as bad as Ardan said they'd be, we need to keep together here in Gosbecks, everyone together. Finally after hours of ruminations she drifted off to sleep just as she started to peak over the ridge in front of Niamh's farm.

CHAPTER 8
THE WAITING GAME

After a restless night, a night full of blustery wind and uneasy dreams Quintus woke with a renewed purpose in Gosbecks. *I need to get the men up and ask if they heard anything during the long night of howling winds. At least it didn't rain again. I don't think I'd be able to deal with the recalcitrant Trinovantes if it was raining, since that is all it does in this gods forsaken place. Where is the sun and how can it be so green here without the sun?* He got up, put on his uniform and rejoined his men who were already stirring.

"Up already Fullo? How was your turn at watch last night?" greeted Quintus.

"Grex and I had fourth watch[113] and it was cold waking up that early! The wind was whipping around like a cold bitch whipping her bratty young ones. I do not think I've heard a wind that loud before. If anyone was mad enough to be about I didn't see it," Fullo replied, stamping his feet to get the feeling to return to them. "I

---

[113] http://penelope.uchicago.edu/Thayer/E/Roman/Texts/Caesar/Gallic_War/Appendices/A*.html

paced the fort at the regular intervals and saw no movement. You might want to ask Bundarus though. He reported hearing music and shouting during the first part of his watch. I heard nothing on the fourth watch. Whatever was going on had ended by the time I got up to take up guard duty. Ask Bundarus."

"Will do and keep moving, it'll help the cold feet," replied Quintus who turned and walked over to Bundarus. Bundarus and Titus both had the third watch. He found the two talking low over their millet breakfast. "Fullo tells me you heard things at the beginning of third watch."

Bundarus nodded: "There was music the likes I've never heard before and shouting coming from the south west about a mille passuum or two away. It was hard to get a bearing on the sounds because the wind was moaning so much."

"Growling is a better description of the sounds coming from the south west. Or it might have just been the wind, it was frightening how loud it was last night," Titus said. "Would you like to have some millet with us?"

"No thanks on the millet. You say it was music? So the Samhain ceremony we saw was not the only Samhain ceremony. We saw what they wanted us to see, sort of their version of Caesars' type of military propaganda? I am not surprised. There must be something they're hiding. The dancing yesterday was pretty spectacular but not bloody like I was expecting. What kind of shouts did you hear? Could it be they were fighting?"

"Hard to say, it was more as if there were a lot of people yelling, no sounds of clashing swords," Bundarus said.

"The wind made the sounds come in and out of hearing as if it were hiding something," Titus mused.

"Yah, that and the woods could have blocked the sound. Plus we have the rivers' noise also covering up the sound. It is almost like the people of Gosbecks led us to this forting spot on purpose, to hide the sounds of any disreputable actions taking place," Bundarus agreed.

"I thought of that myself, I wasn't able to get much rest last night for all the howling wind, maybe I might have heard something too, but it's difficult to make out something with the amount of wind that Boreas[114] sent us last night. Even my Boreas was uneasy and had a hard time calming down for his nights rest. I had to take him for a quick canter to get the demons off his hide," Quintus shook his head. "Since I had first watch with Rufus, I'll go check in with Faber and Coriaro, see how second watch was." Both Bundarus and Titus grunted affirmative and went back to their eating.

Quintus moved over to Faber and Coriaro who were setting up their getting their breakfast as well. "Anything to report for second watch?"

Faber grunted and tossed his head: "It was quiet until the end of second watch then we started to hear music and snippets of yells. The wind was blowing forcefully and we could only hear the noise intermittently. It sounded like the Samhain ceremony was continuing on without us."

"I heard yells but also growling. However it could have been the wind Boreas sent us which was coming from the southwest. I was unable to see anything when we went to look," Coriaro added.

Quintus nodded: "That's what Bundarus and Titus said. They also heard music and shouting. It seemed to have ended about midway through third watch. How far do you estimate it was?"

"Maybe *mille passuum*[115] walk away, but more than a *stade*[116]." Coriaro guessed. Faber grunted agreement.

"But not as far as *Gallic leuga*[117]?" Quintus said.

"No it was definitely closer than a *Gallic leuga* but far enough away that we could not hear the words said. Plus the wind would howl and block out a lot of the noise," Faber said.

---

[114] https://www.britannica.com/topic/Boreas
[115] http://latindictionary.wikidot.com/noun:mille-passus
[116] https://www.britannica.com/science/stade-measurement
[117] http://www.jstor.org/stable/1787545?seq=1#page_scan_tab_contents

"That is what Bundarus said as well. He thought the people of Gosbecks put us here with that in mind, that we wouldn't be able to hear anything. Pretty astute thing to do to hide what really happens on Samhain," Quintus allowed. He scratched his head and crouched down next to the two. "What do you think?"

"Yes, it could be we were put this far from Gosbecks to keep any additional celebrating away from us," agreed Faber. Coriaro nodded.

"Hand me some millet and we'll get going to see what the noise was. I want to see the remains and maybe ask someone about this *"second Samhain ceremony"*, Quintus sat down on the ground by Coriaro. Faber ladled up more millet and handed it to Quintus. They ate quickly and then stood up to get the others ready to leave.

When they were saddling their horses Fullo asked Quintus: "What will we do if we find evidence of a second Samhain ceremony?"

"We'll get answers from whomever we can. I think this was a deliberate act of subterfuge. There is something they did not want us to witness and they took great pains to make sure we were not invited," Quintus answered, tightening his girth on the horse. He swung up in the saddle and said: "If we find the evidence then we will need to let the legatus Marcus Flaccus Antoninus know when we come back in the spring. It will change how we deal with the people of Gosbecks."

"How will it change?" Fullo got his restive mount under him and followed Quintus. The other soldiers fell into line with Quintus as they headed southwest to check out the disturbance.

"It will make the dealings with the people more difficult. There will probably be more cases of enslavement, not just for taxes being in arrears but for the machinations of druids." Quintus said.

Fullo was quiet for a moment and then said: "I thought all the druids were destroyed on that god's forsaken island of Mona."

"Apparently not all of them, they might have pockets of druids hiding out in the villages that serves to incite further atrocities levied on the populace. They can get the people to do terrible things." Returned Quintus.

"How do you know they'll do it here?" Fullo asked

"If you remember the discussion at the bonfire last night? There were several people who voiced dissent about the mill. They were probably goaded on by the druids," Quintus said.

"You mean that old fellow with the beard, the one who was so against the mill and money lenders? Yah, he was an unhappy fellow, very against the Romans. We probably need to keep an eye on him."

Quintus nodded. "He is someone we definitely need to keep under surveillance but there were more than just him. What about the one armed smith Declan? Or the other impaired man Cathmore? They seemed to be hiding something."

They continued forward out of Gosbecks taking a southwesterly trail out. The forest was lush and old, the elms and oaks lining up closely with hawthorn, oak, and yew. The tree tops swaying in the wind like they were dancing. The lane they were on was wide and well-trodden showing that it was recently used. They stopped talking for a few leagues until Bundarus came up the line to ask Quintus: "Do you want us to fan out in a search formation? So we can cover more possible locations for this Samhain ceremony."

"I think we should send out both you and Grex to follow the tracks until we get closer to the *mille passuum* you estimated the celebration took place then we can fan out in a search formation. I am guessing the amount of people that attended will make it fairly easy to find this location. Follow the signs, and report back to me," Quintus ordered.

"Will do Quintus," Bundarus turned his horse and headed to Grex. After a short discourse Grex and Bundarus spurred their mounts to the front and took off.

"That one is sure a stickler for the Roman military way of doing things," Fullo commented, "He is always telling everyone to follow procedure. Do you think he'll be able to transition to civilian life?"

"He is a good soldier but I wonder about his becoming a farmer, despite his name," smirked Quintus.

"Oh that's low, you know he comes from a small land holding around Umbria[118] don't you?" Titus said.

"Yah but it was a rocky mountain outcrop for tilling not like the rich lands like around here," laughed Fullo. "He'll be great with the plow though, he'll just visualize a testudo formation." This generated a lot of laughter up and down the line of horses.

"Or the saw formation, he can visualize it is Celts pushing on his shield instead of just a plow," joined in Rufus. More laughter ensued.

"He'll need something to get the attention of the ladies, he's got that bald pate to compensate for," Coriaro added, more laughs.

"Let's hope your tanners stink doesn't scare away the women too, Coriaro," guffawed Fullo.

"Or your piss stink from your fuller's background Fullo," rejoined Coriaro hotly, his temper flaring at the old jab about his tanner background. The tanning section of the subura[119] of Rome where he came from being infamous for its bad smell. His ego was hurt.

"Now men, that's enough of the insult trading," Quintus stepped in to the fray before tempers escalated. One thing he knew never to step on and that was Coriaro's' background, too many late night drinking bouts had ended with battered bodies that way. Fullo should have known better being the brunt of several of those bouts because of his quick needling wit. They continued to ride in silence for a while before Grex and Bundarus returned.

Thinking of the fights between Fullo and Coriaro had had him remembering a conversation he had with his grandfather. His grandfather would tell him tales of his Contubernium in Gaul under Caesar. He told Quintus about the funny situations and fights between his crew. "Tell me

---

[118] https://en.wikipedia.org/wiki/Umbria

[119] http://www.romeacrosseurope.com/?p=2514#sthash.LYhAVjYu.dpbs

a funny story about your Contubernium, maybe something about Balbus and Pullion," he remembered asking his grandfather.

"Now there were a lot of comings and goings between the two of them," his grandfather said, "They had a running fight between them regarding a Gaulic beauty, Radha who worked at the tavern. I think that was her name or something along those lines so I'll just call her Radha," his grandfather started warming up to the story, "Now Balbus was conniving to have Radha serve only wine to him but leave Pullion out in the dark."

Pullion waylaid Radha and asked why she wasn't serving him. 'I'm only following Balbus' orders, he paid me to keep the wine away from you,' she said.

'Well I'll pay you not to serve Balbus but only me!' Pullion puffed himself up at his quick thinking.

When Balbus saw that Radha and Pullion were talking he got upset and stomped over to the two, 'Why are you talking with this loser?' he asked.

'Pullion will pay me to serve him but not you, and you will pay me to serve you but not him, I am not able to do either so I'll just serve the other tables and you two can go find yourself another barmaid.' With that Radha went off in a huff and left both men speechless.

They looked at each other and Balbus said: 'It's your fault, you should have left Radha alone and found another server!'

At that Pullion said: 'My fault! You are the bastard that started this whole fight getting her to serve only you. What do you think I should do? Just let it ride? You'd get shitfaced and go off and have Radha, but you'd be too drunk and treat her horribly. I on the other hand would treat her with the respect she deserves!' And with that exchange they devolved into a fist fight, Balbus being the bigger soldier got the first punch in and swung at Pullion's face. Pullion being smaller but faster ducked so the punch only landed on his shoulder, he turned and kicked Balbus in the nuts. That ended the fight before it started. Pullion stood over Balbus who was writhing on the ground cursing up a blue storm. That wasn't the end of their fighting, those two were such good buddies that they made up after a week of ignoring and fighting each other until the rest of the Contuberium complained to me about it. I had to listen to them explain the reason. Just goes to show you that men in a Contubernium are a lot like brothers, fighting for the most asinine reasons."

Grex and Bundarus came back after several moments and interrupted Quintus' thoughts. "We've found the location of their ceremony; it is about two *stadium* ahead on the left. There is a better trail at the fork ahead, just take the left fork and follow the tracks from there. The clearing we found looks to be deserted but the bonfire is still smoldering. They burned a large animal on the fire, perhaps a deer or elk, part of whatever ceremony they held," Grex reported. Quintus nodded and began to increase the pace.

Soon they reached the clearing and fanned out to look at the signs of the previous night's Samhain ceremony. In one spot was the butchering area for the sacrificial deer as there was a lot of blood in the dirt from sprays of blood spurting out. "Not very good butchers to leave this much blood on the ground," observed Grex.

Fullo walked over to the bonfire and pushed at the bones with his gladius, "I don't think it was a deer Quintus, look," he pointed out a long thigh bone in the bonfire.

Quintus hurried over to the bonfire and peered at the skeleton laying on top. After the fire there wasn't much left, however the skull was missing, the other bones were twisted in a rictus, the ribcage and spine clear for all to see and identify. The smaller bones of the feet and hands were missing, probably somewhere in the smoldering bonfire.

"Human sacrifice, no wonder they didn't want us to see," breathed Quintus out of his mouth, "They took the skull but left the rest, why I wonder?"

"I heard the Celts drink from the skull like a great bowl," Titus said.

"I also heard in Gaul that burning human sacrifices were done frequently after a battle, they'd tie the victims up into a woven wicker basket and burn more than one together at a time, sometimes up to six at a time," murmured Bundarus who came over to look at the body.[120]

"I heard it was a giant wicker effigy of a man that they'd burn several of them in, sort of like a colossus," Titus said

"I read that too but from Caesar as part of his military propaganda. He had the historian Posidonius[121] come up with that colossus rubbish. But maybe there is more to the propaganda and it was done here last night here for this poor man," Quintus countered.

"How do you know it was a man and not a woman?" asked Rufus.

"Look at the size, even without the skull this was a big guy," said Grex.

Everyone looked at each other; the horror of what they found came to rest. They were going to live in Gosbecks with this underbelly of druidic miasma crawling around through it. "You'll definitely need to tell the legatus about this Quintus," Fullo said.

"Yes, we will need to get to the bottom of this," Quintus murmured. They got on their horses and returned to Gosbecks.

꒰꒰꒰꒰

Once in Gosbecks Quintus made it through to the tavern, there were few that were up this early, most of the people of the village seemed to have decided to sleep late after the night's ceremonies. Inside the tavern owner asked: "Did you have a restful night."

"Not so much with the wind and the noise we heard coming from southwest of Gosbecks. Was there another Samhain ceremony last night, one that we missed?" Quintus replied.

---

[120] https://www.digitalmedievalist.com/opinionated-celtic-faqs/human-sacrifice/ http://news.nationalgeographic.com/news/2009/03/090320-druids-sacrifice-cannibalism.html http://www.irishcentral.com/roots/history/Did-the-ancient-Celts-practice-human-sacrifice.html
[121] http://www-groups.dcs.st-and.ac.uk/~history/Biographies/Posidonius.html

"There are always ceremonies on Samhain, the main one was here, in front of my establishment," the innkeeper said.

"Did you attend the other one too?" Quintus asked.

"Why yes I did, I brought my family out to the Green Man's Clearing for the ceremonies."

"Green Man's Clearing, is that the name of it? What does that mean?" Quintus leaned toward the innkeeper as the others crowded around.

"Why that is the name of the gathering place where Samhain ceremonies are held," the innkeeper uneasily looked at Quintus and the other soldiers noticing how they were circling him.

Fullo came around his other side: "Is it a druid's place of worship?"

The innkeeper whose name was Oisin said: "It is a place of worship but also for gathering together for ceremonies like Samhain."

His wife Grania came out of the back seeing Oisin being interrogated by the Romans she stepped forward. "Do you need any refreshments?" she asked helpfully.

Quintus turned to her: "Yes we all want some of your fine wine to start off this day." Grania nodded and disappeared to the back for the wine and cups. She reappeared and handed out the cups with ale to all the soldiers. When they were all served she left the tavern out the front.

"Now where do you think she's going?" asked Fullo looking at Oisin.

"She probably is looking to get food for this day like she normally does." Oisin said smoothly.

"Uh huh, and not to bring in reinforcements?" Fullo asked.

"No certainly not, she merely wants to feed you first meal as well as the wine. She is very good at being a tavern keeper's wife." Oisin smiled.

"Tell us what transpired last night at the Green Man's Clearing," Quintus said, "I'd like to know what sort of ceremony it was."

"Just a regular ceremony, something we do every Samhain

with music and more dancing that you saw earlier." Oisin said and encouraged everyone to drink up.

"Just a regular ceremony that you have *every* Samhain? Nothing different?" Quintus needled.

"No, it was very regular," Oisin said.

"No sacrifices?" Quintus ground out.

"Oh we might have sacrificed a deer, just a regular offering." Oisin beginning to squirm under the questioning, he brushed the oily hair out of his eyes. He wiped the sweat off of his brow in response to their questions.

Quintus looked up at the ceiling and then back at Oisin: "That's funny because we saw a burnt *human* body on the bonfire and not a deer."

Oisin blanched and said nothing; he looked at everyone in the tavern and rolled his eyes toward the door, looking for a possible escape. Fortunately for Oisin, Grania appeared at that time with Lorcan in tow. Both had packages just as Oisin said she would.

"You made it back Grania, well and good for you. And Lorcan, good to see you this morning!" Oisin gushed out, opening his arms for the packages and ushering them in. "How are you Lorcan? I missed you this morning, you left early to go to your appointment with the other musicians."

"Um, yes the meeting was good. We've decided to put on a performance for the Romans, playing some of our music here at the tavern. And I see they are already here so may I invite you all this evening for more festivities?" Lorcan got out, looking uncomfortable.

"Yes, I think we would be most interested to hear your music. The music you played at the Samhain celebration here was very fine, worthy of being performed even in Rome itself." Quintus said with a smile that didn't quite reach his eyes.

"Yes, Rome would be very interested in the lovely melodies and drumming you performed last night." Fullo also offered, turning to Lorcan. "You have the look of the tavern keeper, are you related?"

"Oisin is my father, Grania is my mother" Lorcan gulped as if to admit the relationship was getting him in trouble but he did not know for what, his handsome face creased in a smile.

"Ah, mother and father, that makes sense, you have the look of both your sire and dam. Good that you have a ready-made place, this tavern, to perform in." Fullo continued.

"Uh … yes it is convenient that we can perform here at a place where people usually meet. It was one of the reasons I became a piper." Lorcan stammered.

"A piper is it, you played beautifully last night and will we hear the same music again?" Fullo asked.

"We will play something different; the music that we played last night was for Samhain alone. You'll get to hear some of the regular music we play for market day and other comings together." Lorcan said warming up to the subject he talked with excitement at performing for new customers, some with deep pockets if he had anything to do about it.

"Good we look forward to listening to your music then and anything else you decide to do or play." Quintus said cryptically

Lorcan smiled and moved back with his mother. Grania stepped forward: "Can I make you first meal?"

"No, I think we are done, what do we owe you?" Quintus asked.

"Three *unciae*[122] or one *quadrans*[123] if you have it," she said and held out her hand.

"Three *unciae*? That is a lot for just eight wines but I'll pay with no haggling. Thank you for the ale and we will be back for the music later." Quintus paid her and they all left the tavern.

Once outside they reverted to Latin, "Why did you stop pressing Oisin for the information about the human sacrifice? He was obviously hiding something," Fullo asked.

"Yes he was hiding something. Did you see how much he

---

[122] http://www.dictionary.com/browse/unciae
[123] http://www.dictionary.com/browse/quadrans?s=t

squirmed when I asked? We'll be back this evening and can continue the line of questioning. I want to get out and see more of Gosbecks and see if I can find the two ladies that escaped from us. I have a notion to question them further. We should get the answers we're looking for," Quintus replied.

"I want to find the one that rode with me as well," Faber said from his place just behind Quintus.

"Of course you do, you want to feel more of her I imagine," laughed Fullo.

"What? You let your hands feel her curves on you ride last night? No wonder she escaped from us, you scared her silly," Quintus turned and looked at him. "Although I felt the one in front of me and would like to hold her again, she felt womanly under that stupid outfit."

They continued on through the village, passing the bonfire still smoldering in the main clearing, the vast space showed the stomped ground showing the revelries of the night before. Next to it was where the food vendors set up their wares with an esplanade running down the center for market day giving an emerald expanse of grass. It seemed the rest of Gosbecks was getting a late start on the day, only a few food stalls were open, the venders moving slowly and tiredly which told of their late night revels. Wandering down the lane which opened out to show an large expanse of the main green. They saw the smithy on the right, but it appeared to be closed and little used, the fire which should have been banked was out cold. The *Contuburnium* continued on down the lane toward the largest stream and pond which would technically be the best spot for a mill. They surveyed the land and desultorily discussed the benefits of building a mill on this location and the benefits one would give Gosbecks. Looking around and getting disgusted at the lack of people out they decided to purchase some foodstuffs for midday meal and return to fort. They returned to the main esplanade where the food stalls were set up.

More people were out now as if the people of Gosbecks decided it was finally time to start their day. Quintus and Titus went over to the first stall, the butchers, and started to pick out the meat for their midday meal. Bundarus and Rufus went to another stall where breads were displayed for purchase and started haggling for a good price for four loaves of bread. Fullo and Faber started looking for olives and greens but settled on older apples instead. Quintus looked over the meat and asked: "So did you attend the Samhain ceremony at the Green Man Clearing?"

The food stall butcher shook his head, "I did not. I had too much work to do so I missed the ceremony."

"Did you hear what occurred there, that there was a sacrifice?"

"I'm sure there was a sacrifice, it was Samhain after all. We normally have a sacrifice to celebrate the end of harvest and beginning of the cold season," the butcher said. "Is there anything else you need, maybe something for the evening meal as well?"

"No this should be the lot for both midday meal and evening meal if we cook it the right away," Titus answered for Quintus.

Out on the esplanade the soldiers met up and found that all had the same answer, that the food stall purveyors did not attend the ceremony. "Looks a little suspicious that no one attended," Fullo grumbled in Latin.

"Even the extra customers at the bread stall claimed they did not attend that Samhain ceremony, just the main one held here," Bundarus said. "Very suspicious, it is as if someone tipped everyone off about what we were going to ask. There was enough noise last night that would require everyone here to attend the ceremony and witnessed the sacrifice."

"Do you think the tavern keepers' wife tipped them all off when she went to purchase the goods for the first meal?" Coriaro asked.

"It's beginning to look like there is something everyone is hiding from us. Maybe if we get to the celebration at the tavern early enough we'll be able to catch someone unaware," Quintus said. He thought for a moment and said: "Wait here I want to ask about the two girls who escaped from us, ask where we can get into contact with them." He went back to the butchers' stall and asked: "Do you know where Edana or Meadghbh are? I would like to congratulate them on their mummer duties they performed last night."

"Edana lives over a *mille passus* away to the west and usually doesn't come in until she has a need or her mother is healing someone. Her mother Bebhinn is the village healer, and very good I might add. Meadghbh lives closer to the village. You might see her soon, it is about time she comes in to buy her daily foodstuffs. Wait around and find out. If you don't want to wait then you might want to ask Eilis, one of the other mummers. She is right over there buying greens, with the raven hair," he pointed the diminutive lady out and then turned to a new customer. Quintus thanked him and went over to the little raven haired woman.

"I wanted to congratulate you on your mummer duties you performed last night," he said as an introduction. "I wanted to ask you about the other mummers, specifically Edana and Meadghbh. Could you introduce me to them to me?"

Eilis looked flustered that he, a man and a Roman, had come up to her and asked her about her friends. Edana and Meadghbh hadn't had time to talk to her so she didn't know that they had met *and* escaped from the Romans. "I haven't seen either one of them since last night. I do not know if they are coming into the village today."

"I understand that Edana lives far away and doesn't get into the village every day, but could you tell me where her farm is? I wanted to congratulate her for her mumming and the lovely dance she performed last night.

"Um, she lives far west of here, about a half days walk from here." She pointed to a dirt track leading out of Gosbecks. "Follow that path that leads to the west and you'll find her farm," Eilis gulped. "You might want to give her time to recuperate from last night. It was a long evening for all of the mummers since we all went to all the farms and homes in Gosbecks to fulfill the propitiation rite for Samhain. It usually takes everyone who performs this rite awhile to rest up afterward."

"Thank you Elis, we will wait here to see if we can meet up with Meadghbh to congratulate her as well," Quintus smiled and walked away from her. He rejoined the men and told them to watch out for Meadghbh, that she should be coming out to do her daily shopping. He kept the information about Edana to himself, thinking that he'll go out there tomorrow on his own. They waited around for a while trying to look like they were interested in all the food stuff tables, and clandestinely asking more questions about last night's Samhain ceremony but to no avail. After waiting and not seeing Meadghbh they decided to go on back to fort and have their midday meal. "Looks like you've scared off the curvy wench that felt so good," Fullo joked with Faber.

"Maybe she is just tired after running away from us," Faber rejoined.

"Maybe, but she didn't show when she normally did her regular shopping," Fullo smirked. They all mounted up and turned to leave the main esplanade.

▭▭▭▭

Down the esplanade Meadghbh came out from behind her mother Eimear, breathing a sigh of relief. When they arrived to do their daily shopping they were told the Romans were in the village asking questions about last night's Samhain held at Green Man's Clearing. Grania had put out the word after she heard the grilling they gave Oisin earlier. After the sad ceremony last night with one of her best friend's father being sacrificed. Meadghbh felt she couldn't bear to go on her own to pick up the days food she talked her mother into going with her to the foodstuff stalls today. Her mother was just as leery about the Romans, especially after hearing what Miach had to say last night. They both watched as the Romans mounted their horses and took off for their fort and breathed a sigh of relief. They both walked over to the butcher's food stall and began to peruse the meat. The butcher Dahy turned and beamed at them, "Ladies I need to let you know that the Romans were looking for you, to congratulate you on the mummer rites done so well last night, so they said,"

"Why would they be congratulating you on your duties?" Eimear said turning to Meadghbh.

"I told you why they might be looking for me Mother, it had nothing to do with the mummers duties. It has everything to do with the big one Faber's interest in me as a woman," Meadghbh replied disgustedly.

"Is that right? It was their leader who asked about you by name," Dahy said.

"Then he wanted to grab me for escaping him last night! I cannot stay here while they are here in Gosbecks. I should go and stay with Edana at her farm to keep away from them," a thoroughly scared Meadghbh said.

"Then you should go and stay with Bebhinn and Edana, stay as long as you need to," replied Eimear who was also as worried as Meadghbh, she was. She remembered the words Miach said about laying down with the Romans but wasn't quite up to the very real possibility of it happening so soon.

"I'll help you finish our daily chores here then I must get going to Edana's farm, thank you for understanding Mother," Meadghbh breathed a sigh of relief. They swiftly finished their foodstuff purchasing chores and left the main esplanade heading back to their farm. They walked as quickly as possible past the end of Gosbecks to the east where their farm was located. The scenery which usually soothed Meadghbh only grated on her nerves as the hawthorn lined lane seemed to continue forever. Finally they made it back to her smart, round, thatched farmhouse, the paddock standing next to their chicken coop surrounded by stately oaks. Inside Meadghbh quickly packed up belongings for her stay and took off, giving her mother a quick kiss. "Take great care Mother, stay out of the Romans way and keep to our farm. Brenna can come and check on you as soon as possible."

"Yes, she will but she has her new family to take care of too. Since she married the widower Ferdia she has his three small boys to take care of. They are quite the little misbehaved hoydens from what she says," Eimear replied.

Meadghbh nodded, "It's not surprising because their mother died two years ago when the youngest Aengus was just born. The other two were left to their own devises as Ferdia tried to make sure the infant was fed. Bebhinn spent a lot of time trying to get him out of infancy. Poor Ferdia was a wreck and needed Brenna as soon as possible. Aengus is just now walking thanks to Brenna."

They said their goodbyes and Meadghbh left the farm as soon as she could. The roads were quiet as most of the inhabitants of Gosbecks were busy at their farms trying to finish getting in the last of their grain and planted foodstuffs. She made it to Edana's farm just after midday meal time. She came up to the front and saw Ailbe out front, just finishing his chores of feeding the chickens. "Meadghbh! I am so glad you're here, Edana will be pleased to see you!" he joyfully sang out in his lovely childish voice.

"Good to see you too this very blustery morning," Meadghbh said. "Where are Edana and Bebhinn right now?"

"Edana's letting the goats out to pasture and Mother is inside still putting away midday meal dishes."

"Good. I'll see Bebhinn first and then go out to check on Edana, to make sure she is doing her chores correctly too," Meadghbh smiled, and went into the farm house.

"Good day Bebhinn, I need to ask a favor of you. Today as mother and I were doing the daily shopping we got word that the Romans were looking for Edana and me. I need to stay here as long as possible, hopefully until they leave and return to their Roman fort and leave Gosbecks all together," Meadghbh got out quickly.

Bebhinn looked up in alarm, "The Romans are looking for both you and Edana? This must be because you escaped from them at Niamh's farm. Of course you must stay here with us; we would love to have you here as long as you need to stay. Do you know how long they'll be staying in Gosbecks? I imagine it will be until the village decides what to do about the mill. You are welcome to stay that long. It could be many days but from what Miach said it will probably be an answer they do not want to hear."

"Thank you Bebhinn, I could not stand to stay in Gosbecks a moment longer with that hulking Roman who touched me. I know Miach wants to have the unattached women lay down with the Romans but I cannot be one of them. I am too afraid," Meadghbh said miserably.

"And you shall not, stay here with us and do not worry, we'll take care of you. Speaking of taking care, please eat some of our midday soup, there is plenty left and you will feel better after you eat something," Bebhinn said. "Edana will be back shortly and then we can all go to the garden and finish up with the preparations for the winter, I think I have to pick some late season peas turnips for soups and harvest chestnuts."

"All right, I'd love to have some soup since I practically ran from Gosbecks without eating the midday meal."

Bebhinn quickly got the soup for Meadghbh and sat down next to her as she ate. "I'm glad Edana has you for a friend, not many would have thought to come all the way out here to let us know the danger in Gosbecks from the Romans. You could have easily gone to your sister Brenna's farm to escape. They live far on the east side of Gosbecks."

"Yes but she would have put me to work with those young boys she has to take care of. I also wanted to talk to you and Edana about last night's Samhain. We received a message from Addis about the upcoming seasons. It was most depressing and scary. He talked about something that we have will be taken away or "stripped" from us," Meadghbh said earnestly. "With that message from the other realm and the Romans here in this one I wanted to come to a place of safety."

"We also received a distressing message from Ardan. I'm sure we will all be together in the next seasons to withstand the challenges we have facing us. We need to stay true to the old ways even more now than ever before." They continued to discuss the possible meanings of their messages from their loved ones.

Presently Edana came inside with Ailbe: "Meadghbh! I'm so glad to see you. Ailbe told me you just arrived. What news do you have?"

"I came to let you know that the Romans are looking for us both. Quintus came to the main esplanade and asked Dahy about us. He says he wanted to congratulate us on our performance at the Samhain ceremony but I think it's more likely that they want to take us back as prisoners," Meadghbh gushed.

"NO! I do not want that! You must stay here with us, stay away from Gosbecks. I understood that they'll be leaving to bring back information to their general about what we want the Romans to build, about the mill and bridges. They will be leaving soon," Edana shouted, her worry escalating the more she talked.

"Calm down Edana! We were already discussing that Meadghbh will be staying here while the Romans are in Gosbecks, that is already decided. Miach' has said the people will need to send back a resounding no answer to their building anything here. It will take time for the leaders to decide exactly what they'll tell Quintus and his group. We must be clever in our response, not seeming to be needy like children who want the goods from an overbearing parent. Too many open ended issues to be left without a reason," Bebhinn responded soothingly.

"What is a mill Mother?" Ailbe asked.

"It is a large building holding a giant wheel that will grind wheat into flour, the Romans have built several in Camulodunum and would like to build one here in Gosbecks," she answered.

"Why would we want one? We do all our own grinding in the kitchen," Ailbe who had just come in from outside said.

"And so we do, that is one of the questions we need to answer the Romans. They think we can build one to grind more than just one family's at a time but for everyone and make money at it for all of Gosbecks and the surrounding areas," Bebhinn answered.

"How would that make money? The women do all the grinding for without charging a fee for it," Ailbe persisted

"Yes but the Romans think that the mill will free all the women from having to take the time to grind their wheat for their families and can let the mill do it for a lot of people at once instead of one by one," Bebhinn explained.

"Well then maybe it is a good idea, to let everyone have the mill grind their wheat instead of just the women doing it," Ailbe said uneasily.

Edana shook her head: "The Romans would charge us for building the mill and will run it until the people of Gosbecks can pay it back, if that is even possible," looking sideways she said under her breath.

"Then we shouldn't do it, we'll tell the Romans no we don't want a mill," Ailbe shook his head.

"Well said Ailbe!" Meadghbh said, "I agree with you there."

"Let's get back to the Romans wanting to find us Meadghbh, if we stay here until they leave, that might work but what if they ask where I live?" Edana asked.

"I'll go to the village and put out word to keep our farm off limits to the Romans. I'll explain that you are very sick and not to come because it might be catching," Bebhinn looked down thoughtfully, "Maybe say that you do not want to entertain anyone because of it. Of course I'll need to go to Gosbecks right away to explain, make sure Dahy and the most talkative food sellers don't tell the Romans inadvertently. I'll pack and go right now; you girls can pick the peas, turnips and chestnuts this afternoon." With that Bebhinn got up, packed her medicinal kit that she never was without and left.

"We need a strategy Meadghbh; we need to figure out what we'll do if they show up at the farm. We'll need an escape route," Edana was already planning on any unforeseen contingencies.

"Why don't we all meet at the rabbit warren if we see the Romans coming? We might be in different areas when they come but we'll know to regroup at the warren." Meadghbh suggested.

"Good thinking, it is at least a full half days walk from here and out of sight from the farm house. Ailbe can you keep this a secret if they show up? If we are not here at the time?" queried Edana.

"Yes Edana I will not tell the Romans if they come where you are," Ailbe solemnly said.

"If they do come here and we meet at the rabbit warren where will we go after that?" asked Meadghbh.

"We can plan on going to Niamh's farm from there, they'll help us out, or we can even plan on going to Brenna and Ferdia's farm since the Romans know that Niamh helped us out before and might again," Edana reasoned.

"Yes and they will not know the connection between Brenna and I. I think that is the better plan," Meadghbh nodded.

"Then it's settled we'll meet at the rabbits warren then take off for Brenna and Ferdia's farm," satisfied Edana ended the discussion. "Now how about getting those carrots and turnips?"

֍ ֍ ֍ ֍

When it was time to listen to the music by Lorcan at the tavern the Romans all mounted up again. They planned on separating as soon as possible and talking to as many of those attending to get the information about the human sacrifice. By pairing up they could get the most coverage of the crowd, a typical Roman military tactic, divide and conquer. When they arrived at the tavern it was already crowded, seemed word of the impromptu music for the Romans had been spread. They walked in and immediately were hailed by Oisin: "Seems like word of the music has gotten out; Lorcan will play a lot of music for you tonight. Would you like wine while you wait?"

"Yes we'll take a round," Quintus replied.

"As you wish, Grania will be back with your wine shortly," Oisin bustled off to give their orders to his wife. Soon they were all served. They looked around at the crowd then paired up and melted into the crowd. Fullo stood next to Quintus: "So should we go find someone to ask?" and he ushered Quintus to a group of young ladies who were talking amongst themselves.

"Ladies we are obviously looking forward to hearing the fine music in this town, do you normally have music on a regular basis in Gosbecks?" Fullo was at his charming best.

"No, we don't have music on a regular day, I understood it was for you Romans since you seemed to enjoy our music at the Samhain ceremony last night," an older brown haired lady answered.

"We did enjoy the ceremony last night, the music and dancing was enchanting," Quintus said as he stood near the ladies. The ladies looked at him and pondered that both the Romans were very handsome.

"We have great music and you will be even more enchanted tonight," a young blond haired woman said. "My husband is the drummer Iollan, the best in town."

"Hang on, my husband Glendon is the best drummer," the voluptuous redhead standing next to her said.

"They're both great drummers if you ask me," the older woman said, trying to placate both the young women who looked ready to start fighting. "I'm Muirne, wife of Dahy the butcher." She smiled at Quintus and Fullo and then leaned in closer to say, "Never say one musician is better than another, in this room you have a lot of very partial fans."

"I see that thank you Muirne; we'll keep our opinions to ourselves," smiled Quintus.

He turned as Lorcan appeared at his side. "We've been waiting for you all to arrive before we started. Now that you're here we'll begin," and with a flourish he stepped back into the crowd. Soon the talking around them stopped as he got into the middle of the tavern and called for everyone's attention: "Our Roman guests have arrived, we will get this celebration started. We'll play some tunes and if anyone wants to join in singing please do so." With that quick start the other musicians formed around him, three drummers, four pipers and one who played an unusual looking instrument with strings that reminded the Romans of a lyre but was shaped very differently. The musicians began to play a lively melody that made the patrons of the tavern clap and start to sway. Then several of them stepped forward and started to sing, adding their dynamic harmonious voices to the sound of the instruments. The song was once again unintelligible to the Romans but they enjoyed the music nonetheless. The people of Gosbecks started to gyrate and dance, including the ladies that Quintus and Fullo were standing with. Dahy came over to his wife and picked up her hand; the two began to twirl in a circle to the music. Other couples appeared to do the same thing, starting to spin in time to the music, so all the movements were fitting, seeming to work with the music and the singers. Fullo's hand was grabbed by the voluptuous redhead who twirled into a circle with him. At first he did not know what to do, but he followed her lead, letting her set the speed and timing, after a moment understood what she was doing and mimicked her. They too started to dance like the rest of the dancers. The blond woman next to Quintus took his hand and did the same. While not as swift to pick up the dance he smiled and began to relax into the rhythm, swaying with her like she wanted him to. Soon everyone was dancing together, holding hands and beginning to link together so streams of people flowed past each other, their steps intricate but easy enough to follow since all of the Romans had joined the dance too. Stomp, slide, step, step slide, stomp, slide, step, step, slide and it repeated endlessly.

Soon the song ended and the dancers dropped their hands to clap them together. Hearty cries of: "Well played," and "Good drumming," and "More!" was heard. The singers laughed once again took up the song and added their voices to the mix. The musicians began to play another tune that was even livelier than the last one. The people of Gosbecks settled into more dancing, this time a little different, more individuals jumping and moving their feet in intricate steps. This dance was quite different with each participant seeming to dance for a little bit then pointing to another one and that person dancing, adding his or her steps differently. The song continued and everyone clapped their hands in time to the music.

Quintus had never seen this type of celebration; most of the Roman dances were stately and choreographed, slow and dignified and usually performed by professional dancers. This however was more loose, the type of dance that didn't have rules. He began to see the fun in it despite not knowing the rules and joined in the clapping, like his other soldiers were doing. Bundarus sidled over to him from the back: "Should we be ready for conflict? I do not understand what they are doing here."

"I don't either but I am enjoying the intricate dancing. Keep alert, I do not think they will try anything," Quintus said over the noise. "You and Rufus should keep on your guard up though." Bundarus nodded and stepped back, beginning to clap with the others around him. The mood of the room was jubilant and energetic. Circling through the room was Oisin and Grania, refreshing everyone's ale and wine as they went, obviously used to this type of gathering. They had an unidentified woman helper who also poured ale to those around her. She caught up with Quintus and refilled his cup without asking. The song ended and another one much slower started, one of the singers stepped forward and started singing a slow, lilting song in his pleasing tenor voice. Once again the words were unintelligible but pleasing, the sound forlorn and wanting. Quintus turned to the blond next to him to ask: "What is this song about, I recognize the singer but sounds sad."

The blond turned to him and replied: "It is a sad song about lost love. The singer is saying he cannot live without his only love that has died."

"How sad, the song sounds like he is mourning. I can't understand all the words but the feeling of grief is audible," Quintus said.

"I haven't had the pleasure of knowing your name; I'm Quintus by the way."

"My name is Gormley," she replied, "My friend over next to your soldier is Aileen."

"Nice to meet you Aileen, my name is Fullo," Fullo turned to Aileen and smiled.

"And good to talk with you Fullo," smiled Aileen. They listened to the song in silence, both Romans amazed at the lovely sounds coming from the musicians and singer. "Who is the singer, I've seen him before," Fullo asked.

"That is Cathmore, he is one of the best singers in Gosbecks and he always sings this song. The word is this was the song that got his wife Meara to join with him," Aileen answered.

"I can certainly see why, this song is beautiful," Fullo said. They listened in silence for a while until the song ended. The audience clapped their appreciation at the end. The next musicians struck up the next song that was once again lively and the audience started to clap their gratitude for another longtime favorite. The singers stepped forward to lend their voices and the room once again erupted in happy movements. Quintus excused himself and made his way over to Dahy and Muirne. "I enjoy the music here; we Romans are all impressed with the singing and musicians."

"I'm glad to hear that you like our music, we enjoy the opportunity to show you we in Gosbecks can do more than just grow wheat," said Dahy. "I need to introduce you to more of our people." Turning to his side he introduced Meara and her daughters Aine and Flann. "Meara is the wife of Cathmore, the one who sang the last song. Actually Meara, Aine and Flann also sing as well. They have very melodic voices."

"Your husband has a fine voice, it is good enough to sing for the General should he ever come to Gosbecks," Quintus commented hoping they understood the compliment. They listened to the song a little more than Quintus turned to Meara, "Could you introduce me to your husband when he is finished singing? I would like to personally compliment him for his melodic ability."

"Certainly, when he is done I will introduce you to him," Meara replied. They stood and listened to the song. Aine and Flann went off to dance some more. Quintus then turned back to Dahy: "Do they always dance during song recitals here? This is different than where I come from."

Dahy looked surprised: "Don't you have dancing at your merriments?"

"Not like this, it is much more controlled. Dancing together like this is not done in Roman society, but I am enjoying the freedom here," Quintus answered.

Muirne asked: "Is there no dancing in Rome?"

"There is dancing but it is all choreographed and performed by professional entertainers. You would never see something like this in a tavern back in Rome; taverns are just for eating and drinking. You would have to go to the theater for something along these lines."

"How different that is," murmured Dahy, "We need t to have music around us all the time. It helps to pass the time. You'll hear everyone singing when we are doing our daily chores even."

"You hear our slaves singing but not the Roman freemen, we are usually too busy for that type of frivolity," laughed Fullo.

"How sad that you don't feel the need to sing during the day," Meara said, "I would not like to be in Rome for that reason alone, I would be constantly mistaken for a slave."

"Then it is good we are in Gosbecks, I would not want to think of never hearing your husband and I suspect you are just as talented a singer as he is," Fullo said.

"She is that talented," added Muirne.

Soon the song ended and the musicians called a break, the singers returned to the crowd. Cathmore walked up to his wife and greeted everyone standing around her. He accepted her cup of ale to wet his mouth after singing so much. "We were talking about your amazing voice, I wanted to congratulate you on your singing," Quintus stepped forward to offer.

"Thank you, it is a gift the gods have given me that I am sure to share with all," Cathmore said with dignity.

"I'd also like to ask you more about Gosbecks. Since you are a recognized leader here please tell me about the needs of the people here. Since there are many streams and rivers do you need any bridges built? I know you will be holding meetings about the mill but what are your thoughts about it?" Quintus asked.

"We seem to have all our bridges that we need. As far as the mill I am not sure Gosbecks needs one. All of the family's take care to grind their own wheat on a daily basis. We do not seem to have a need for one, we are still too small of a village to need one," Cathmore replied.

"Do you want to Gosbecks to grow at all?" Quintus asked.

Cathmore shook his head, "No, we are the correct size; we are down people from the losses of the rebellion."

"Yes I see that," replied Quintus looking around at the crowd that was heavy with females and not so many males. "So you do not think we Romans can build the people of Gosbecks anything? What about roads, are there roads that wash out on a regular basis that need to be drained and paved?"

"That might be something we can talk about in the meetings," Cathmore replied grudgingly.

"Fair enough thank you. I do have another item to ask you about, did you attend the Samhain ceremony at the Green Man Clearing?" Quintus asked.

"We attended the ceremony, yes," Cathmore looked at him sharply.

"Did they have a sacrifice there?" Quintus looked at him squarely.

"We did have a sacrifice because it was Samhain," Cathmore told him.

"Was it a human sacrifice, performed by the druids?"

Cathmore looked at him pointedly: "We performed a sacrifice on Samhain but it was a normal sacrifice, not human but a deer. I killed the deer myself."

"We saw the smoldering bonfire at the Green Man Clearing, the remains on it was not a deer but a human man," Quintus said quietly.

"There was an older man that expired last night; we put his body on the bonfire because it was already consecrated and therefore holy. That is all that happened and nothing more," Cathmore replied with a steely expression.

"I can vouch for that," Dahy said, "The man was our smith that lost his arm in a skirmish. He danced so much that he had fit and died on the spot. Very tragic that."

"Are you talking about the one I met last night, Declan was his name?" Quintus asked.

"Yes that was his name," Meara offered, "We are all very sorry for his death and the best thing to celebrate his life is through music."

"So this music festival wasn't just for us Romans but for Declan?" Fullo asked.

"Yes it was for both you Romans and Declan," Cathmore said showing he was impatient with this line of questioning.

"Then Fullo it seems we have the answer to our inquiry, who was the man on the bonfire, but I'm still a little confused, why were his skull missing?" Quintus turned to Cathmore.

"Because it is part of our grieving, we take the skull of the one who passed and purify them. Once they are purified we use them in ceremonies to celebrate the life of the man who passed, in this case Declan's life." Cathmore replied.

"Ah yes, more ceremonies, I understand. Thank you for clarifying that up for me," Quintus nodded. The musicians began to regroup and Cathmore excused himself again to sing. The songs lasted longer and there was more dancing. At the end the Romans thanked Lorcan and the musicians for their great performance then turned to pay their bill with Oisin. Once they had paid they thanked their new friends and left for their fort.

Outside Fullo turned to Quintus: "I know that look; you don't believe that story about Declan dying do you?"

"No I do not! I still believe they are hiding a human sacrifice and the druids' involvement. We need to ask the others what they heard from their conversations," Quintus answered.

Soon the Romans were all mounted up on their horses and heading back to fort. Once on the road and out of sight of the tavern Quintus turned: "Report, what have you found?"

Bundarus and Titus rode up first: "We found that there were some in the crowd we talked to that went to the Green Man's Clearing but none admitted to a human sacrifice," Bundarus rumbled disgustedly. Titus added: "Only dancing and a sacrifice of a deer." They both turned their horses to the rear. Faber and Coriaro rode up next.

"We received the same answers, no human sacrifice but only the sacrifice of a deer," Faber said quietly. Coriaro only nodded his head. Grex and Rufus rode up next.

Grex started: "All of the people we talked to did not go to the Green Man's Clearing. They claimed to have important work on their farms to have to do the next day so they didn't go to the second Samhain ceremony." Rufus agreed: "I found it very curious that out of the eight people we talked to none went to the ceremony."

Very interesting and a bit too convenient, thought Quintus.

CHAPTER 9
HUNTING WILD GAME

By midday Bebhinn returned to the farm exhausted from her haste to get back to Edana and Meadghbh. She had interesting meetings with the food vendors and was able to tell them what she wanted to. Dahy was especially helpful, he told her where the Romans were at the moment and where they will probably be. "Don't worry about anyone going to your farm, I'll pass on that Edana is feeling poorly. I hope she feels better soon."

"She'll be better in a week or so, I think the excitement of Samhain got to her. She just needs to rest," Bebhinn smiled at Dahy and purchased some pork from him.

"Where is everyone Ailbe," she said as she mounted the steps up to the farm house."

"They are out at the rabbit warren setting snares for dinner tonight," he replied as he continued in his chore of feeding the chickens and ducks.

"How long ago did they leave?"

"They left right after they picked all the peas, turnips, and chestnuts, which took some time since we had a good crop of them this season. They should be getting back soon," Ailbe smiled at his mother. Bebhinn's heart skipped a beat; Ailbe looked so much like Carrick did at this age, in the sunlight they both had the same crooked smile and tow headed hair that ended in wispy curls whipping about in the wind. It made her doubly sad to know he would not grow up together with Carrick, learning new things from his older brother. It is the way of life, she thought, brutal circumstances altering a carefully planned out life. She shook her head and went on into the house to put down her medicine bag. Inside she chastised herself for letting the past intrude on her very present circumstances. She had more pressing matters to prepare for. She had learned some important information in the village about the Romans that she needed to tell Edana and Meadghbh about.

At the voices coming from outside she turned and went to the door, "I have news for the both of you about the Romans, come inside and I'll tell you everything while I unpack my purchases from the food stalls," Bebhinn beckoned them inside.

"I hope it is good news Bebhinn. I could sure use some," Meadghbh said.

"It is good news for us; the musicians are planning on playing music for Declan to celebrate his willing sacrifice this evening. They are telling the Romans it is for them since they have been talking about how much they liked our music. Anything to flatter the Romans. This means we will not have to worry about seeing the Romans today, possibly even tomorrow since I put out word at the food stalls that you are not feeling well Edana," Beaming Bebhinn felt very satisfied. She continued. "The Romans believe they are so important, they will believe the music is just for them and not a celebration for Declan's selfless sacrifice."

"What did the Romans say about the celebration, are they interested?" Meadghbh said.

"They were flattered and will be there. What else is there to say? We cannot see their perspective, it is so different from ours," Edana said dismissively waving her hand.

"Do not be so flippant of them my daughter. They were asking about you earlier," Bebhinn said gently. "We must be careful with the Romans, they have great pride and once hurt it is dangerous."

"We have been making contingencies for that possibility. We decided to have an escape plan if the Romans come to our farm. Meadghbh and I will get to the rabbit warren as soon as possible if they show up here. We'll regroup there and escape to Brenna's farm. The Romans do not know our connection to Brenna and will not know to go there. If we are separate when the Romans show up we'll still get to the rabbit warren separately. We've already set up some supplies up there in case this comes to pass," Edana told her mother.

"And what about Ailbe and I, should we feign ignorance if they come and point them to the lake?" Bebhinn asked.

"Yes that is a good plan. Point them to the lake which is even further away from us than the rabbit warren and on the opposite side," Meadghbh sounded out, getting excited. "Ailbe has already said he'd feign ignorance and shrug his shoulders when asked."

"Good, then that is what we'll do," Bebhinn said definitively. "Why don't you go back to the rabbit warren and check your snares. Evening meal time is coming on fast and it will be dark before you know it."

"You'll find the snares full Edana, time to go get the rabbits. I'll get the greens that you picked earlier for Mother," Ailbe said in his uncannily calm way. All three women turned to look at him with a slight shiver going up all their backs. Would they ever be used to his confident predictions? It was becoming more prevalent the older he became, having a family member so tied to the other realm was unnerving.

Edana and Meadghbh got their satchels and headed out the door. Bebhinn thanked Ailbe when he returned with the greens. She looked at him sideways as she prepared the greens for the evening meal. "Do you have any signs that the girls will escape the Romans?"

"They will not be taken by the Romans now but will be later.

Both will find themselves just as ensnared as the rabbits they'll find tonight," intoned Ailbe in a hollow voice, coming from beyond the room, from another realm. He turned and went outside.

Bebhinn heard the voice with dread. It seemed that the Romans had already invaded Gosbecks and now their home. She had already suspected it from the message they'd received from Arden last night. They would have to learn to live within the Roman parameters, as if they were standing over their shoulders all of the time. It would make for tense seasons. As they did their chores waiting for Edana and Meadghbh to return Bebhinn looked over at Ailbe. He was doing his chores of getting the chickens and ducks into their coop for the night. He was so serious but serene at the same time. There were no childish behaviors about him; he worked with the knowledge that what he did was needed. So unlike Carrick at the same age Bebhinn mused. Carrick would turn any chore into an opportunity to play. The ducks and chickens would be little soldiers or armies fighting each other. Bebhinn smiled at the memories she was suddenly assailed with. "Goodbye my son Carrick," she murmured sorrowfully.

Soon Edana and Meadghbh returned with four rabbits, each exclaiming that all but one snare had a rabbit. They all began to get their evening meal together and when they were finished all settled before the fire doing the end of day chores. All of them taking the time to stretch the rabbit hide for later use, each rubbing the fat and sinew off the hide. "Looks like we can include more mittens for everyone after this bunch are prepared[124]," Bebhinn said, as she did her work.

"If we continue at this pace the warren might move or be depleted, we'll need to find another source for meats. Tomorrow we can try to fish but as it gets colder the fish become more sleepy and harder to catch," Edana said, looking worried.

---

[124] https://www.pinterest.com/pin/390616967653521085/

"What about hunting for duck or geese? We can do that instead of fishing," Meadghbh offered.

"What do you think Ailbe? Should we go after the ducks and geese?" Edana asked hopefully.

Ailbe just shook his head, "I don't know which would be better, I'll have to sleep and let the dreams come to me about it."

"Alright, we'll do one or the other tomorrow. Either way is fine with me," Edana said. They prepared for sleep and went to bed. That night Edana and Meadghbh stayed awake on their pallet and discussed what to do for the next few days: "I think we should just go about the regular business of daily living and preparations for the winter. There is plenty for you to do here and you can take whatever you want back to your farm when the Romans leave," Edana whispered.

"Alright, but we need to keep making contingencies in case the Romans come to the farm. I cannot help but believe a simple misplaced bit of information from someone back in Gosbecks will lead them here," Meadghbh whispered back.

"We've already decided to escape to the rabbit warren at the first case of them coming. Then to Brenna's farm after that, what more do you need. We'll need to be nimble in all the possible outcomes. The more we keep planning the greater the problems seem. Just go to sleep and we'll be fine," Edana drowsily whispered.

The next day they were advised by Ailbe to hunt ducks and geese, but with the admonishment of staying close to the southern side of the lake. There was more trees and they were not to venture around to the west where there was more open areas with cattails and sedges. Armed with his instructions they took off before first light, hoping to get to the ducks first. "We'll be out all day Mother so don't worry about midday meal for us. I've already packed a meal for Meadghbh and I for us to eat at the lakeside," Edana told her Bebhinn on the way out the door. Back at home Bebhinn looked at Ailbe who was preparing to start his day of chores and getting bundled up because it was cold. "Why were you so specific about where Edana and Meadghbh should go? You know the best place to hunt ducks is on the west side. There are more places to hide from the ducks than the southern side."

"I was lead to the information from my dreams. I have the picture of Romans coming today and having Edana and Meadghbh out on the lake hunting will put them out of the way," Ailbe told her.

"Romans coming here today, even after all the information I told Dahy, Muirne and the other food stuff vendors?!" Bebhinn exclaimed.

"The leader of the Romans is drawn to Edana. The relationship that blossoms from this will be to our benefit," Ailbe said with that hollow voice from beyond. He shook his head when he stopped speaking and turned to finish getting his furs on. He turned to his mother, smiled and left out to do his daily chores starting with getting the goats up to the far pasture.

▰▰▰▰

That morning at the Roman camp Quintus and Fullo rode out to look for Edana and Meadghbh. They followed the track pointed out by Eilis the other day and rode just over a *mille passuum* and *stadium* to her farm. When they got to the farm the front paddock was open. It looked like whatever animals were in the paddock were being led to another. In the chicken coop a small boy was standing as if waiting for them to notice him.

"Boy, is this where Edana lives?" Quintus asked him.

Despite his heavily accented Celt the boy answered him easily, "Yes, Edana lives here at this farm."

"Where is she? I want to talk with her," Quintus said.

"She is out hunting," Ailbe answered.

"When will she return?" Quintus asked

"Later, probably sometime after midday meal but not later than the end of day meal," the boy said.

"Is your mother or father home?"

"Mother is letting the goats out into the upper pasture for foraging. Father is dead," Ailbe answered in a flat voice.

"We'll wait for her then," Quintus said and dismounted from his horse. He looked at the farm with a critical eye and could see that while it was well run it had a lot of fallow fields surrounding the farmhouse. The house itself was well built but could use some fixing from the look of its' odd shape, very different from the Roman construction he was used to. The building interested Quintus in the strange way it was built. It was a round building with an enlarged entry way topped with a thatched roof and supported by walls made of stone on the bottom and wattle and daub on the top. It appeared big enough for a large number of people, but was only one story with no windows. The outside walls were low to the ground with the gray thatched roof hanging over it resembling an old man with a straw hat. The outer walls were painted with lime which made them lighter but they were hard to see unless you walked up to the house.[125] It didn't look anything like a Roman home which had windows, an atrium and an open courtyard. He recognized that the closed off interior would make it substantially easier to warm. He wanted to see inside but had to wait for the boys' mother to return before he walked in to view it from the interior.

Presently his mother showed up with large satchel tied and on her back. "Ailbe look at what I found, late season mushrooms!" Bebhinn was looking down as she walked and as she rounded the chicken coop suddenly saw the Romans. "Oh! We have visitors!" She slowed to a stop and stood there looking at them, not knowing what to do.

Quintus stepped forward "We are seeking Edana, the mummer from Samhain's activities."

"Oh! Alright." She said in a flustered way. "What do you want

---

[125] http://resourcesforhistory.com/Celtic_round_houses.htm http://resources.woodlands-junior.kent.sch.uk/Homework/celts/index.html

with Edana exactly?" Bebhinn asked, her heart beating wildly in her chest at her audacity.

"We want to congratulate her on her method of escaping from us last night. It was a ploy worthy of any foe we've yet had." Quintus replied, a smile meant to sooth her worry.

"Why did you take Edana and Meadghbh last night while they were performing their mummer's rites?" Bebhinn asked

"We were looking for someone to take us to the farm on the ridge," Quintus searched his mind for the name, "Niamh's farm. They said they were on the way to her farm and we offered to escort them. They were not captured at all, simply riding with us," he replied.

"Edana is out hunting right now, I don't expect her back until much later, why don't you come back later, maybe tomorrow?" Bebhinn said.

"We would prefer to wait for Edana now," Quintus rejoined, his tone brooking no argument. "I'd like to see your farm house; I've not seen one up close before."

"Alright, then come inside and partake of some of our mushrooms," Bebhinn said, suddenly remembering her manners. "Do you like mushrooms?"

"Yes, we do thank you," Quintus smiled.

"Come in," Bebhinn led the way thinking it very unusual for these men to be interested in her home. She couldn't' help but remember what Miach said about Roman interest in the farms. She uneasily led them inside.

Once inside the Romans were impressed with the interior. It was a large room with hard beaten dirt floors. There were work areas carefully defined with baskets and containers filled with items that were being worked on. A hearth stood in the middle with no chimney in site, the smoke just disappearing up to the ceiling leaving upper roof in a haze of smoke. Various meats for smoking hung near the hearth area. The inner portion showed walls that where white from a lime wash and was and beautifully decorated with strange swirling, circular symbols painted in red ochre, yellow Sulphur and blue woad[126]. The cooking hearth had a domed oven next to it for baking, on the outside it was painted with the white lime wash and circular symbols. A large cauldron was suspended from a brace of interlocking branches over a banked fire; next to it was a long branch suspended by wooden supports for cooking pieces of meat. Additional iron pots and pans were neatly stowed away on shelves along the wall. Large baskets were interspersed around the walls for storage. Pallets for sleeping were neatly rolled up and put away by the walls. Small tripod tables and tree stumps were interspersed around the floor at work sites, unfinished bits of fur and woven cloth hung by them.

"This is certainly a spacious farm house, it is much larger on the inside than it looks from the outside," Quintus said, clearly impressed with how large home was.

"All of our homes are constructed much like this one. My husband built it by hand many seasons ago, we've been adding to it since then," Bebhinn proudly said.

"What do these symbols mean?" Fullo asked pointing to the walls.

"They are blessings for the inhabitants of this home, each season there are more blessings that we add to the walls. The ones on our oven celebrates Bris[127], the god of all growing crops and fertility, that he may continue to bless this home every time we bake," Bebhinn said.

"Very nice," Fullo said running his hand over a large circular symbol on the wall.

Bebhinn began to prepare the mushrooms, washing with water from a jar standing next to the hearth. She then reached up to get

---

[126] https://www.pinterest.com/pin/354447433148952957/

[127] https://www.google.com/search?q=bris+celtic+god+of+fertility&tbm=isch&source=univ&sa=X&ved=2ahUKEwjJpteih PHjAhVHA6wKHW2nCnkQsAR6BAgFEAE&biw=1034&bih=630

one of the slabs of meat, venison, and cut a generous portion for their midday meal. She dropped it on the table near the hearth and began to slice off portions. Next the mushrooms and venison went into a low pot that she suspended over the hearth. After coaxing the flames up Bebhinn put the pot over the hearth. Soon the room became warmer and the stew began to bubble. Into the stew she put some turnips, peas,, wild onion and herbs from her store kept by the hearth. Bebhinn moved methodically but surely to get the meal going, while she cooked Quintus and Fullo looked around the room, occasionally commenting to each other in Latin about the home and pointing different items out to each other. Ailbe had come in earlier and was nearby to answer any questions if needed.

"What are you working on here?" Quintus pointed to the scraps of rabbit fur.

Ailbe picked up an unfinished mitten and held it up: "These are mittens for the cold weather; they are not quite finished yet."

"Is this the hunting that Edana is doing now, more rabbits?" Fullo asked.

"No she is hunting ducks and geese today, on the far side of the lake. She'll be back much later today than I thought because of the time it will take her to travel," Ailbe answered.

The men looked at each other for a moment. An understanding passed between them. Quintus asked: "If we were to ride out to the lake, where would we find Edana?"

"She will be roaming around the west side, where there are sedges and grasses you can hide in. You know when you are hunting ducks and geese you hide amongst the grasses waiting for the right moment to let your sling fly," Ailbe advised looking much older than his young years.

"After the midday meal we will leave to join up with Edana. We'll bring her back to the house when we catch up," Quintus said.

They ate the midday meal with relish, and complimented Bebhinn on her dish. Then they went outside to mount up, taking the time to thank Ailbe for his information. Quintus felt for the small serious boy whose father was no longer around to help out and took the time normally not something done by Romans to talk with him. "You do a fine job of looking after your sister and mother Ailbe." He swung up into the saddle, Fullo and he turned to leave, waving at them both.

"Will they find the girls?" Bebhinn asked anxiously.

"If the girls stay on the south side they'll miss them. If the Romans decide to look for them then they might be found. I don't think they'll do anything, they are interested just to see the girls, I know that is what Quintus wants," Ailbe said.

"Should I be worried at that?" Bebhinn asked, even more worried now.

"They will do nothing now. They will leave shortly to go back to their Roman general with all the information they've gathered up till now and will return. Then the Romans will be part of Gosbecks in earnest. Then you should worry." Ailbe replied in his hollow voice, the one he channeled from beyond.

"Let it be as the gods will," Bebhinn sighed.

Quintus and Fullo made to the west side of the lake, through a lush wooded meadow and over a ridge. The weather was cold but not as windy as it was the last two days; the clouds scudded across the sky overhead. As they passed the grassy ridge they could see the lake just as described by Ailbe, sedges and grasses moved up to the lake, perfect for hunters to hide in. But upon inspection there were very few ducks or geese in the area despite it being the top time in the oncoming evening for them to come in to feed. Looking toward the shoreline they saw movement in the sky over to the south side, a flock of geese were circling and looked ready to land in the water. From where they were mounted they heard the sound of a stone hitting a goose and the fowl plummeting to the water landing close by the shore.

"I think we found where the hunters are, not on the west side but on the south side," Fullo observed.

"We should make our way over there as quickly as possible.

Looks like more geese are coming in for their evening feeding over there," Quintus replied.

They made their way to the southern more wooded area, and having rounded a large tree they caught sight of both of the girls. They were looking up at the sky and gesturing to another flock of incoming geese. Both of them were wet from the thighs down from frequent trips to retrieve the birds and from the brace beside them they looked to be pretty successful in their hunting ducks and geese[128].

"I don't think they'll be here much longer from the look of their catch," Quintus murmured. They continued to watch the girls take down one more goose and collect it from the water. Edana came out of the water with her graylag goose and happened to look up as see the Romans as they were mounted watching them from the shore. She squealed out a strangled cry and pointed to them. Her friend Meadghbh turned and saw them as well. Both the girls hurried to gather their catches and bundle them together. As they did they were almost crying in their haste to gather everything as fast as they could. Quintus and Fullo watched them in bemusement, not realizing they were the cause of Edana and Meadghbh's stress. Finally they stopped trying to get everything together and spoke quietly to each other. They turned their faces to the Romans and just dropped their geese and ducks. They stood and waited for the Romans to come to them instead of trying to leave. The Romans obliged them and rode up quickly. Once they were close Quintus said: "You are to be congratulated, that was a most impressive brace of duck and geese."

"Oh ... thank you," gulped Edana, she looked up at the Romans with interest. This was the first time she saw them and was impressed by their good looks. Both men had darker complexions than she was used to but were pleasing to look upon. It was hard

---

[128] https://www.youtube.com/watch?v=NixPfpA-w-Q
https://www.youtube.com/watch?v=RXASb6V0O8U

to tell how tall each was since they were still on their horses. but they looked to be tall and well built. Quintus had darker hair than his companion but it was a pleasing curly dark brown. His face was thoughtful and serious, but there were laugh lines around his eyes indicating a pleasant demeanor. She realized with a start that she found him quite attractive. Unexpectedly wishing to keep him by her she asked: "Do you wish to share in our evening meal today? We have plenty of geese and ducks for everyone." Meadghbh looked at her sharply with surprise, not expecting that from Edana.

"Yes, I think Fullo and I would be interested in partaking the evening meal with you," Quintus replied with a smile. Seeing her he also wanted to extend their time together. He was pleasantly surprised at how beautiful Edana looked with her curly blond hair pulled back from her face and secured in elaborate braids. Her face was blushed from exertion and probably excitement, the planes of her face were exquisitely stark in the autumn light, her clear skin blushed from the cold and glowing. He realized that she had startlingly gray eyes that watched him warily but with interest. Fullo at his side was also looking at the two girls and focused on Meadghbh. Meadghbh was taller than Edana, had dark brown hair and eyes, and very womanly curves. She was uneasily watching the expressions of Quintus as he perused Edana and recognized the interest in both their faces. She quickly glanced at Fullo and her eyes widened in surprise. She also found his face as intriguing as well with his easy smile and light brown curly hair. She was so worried that she didn't want to talk to him. She looked away quickly.

Fullo took pity on her on her during her stare and said: "Do you want assistance in bundling up your catch? We can ride double back to your farm house and easily carry all the birds tied on back."

Before she could answer Edana said: "We'll get it all together then ride with you." She quickly bent and began to tie the fowl together to carry them home. Once she'd bound all the geese and ducks she moved over to Quintus with her brace. Quintus dismounted and tied the birds to the back of the saddle then gripped her waist and placed her on the horse. He mounted up behind Edana and turned to go. Watching this Meadghbh also began to tie her birds together and carried her bundle over to Fullo, who did the same. Once on board he said: "Don't worry about me taking advantage of you and feeling your curves. I am not Faber. You are safe with me."

Meadghbh just nodded. Her heart was hammering from the unexpected change in plans from Edana. Why did she so easily change her plans? Did she not see they are in the same predicament as they were on Samhain, with the Romans in control of them? They rode in silence, no one breaking the quiet until they made the meadow before their farm house. In front Edana asked Quintus: "Why are you here today, close to my farm?"

"I wanted to see the two girls that escaped me on Samhain night, and quite well I must add. Going through the paddock to mask your tracks was the best bit of planning anyone could have arranged. My trackers couldn't follow you because of it," Quintus answered. She could hear his smile in his voice and grinned.

She was uneasy about her actions. She realized they were in the exact place they'd been during Samhain but she surprisingly wasn't worried. His easy going manner calmed her stuttering heart. Seeing the Romans unexpectedly showing up she wondered if Ailbe sent them toward their hunting spot, but discarded that thought since all the ducks and geese were located on the southern side, not the usual spot of the west side of the lake. She looked up to see them watching Meadghbh and herself quietly, not stepping forward until they saw the girls had seen them. There was no time to escape to the rabbit warren, they were mounted and could easily have caught up with Edana and Meadghbh. When she turned to look at them again she was struck by how handsome Quintus was. She'd never considered men in the village as that interesting so it surprised her with the strength of her attraction. She was struck by how strong he looked, how imposing. His face was interesting, strong chin, full lips and a slightly aquiline nose, so different from the noses around here. His eyes were dark and beguiling, with lush brows above. She had the urge to see him smile with those generous lips.

With all her thoughts of Quintus she shook her head at herself and looked back to Meadghbh and the second fellow. At least it wasn't the big one that rode with her last night. Meadghbh looked grim but not as scared as Edana thought she might be. She asked Quintus: "Who is your companion back there?"

"That is Fullo; he was with us last night but not the one who road with Meadghbh last night," Quintus murmured as he maneuvered the horse up a small ridge and into the meadow. The night was quickly coming and they had at least a *mille passus* still to travel before getting back to the farm house. Quintus urged his horse to a faster pace.

"Are you staying in Gosbecks until the leaders give you an answer about building your mill?" asked Edana wanting to keep him talking.

"Yes, when they have their answer my men and I will return to the Roman fort back west," Quintus replied. "Are you Celts all so willing for us Romans to leave?"

"It is just that winter is not a season to be forting out of doors in tents, it will soon start getting colder and start to rain, possibly snow," Edana answered.

"Are you willing to let us stay with you then, at your farm?" Quintus asked laughing.

"Oh! That is not what I meant at all. Just that forting out in tents is not the best place to be during the cold winter season," a flummoxed Edana said.

"I know what you meant but where we should stay is the next logical thing to do, we will simply move in with several families and take advantage of their houses and no longer living in the tents in the fort," Quintus grinned.

"Is this what you normally do? Just move into houses of the village you wish to?" Edana turned to look at Quintus with a quizzical look on her face.

Quintus shrugged: "Sometimes, especially when we are somewhere that requires time to negotiate. I think this might be one of those places, since the mill and building roads will take time for your leaders to agree to. We will pay for the lodgings."

"Wouldn't you want to stay in Gosbecks and not all the way out here at my farm house?" Edana pressed.

"You are not too far from Gosbecks, plus I like the farm, it is quite nice," he rejoined.

"It is a beautiful farm is it not," Edana replied, "The animals and plants seem to thrive."

"I understand your father is no longer here to help with the plowing and harvesting, how did you and your mother get it all done?" Quintus asked.

"We worked hard but last season we had to leave a few fields fallow. We toiled and brought in the harvest and still had enough to put some aside for the winter," Edana told him proudly.

"Maybe if I stay at your farm I'll be able to help with some of the bigger items that a farm needs. I know winter is the time to do building or repairs on your roofs and fences around your paddocks," Quintus said.

Edana turned to look at him, surprised that he would know so much about the needs during different seasons on the farm. "You sound like you know about farming?"

"I am from Apulia[129], far from Rome. My family has been farming there for hundreds of years. I got my start as a farmer first, soldier second," Quintus said. "I know winter is the season for shoring up the buildings and fencing on a farm, for preparing the ground for the next spring's plantings."

"Well now that makes sense that you would know about the duties to run a farm if you have experience. We do have some sheds that need to be seen to, the chicken coop needs fixing since I've seen a family of foxes not too far from our farm house. There is

---

[129] https://en.wikipedia.org/wiki/Apulia

always more fields that need preparations for next spring," Edana was warming up to the thought of relaying all the jobs that needed to be taken care of.

Quintus started laughing: "Wait, I'll need to see if I can get to that long list on top of my other duties . My soldiers and their places of living must come first and then I'll still need to talk with the leaders of Gosbecks." They topped the last ridge as the sun began to sink behind in the west. They could see the farm from this vantage point.

She stayed calm in his arms, knowing that even though he was Roman he would be able to help them out with those jobs they sorely needed. Once in the courtyard they dismounted and retrieved the birds from the saddle. Ailbe and Bebhinn came out the front to greet them, Bebhinn smiling but looked a bit surprised they all came in together. "How was the hunt?"

"We got plenty of duck and geese for dinner tonight and tomorrow. Let us get them prepared for dinner. I've also invited these Romans for dinner tonight," Edana said as she showed the ducks and geese to her mother. They all made their way into the farm house after the Romans let the horses out to the paddock. Meadghbh and Edana set out to pluck the geese and ducks and soon had them over the fire pit with the other geese hanging over the fire pit getting smoked. Soon the dinner was prepared and they all sat down together.

"So tell me how you four all met up on the lake," Bebhinn said

Quintus smiled at Ailbe: "We started on the west side of the lake but there were no ducks or geese in the area. We watched some geese fly over to the south side and saw one felled by a rock. We simply made our way over to the south side and met up with Edana and Meadghbh. They are quite good huntresses."

"We were in the right place at the right time. We got ducks in the morning and geese in the afternoon," Edana smiled at her mother and Ailbe. They all kept eating the bounty of geese that Edana and Meadghbh provided.

"Tell me which one of you was the better shot with her sling, Edana or Meadghbh?" Fullo asked.

Both girls looked at each other in surprise, never having thought of themselves as competitive. Edana said: "We both got equal amounts of the duck and geese. The ducks were harder to bring down because they are smaller and more spooked by noises. Geese are easier because they offer a bigger target and they fly slower."

"We were both wet from the thighs down from retrieving the birds when you met up with us," Meadghbh said. She pointed to their leggings drying by the hearth. She ducked her head when Fullo smiled at her.

"It seems the maids were blessed by Diana[130] today," Fullo smiled

"No, they were blessed by Cernunnus[131]," said Ailbe in a surprisingly strong voice.

Quintus looked at Ailbe: "Is this the Celtic god of hunting?"

"Yes, he is the god hunting. Who is this Diana?" Ailbe asked.

"She is the goddess of hunting for us Romans, so maybe here she can also lend a hand to those who hunt here," Quintus answered.

"Cernunnus is the one here for us Celts, no Roman goddesses are needed," Ailbe insisted, his voice becoming stronger as he spoke.

"Peace young Ailbe, your Cernunnus definitely blessed Edana and Meadghbh this day. I do not think they will need to offer propitiations to Diana just to Cernunnus," Quintus said with his hands raised in supplication. "Are your hunting parties this successful normally?"

"We normally hunt ducks and geese this time of year, catching them before they leave for winter. We also hunt deer too,"

---

[130] http://www.crystalinks.com/diana.html http://www.mythencyclopedia.com/Cr-Dr/Diana.html

[131] http://paganwiccan.about.com/od/godsandgoddesses/p/Cernunnos.htm

Edana said. "We were unusually blessed today, thank the gods." She looked at Quintus and smiled proud to show that she helped to provide for her family. They finished their food quietly after that. Bebhinn and Meadghbh stood up to start clearing the plates. Edana moved over to Quintus: "Can you tell us about your farm in Apulia?"

"Well let me see, it is a smaller farm than yours but at one time it was much larger. On the farm we grew barley, beans, garden vegetables, and had olive trees and grape vines. The land is very different, much hillier and drier, not as green and wet as it is here. We had several fields for each of the crops that we rotated each season. It is a small but profitable operation," Quintus said.

"What are your most successful crops?" Edana asked curiously.

"Olives and grapes, we were fortunate to have healthy, producing olive trees and grape vines."

"Could we plant olive trees and grape vines here?" Edana asked.

Quintus shook his head: "I do not think so. The land is very different back in Apulia or even the surrounding areas of Italy. The olive trees and grape vines do best in sunny climates, with not that much rain. I've not seen any grapes or olives growing in Britannia."

"Can it be there are grapes or olives being grown here that you do not know about?" asked Bebhinn.

"Maybe, but I do not see the type of ground that the olive and grape loves here. Sun and warmth is also required for them both," Quintus replied.

"Maybe. Grapes grow here but we do make drinks that are close to your wine with apples and our native berries," Bebhinn countered.

"I've had some of your local spirits and while they are good it is not wine that we make in Italy, or like mine in Apulia," Quintus said, not allowing the fact to sway his argument. "Tell me about your farm, what do you grow?"

"We grow barley and wheat, vegetables and medicinal plants for mother's healing arts," Edana said.

"You are a healer?" Quintus asked Bebhinn.

"Yes, I am trained in the healing arts and it is my duty to serve this community," Bebhinn answered.

"I'm not sure I understand, does this mean you are a surgeon for all the people of Gosbecks?" Quintus asked.

"I am a healer, I do not know the meaning of surgeon," Bebhinn said not sure what he meant.

"A surgeon is the person assigned to render aid on a battlefield. They can heal sword cuts, spear throws and amputated limbs," Quintus said.

"I help those who have been injured in battles but also on farms and in everyday life. If someone is sick I seek to heal them, or I will assist in childbirth," Bebhinn replied.

"So you are more than a surgeon, most likely on the level of a doctor," Quintus mused. "Are you the only one in Gosbecks?"

"Yes but where I come from there are more healers, if I come across a patient that I cannot heal I'll send them to one of healers," Bebhinn replied.

"I would like to see your medicinal garden. It would be interesting to discuss some of the herbs you have to see if I have knowledge of the same type," Quintus said. "Maybe you can teach me of some of the local plants and what they are used for, I can tell my surgeon."

"Alright, but Edana can also help you with that, I've been instructing her in pharmacology," Bebhinn said.

"Pharmacology? I do not understand the word," Quintus asked

Bebhinn smiled: "It means what the plant is used for when you are trying to cure someone."

"Ah, what the plant does, their properties," Quintus smiled in understanding.

"I think so, I do not know the word properties but yes what the plant does, the efficacies of the medicine," Bebhinn said.

Quintus smiled, "I have a good ear for languages and picked up a lot of Celtic in Gaul. It is different from here but there are a lot of similar words that I am able to understand you better than others in my group. My tracker Grex is even better at Celtic than I am, you should speak with him."

"All right, I look forward to speaking with him," she replied.

"You would do well to learn my language, Latin." Quintus said to them looking at them with a meaningful stare.

Edana and Bebhinn looked at each other with astonishment. "We need to learn Latin? Why?" Bebhinn asked

"Because we will be moving a lot of Roman veterans here in the next couple of months. Gosbecks will be another Roman colonia," Fullo volunteered.

"I think I'll look forward to speaking with Grex, since he is your tracker Quintus," Edana said. "I need to ask him some of the possible ways to elude you even more next time I need to." She smiled at Quintus. He smiled back, not sure why but he felt the need to keep the conversation going with Edana. They looked at each other for a moment longer wanting to ask the other more questions but couldn't find the words at that time.

Finally Fullo interrupted. "I think we should get back on the horses and return to our fort before it gets much later," Fullo said in Latin breaking in on the moment between the two. "We need to let the others know we are fine and nothing nefarious has occurred."

"Yes we need to do that," Quintus not yet willing to leave but knowing he had to. He turned to the others and in Celt said: "We will need to get going before it gets much later. The other soldiers will be wondering where we are."

"Are you going to tell them that you wish to stay with us the next time we see you?" Edana asked, not willing to let this be the only time they are together.

"So you are inviting me to stay at the farm?" Quintus smiled.

"It is better than staying in a tent outside," Edana rejoined with her own smile. Meadghbh looked at her sharply, not liking what she was hearing.

Quintus turned to Bebhinn: "Well that is up to your mother, would it be acceptable if we come back and stay in your home until the leaders of Gosbecks make a decision on the mill? It would be preferable than staying in the tent back at fort."

Bebhinn looked nonplussed and glanced at the girls and Ailbe. Once she caught Ailbe's' eye, he merely looked at her and nodded. "All right you can stay here with us."

"Thank you Bebhinn, Edana and Ailbe," Quintus stood up and began to gather his things from the doorway. Soon both of the Romans were striding out into the cold night to get their horses from the paddock. He turned and said to Edana: "Fullo and I will come tomorrow with our things but it might be after midday meal before we get here. I look forward to staying here at your farm, it is a nice place." With that he went off to catch his horse and took off in the direction of Gosbecks.

"Why did you invite them to stay at the farm Edana?" Meadghbh said in exasperation. "Now they are going to be in our home! We cannot get away from them now!"

"It is not like the big guy will be staying here Meadghbh, just Quintus and Fullo. They already know where we live and they did not do anything to us when they caught up with us at the lake. We had no chance to escape from them then and they just rode us back home to the farm. I do not think they mean us harm. Look at how easily they answered my questions about his farm," Edana said

"Of course he was open to answering your questions; he wants to have you for a tussle in your pallet. Just look at how he was watching you like a little bird that he wants to eat," Meadghbh threw her hands up in disgust.

Edana's eyes opened wide at the insinuation: "I am sure he doesn't want to tussle with me on the pallet like you mean."

"I'm sure he is more interested in you than you think Edana. Did you not see his eyes when he looked at you on the lakeside? He was giving you an appraising look, and I guess he liked what he saw." Meadghbh rebutted. "Don't be so sure to give yourself a way to this Roman, remember what Cathmore said about he knows Quintus Agricolanus was the one who killed your father."

"Is this true Edana? Quintus was the killing sword for your father?" Bebhinn asked stridently.

"Oh gods, yes that is just what Cathmore said. He knows the man who saw the fight and was sure it was Quintus Agricolanus that killed father. Carrick was killed by an archer," Edana said with resignation. She had forgotten what Cathmore said. The weight of what he told her came back and hit her in the chest. She just found a man who caused her heart to beat faster and her eyes to seek his but it was not meant to be. Now because of her inadvertent meddling he would be staying with them. The man who killed her father was now their honored guest.

"I am so sorry Mother. I don't know what came over me. He is so fascinating, I feel like I need to be around him. But I cannot now that I realize who he is and what he has done. Why did I not remember what Cathmore said? I'll try to talk him out of staying with us," Edana tremulously said, big tears welling up in her eyes at the situation.

Bebhinn shook her head: "It is too late, he asked formally for my permission and I granted it. By our laws of hospitality we must abide by them and let them stay here despite what he may have done. We must treat them as honored guests and give them what they require. If that means he wants to lay with you then we'll deal with it when that time comes. You do not have to give him your honor if you do not want to. However we are well and truly caught with allowing them to stay here at the farm. I will need to readjust my thinking here, maybe even talk to Miach about it."

"How is it he knew just what to do by formally asking for your permission to stay here? Did he come here with an ulterior motive hoping to live here with Edana or does he know he killed your husband Bebhinn?" Meadghbh said with worry.

"I don't know if he meant to do this all along and does he even remember killing Ardan? He could have been one more Celt to dispatch in war. We will need to find that out." Bebhinn said tiredly.

"I am so sorry Mother; it is all my doing. Why could I not remember what Cathmore said? I will stay out of their way and work on the farm since I have those duties to take care of anyway." Edana said. "Meadghbh you will stay with me at this time and out of Faber's grasp."

"We need to find out for sure just what game the Romans are playing. I will stay here and out of the big Faber's grip a little longer but it might be too late for you Edana." Meadghbh said with fervor.

"And I'll stay out of Quintus' way and keep apart from him. I won't let him have me either," Edana said with conviction. "No matter what my heart wants to do I will stay strong and ignore it. How could I do otherwise?"

Bebhinn answered. "We just don't know how to deal with the Romans now that we know Quintus is the one that killed Ardan." She smoothed her hair back from her face with an impatient gesture. "If only events would be easy to see before they happen, and not after when decisions have been made that you wish to rescind. Ailbe is there something you can see about this situation?'

Ailbe just shook his head, "It doesn't work that way, I need to dream and see if the gods have anything to say. I might dream tonight and if they deem it important I will receive a message, then again I might not dream of this situation at all. You might be better served to ask what Miach thinks of the situation."

"We will have to deal with the Romans together Mother," Edana held her mother close and rested her head on Bebhinn's shoulder.

回回回回

The night began to get progressively colder as time went on and the Romans made it back to fort in record time because of it. They arrived at first watch and saw Grex and Titus on duty. "Where have you been all day?" Titus asked.

"We've been out looking for the two girls that eluded us on Samhain. We found them at their farm to the west of Gosbecks. Fullo and I will be staying there at that farm. Now I need to get places for all of you to stay to get out of our fortsite tents and into houses that are more comfortable," Quintus said. "The place to start would be to ask at the tavern to find names of suitable homes to pair everyone else off."

"Good to hear, I would like to be able to feel my feet at the beginning of day instead of the blocks of ice I've been waking up to," Titus replied.

"Funny smart ass," Fullo grunted. "This is just like the last winter in Gaul we forted, waking up with frost on the blankets. We had no place but the fort to stay in. You whined back then too."

"Well at least I'm consistent," Laughed Titus.

"We are lucky to have places to move into in Gosbecks. We just need to get that set up the right way, with the locals' permission," Quintus said.

"Where do we get their permission from?" Grex asked.

"From their leaders, I can talk to Oisin at the tavern first then go ask the other leaders like Cathmore. It will have to wait until morning though, I am tired tonight and would like to sleep in my cold bed in the tent," Quintus replied.

"You think you're tired? I have stiff hands from holding the reins in the wind tonight, and a tired seat from riding all day long," Fullo laughed. "Too bad we couldn't go to the tavern tonight and take a little of that ale. That should loosen up my joints a bit."

"It is a little far to walk so you'd have to get back on your horse but I'm game if you want to," Titus said.

"What about your turn to do guard duty, you've got first watch with me," Grex put in.

"Maybe I'll be able to switch with Rufus and do second watch," Titus said warming up to the idea.

"You'll do the first watch tonight Titus," Quintus said putting an end to the discussion, "I'm turning in to bed. Fullo you should too and get some rest for your turn at fourth watch with me in the morning. So if there isn't anything to report tonight I will turn in and go to sleep."

"Good night sir," said Grex and Titus in unison. Fullo just turned and followed Quintus back to their tent. On the way there Quintus stopped by Bundarus' tent to check on the goings on at the fort.

Bundarus said: "It was quiet this day in town. We just did the daily shopping and checked in on the tavern owner for news. We found tomorrow is market day so it will be a good opportunity to talk with more local merchants about the mill and possible roads and bridges."

Quintus could always count on Bundarus for thinking about Roman interests. It was why he liked to talk with Bundarus before the others with their self-interests. He thanked Bundarus and left his tent. Then he went to Faber and Coriaro's' tent. They reported the same as Bundarus and had little to add to the goings on except that the man who died on Samhain was the only blacksmith for the area. That was an important bit of information for Quintus because with Faber's former background as a blacksmith it would be an advantageous thing for them when they returned in the spring.

"Let us go to bed Fullo, tomorrow will be another day." Quintus said tiredly.

⌐⌐⌐⌐

The next morning they all had their morning meal at the tavern. "Fullo and I will be packing up our forting gear and moving it to Bebhinn's farm. It is located on the west side of Gosbecks, follow the main road until you get to a lane branching off further west. There is a large oak that you can use as the marker. It is surrounded by crab apple trees. Take the lane up about two *mille passuum* and veer to the right. The lane will end at Bebhinn's farm. If you need to contact me you'll find me there," All of the men nodded.

"What should we do today?" Asked Grex.

Quintus looked at the men. "Since we'll be breaking up the fort soon start the process of getting ready. You might want to bury all waste products. It will keep you warm at least. Every man is responsible for his own waste removal." The men all groaned in response to that. The burying of their waste products was the one duty every soldier had to perform but they all hated it.

"At least you will be dealing with the same stink Coriaro." Fullo laughed. "I'll be leaving with Quintus and someone else will be burying my waste."

"We'll be doing all of our own before we leave Gosbecks for the farm so that's fair Fullo." Quintus said.

Coriaro just shot Fullo a dark look. "You'll be burying the piss you are so used to smelling. It should be like a home coming for you." He grinned triumphantly and laughed at Fullo's comeuppance.

"Everyone keep your eyes open and your ears to the ground when you have dealings with the people here in Gosbecks. I'd like to get at the end of that Samhain mystery of the human sacrifice. Even one human sacrifice by the druids is one too many. The gods here must be blood thirsty," Quintus said darkly.

"Yes sir!" All the men said.

Then the *Contubernium* left the tavern to get their duties done and start their day. In record time the men had dug their pits to dump their sewage and trash in and then they finished the aromatic chore. Fullo and Quintus then packed up their belongings. They began preparations to tear down their tents the next morning and break up fort. . Boreas seeing them break down their tent sensed a big change in their move. He was quite restive when Quintus came to tack him up and get their belongings packed. He sidled away and wouldn't stand still. Finally Quintus got him tacked up. Fullo had a much better time of it with his bay Quirinus. His bay was much more resigned to standing patiently while being tacked up. Soon they were both done and they led the horses out to the road. "Contact us if you need to, ." Quintus said to the men.

Bundarus rumbled: "We know where to find you. Gods speed."

Chapter 10
Market Day

The next morning Quintus got up for the fourth watch with Fullo, the sky was still dark and cold but it wasn't raining. "Thank the gods," mumbled Quintus into his cloak as he trudged up to Faber and Coriaro to relieve them from their watch duty. "Report," he said as he and Fullo stopped in front of them.

"Third watch was uneventful, we saw nothing and no one," Coriaro told them. "Bundarus and Rufus also had nothing to report. It would seem all the inhabitants of Gosbecks bed down quietly."

"Good, you are relieved of duty go finish your night," Quintus said. He turned to Fullo and they took the first turn around the perimeter per the military rules. As the time progressed they began to hear movement on the main road which turned out to be vendors and farmers coming in for market day. As the morning drew on the traffic picked up. More farmers and herders were moving their herds and flocks into Gosbecks. Sellers with their carts being pulled into the area for set up on the green space where the bonfire was held. It was interesting seeing the farmers startle at the presence of the Roman soldier fort at the edge of Gosbecks. Soon the

Romans began to rouse at the sounds of the population coming by the fort which was located the south side of Gosbecks. More of them woke up and began to get their morning meal the vendors and farmers hurried to get by their fort causing the Romans to laugh in response.

"Look at them scuttling around us as if we might bite!" Titus laughed at one farmer who hurried his cart away from them, causing the load to sway precariously. Rufus and Bundarus laughed with him. Another drover hurried by with his herd of cattle, careful not to make eye contact with the Romans as he hustled the small herd pass. Behind him a farmer moved his cart slowly but didn't stop to ask any questions, just struggled pass with his cart laden with vegetables to sell.

"Leave the vendors and market day customers alone and help me make some millet[132] this morning," Grex said as he prepared their breakfast. The others turned to look at Grex and laughed again at his disgruntled look. They meandered over to him and began to pass out the eating utensils to the others sitting there. Bundarus and Rufus started to gulp down their morning millet. Faber and Coriaro moved over to the impromptu mess tent for the morning. Quintus and Fullo came up last and began to eat with everyone.

"Today we will be looking for places to stay to get out of these tents while we wait for the leaders of Gosbecks to decide what they want to do about the mill and roads. Also today is market day and we can spread out and talk to the people about the benefits of Roman building in the area. It is a good opportunity to do some politicking. I also want to ask about the human sacrifice. I'll take the opportunity to do that today." Quintus said around his mouthfuls of millet as he shoveled it in.

---

[132] http://pass-the-garum.blogspot.com/2013/03/punic-wars-and-porridge-part-4-of-6.html   https://notjustdormice.wordpress.com/2015/05/06/millet-in-the-roman-diet/

"Understood, do you wish us to pair up again and make our rounds for information?" Bundarus said.

Quintus nodded: "Yes that would be good to do, but leave the question of places to stay to me to discuss with the leaders. We need to make it as palatable for them as possible to let us stay in their homes. It is a good non-intrusive way to introduce ourselves to the locals." They finished their morning meal and gathered up their items for the day. Once they were mounted up they left their fort and joined the streaming crowd into Gosbecks.

The crowd had increased as the time went on and it was surprising just how many vendors there were in the main gathering spot. All traces of the bonfire were gone and in its stead were food stalls and market carts up and down on four sides of the main esplanade near the tavern. The center grassy esplanade was transformed into sectioned off areas for livestock for sale or trade. The many farmers and drovers were friendly and discussed their wares and livestock with anyone. Vendors had set up their carts on the east, west, north, and south sides of the patchy dirt of the esplanade, sometimes setting up so close together it was hard to get in between the sellers carts. Despite the close quarters there was little bickering between the vendors, more good natured taunts between each other. There were enough people to get the market day started; the many members of Gosbecks intermingled with the farmers and sellers[133]. Quintus and Fullo went to the tavern first and left the others to pair up and make their way around the market.

"How are you this morning Oisin?" Quintus asked when they entered the tavern.

"Good market day to you Quintus and Fullo. I am fine thank you for asking. You'll be able to see how we in Gosbecks do commerce today." Always one to promote his village Oisin answered. He wiped his wet hands on his drab tartan.

---

[133] https://en.wikipedia.org/wiki/Gaelic_Ireland
http://www.british-history.ac.uk/vch/yorks/city-of-york/pp481-491

"I have another thing to ask you today. We Romans are a hardy bunch but I suspect the decision on the mill will take more time. Since that will be the case we would like to pair up our men and put them in homes here in Gosbecks. It is getting colder and wetter and it is very uncomfortable in our tents," Quintus looked at Oisin when he made the request.

Oisin scratched his head: "So you're looking at different places to billet out your soldiers here in Gosbecks, hmm ... let me think," he stopped to scratch his head as he thought, "You might need to talk with some of the leaders in Gosbecks to ask them first. There are a lot of homes that are missing members of the families because they were killed in the rebellion but I daresay they wouldn't want to share their homes with Romans, no offense meant. You are better off talking with someone like Cathmore or Ronan who are considered leaders here in Gosbecks. They would be the two to start with."

"My thanks for that bit of information. Do you think they'll be here for market day?"

"Most likely they'll both be here. Ronan and his wife Fingula have a cart where they sell woven textiles on market day. They usually set up on the north side toward the smithy where all the carts that have wearables are," Oisin said. He wiped his greasy forehead and ran his dirty hand back through his oily hair. He beamed, his weasel-like face creasing in a smile.

"Once again my thanks for the information Oisin," Quintus nodded and left with Fullo. They headed out and turned toward the smithy on the north side of the main esplanade. As they walked through Gosbecks they were hailed by some of the vendors looking to sell to rich Romans but Quintus just shook his head and continued on. They made it to the smithy and beside it where they found the cart displaying woven textiles. "Are you Ronan, one of the leaders here in Gosbecks?" Quintus asked the short, round, dark haired man behind the cart.

"Yes I am Ronan and some call me one of the leaders here in Gosbecks. How can I help you?" Ronan stepped forward, his petite, dark haired wife Fingula whom he introduced stepped forward to help as well. Their daughter Eilis just ducked her head and continued to arrange the scarves and tartans on the cart. The cart was a gaily painted affair, yellow with Green trim. The tartans and scarves were displayed in shelves and on some tables that the proprietors stood behind.

"We are looking for some places to billet my soldiers since winter is bearing down on us.. Is it possible to have someone agree to house two of my soldiers in their homes for a short period of time? We will be gone as soon as the decision is made to have a mill built or not? I will pay for the rooms." Quintus asked.

Ronan stroked his beard thinking: "How many houses will you need?"

"We would need three homes. I've already made arrangements for myself and Fullo here to stay with Bebhinn," Quintus said.

"You'll be staying with Bebhinn? That is far from Gosbecks, why don't you stay closer in?" Ronan looked at him quizzically.

"No, it is fine and with our horses is closer than it appears. I met Bebhinn's daughter Edana and the other girl Meadghbh during Samhain. They were kind enough to show me where Niamh's farm was located. Niamh took me into Gosbecks that night," Quintus said patiently.

"Oh, then alright if that is the case, we can take two of your soldiers, Cathmore can probably take two more but you'll need to ask him first. Our best piper Lorcan is a bachelor. He has a home on the east side of Gosbecks where a lot of the musicians stay. He could take the last two there. You'll need to let Lorcan know. He is the son of the tavern owner Oisin. When will you need the homes for your soldiers?" Ronan asked.

"If possible tonight would be the best. I can billet Bundarus and Rufus with you, let me find them and I'll introduce you to them. I can pay you a *dupondius*[134] per night for the duration of our stay.

---

[134] http://www.unrv.com/economy/roman-coin-denominations.php

The others will be distributed out to the right homes." Quintus smiled his thanks and turned to look at the wares hanging in the cart, seeing the woven textiles were well made and beautiful. "Your textiles are very beautiful, you must do good business."

"Our cloths are well thought of but there aren't a lot of people who can buy right now. Too many have lost their loved ones and there isn't that much money floating around," Ronan smiled sheepishly.

"If that is the case then I'll take this blue scarf hanging here, how much do I owe you?"

Ronan looked at his most expensive piece that Quintus was fingering. "I normally ask for two *quadrans* but for you I'll half the amount, only one *quadrans*."

"No I'll pay the two *quadrans,* it is a fine piece of textile, and you are offering to put up two of my soldiers in your home. Here you go. And for every day you need to keep the soldiers at your home I'll pay you one uncia." Quintus paid the money and retrieved the cloth from Ronan.

"Thank you, I'll make sure your soldiers are well seen to at my home," Ronan smiled. "You might find Cathmore at the drovers' pen. He has been talking about needing a milk cow for his farm. You'll find the drovers pen in the middle of the esplanade to the east side."

"You have my thanks, I'll be back later with Bundarus and Rufus to introduce you to them," Quintus said. Quintus and Fullo turned to leave and make their way to the drover's pen. The crowd was swelling with people from the surrounding areas coming in to do their weekly shopping. They saw some familiar faces but more were unfamiliar. When people caught site of their uniforms they gave the Romans a wide berth. They got to the drover's pen without delay but there was no Cathmore at the pen. "I am looking for Cathmore and I've been told he'll be coming here today. Was he here?" Quintus asked the drover manning the herd.

"Cathmore was here earlier looking at my dairy cows but left without making a deal. He did say he'll be back later today, I just don't know when," the drover said, eyeing their Roman uniforms uneasily.

"Alright, let him know Quintus Agricolanus would like to speak with him. I'll be over at the tavern," Quintus nodded his thanks and turned to go but stopped for a moment. "Would you happen to know where Lorcan is?"

"I saw him earlier over by the musicians cart on the south side of the esplanade near here on the east side, just over there," he pointed toward a little knot of young men around a cart not far from the end on the east side.

"Thank you, and please tell Cathmore if you see him again that I am looking for him," Quintus requested. He smiled his thanks. Fullo and Quintus turned to leave and made their way over to the musicians' cart. There were quite a few young musicians over at the cart but it didn't look like a lot of commerce was going on, just discussions on different tunes from what they heard.

"Good morning I'm looking for Lorcan, is he here or have you seen him?" Quintus asked the crowd of young musicians.

Iollan and Lorcan turned and said: "Good morn Quintus," they both said in unison. Lorcan said: "I am Lorcan. What brings you to the musician's cart today, looking to purchase a drum or pipe?"

"No, I am looking for you and would like to ask you a question. I understand you have a home here in Gosbecks that you share with some of your musician friends. It looks like we'll be here a little longer than anticipated, and as such I am looking for some homes to billet my men. I need homes to place them in two at a time here in Gosbecks. I would like to ask you to take two of my men. I am willing to pay you for the short time you will be billeting them. We are looking to get out of our cold tents and into something a little warmer," Quintus smiled at the admission hoping to sway Lorcan.

"Um … alright I'll be able to take two of your men at my house. How much do you think to pay for billeting the men?" Lorcan said always looking to benefit monetarily from those who wanted something from him.

"I can pay you a *dupondius* a day for as long as we stay in Gosbecks. We'll need to have them billeted tonight if that is possible. I'll billet Faber and Coriaro with you at your home. I can bring them by later to meet with you and get the directions to your home."

"Alright I'll meet you at the tavern for midday meal," Lorcan said happy to be fed.

"Good that will be fine," Fullo replied for them both, Quintus nodded. "Have you seen Cathmore this morning? We are looking for him as well."

"No, I haven't but he will be here today to this cart. He manages to keep abreast of the newer tunes from the surrounding areas. He is Gosbecks best tenor singer you know," Lorcan said. Quintus just nodded that he knew. They turned and saw Grex and Titus coming towards them from the esplanade, both carried goods for their midday meal later.

They hailed each other: "How is your market day? I see you already have food, you're not going to the tavern like everyone else?" Fullo asked.

"If we go to the tavern for midday meal we'll just save this for later," Grex held up the haunch of beef. "It will feed all of us tonight."

"I can see that but we are already making plans to have everyone to be billeted in different homes so keep that by you, if everything works out I'll have you and Titus bunking with Cathmore and his family. A beef haunch will help sway them to take you two in," Quintus said.

"Alright we'll do that. I saw Cathmore over at the drovers' pen just now. It looked like they were haggling over the price of a cow," Grex responded.

"Good, we might have all our business taken care of here then. Stay with us and I'll introduce you to Cathmore and his family if they are all here at market day. Is there anything else to let us know? Have you heard anything else about the *potential sacrifice* at Green Man's Clearing we saw the day after Samhain?" Quintus questioned.

Titus and Grex shook their heads, Titus said: "We've been mainly mingling with the people of Gosbecks this morning. There are a lot of other people from the surrounding areas, some from as far as Camulodenum that we ran into but there was nothing about Samhain. The people here are much more interested in their daily shopping than what happened the night before last."

Quintus nodded: "Then let's just keep today for politicking for the mill and roads." He turned toward the drovers' pen and saw Cathmore talking to the drover. Quintus motioned to the others to follow him over toward them and stopped a polite distance away from the two haggling over the price of the dairy cow. After a few more moments they seemed to come to an agreement and Cathmore turned to Quintus: "I hear you are looking for me?"

"Yes, I've been arranging additional billeting for my soldiers and have them all taken care of except for these two men. It appears the decision to be made by Gosbecks about the mill and additional roads will be taking longer than I anticipated. Until a decision can be made we will stay but my men are looking for a warmer place to stay other than our tents. I've made arrangements for everyone except for Titus and Grex." Here Quintus indicated the two men, "What I wanted to ask you is the chance to billet them with your family until the decision is made. We can pay you for the extra mouths to feed and for the hospitality of your home," Quintus said with dignity.

"You say you've made arrangements for the others to stay here in Gosbecks? Where are they billeted?" Cathmore asked curious to see where they would be housed.

"Faber and Coriaro will be billeted with Lorcan, Bundarus and Rufus will be staying with Ronan and his family, and Fullo and I will be staying with Bebhinn and her family," Quintus answered.

"You and Fullo are staying with Bebhinn? Isn't that far from Gosbecks to be billeted wouldn't you prefer something closer in?" Cathmore asked.

"I've already asked for her permission to stay out at their farm. With our horses it isn't that far from Gosbecks, they make the distance doable. Plus I do not think the time will be long to stay there with them," Quintus said.

Cathmore looked at Quintus with a speculative look: "I can take your two men here until we make a decision on the mill. When will they be coming to my farm, it is not that close to Gosbecks either."

Quintus nodded satisfied: "They can come tonight to stay with you at your farm. I can pay you a *dupondius* per day until the decision is made by all the leaders of Gosbecks regarding the mill. Speaking of the mill have you had your meetings yet and if not will they be scheduled soon?"

"We have not met yet but will be meeting tomorrow evening. Market day is one of the best ways for us to get our message out to the people of Gosbecks. You'll see the leaders talking with a lot of people from Gosbecks and the surrounding areas who would be interested in the mill." Cathmore said

"Thank you, Grex and Titus will go back to fort and pack up their belongings and be ready for you here at the end of today. They will even be bringing this haunch of beef for your evening meal," Quintus gestured to Grex who was holding the meat. Cathmore's face brightened at the thought of having beef tonight. It had been awhile since they had had that luxury.

"That should be fine, we'll meet up here before market day closes and we'll all go back to my farm. I could use the help of two mounted soldiers moving my new dairy cow and her calf to my farm." Cathmore smiled happy for the extra help and relieved at the extra income.

The men shook hands and turned to leave. Grex and Titus to go back to their fort and pack up their equipment and Fullo and Quintus to go find the others. They took a leisurely walk down the south side of the esplanade to find the rest of their *Contuberium*. They passed many busy carts with the wares out for sale, the most prominent being food stuffs such as specialty cuts of meat from pigs and cows or the cheeses, clotted cream,butter and milk which was consumed in great quantities by the Celts and specialty carts like the honey trader. The food vendors called out their wares with earnest cries to get the attention of customers who sauntered up and down the esplanade perusing the carts. There were several specialty carts that had honey or preserved fruits and nuts lay out invitingly but did not have the attention of the people like the cheeses, creams, milk and butter carts did.

In the distance they spied Faber and Coriaro talking with the butcher Dahy and Muirne at their cart and made their way over to them. Once they got there they overheard Faber ask: "So you do not know where Meadghbh is? She lives in this village, where is her home?"

Dahy shook his head: "She is not at her home right now; she has left to visit a friend of hers and is staying at their farm for now."

"Do you know which farm she's at? Faber pressed.

"Not off the top of my head. Muirne do you know?" Dahy turned to his wife and asked. Muirne just shrugged her shoulders and turned to a new customer. "Guess you'll just have to wait and see her later then." Dahy then turned to Quintus and Fullo: "Good to see you two again, can I help you with some meat?"

"Yes I think some fine beef would be best. Fullo and I will be staying with Bebhinn for the time being and would like to bring some good cuts for her for dinner tonight but I have some business with these two," Quintus indicated Faber and Coriaro. "Just put the meat in a package and Fullo will pay for it." He turned to the two men and gestured for them to follow. After they had walked away from the bustling butchers cart he turned to the two: "I've made arrangements for you two to stay with Lorcan at his home. We'll go meet him for midday meal at the tavern."

"Do you wish to go now since it is almost midday?" Fullo asked at his side holding a haunch of beef on his shoulder. "We also need to find Bundarus and Rufus to let them know where we've made arrangements for them to stay."

"We just saw Bundarus and Rufus over at a cart selling knives and swords on the north side of the esplanade. You should know the cart was doing brisk business. Do you want us to show you where?" Coriaro said.

"Yes let's all go over to the cart and find them," Quintus said. They turned and started walking over to the cart on the north east side of the esplanade quickly coming upon the cart. Sure enough the cart had a lot of Celts surrounding it listening to the discussion between Bundarus and the seller.

"But your swords are too long to wield with any accuracy," they heard Bundarus' deep voice say to the seller.

"This is the length they've always been. The sword is good for slashing in a wide swing, good for chopping your adversaries arm or head or even taking their shields in one good swipe[135]," the seller rejoined, sounding annoyed.

Bundarus stood and shook his head: "But you'll have to have the space to wield the sword, in close quarters you lose the advantage when you fight."

The cart owner looked livid. "Is this from personal experience?" the seller said looking increasingly angry, his face flushing with blood.

"Yes, we went head to head with a lot of Celts during the fight at the Isle of Mona and at Boudicca's rebellion. The Roman way was much more efficient to fight the large number of Celts coming at us. Our method of fighting in close formation ultimately won the day against the overwhelming number of Celts."

"Are you saying we Celts couldn't fight?" a man in the crowd said loudly.

---

[135] http://deadliestwarrior.wikia.com/wiki/Long_Sword_(Celt) http://myarmoury.com/nateb_swor_mrl_celt.html

Rufus put his hand on Bundarus' shoulder to caution him but Bundarus shrugged him off. "No but I'm simply explaining what happened. We stayed in formation and fought as we normally do, behind our shields and with our shorter swords, our gladius[136]. As a unit working together." Bundarus patiently said not realizing the crowd of men around him were listening in as well and building in anger, they were fuming.

"So now you're saying that we Celts can't fight in battle as well as the Romans?" the seller said in a raised voice. More voices rose in agreement supporting his side in the altercation.

"No I'm just pointing out what we saw at the rebellion and before when we had skirmishes with Celts," Bundarus tried to reply reasonably still not realizing the anger of the crowd. The air around them was rife with danger, mutterings could be heard.

A red headed Celt moved forward into the argument: "You're saying we Celts don't know how to fight? That we just wave our swords around but ineffectually," he yelled his face red in response.

Bundarus looked at him patiently and said: "That is not what I meant at all, I'm just pointing out the ineffective way to fight with the long sword as opposed to the better Roman tactics."

"You ARE saying we Celts don't know how to fight! That the Romans are SUPERIOR to us!" the red headed Celt spat, spittle flying from his lips as he yelled.

"You tell him Kearney!" Yelled a tall Celt named Fintan.

"Yes you are right, the Roman way of fighting is superior to the Celtic way of fighting," Bundarus said reasonably, moving his hands in a placating manner to calm red headed Kearney down.

Hearing the discussion Quintus said under his breath to the others: "This will not end well. We need to diffuse the situation

---

[136] https://images.search.yahoo.com/yhs/search?p=Roman+Gladius+ Sword&hspart=att&hsimp=yhs-att_001 https://www.amazon.com/s?ie= UTF8&page=1&rh=i%3Aaps%2Ck%3Aroman%20swords

as quickly as possible. Come with me and back me up," Quintus pushed to the front of this crowd.

"Oh so now your men are coming to your rescue?" a man in the back of the crowd said loudly as Quintus and the others brushed by him to move to the front. Heads turned in unison as Quintus, Fullo, Titus, Grex, Faber, and Coriaro made their way towards Bundarus and Rufus thru the crowd.

Quintus got up to Bundarus and took him aside and said in Latin: "What the fuck are you doing inciting a mob? Now is not the time to discuss the rebellion. Look around you; the men here are upset at what you are saying. We are greatly outnumbered!"

Bundarus guiltily looked around at everyone, seeming surprised at the number of people in the crowd looking at him furiously and muttering and pointing at him. "I was discussing the Celtic sword with the seller. It is vastly ill prepared for close quarter fighting."

"Perhaps but now is not the time to discuss this you shit for brains! You are supposed to be passively mingling not starting another rebellion," Quintus ground out. He turned to the crowd and in Celtic said: "Peace good people, my soldier did not mean to imply your swords are not good for battle. He was just explaining, but not very well," a quick look of derision in Bundarus' direction, "what happened in the rebellion. We want to work together with the good people of Gosbecks. We wish to move forward past the problems from before."

"Are you saying that your soldier was not speaking for Rome?" a familiar voice said from the back. Miach came into view and moved forward, the crowd parted and let him as he stepped forward, he moved forward in a stately manner walking with his long staff, his long gray robes flowing around him.

"He was speaking his own opinion, not ours," Quintus turned toward Miach to answer him.

"Was he also elucidating why we lost to you Romans?" Miach said quietly. The crowd became deathly still as they were interested in the answer. The surrounding faces watched Quintus with interest.

"There are many reasons why you did not win the rebellion," Quintus said.

Tense silence met this remark from Quintus, many faces glancing at Miach for his response. Miach' looked coldly at the Romans for a few moments before he asked: "What is *your opinion* then."

"I believe we fought as Romans do, as a cohesive unit which allowed us to win," said Quintus keeping his eyes on Miach face.

"And we Celts fought as individuals?" Miach pressed.

"It is just a different fighting style from the Romans. Our general chose a good tactical area to fight in, with the Romans on the high ground and the Celts coming at us in the bowl shape of the meadow rimmed with forest and boulders. They were naturally squeezed together which limited their ability to wield their swords effectively. The crush of their numbers further impeded them. The forward momentum of the troops from the back pressed them forward into our formation, then our cavalry swept in from the right and finished off the remaining Celts." Quintus explained as succinctly as he would not embellish on any aspect.

The murmurs in the crowd lessened with this explanation, then someone said: "He's right, I was there that is what happened." Murmurs between the men seemed to accept his account despite the negative light it shone on the Celts rebellion.

"That's not what happened; we were butchered by the Romans. There was nothing that we Celts did wrong! We fought valiantly! The Romans placed a bloody curse on us!" the red headed Kearney yelled.

"Peace Kearney. Let us discuss this some more without hurling insults at the Romans," Miach said quietly, giving Kearney a look that brooked no dissention. Kearney huffed but stayed quiet, his face betraying his anger at being chastised in front of everyone, embarrassed he looked away. Several of the men around him patted him on the back and murmured.

Murtagh a big dark haired Celt standing next to Kearney patted him on the arm as said: "It's alright, I agree with what you're saying. We lost to the Roman scum through evil forces."

Miach turned to Quintus then nodded to him: "Your explanation makes sense even though it is not palatable to us and all the members who lost their family members to the battle. I just question the glib way your soldier is lecturing us on our weapons that we have used since our grandfathers time."

The crowd murmured in agreement. "Yah, I have my grandfather's sword and it is still as sharp as ever," one man yelled.

"I apologize for his insensitivity. He is only a soldier at heart and thinks in terms of his experiences but not of anything else. I will punish him for this incident and hopefully we will all move on,"

Quintus grabbed Bundarus' arm and hauled him off to the back of the crowd which let them go without incident. In the back was heard the last catcalls: "We're not sure we want your mill Roman and this is *the true opinion of us Celts.*"

Another yelled out. "We don't want your roads either!"

Quintus just grimaced and continued to move on. Faber, Coriaro, Rufus, Fullo, Titus, Grex, and Bundarus just kept their heads down and walked on. From the back a small boy threw a rock at Bundarus which hit him in the back. Bundarus just kept going forward as if he didn't feel the rock hit him. They made their way to the tavern in grim silence relieved that the crowd did not follow them. Quintus trying to understand how bull headed Bundarus had acted but knowing his personality type it didn't surprise him. He decided to give Bundarus the most onerous job in the fort to do as punishment by himself. The burying of all the waste from the midden and the men's latrines. The hard cold ground will make the job that much more difficult and the smelly garbage and sewage would be its own punishment.

Once at the tavern Quintus hailed Oisin and ordered wine and the midday meal for all his men. Oisin saluted and ran to do his bidding. Quintus turned to Faber and Coriaro: "We will be meeting up with Lorcan to introduce you since he is billeting you two in his home. Please do not have a repeat of this day with the almost mob riot incited by Bundarus' stupidity. Remember we will be living here at least for a couple more weeks until the people of Gosbecks make their decision on the mill and roads. Although I think this little incident will turn them against the mill at least."

"Understood sir," the men said in unison.

"As for you Bundarus your punishment will be to bury all the waste from the last few days at the camp site. You will be doing it alone, no one is to help you, and you will do it by the end of today. Before you start I need to introduce you and Rufus to Ronan and his family. They have agreed to billet you two. No more discussions on the Celtic rebellion or Roman superiority will pass your lips while we are in Gosbecks. Keep your mouth shut!" Quintus shook his head at the close call they just had on the esplanade with the crowd. "Now has anyone gotten any information about the sacrifice in the Green Man clearing?"

Faber nodded: "Dahy said it looked like the dancing caused Declan to have a fit and die." Coriaro also nodded in agreement.

"Anyone else? That seems an altogether too convenient explanation for me," Quintus commented. Everyone just shook their heads.

Presently Lorcan came in to the tavern and made his way over to their table: "I see you're already here and I am able to take your men to my home now. I'm free for the rest of the afternoon and can show the men around Gosbecks as well."

"Why don't you have midday meal with us here first? I've already ordered the meal for us. Plus the men will need to pack up their gear from the camp site. That leaves you a little time to get to know these two men who will be bunking with you for a few days," Quintus said smiling at Lorcan.

"All right, thanks for the invitation, I think I will have midday meal with you," Lorcan looked relieved at not having to pay for lunch. They discussed what Lorcan could teach Faber and Coriaro about Gosbecks. They settled on having him give them a tour of all the most important places and people.

Presently Oisin and Grania came in with the midday meal and their wine. Once they've all been served everyone sat down to eat. Quintus turned to Fullo and said: "When we finish here we'll take Bundarus and Rufus to introduce them to Ronan and Fingula so they'll have all the information for their new billet. Then we need to get back to fort and pack up so we can get back to Bebhinn's farm. Good thing we picked up some beef from Dahy's cart to make it easier for them to billet us."

"Yes that was good thinking on your part, " Fullo replied.

"Yes let's plan on getting packed up and going to Bebhinn's farm quickly," Quintus said around his meal and thinking about the enchanting Edana.

While they were talking Niamh and her family came in the door of the tavern and started ordering their midday meal from Oisin. Niamh caught Quintus' eye and walked over to him: "Good day Quintus, I see you have all your men with you, have you been enjoying a fine market day?"

"Yes Niamh we have and we'll be neighbors soon. Fullo and I will be staying with Bebhinn. The rest of my soldiers will be billeted out to several of the fine people of Gosbecks," Quintus smiled.

"Why are you moving in with Bebhinn and other soldiers in Gosbecks?" Niamh asked looking skeptical.

"Staying in the tents is getting harder to take as the cold weather moves in. We'll only be in these billets until the leaders give us the decision on the mill and roads then we'll be leaving to take your answers to the governor," Quintus answered.

"Ah, so when we give you the answer you'll leave and take the information back to your general? We should be getting you the answer for building the mill and roads as soon as possible, it has just been too quick for the slower life at Gosbecks, between Samhain and now," Niamh nodded as if that responded to all of his questions.

Quintus smiled again, realizing that Niamh liked to be in

charge of any situation, even if she had little control over them. "You are probably right Niamh. We just need to slow ourselves down a bit while we are here in Gosbecks. Speaking of Samhain, did you attend the ceremony that took place at the Green Man Clearing?"

Niamh's eyebrows rose up in surprise at the question and the fact he knew the name of the clearing: "We did attend the ceremony. What do you know about it and why do you ask?"

"I'm asking because we found a burned skeleton of someone on the bonfire there. Do you know who it was and what happened?" Quintus looked at her.

Niamh looked at Quintus closely and nodded: "I do know who it was; it was Gosbecks only smith Declan that died because he had a fit during the Samhain ceremony. We had a sanctified bonfire that we placed his body on because it was already there. It was a way to cleanse the body and offer it up to the gods. The death was very sudden and we are sad because he was a cherished member of Gosbecks."

"Thank you Niamh that is exactly the information we needed. I was very surprised to see the body remains there on the smoldering remnants of the bonfire. What happened to his head though? It was missing," Quintus asked.

"We take the head and perform a purification ceremony; the skull will therefore be relegated to the people of Gosbecks to be celebrated," Niamh relayed. She looked at him and said: "I'll answer any questions you might have regarding what happened at Samhain. It must be a confusing celebration for you Romans." She smiled and looked superior.

Quintus smiled. "Yes it is confusing but I'm sure our own Roman religious ceremonies seem just as confusing to you. Thank you for your explanation and I will take you up on asking questions about Gosbecks because you are one of the most approachable leaders that Gosbecks has."

Niamh smiled and said: "Ask me anything, if I don't know the answer I'll find it for you." She waved and moved back to her family. They all turned to the Romans and waved a polite hand. The youngest daughter Nola blew a cheeky kiss. The Romans shook their heads in amazement that they would be the recipient of such a bold action from a young lady and in the presence of her mother and grandparents, shameful.

"We have a lot to learn about the residents of Gosbecks," said Titus as he smiled and waved back at Nola.

"Just remember we'll be coming back in the spring to live, don't make any bad first impressions now," Fullo rejoined as he waved to Nola as well.

"If we're done with the flirting then we can discuss the living arrangements with everyone. Fullo and I will be billeting with Bebhinn on the outskirts of Gosbecks to the west. Should you need to get to the farm take the lane heading due west, at the fork at the end of Gosbecks take the left hand lane and follow the road up to the farm. It is about a *mille passuum* and *stadium* from Gosbecks, you'll come to the farm without turning off the lane, it is a meandering lane but you won't have to turn off. It should take you no longer than half a day to get there on foot, less on horseback at a good trot. Now Bundarus and Rufus will be billeted with Ronan and his family. I need to take you to meet them after we eat Bundarus and Rufus. You'll still need to clean up the forts trash." Quintus looked at Bundarus with a jaundiced eye, "No more out bursts about the incompatibility of Celtic warfare versus Roman might." Bundarus just nodded shamefacedly and continued eating.

Rufus said: "I'll be there to make sure he does not make any more unwise comments."

"Good, next I have Grex and Titus staying with Cathmore and his family. They are also on a farm to the west of Gosbecks and you'll have to let us know exactly where it is when we regroup again. When we get back to our fort get packed up and plan to meet with Cathmore and his family then. I'll take you over to them." Grex and Titus both nodded their heads.

"Last but not least we have Coriaro and Faber staying in Gosbecks at Lorcan's home," Quintus indicated to Lorcan to stand up and address the meeting.

Lorcan stood up and waved to everyone. "I'll take you to my home after we get you packed up from the campsite. My house is located at the beginning of Gosbecks on the east side, right next to the smithy, not far from where the bonfire was held. Ask anyone in Gosbecks and they'll be happy to point it out to you. I usually have a parade of musicians traipsing through the door at all hours of the day and night." He stopped and looked at Faber and Coriaro, "I think it will be great having you two in residence with me. My home is roomy and there is plenty of space for you."

"Thank you Lorcan I'm sure Faber and Coriaro will be quite comfortable with you. We'll need to regroup at the beginning of each day and we'll meet here at the tavern for our morning assembly. We should also meet at the end of day for the evening meal just until a routine gets set. I don't know how long it will take for the good people of Gosbecks to make a decision on the mill but we'll stay until they do. Remember to be good guests in your billets. We'll pitch in to help where you see the need to. It will help the members of the families that we are staying with. I know after talking with Bebhinn's daughter Edana there are quite a few things I'll be starting on for them at their farm. I imagine Grex and Titus you will have the same thing happen at Cathmore's farm. Cathmore has lost the use of his left arm. I'm sure he'll have a lot of chores for you to do. Let's be good guests and pitch in as much as we can. I expect all of us will be busy helping our host families however we can," Quintus smiled at his *Contuberium.* "Anyone have questions?"

Bundarus rumbled: "How do we get a hold of anyone it there is an emergency?"

"When we regroup in the morning we'll give each other the locations of our billets, where and how to get into contact with you. If in the case of an emergency we'll send a message via fast canter to me then to the other members of our *Contuberium*. Once we've gotten everyone's location we'll be able to better coordinate the logistics. If we find that Cathmore's farm is closer to me than it should make sense that they will contact me or Fullo first. If we find that Bundarus and Rufus are on the east side then they will need to coordinate with Faber and Coriaro first and then send me notice as soon as possible. Do what makes sense. I just don't want to get notice of another mob Bundarus," Quintus looked at Bundarus with a stern face. "We will never have a situation like that again, am I clear?"

"Clear as a stream of icy water in the alps," Bundarus said.

"What if we find the billeting family has problems with us? What do we do then?" Titus asked.

"Let me be understood on this, I don't want any of the billeting families to have a problem with any of us. We are their guests and as such treat them as an honored host. If they should they ask you to plow a field in the middle of a snow storm then do it with a smile on your face. If they should ask you to paint their interior walls with Celtic designs, just ask them to show you how and then do it with a smile on your face. Should they ask you to help them weave their textiles so they can sell them at market day, do it without saying you don't know how, and then plaster a smile on your face. Should Lorcan ask for help playing a pipe or drum, tell him you'll do your best to play the pipe or drum. Play a good marching tune with a smile on your face. We will be the best guests Gosbecks has ever seen," Quintus finished vehemently.

The men nodded and said: "Yes sir."

"Alright men we are done, let us get our gear packed up and move to our new billets. Bundarus and Rufus, you will follow me to meet Ronan, Fingula and their daughter Eilis. They have a cart selling textiles for clothing, I picked up this one," Quintus pulled out the blue plaid scarf that he had bought earlier. The men all expressed surprise and interest at the fine craftsmanship of the scarf. The scarf was passed down the table and marveled at for its fine quality, the men were surprised to find something so well wrought in Gosbecks. "So like I said you might be asked to help them do something with their cart if we are here next market day. Finish performing your punishment Bundarus and I'll take you both over to them."

"Yes sir," Bundarus was embarrassed enough to look chagrined, the repeated admonishments finally getting through to him.

"Then men let's get going and packed up. I'll pay Oisin so get going now." Quintus finished the meeting. The men stood and made their way to their horses which were next door at the Gosbecks livery. Quintus paid Oisin and let him know that they would all be back in the morning. He made arrangements to have a standing tab at the tavern.

Quintus left to join the men back at fort to pack up and finish getting his gear all stashed back on Boreas. He was impatiently tossing his head and stamping the ground in excitement for the upcoming trip. The men quickly got their gear and tied it together for their departure with the practiced ease of a well-oiled machine, used breaking down forts and moving on per their orders. Bundarus wordlessly went about his punishment of burying all the forts debris and offal. Attacking the frozen ground with renewed vigor, as if he wanted to bury his embarrassment at the whole affair with the forts detritus. The ground suffered under his onslaught of shoveling as he relentlessly widened and deepened the hole until he had it big and deep enough per Roman regulations. He dumped the trash and offal into the hole and then covered it up with dirt.

"I thought you'd break your shovel or at least pull a muscle you were so intent on getting the job done," laughed Titus. Rufus who had helped Bundarus by packing up his gear laughed too. They both stood and watched as he finished up with the final pats to the freshly turned earth. "There, I think that is done per the regulation." They turned to get on their mounts and moved to meet up with Quintus as he got on his excited mount. The group of Romans all went off to meet up with their perspective billeting families.

At the tavern Faber and Coriaro met up with Lorcan. Cathmore and his family were at the tavern as well so Grex and Titus were able to meet up with them. Bundarus and Rufus followed Quintus and Fullo over to Ronan's cart on the green. Market day was winding down and a lot of the owners of the carts were breaking them down and repacking them. When they met up with Ronan they saw that the family was in the process of breaking down theirs as well.

"How was market day? Profitable I hope," Quintus greeted Ronan.

Ronan nodded his small dark head. "It was reasonably profitable; I was able to sell several yards of textiles today, none of the expensive stuff though."

"I'm glad it was profitable today. As we spoke earlier here are the two soldiers that will be staying with you, Bundarus and Rufus," Quintus indicated the men as they sat their horses. "Do you need any assistance in breaking down your cart? These soldiers are more than capable of helping you out."

"No I think we've got most of what we need to do. We'll be leaving shortly for our farm on the south side of Gosbecks," Ronan said as he finished pulling up some stakes that had been propping up the front of his cart. Fingula and Eilis were already finishing folding up the textiles and were storing them away in drawers that were built into the cart itself. Eilis looked up and let out a strangled squeak at the soldiers. She was very intimidated by their size and stern demeanors. Fingula reached over and patted her arm measuredly, trying to impart support for her shy daughter. Eilis looked away quickly and kept her eyes locked on the plaid tartan she was folding. She kept her face averted from the Roman soldiers as she redoubled her efforts to fold up the textiles and pack them away into the clever drawers built into the cart at the bottom. Rufus saw what she was doing and smiled: "Looks like we intimidate our host family already Bundarus, we'll need to change that." Bundarus nodded and got off his mount passing the reins to Rufus. "Here let me assist you in folding away the textiles and scarfs for you." He bent over Eilis and took up some of the textiles and folded them. He took infinite care to do it the way Eilis was folding hers, rolling them with the textile showing on outside. Eilis looked up at him in surprise but smiled when she saw him exquisitely folding the scarf. She was surprised that such a big man would take the time to fold the textiles with such care. She gave him a hesitant smile.

Seeing things progressing well Quintus said: "I will leave you to finishing up packing your cart. We have a long journey to get to Bebhinn's farm before dark. Bundarus and Rufus are at your disposal so if you need anything done don't hesitate to ask them for help." He saluted Fingula and Eilis. Signaling to Fullo he took their leave riding off at a good clip towards the west and Bebhinn's farm.

"Do you think Bundarus will behave himself?" Fullo asked as they got out of earshot of Ronan's cart.

Quintus shrugged. "I hope so. I was amazed to see him help Eilis fold the scarves so carefully. It's a good sign he took the time to watch how cautiously Eilis folded the wares and he repeated it. It was funny seeing him use those big hands of his to carefully fold the scarf."

"I thought that was funny too, his big beefy hand tenderly folding that scrap of textile so lovingly. Maybe he'll find a new craft to make money at. Wouldn't it be funny to see him spinning wool and making those textiles with Fingula and Eilis?" Fullo laughed at the picture he wrought from his words.

Quintus barked out laughter at that mind picture too. " Could you have imagined he'd find such a dainty craft to do than that? Who knows maybe he'll find a talent for it. And make us look bad for making a lot of money at it."

"The next thing you know is he'll become a good cook, he'll be able to run his own tavern. Heck Gosbecks only has one tavern it could easily support one more." Laughed Fullo.

Quintus laughed too. "With more soldiers moving to Gosbecks maybe he will do that. I'd be a regular customer then at his tavern."

"He'll name it 'The Testudo'," Fullo guffawed, "Or even 'The Saw Movement'."

Quintus laughed at the names although he could see the potential of a new business proposition. There was something to it to think about. "At the rate this is going maybe I'll open one."

"No I got dibs on the tavern, it was my idea anyway," Fullo said sobering up as he too saw the benefit, he also thought of the benefit for running his own brothel as a side business, a never ending supply of women began to form in his mind making him smile, they all were dark headed and tall with womanly curves like Meadghbh. At that thought he was surprised and stopped his ruminations, it bothered him to think of Meadghbh being passed around to soldiers for a quick tussle on the pallet for money, a never ending succession of them. He would much prefer if he was the only man in her life and no one else. The thought was so surprising to him he was quiet for the rest of the ride to Bebhinn's farm.

On Quintus' side he was ruminating about the possible human sacrifice. The explanations they had gotten from Dahy and Niamh were too easily fabricated. They didn't sit well with Quintus' suspicious nature. He thought about the story told to him when he was in Gaul about the Celts performing human sacrifices to their gods. One included a large wicker basket where the multiple victims were caged inside and immolated in a bonfire. It was never clear if the victims were willing or prisoners of war. One place had a basket with five bodies burned in it. That was reported by Caesar to the Roman senate so it must be true. He wanted to know the truth. Was the body found in Green Man's clearing a victim of a human sacrifice? The setting sun cast long shadows, a chill wind started to blow matching Quintus' chilly thoughts.

As they rode up to the farm dusk was descending in quick fashion. darkening the surroundings like a smoky curtain being drawn around the world. The deepening shadows amongst the trees as they passed the main gate of the courtyard showed the main paddock getting darker as they rode up to the farm. Outside they saw

Ailbe herding the chickens and ducks into the coop. He was intent on his work as a recalcitrant duck kept trying to escape around him and go out to the courtyard.

"Keep up the good work Ailbe, the duck will eventually understand that darkness means hunting foxes, hawks and owls," Fullo said to him as they dismounted from their horses. Ailbe looked up and grinned as he kept herding the duck toward the coop. Eventually he was able to close the gate once the duck had rushed into the coop, startled by the Roman horses' arrival.

"Did you have a good Market Day?" he asked.

Fullo nodded. "We had a very good market day and came home with a haunch of beef for dinner tonight, could you take it into you mother while we unload our gear and turn the horses out to the pasture?" Fullo handed the haunch to Ailbe to take into the house. It was almost too big for the boy to carry but he managed to heft it over his shoulder and carry it on his back. The Romans laughed at his discomfort. "Well done Ailbe, you've got it and will be able to take it inside now." Ailbe tottered under the heavy slab of beef and moved unsteadily toward the entry way, almost dropping it several times.

"Why don't you help him Fullo, it looks like he'll hurt himself," Quintus said as he was unloading his gear from the fort.

"Yes, but I wanted him to try and he's doing a great job already," Fullo said but he followed Ailbe's unsteady gait to the front door of the farmhouse. Quintus continued to unload his horse, Boreas stood quietly while he finished. Once all the gear was off the horse Quintus continued to talk softly and started to untack and rub him down. Soon he was let loose in the paddock with the goats to trot off and forage for dinner. Quintus smiled at his lively gelding, as he lovingly watched the horse find a patch of grass to eat with gusto. Fullo had come out and was finishing unloading his horse. He then untacked his horse and rubbed him down as well. When he'd turned out his horse they both walked over to the farmhouse.

Inside they hailed everyone and walked over to Bebhinn to

greet her formally: "Good tidings Bebhinn how was your day?" Quintus courteously asked her.

"It was productive thank you. And thank you for the beef haunch, we'll have that for dinner tomorrow," She indicated the beef hanging over the center fire pit slowly smoking. "We're having goose tonight, from the hunt yesterday. Ailbe has been clamoring for goose ever since this morning."

"Good, a fine goose will be much appreciated," Fullo said good-naturedly. "I was impressed with Ailbe's strength. He was able to bring the big beef haunch inside without my help."

"Well done Ailbe, well done," Quintus also said, Ailbe grinned and preened under the compliments. "Bebhinn and Edana you'll be glad to know that Eilis' family will be hosting another two of our soldiers at their home. Bundarus and Rufus will be lodging with them starting tonight. Also Cathmore and his family will be hosting Grex and Titus. Faber and Coriaro will be staying with Lorcan at his home in Gosbecks. So now we all have farms and homes to billet us. No more cold tents, thank you very much."

"I'm glad that Gosbecks was able to help you out. We are a hospitable village. I don't think it will take long for the leaders to give you an answer about building a mill. Once they make a decision they will abide by it," Edana said.

"I'm happy to hear it. In the meantime while Fullo and I are here you might want to put us to work. You mentioned several things that are needed. Like your chicken and duck coop since you've seen foxes in the area. You mentioned it needs to be repaired. Or maybe preparing some of the fallow fields for planting come spring. We are at your disposal."

Bebhinn nodded and Edana said: "We would greatly appreciate the help, the chicken and duck coop will be the first to work on. There are some loose boards on the south side that would be a quick entry for those sly foxes. Next maybe the goat shed, it needs a new roof because the old one is falling apart from last winters' heavy snows. That should get you started."

Quintus smiled and nodded. "Then tomorrow we'll start on the chicken and duck coop. The first thing in the morning we need to go to our early morning meeting so we'll be leaving before first meal. We should get the chicken and duck coop taken care of tomorrow though. Between Fullo and me we'll get the coop fox proofed."

"Where will we be sleeping tonight? We have gear to stow away for our area," Fullo asked as they began to move into the farmhouse.

Bebhinn motioned to the left side of the farmhouse, by the area with the rabbit mittens and skins. "You can stay in this area."

"Fine, we'll get our gear stowed away before dinner," Quintus said as he moved back outside to get their gear. They toted it in and laid their sleeping pallets side by side. Quintus was interested to find just where Edana slept tonight; he hoped it was fairly close to their bedding so he could look at her, maybe even converse in quiet tones. He hoped so.

Dinner was a quiet affair, the goose was excellent complete with roasted turnips, peas, and winter cabbage to top off the entire meal. Quintus was impressed with the subtle herbs used to flavor the meal, much better than the plain soldier fare he'd been used to up until now. Ailbe kept up a lively conversation with the soldiers a he regaled them with his childish exploits on the farm. "I'm beginning to teach our hound Cabhan to keep the foxes from our chickens and ducks. He is doing well but he keeps mistaking the ducks for foxes and gets after them. I need to catch a fox to show him the difference." Ailbe petted his large tricolored hound's head lovingly. Cabhan thumped his tail in thanks then returned his attention to a bone he was chewing on.

Fullo laughed. "All it would take is to show him the entrance to the chicken coop that the foxes have been trying to get in. He'll get it. Scent is the best training you can show him. Tomorrow we'll find a good fox trail and get him excited about hunting those foxes. His nature will take over from there."

"That would be great, thanks!" Enthused Ailbe and he hugged Cabhan's head. The tricolored dog again thumped his tail in thanks.

"Soon our young hound will hit his stride as a good farm hound," Edana smiled and looked at Cabhan lovingly. She had done the most in training the young dog for their farm since Carrick and Ardan left for the rebellion. She was proud at how well he was doing even though he was young. He had a good guarding instinct. Cabhan's sire was Ardan's dog and he passed away shortly after the rebellion. Edana thought it was the sadness of losing his master. They were inseparable and Edana hoped Cabhan would be that close with Ailbe. They seemed to be getting that close now. A good training exercise will seal that bond.

"I think that would be wonderful to do, Ailbe needs to see how good training will be for Cabhan's work on the farm. Ailbe you should make sure to pay attention to Fullo when he trains Cabhan. Ask questions if you don't understand what is going on," Edana said. She turned to Fullo. "Thank you for offering to do this with Ailbe."

"He reminds me of my younger brother Drusus. Drusus and I got into all sorts of trouble growing up when I was at home. One of the things involved our family guard dog Cerberus and our neighbors' scrawny tomcat. I'll tell you the story tomorrow Ailbe, it's not one your sister would like to hear," Fullo laughed.

"Oh now you have to tell the story Fullo," Meadghbh said smiling as she got into the conversation. She and Edana were finished clearing the dishes from dinner and cleaning up the remains.

"Oh so I'll tell everyone what Drusus and I did with our dog Cerberus and the cat. We had a yowling, scrawny tomcat that lived next to us and kept us awake night after night doing his tomcat duties to the ladies in the area. After a seriously annoying night Drusus and I made a plan to get rid of the cat by egging on Cerberus to maul him. Cerberus didn't like cats anyway so it was easy to get him to go after that scrawny tomcat." Fullo said in an aside to Ailbe, "So the next night after he started yowling we set Cerberus on the cat. He went after the tom like an imp out of Hades, snarling and lunging. What we didn't know was the tomcat was a survivor of other run-ins with dogs. Cerberus lunged at the cat and causing the cat to leap and land on Cerberus' head, the cat then proceeded to scratch the devil out of his right eye. Cerberus twisted and dropped the cat and took off yelping like a crybaby. He was badly scratched and lost his right eye from that fight. After that he was worthless if it came to cats, he always gave them a wide berth, always thinking of the scrawny tomcat thereafter. What a baby and he was an older dog too. He should have known better," Fullo laughed. Ailbe, Edana and Meadghbh all laughed with him.

"Why didn't you want to tell us the story?" Meadghbh asked.

"Because you would think I was cruel to go after the scrawny tomcat but we got so tired of hearing the damn thing yowl at night, *every* night, *every single night,*" Fullo explained rolling his eyes in vexation.

"I would get mad too," said Ailbe "Our tomcat doesn't do that, he just chases mice and rats like a good cat. Plus he's very sweet; Edana is always petting him and giving him extra goat milk."

"Well no wonder he is a good tomcat, I'd get the mice too for extra goats milk," Fullo winked at Edana. She laughed and ducked her head. She went back to working on the rabbit fur mittens like Bebhinn. Quintus looked over at them as he was polishing his gladius, his short sword and pilum, his long spear. Ailbe came over to look at the gladius and fingered his pilum. Quintus looked at him and said: "Don't touch my pilum unless you want to learn how to use one."

Ailbe quickly moved his hand away from the spear and asked: "Why is it so long and heavy? Don't you throw them at the enemy?"

"You do but it is designed be heavy and to bend at the iron shank so the enemy cannot turn around and throw back at me. It is also used to jab at the enemy when we are in an iron turtle formation, or testudo as it is called," Quintus told him.

"But wouldn't that cause it to bend at the shank too?" Ailbe asked.

"Sometimes but you need more force to bend it badly, like when you throw it at the enemy, that will bend the shank and make it unusable to the enemy."

"Did you use it during the rebellion in the iron turtle formation?" asked Edana from her position by the mittens a little to the left of Quintus. He turned and nodded at her, not willing to go into further explanations of the rebellion since her father and brother were killed by the Romans.

"Was it as terrible as we heard? Was it true that Boudicca had a massive army and the Romans had a little one but still they won the battle?" Edana asked her face tense and she worried her lip waiting on his answer.

Quintus stopped polishing his gladius and turned to look her full in the face, his own pensive as he weighed his response: "It was terrible, for both sides. Yes Boudicca had 100,000 members of the tribes in her army. It was massive, terrible to see and hear as they were all yelling out their war cries. But what she didn't take into consideration was the Roman warfare tactics. The general and our governor, Gaius Suetonius Paulinus, chose his spot carefully to engage the Celts to his advantage. It was in a bowl shaped depression giving the Romans the advantage of the high ground and he funneled the Celts into this bowl just as he wanted where he wanted them to go. Once they came, and they came in masses all at once, he let them get as close as possible then ordered the infantry to attack in tight formation. To the side was the Roman cavalry that waited until signaled and came in to finish the job. This was something the Celts didn't expect because they were used to coming in mass at the enemy, leaving little space between the fighting men. The Romans didn't give them that opportunity. We were able to defeat them by this one simple tactic, fight in close quarters, kept our shields up and jabbed with our shorter gladius and pila. We were a devastating unit to the Celts."

"Just like that you managed to kill us off with your Roman military tactics? I don't understand how the small Roman army beat the vastly bigger Celtic one." Edana threw up her arms in disbelief.

Quintus shook his head, at a loss to explain military tactics to a woman but he tried: "It was all about *where* the battle was fought and how the general set up his troops. He made sure to place the Romans in an advantageous place *before* the battle was fought. The Celts had the disadvantage of being forced to come at us through a bottleneck caused by the terrain. There was a natural break in trees and boulders at the top of the meadow and around the edge and the Roman general took advantage of it. The Celts didn't take that into their tactics they just came at us in a large mass, not with any generalship shown. Whoever was in charge in the Celtic army did them a disservice."

Edana, Bebhinn and Meadghbh were all silent and looked at the Romans in disbelief that he could explain the battle so succinctly and without emotion. All of them wanted to cry, to yell out that it had to have been so much more to the battle than the cut and dry explanation of Quintus. But because they had no experience with battle they held their tongues, just looked at him with haunted eyes. "So it really was just the terrain and the general's decision to hold the battle in that field that made the difference," Bebhinn said in a hollow voice, sadness in her eyes as if she might start crying at any moment. The thought of losing based solely on location was not in her realm of understanding. There was logic in the argument but it still made it hard to accept.

"Yes, most battles are won or lost on where the battle is fought. In this instance it definitely put the Celts in a vastly detrimental location," Quintus said quietly, his serious face sad for their loss.

Bebhinn nodded and went back to her work wordlessly, what more was there to say? But Edana wasn't done she asked: "So if Boudicca had chosen a different field to fight things might have gone differently?"

"Possibly, if she had held back her army and chosen a different spot there might have been a very different outcome," Quintus allowed. He didn't talk about the different fighting styles that were also the problem with the Celts when they engaged the Romans.

He'd had enough of that from earlier today. He just wanted to let the room clear of the bad state of mind for the Romans. Let them get to know each other first before he let them know how truly outclassed the Celts were when it came to their battle tactics. The loose confederation of tribes caused them to not fight as a single unified army, as a single unit, but as individuals fighting one on one. That was the Celts' downfall."

"But the Celts still fought bravely and savagely, right?" Edana asked, grasping at any reason to celebrate the Celts.

Quintus nodded and said: "Of course they did, I've been in battles before and that one was fought savagely, it lasted far longer than it normally would have. I know because I was there until the very end."

Edana looked at him with tears in her eyes. "So how many Celts did you slay in the battle?"

"I don't know. I don't keep count in battles, the action takes place so fast that there is no time to keep a running count going," he rubbed his face looking tired, tired of the conversation and the direction it was taking.

"What are you taking about tens of Celts, twenty, or hundreds? Is it so hard to keep a tally of the ones you slay?" Edana asked, her tears streaming down her face. Meadghbh and Bebhinn were looking at him in consternation now, each with a stricken look on their faces.

Quintus shook his head and looked out of sorts. "I told you I don't keep a tally of the people I kill in battle. No soldier does. If you did it would slowly be eating your soul bit by bit by keeping a tally of all the ones you kill in battle. Even the officers don't do that. The general would be closer to Hades if he kept a tab of all the deaths he was responsible for."

"So General Gaius Suetonius Paulinus is responsible for the deaths of 100,000 of my kinsmen, he should go to your Hades! He is already damned!" and Edana got up and ran from the room, wiping her tears as she ran out the doorway.

"Edana wait, don't cry," Quintus got up to follow her, unsure at how she had reacted to his discussion of the battle and what he should do when he caught up with her. Quintus followed her out into the courtyard where she had stopped, bent over and crying in a heap as if she was feeling all the hurt of the 100,000 dead Celts. He hesitated, not sure what to do, and then continued to her feeling grief for her sadness. A soul crushing sadness. This was a new feeling, having never thought about the deaths he caused as a reason to feel something about. He crouched down next to Edana, and tentatively put out a hand to smooth her beautiful blond hair back from her tear-stained face. Edana, not wanting him to touch her, knocked his hand away.

"Go away you murderer! I don't want you here at the farm anymore, you've done enough to us you Roman bastard! Get off my farm and return to Gosbecks!" she cried harder at that, grief pouring out of her as if she was feeling the slashes of all his pitiless gladius jabs.

At a loss for what to say Quintus just stood up and stood there over her. He wanted to do something but didn't know what. He wanted to caress her hair, touch her face and dry her tears that were coming out in earnest now, along with long gulping sobs. "Please don't cry. I am sorry you lost, so sorry. Please be calm and stop crying."

"GO AWAY! LEAVE AND NEVER COME BACK!" Edana yelled, then quieter "Forget you even know me and my family," she sobbed more quietly now that her storm of grief was abating, she slowed to quiet sobs, small hiccups and swiped her hand over her nose.

Unable to stop himself Quintus crouched down and gathered her into his arms. She fought him, slapping away his arms and hands but after so much grief she was exhausted and stopped, unable to prevent him from encircling her in his arms. He stood with her in his arms and held her close, cradling her in his arms as he used his voice to sooth her, like he soothed Boreas after he'd shied. He murmured in deep crooning noises with nonsense words in lilting Latin, melodic syllables that soothed her despite her not understanding what he was saying. If she had known she would have been even more upset because he was telling her: "My beautiful Edana, please don't cry, you are breaking my heart with your tears. If only I had known you'd be so hurt I would never have had this conversation with you. I'd tear out my heart instead." Slowly she began to calm down. Just like Boreas when he had shied and got frightened by a flickering light caught out from the side of his eyes. She calmed down.

Quintus pulled back and turned her face to him, he looked at her tear streaked face, so beautiful even after the crying, her eyes still leaking tears. He carefully put his hand up to her cheek and with his thumb wiped her tears, softly. She looked at him with surprise but also liked the tender way he was treating her. She tilted her head into his hand and looked up into his kind brown eyes and concentrated on his beautiful full lips. "Do you know Cathmore knows of someone who saw you kill my father?"

"No, I didn't know I killed your father." But after he said that and looking at her beautiful hair he remembered the pair of blond Celts that attacked him before the rebellion. He looked closely at her face and realized that it was, in fact, that Celt that was her father and the younger Celt had to have been her brother. More reasons for her to hate him. He knew he couldn't make it up to her or her family but he'd try. "I'm so sorry, please forgive me," he said as he looked into her lovely gray eyes and willed her to believe him. Then without thinking he leaned in and quickly kissed her. Tentatively at first then when he met no resistance he deepened the kiss. His tongue opening her mouth with a groan, she whimpered and opened her mouth in surprise. Their tongues met tentatively at first, then with more eagerness they met and clashed. Going at each other deeper the more they kissed, feeling each other, deeper with the glory they felt at the entwining of their tongues, deeper and faster. Each of them losing their thoughts as they continued, just seeking more, just feeling.

Finally Edana stopped the kiss and came up panting; looking at Quintus with a somber look that was surprised at the ardor they felt. They looked at each other for a moment, not wanting to break the spell by speaking, just looking at each other with surprised wonderment, their hearts beating fast in concert.

Behind them Bebhinn and Meadghbh witnessed the kiss, both looked stricken at the kiss and obvious enjoyment of both participants. They looked at each other in surprise and by mutual agreement sidled back into the farmhouse. They guiltily sat down and resumed their chores. Both Ailbe and Fullo were looking at Quintus' sword and spear, discussing the finer points of both. Fullo seemed to be perfectly at home speaking with the young Ailbe, very patient with him as well. Both looked up at Bebhinn and Meadghbh as they came in.

"They are discussing their previous conversation and will be a few moments before they are done," Bebhinn said quietly, avoiding eye contact as she went back to working on their rabbit mittens. Meadghbh just nodded and went over to Bebhinn and picked up a stretched rabbit skin to work the leather and begin to make more mittens like Bebhinn. They continued to work wordlessly. Ailbe and Fullo went back to their discussion.

Outside Quintus looked at Edana, his breathing getting back to normal. "I want more. I want to join with you."

"What? I don't understand what you mean, *join with you?*" Edana breathlessly said, looking at Quintus with wide eyes.

"I want to come together as a man and woman does, I want to touch you all over, to kiss you all over, taste all of you." Quintus breathed

"Oh! I … I don't know … I've never done that before," Edana whispered fearfully, looking deeply in Quintus' eyes hoping he understood what she meant.

Joy sprouted in Quintus' heart, he'd be the first for her and she'd never experienced sex with any other man. "I will be slow and kind. I'll treat you as you should be treated. I'll make you feel the things you always wanted when we join."

"I … I … I don't know, I need to think about this first, we'll be here together for a while at the farm, let me think this through. I still need to reason through the fact that you've killed my father and brother. You are part of the Romans who destroyed the Celtic army. I'll need time to think this all through," Edana moaned.

"And I want to join with you, tomorrow. Fullo will take Ailbe and Meadghbh to hunt the foxes. Bebhinn can go with them too. We'll be alone to explore each other, to be with each other." He breathed, his lips inching closer to her mouth as he watched her red puffy lips.

"I don't know, you are still a Roman, one that killed my people," she gasped.

"I'll give you time, just think about it tonight. I will make you happy when I join with you," Quintus breathed fast, looking at her face and swollen lips, wanting to kiss her some more but knowing he needed to wait. He let her go reluctantly, his arms dropping to his sides, wanting to keep holding her so his hands clasped reflexively. They separated and looked at each other, he with repressed desire and she with that unknown want that she still felt. They sheepishly smiled and turned to go back inside, walking awkwardly back to the farmhouse. Once inside they separated, she to go back to work on the rabbit mittens, he to finish polishing his weapons. They both smiled to themselves. "Tomorrow," Quintus mumbled to himself.

Fullo spoke to Ailbe. "Would you like to learn how to fight with a gladius and pilum?"

Ailbe's face brightened. "Can I?' He eagerly asked. "Now that my father's gone as is my brother I have no one to teach me to use a sword. Plus your sword is so different. So much smaller than our long swords which I can't even pick up let alone wield it."

Fullo laughed. "Yah. I can imagine you would have a problem not being able to wield a Celtic long sword. I imagine you Celts start a little later in your martial training than we Romans do."

"How early do you start training your boys?" Meadghbh asked. She had been listening in as she worked on the rabbit mittens.

"We start when they are about five summers old. The games they play prepare them for fighting. There is one that involves a stick. The two combatants try to knock the stick out of the others hand." Fullo told them looking excited. "I spent many a day doing that particular game with my brother. And I was pretty good at it too. Maybe Ailbe and I can do it tomorrow."

Bebhinn stepped into the conversation. "I would prefer for him to not learn to use your weapons and your games. There is plenty of things for him to do around here."

Ailbe cried out at the indignity of having his mother step in and forbid him this fun. "But Mother why? I want to learn! There's no one else to teach me."

"There's Cathmore to teach you. He's already set aside his sword for you." Bebhinn patiently explained.

"But that's a long sword. Not the Roman gladius. I want to learn how to fight with the Roman gladius and Roman pilum." Ailbe whined.

"That is all you need to know about, a good Celtic long sword." Bebhinn asserted. She was getting a tension headache from the discussion and what she saw outside. She hated Quintus. The man killed her husband and oldest son Carrick. She couldn't bear to have him take Edana from her now. She was also very angry with herself for agreeing to house the Romans. They were more dangerous with their talk. She'd have to be careful with Ailbe, explain to him he needed to be careful around the Romans. She did not want them to know he was a special child with ability to read the future in his dreams. That was his gift from the gods. She wanted to keep it that way.

回回回回

"That should give us plenty of time for our early morning meeting." Fullo allowed. "I like it. Perhaps Cabhan will find one and kill it. Then we'll be done with the foxes. Maybe even get a pelt out of it. Fox pelts are very nice."

"Then it's a plan. We'll do it tomorrow. There is plenty of food left over from our meal and then there is the garden outside that still has vegetables we need to pick. Bebhinn, I'll help you do this tomorrow." Meadghbh said. Bebhinn nodded her agreement. Meadghbh looked forward to spending more time with Fullo. He was very easy to be around. Very entertaining. She liked how he treated Ailbe, with patience and showing interest in what the young man had to say. It showed he was kind hearted. She liked that.

"Sounds like a plan then." Fullo said as he looked at Quintus. Quintus nodded his assent.

"I'm looking forward to it." Quintus said and he looked at Edana. She blushed even more. Tonight, he mouthed and pointed to his pallet. Edana looked at him with a mixture of fear and longing. She nodded again.. Bebhinn got up to go to bed. "Come on Ailbe it is time to get ready for bed. Tomorrow will come early enough." She collected Ailbe. They went over to his pallet. Ailbe started to pull off his clothes and lay down on his pallet with just his tunic on. Quintus grimaced. He was uncomfortable with their lack of cleanliness. Ailbe was still dirty from the day and needed to wash. At the very least he needed to wash his face and hands. His feet were another thing. They were just about as dirty as could be imagined. He needed a good bath. Quintus watched as Bebhinn went to the kitchen and got a bowl filled with water. She washed her face and hands. Then lifted her tunic to wash her underarms, bottom and feet. Edana and Meadghbh came over and did the same. Each wanted to stay behind the hearth to shield themselves from Fullo and Quintus' gazes. Once they had finished they all returned to their pallets. Each divested of their tartans and slept in their daily tunics.

Fullo turned to Quintus and murmured in Latin. "At least they washed."

Quintus grunted. "They all need to take a true bath. Getting their entire bodies dunked in water and washing their hair. They need to visit a Roman bath house."

"I do too. I can't wait until we get the colonia built. It will include a proper Roman bath house." Fullo muttered.

"Yes it will. I cannot wait for it. But for now it is just cold water and a bowl to wash out of." He groaned and got up. He went over to the hearth and picked up the bowl. He went outside to throw the water out, went over to the stream and refilled it. He came back inside and set the bowl down between their pallets. Both men stripped down to nothing. They grabbed their soaps and started lathering their bodies. In the shadows Edana and Meadghbh were watching the men wash. They were amazed at the thoroughness of how the men were washing their bodies. Paying close attention to the men's private parts the girls held their breaths. Soon each man finished and then they took turns rinsing off. When they were done they got out fresh tunics to sleep in and laid down on their pallets.

"Do you think we gave them something to see?" Fullo chuckled to Quintus under his breath.

"I hope so. I plan on staying here with Edana and not going with you to fox hunt. I want to join with her tonight. She is so beautiful I cannot wait any longer. So get to sleep fast," Quintus said and smiled.

"Already? You work faster than I do. But I'll just get to bed Meadghbh later." Fullo chortled.

"You do that. We'll both be better off." Quintus said and turned over to go to sleep. Outside the wind picked up and blew a gale. Tomorrow would prove to be stormy.

Later that night when everyone was asleep Edana snuck out of her pallet and tremblingly snuck over to Quintus' pallet. Quintus lifted his blanket inviting her into his bed. Before she lost her confidence Edana dove under the covers only to feel a naked Quintus. She jerked and gasped as her hand accidentally grasped his cock. He quickly covered her mouth and simultaneously covered her hand grasping his manhood. "Calm, my Edana. Just feel how much I want you." He took her grasping hand and moved it up and down the shaft.

"Your cock is so hard but the skin is soft," Edana whispered wonderingly "Is it always this way?"

"Yes, it is always that way when I want to couple. Normally it isn't hard but soft. When men want to lay with a woman it gets hard like this," explained Quintus patiently. "You see men put their cocks inside women's vaginas so it must be hard. That's how you can tell a man is aroused and wants to couple."

Edana took the opportunity to run her hand up and down his penis in fascination, exploring the hard length in the dark by touch. "It is so long and wide. Will it fit in me?"

"Yes, you will take it and be pleasured by it. Let's get you out of your tunic." Quintus pulled the tunic up, getting it over her hips and up further to her breasts. When he got to her breasts he stopped, bent his head and took one of her nipples into his mouth and started to suck. Edana's face was covered with the tunic and was caught by surprise. "Oh!" she gasped as he continued to apply harder sucking. Edana pulled the tunic over her head and threw it to the floor. She arched her back to push her breast further into Quintus' mouth. He responded by opening his mouth wider to pull more of her nipple and the surrounding areola into it. He sucked harder.

Then Quintus moved his face down her body kissing her belly, moving lower to her love garden. Edana was shocked and tried to pull him up back to her breasts but Quintus had another idea. He successfully got his head where he wanted it, right in front of her womanhood. He licked his lips then licked hers. Edana gasped at this intimate intrusion. Quintus licked up to her clitoris and then licked it in circles, She felt an immediate wave of gratification but with an underlying feeling of urgency, a feeling of something greater to come. He then affixed his lips to her clitoris and licked rapidly, causing Edana to fall over that cliff to mind blowing ecstasy.

Quintus moved back up to her head which he grabbed her face. "Now you are ready to couple, follow me." He settled his hips in between her legs. She felt the hard blunt tip of his manhood at her entrance. Quintus pushed it forward into her depths slowly. "One bit of pain then you are a woman." With that cryptic warning he surged forward and breeched her maidenhood. Edana whimpered at the abruptness of the action and at the pain. Quintus stayed motionless, letting her get used to the feel of his penis despite it being hell to not move in her hot, tight depths. He started to kiss her mouth, deep, passionate kisses to get her mind off the pain. She returned his kisses with growing enthusiasm. Quintus then started to move, long slow strokes. When Edana met his strokes with her own hip thrusts. He began to thrust faster and she met his thrusts. His urgency met hers and they both moved until she met her completion. Then he followed her down to fulfillment.

They panted to catch their breath. "Did you enjoy your first time, my Edana?" he breathed.

"Oh yes!"

CHAPTER 12
THE MILL

Quintus and Fullo took off to the tavern before first light in the late autumn morning. The wind was bracing and heading out of the north into their backs as they headed into Gosbecks at a trot on their horses. Fullo's gelding Janus[137] danced sideways as the bare branches of hawthorn creaked and rubbed together causing him to shy and bolt to the side. Fullo pulled back on the reins to get him under control. "It is as cold as the river Styx[138] and my Janus sees imps everywhere," Fullo said as he got his gelding under control.

"At least you're warming up together, Boreas is still half asleep this morning," Quintus rumbled as he expertly got Boreas to catch up with Janus, a feat that was no small thing since Boreas was very spirited and would take off at even a small nudge of his heels. "I'm interested to see if Faber and Coriaro have any more information on Kearney and his group of friends. I'm also interested in the decision the people of Gosbecks will make regarding the mill and

---

[137] https://www.britannica.com/topic/Janus-Roman-god
[138] http://www.theoi.com/Khthonios/PotamosStyx.html

roads. We should start to get information on that shortly and I'm hoping it would be in the affirmative. Weren't their leaders going to have a meeting shortly after market day to determine if they want it or not?"

"Yes that sounds correct from what Cathmore was saying. Maybe we'll be able to get more information on that from Grex and Titus," Fullo said as he slowed Janus down to a steady trot. They continued on in silence until they got to Gosbecks, the town was just waking up but there was all of the *Contubernium* were waiting for them at the tavern. They came in and got their meal order into Oisin.

Oisin pulled Quintus aside to tell him: "There will be a big meeting here at the tavern today regarding the mill. Cathmore let me know yesterday. Word went out to all those who attended market day about the mill and we would regroup here at the tavern after midday meal. One item to note is the surrounding populous has been showing enthusiasm for the mill. You might want to stay and go to the meeting after midday meal."

"That is good news, and I will attend the meeting today, we need to get the people of Gosbecks on board with building the mill. Camulodunum is doing quite well with their mills and there is no reason Gosbecks will be just like them," Quintus said enthusiastically. "I'll give the good news to the others."

Quintus turned and went to the table where his *Contubernium* was sitting and told them: "Oisin has just let me know that Gosbecks will be having a meeting regarding the mill. It will be here at the tavern after midday meal. I intend to be present at this meeting and I want all of you to be present as well. I don't anticipate any hard questions but it would be best if we are a united front of Romans here in Gosbecks. After this meeting you can return to your farms to let the sponsors know we will be busy most of this day with this meeting. I imagine Cathmore and Ronan will both be attending but I don't know about Lorcan or Bebhinn. We'll just let them know that we will be spending the majority of the day in Gosbecks and to conduct their day normally. Now do you have anything to add to the meeting. What say you? "

"Nothing to add from last night's meeting, the musicians were quiet, only Iollan and the other drummer Glendon dropped by to discuss more music with Lorcan. No interference from Kearney and his group," Coriaro said around his mouthful of food.

"Good, maybe they'll be so busy with the mid-winter festival that we won't have to worry about Kearney and his group," Quintus said still worried about this pool of fomenting young men.

"Cathmore also talked about this meeting as well. He'll be coming into Gosbecks in time for the meeting with his wife Meara. He also said that it should be a large gathering because there were a lot of people who voiced their positive opinion," Grex said smiling.

Bundarus sat up and said: "Ronan also said essentially the same thing. It seems the farmers around Gosbecks are excited about the prospect of having their own mill. The ones that have business in Camulodunum couldn't say enough good things about their mills. We might see a groundswell of those in favor to build a mill here in Gosbecks."

"This is good news indeed. Then maybe what we need to do is call this meeting over so everyone can go back to their billets and return in time for midday meal here at the tavern," Quintus said with alacrity. Everyone finished their meal quickly and left to go back to their prospective places of billets.

"That was a nice short meeting and we'll surprise Bebhinn when we return so early to the farm," Fullo said as he maneuvered Janus onto the path towards Bebhinn's farm. The gelding seemed to know the way and moved smartly at a fast trot. Boreas rode alongside his stable mate at the same quick ground eating clip. Quintus had to fight to keep him from charging ahead into a full blown canter.

"Yes it was the right length of meeting since we'll need our wits about us this afternoon," Quintus grinned and kept Boreas at a fast trot. Before they knew it they returned back to Bebhinn's farm in time to see Edana and Meadghbh lead the goats into the upper pasture.

Ailbe was doing his chore of feeding the chickens and ducks in the coop by spreading wheat on the ground. He looked up to see the men come in: "That was a fast meeting in Gosbecks. We didn't expect you until shortly before midday."

"Well now you know we won't be here for the midday meal because we will be going back into Gosbecks for another meeting. That was why we cut short our meeting this morning," Quintus laughed.

"It seems all we do in Gosbecks is meet," Fullo chuckled as well

Bebhinn came out of the farmhouse upon hearing the Romans return, she stood in the entryway and asked: "You'll be gone for midday meal? What is this next meeting about?" she asked.

"It is for the mill, the leaders and members of Gosbecks have all determined that today is the day to make the decision either for or against the mill," Quintus told her as he dismounted from Boreas and turned to look at her. "I am hoping for them to approve the mill, it would be best for the farmers and people of Gosbecks."

"It is for the members of Gosbecks to decide, not you Romans who come into communities and change the situation to better fit your view of the world as primarily Roman. You discount what the locals want," Bebhinn said quietly for the first time putting into words her true feelings about the Romans. Fullo and Quintus looked at her in surprise but also resignation.

"I'm sorry you believe that but you are wrong. Getting a mill for Gosbecks and the surrounding area will be the best. It will take the burden away and allow the farmers and peoples to grind their own wheat," Quintus told her. "Are you going to the meeting?"

Bebhinn nodded her head "I will attend the meeting as soon as I tell Edana and Meadghbh what needs to be done today. I'll get on the road as soon as possible."

"We can give you a ride into town with us. It will be much shorter than you having to walk all the way," Fullo offered.

"I will walk, it will give me time to mull over my decision more," Bebhinn said. Not admitting that she wanted to catch up with Cathmore on the trail to discuss the decision with him, plus it would look to the others in Gosbecks that she had already thrown in with the Romans since she had them staying with her.

"I understand, we'll get going after we get the horses turned out for a little while. The rest in your pasture is much appreciated," Quintus relayed. He turned to the horses and started to untack Boreas. Fullo did the same with Janus and soon both horses were turned out into the pasture. The two Romans stood and then looked at Ailbe. "What do you have planned for this day young Ailbe," Fullo asked.

"I'm going to finish my chores with the chickens and ducks then I'll take Cabhan to go look for the foxes. We'll hunt them together now that he has their scent," Ailbe told him, puffing out his chest as he did so. He clapped his hand on Cabhan's head to pet him, Cabhan thumped his tail obligingly.

"Watch that he doesn't lose their trail. Stay close to him and follow his lead, encourage him as he is casting about for their scents," Fullo offered advice since he would not be there to guide Ailbe. Ailbe grinned and nodded, Cabhan just thumped his tail as Ailbe petted him.

Presently Edana and Meadghbh returned from the upper pasture, each moving faster once they saw the Romans standing by the chicken and duck coop. When they got up to the coop Edana asked: "We weren't expecting you until shortly before midday meal, why are you already here?" She smoothed her hair behind her ear as she waited for Quintus to answer.

Quintus said: "Good morn but alas there will be another meeting in Gosbecks about the mill decision shortly after midday meal, we are going to that meeting and will be leaving here shortly. We just wanted you to know so you can plan out your day accordingly. We'll be back before the end of day meal." Quintus smiled as she squirmed and looked up at him with a slight smile, wanting to touch him. She met his gaze and her eyes crinkled in happiness, her lips turned up in a smile. He wanted to touch her but also saw that now was not the appropriate time to grab and kiss her which is what he wanted to do. They'd have to wait until they were alone to do what they wanted.

Fullo smiled and said: "We'll be leaving but if you get all of your duties done by the time we get back there will be more time to do something together, something for amusement like learning to play draughts. Could you get everything done so we'll have time? You'll need to since Bebhinn has duties to give you." He looked at the girls and anticipated them saying yes which is what they did in unison when he looked at them. Meadghbh looked at him with the dewy eyed look of the entranced, one who wants more but doesn't know exactly what. Fullo smiled and nodded at her as if to say "I understand and will get you what you want later."

The men stepped back as Bebhinn came forward and rolled out her list of things to do mainly centering on finishing up the late autumn vegetables in the garden like collecting the peas, turnips, and cabbages then picking some of her medicinal plants for elixirs and unguents to be made later when the days got darker and they were stuck inside. The directions were quite extensive and it looked like it would take the girls all day to finish. When she was done she smiled at them and looked for their agreements to the duties she laid out for them. Both nodded and went into the farmhouse with her to get the baskets needed and more instructions from her. They needed instructions particularly on clipping the right feverfew, coltsfoot, vervain and comfrey sprigs for the elixirs she needed since this was the most important. Bebhinn would go out with them later to harvest willow bark for teas to alleviate pains. Both girls understood she was entrusting them to very important duties and would finish them. Bebhinn said to them: "Good, now I'll be leaving for the meeting in Gosbecks about the mill, I'll be back before the end of day meal so go ahead and get prepared for getting Ailbe fed for midday meal. He will be off trying to find foxes so he'll be hungry when he gets back. Be prepared." She nodded to both of them and got her satchel and left the farmhouse.

"Why is she walking, couldn't Fullo or Quintus give her a ride into Gosbecks?" Meadghbh asked.

"Knowing mother she would probably prefer to walk and not ride with the Romans. She might want to catch up with someone on the way to the meeting, maybe Cathmore or Niamh. She is more likely to talk to them," Edana told her. Meadghbh gathered the extra basket and small hanging satchel for the medicinal herbs. She made sure she had her knife well sharpened for taking the snippets from the plants. She nodded and looked at Edana as Edana gathered her basket and hanging satchel. en they were both ready they left together for the large garden hauling their baskets. "Mother left us with a lot of duties to do so let's get going." Both of them looked at each other and broke into giggles.

Outside the Romans were still talking with Ailbe near the chicken and duck coop. They seemed to be waiting on Edana and Meadghbh. and when they came out of the farmhouse they let Ailbe go on his fox hunt. Ailbe ran off with Cabhan jumping joyfully at his feet. Quintus turned to Edana and said: "Now both Bebhinn and Ailbe are gone off on their own, we have enough time to stay with you for a while before we need to leave. I want to kiss you once more. Let us go back into the farmhouse out of the cold." He held out his hand to her and she took it. They walked back to the farmhouse and disappeared inside.

Fullo stayed with Meadghbh and watched them leave. "We'll stay here and I wish to kiss you as well, it is a pretty morning but a little windy so let's walk over to the wall of the coop to block the wind. I want to kiss you as well but I'm not sure we have enough time to do what I want to do, I would prefer not to be hurried since you and I have not been together yet."

"All right, I'm not sure what you mean exactly but I'll follow your lead," Meadghbh said vibrantly not really understanding what Fullo meant. Fullo grinned and took her hand, he then lead her around the edge of the chicken and duck coop. Once there Fullo pulled her to him and with his other hand softly traced her jaw and lips with his thumb. He bent his head and pressed his lips to hers, lightly at first then with more urgency. Meadghbh just stood there in the weak late autumn morning sun and tilted her head to the side, giving him more access to her mouth. He took advantage and moved his mouth over hers with more fervor opening her lips to push his tongue inside. They stood there, entwining their tongues as they delicately explored the other's mouth. Softly with no sense of urgency but only with discovery they delved. Fullo ended the kiss and stopped to look at Meadghbh as she opened her eyes. "That is how we should always kiss, simply and with no urgency. Just the two of us enjoying the taste of the other and finishing the kiss together."

"All right," Meadghbh breathed into his face, her lips so close to his and smiled. He kissed her one more time and stopped. They stood looking at each other.

Inside the farmhouse Quintus and Edana fell to each other quickly as soon as they got out of eyesight, he moved her closer inside and took her to his pallet where he turned to her and grabbed her hips. He turned her towards him and bent his head, seeking her lips quickly, unerringly finding them and capturing them in a kiss. Soft at first then with more intensity as they continued to seek each other, he found her soft ones under his onslaught of lips and tongue. Edana moaned and opened her mouth to his, opening it to allow him greater access to her mouth. Quintus groaned and took it, delving his tongue into her mouth deeper with a little more urgency, but backed off as soon as she moaned. He loved the way she tasted but felt but he didn't have the luxury of time to spend with her. He knew not to continue and moved his mouth to spread soft kisses around her lips and nose. He moved his hands over her face and throat, circling it with care and soft hands. He placed his hands on her hips.

"We can't do more than kiss, we do not have time to continue as I want but we'll revisit this moment again," Quintus breathed into her mouth as he rained down small kisses on her lips and nose. "We'll take our time later and finish this."

"All right," Edana murmured into his mouth, "I have a lot of chores to finish and you have your meeting to attend." They smiled at each other and stopped kissing. Edana leaned down to grab her basket and satchel that she had flung down in her haste to kiss Quintus. Once she had both they moved to the entryway of the farmhouse and out into the blustery autumn morning. "I look forward to this evening then, whether it is to play draughts or else." Edana gave Quintus a sidelong look and moved off into the morning light. He laughed and followed her. They spied Meadghbh and Fullo standing next to the chicken and duck coop standing and talking. Quintus took her hand and walked over to the two.

"We need to leave so let's go get the horses and return to Gosbecks," Quintus said to Fullo. Fullo nodded his head and turned to Meadghbh who smiled and motioned for him to go ahead and get the horse.

Edana said to Meadghbh: "We better get moving on the chores mother assigned to us. It should take us all day to complete if we start now."

"Let's get going then," Meadghbh responded and she hefted her basket on her hip, the satchel already on her other shoulder. The girls moved off to the garden with purpose, both keeping an eye on the Romans as they collected their horses. "Did you get your kiss like Quintus said he'd give you one?"

"Of course but we didn't do anything else even though we were by his pallet. He kept saying he didn't have time and said we'd have to finish later," Edana told her.

"Funny that is what Fullo told me after he kissed me again. I love it when he kisses me. I can't wait to see what else he'll do when we have time. We'll probably need a whole afternoon to finish according to Fullo," Meadghbh said longingly.

"Yes you will need a whole afternoon for that. You need to

experience the wonder that coupling can be. I can't wait until we couple again," Edana purred and smiled. The girls then giggled and went off to the garden to begin the chores set to them by her mother to pull more of the winter vegetables.

The men gathered their horses and took them to the courtyard to tack up. They expertly got their saddles and bridles on the horses despite the way the horses danced around in the courtyard not wanting to be put back into their tack, that short period of freedom was too little for them. Once mounted the men took off at a good ground eating trot back to Gosbecks. On the way they ran into Bebhinn and Cathmore with his wife Meara who were deep in conversation with each other. The men passed with a greeting: "We'll see you in Gosbecks for the meeting," and waved.

Cathmore said to Bebhinn: "How is it having those two at the farm?"

"They are easy and yesterday Quintus fixed out chicken and duck coop, next they'll work on fixing the goat shed, maybe even enlarging it so I may get a milk cow next. I know Edana is getting them to do other chores for us such as fix some of the fences that have gotten into disrepair," Bebhinn shrugged as if it wasn't that big of a problem to have the Romans at her farm.

"I have the two Romans staying at my farm doing some of the same type of chores around my farm. They will be plowing under some of my fields that I didn't get to during reaping time. I am looking forward to them getting this heavy work out of the way and done before the Roman tax assessors come. Even though we got little done this fall we can make it look more profitable," Cathmore said, "Plus since I've gotten the milk cow we've been able to do more work around the farm. A little milk in the morning does you well for the whole day."

"I've got the goats so I know what you're talking about. The goats' milk is better for young ones that aren't thriving on their mother's milk but I'm beginning to prefer it over cows' milk now," Bebhinn told them as they walked. "Now tell me about the mill what is the vote going to be?"

"Surprisingly there is more of the people that are looking forward to a mill than I thought. They know about the mills in Camulodunum and the surrounding areas, they see how it makes sense to have a large mill do the grinding for the surrounding farmers. However they do not know the cost of the mills and how the Roman moneylenders that make it burdensome to run the mills without tacking on a high surcharge on the cost. For every bag of wheat milled the millers are taking a tenth of the next one. So for every ten bags you grind the miller keeps a bag. That doesn't sound too bad but when you don't have that much wheat to be ground it takes rather toll," Cathmore told her.

"Are you going to explain that to these smaller farmers?"

"We'll try, but the idea of Gosbecks getting its own mill might be too attractive to the farmers. They won't see the true cost until the mill is built and the grain ground. Then when they see the cost they'll remember it was explained to them before the mill was built," Cathmore said.

"What does Miach say?" Bebhinn wanted to know.

"He has much the same mind as I do, he wants the people to know about the cost of building the mill but he also knows that the people will want one. I don't precisely know what he'll do, he is a closed lipped when it is needed you know," Cathmore conveyed.

Bebhinn nodded she knew how Miach would turn when the wind blew him in the right direction. She trusted his decisions though. She'd seen him get desperate people having arguments agree through intense arbitrations when none could be found before. "Let's hope Miach can see the light in this dark night. We'll need his wisdom in this meeting."

"Let's hope and the gods be willing," Bebhinn replied. They walked for a while then came up to the forks that lead to Niamh's farm. They saw ahead of them Niamh, Drust, Ealga and Aibhlinn. "I'd like to get what Niamh's decision is as well." Bebhinn hurried to catch up with them and hailed: "Niamh, Drust, Ealga and Aibhlinn wait up for us!" The ones in front stopped and turned around to see them. Niamh turned and waved to them as they hurried to catch up.

"It's good to see you this morning, we just saw the two Romans who are staying with you come pass us as we got to the road. We knew you wouldn't be far behind them. Are you ready for the meeting? How do you stand on the decision of the mill?" Niamh said as they caught up with them.

"We are not for it because of the cost. The Romans will find a way to get the money out of us one way or another whether by the taxes or the cost by the miller that levies on each unsuspecting farmer," Cathmore said to Niamh. Bebhinn nodded to show she agreed with Cathmore.

"The cost is the most important, whether it is the cost of the building or the person who is assigned to run the mill the Romans will get their money back. I think a mill is needed for Gosbecks. It will free us up on time spent grinding our own wheat and if we can get it done all at once it would be a major time saver. I think it will also depend on the terms of the grinding. Some of the mills in Camulodunum only charge one twentieth per load so only one bag out of twenty will go to the miller. I don't think that is a bad amount to charge a farmer," Niamh relayed as she walked along on the path.

"What do think Drust?" Cathmore asked.

Drust cleared his throat and hawked a bit of sputum then said "I think we should let the Romans build a mill and we'll get the business here in Gosbecks like we should. We should get the business that Camulodunum gets."

"And Ealga what do you think?"

"I think we should keep the Romans out of Gosbecks. We need to leave Gosbecks for the residents to deal with, not the Romans to mess up," Ealga said angrily, clearly not in line with her daughter or husband.

"All right then, what about you Aibhlinn, do you think we should have a mill or not?" Cathmore asked her.

Aibhlinn cocked her head to the side and moved her dark hair to behind her ear. She said: "I think we should put it to a vote, the more progressive thinkers say yes, the more traditionalists say no. I am inclined to be more forward thinking and go with yes to the mill. We might have to pay for it but I think the surrounding farmers will be able to. I know we can."

"Well you've all thought it through pretty thoroughly, some for some against. We are still mulling our decision and would like to see what everyone is thinking. I would like to know what Miach is going to say, whether he is for or against it. I guess that will have more sway for my vote than anything," Cathmore said as he continued to walk looking down at his feet as they ate up the road on the way to Gosbecks. They all continued on their way to the meeting with no further talking between them.

Presently they arrived in Gosbecks and were amazed at the amount of people who were able to show up for the meeting. Many farmers from the outlying area were in attendance including those that normally went to Camulodunum to grind their wheat at the mills there. It seemed the idea of a mill in Gosbecks pulled in the ancillary people, those who supported the farmers. There were also business men that normally would only come to Gosbecks on market day attending. From the discussions between everyone it seemed that the mood was very positive for the mill, or at least those who were against it were silent. As they moved through the crowd they ran into Dahy and Muirne who were talking with Eimear, Meadghbh's mother. They hailed everyone. Bebhinn was able to talk to Eimear about her daughter: "Meadghbh is doing fine and is such a help to us. Do you need her back home?"

"No, I think she should stay. The big Roman is staying in Gosbecks at Lorcan's home, which is too close to us for her to feel comfortable. He really scared her on Samhain," Eimear answered anxiously.

"Yes he did but you should know that I have two Romans staying with me now. One of them has spent time with Meadghbh and they seem to get along more than just fine. Yesterday they were laughing together about hunting foxes with my son Ailbe. They seem to find happiness in the time they spend together. You should know before it gets too far," Bebhinn let her know.

"So you are worried it would go farther?" Eimear asked.

Bebhinn looked at her and said: "It might go further with the way they are spending time together. His name is Fullo and he is quite kind to her. He also spends a lot of time with Ailbe and plays with him, he exchanges jokes with him and makes Ailbe laugh. I quite like the young man. He's here at the meeting and I will point him out to you. He spends a lot of time with Quintus who is their leader."

"Thank you Bebhinn, I'd like that. I know Miach said to let our girls go pair up with Romans but I didn't think it would be so fast," Eimear said with a worried look on her face. "If you can I would like to meet him tonight."

"All right I'll do what I can to introduce you to him," Bebhinn said and turned to Dahy and Muirne. They were listening in on the conversation and Dahy said: "I know Fullo. He is a good man, he is always smiling for Muirne and I when we wait on him at the butcher's stall. You know one of the ways to see how a person is like is when they deal with someone secondary to them like a butcher. We have many stories of good people and also not so good people. We can tell he is one of the better ones."

"Thank you Dahy, that makes me feel better." Eimear said, "I trust your judgment."

Niamh stepped in and said: "So what are your thoughts on the mill Eimear, Muirne and Dahy?"

"I love how you come in right for the subject Niamh! Of course I'm for the mill. We need one in this large village. It will help us to compete with Camulodunum and bring in more people to trade on market day." Dahy enthused. Muirne nodded agreement.

Eimear didn't look so encouraged: "I worry that the more the Romans do the more there will be reasons for the Romans to come into Gosbecks. I would prefer they stay in Camulodunum and leave Gosbecks alone."

"You don't think the more we get better roads and a mill the better Gosbecks will become? If we get the mill other businesses will come with it, more merchants, more food processing and more people will be attracted to Gosbecks," Niamh said with a smile.

"Yes but also more Romans which means more tax assessors, more land speculators and more involvement by Roman money lenders," Eimear replied.

"My dear they are already involved with Gosbecks, just look at the soldiers that have come to Gosbecks, they will be living here just give it time. Word has it that Gosbecks will be getting some retiring soldiers to live here and I'm sure that includes the ones already here," Niamh said apologetically. "Rome has been looking at the surrounding area of Camulodunum for a while and they see Gosbecks as an addition to their already vast influence. We might as well take them for all they are worth and ride the forefront of this invasion."

"I didn't look at it that way, I want nothing to do with the Romans and wish they would look elsewhere for their invasion," Eimear worried biting her lip. She still felt uneasy about having the Romans in Gosbecks despite the information Niamh was giving her. She shook her head dislodging some of her graying brown hair.

"Let's see what Miach thinks about this whole mill and roads idea. He might be in favor of them just you wait and see," Niamh said to Eimear. Then she turned and followed the stream of people going into the tavern. Eimear looked at Bebhinn, Dahy and Muirne and they all followed Niamh into the tavern.

The tavern was almost full to bursting with people who had come to attend the meeting, each person standing with those they knew and agreed with as was expected. The murmuring of people was a dull sound as if it was a tide at the beach rising and falling with each new group that walked in. More murmurs greeted Niamh as she walked in, then more to greet the local healer Bebhinn in time like the susurrating ebb and flow of the tide. As the room became full the sound was now a dull roar with no ebb. The people were mixing freely from one group to another in greeting. Soon the dull roar quieted as the one who everyone was waiting for entered the room. Miach strode in with authority handling his staff in his hand and his look of command on his face. Many of those in the room surged forward to get his take on the meeting but he just smiled and said it would have to wait for the meeting to start for them to hear what he proposed. In confidence to his authority they nodded and stepped back giving him space, nodding their heads in unison.

In the back the Romans gathered together to see the meeting, interested in the final word but not really worried about it. They realized that their numbers were small and negligible and they were easily dismissed. They also knew that whatever the final decision wouldn't matter to them as they would get what they wanted when they returned to the general. Rome was not to be ignored despite what these provincials wanted. The Romans patiently waited for the meeting to convene. "What do you think the people of Gosbecks will agree to?" Fullo asked Quintus in Latin as they stood in the back.

"It might be positive and they'll vote for the mill on their own but it really doesn't matter. The general, who will continue in power as governor and Rome will get their mill one way or the other," Quintus replied quietly in Latin. Fullo nodded in agreement and turned to the crowd as they seemed to begin the meeting with Miach's advent. The Romans took note of how they paid respect to the old man and realized that he was definitely a leader in Gosbecks but didn't really know why. Fullo elbowed Quintus and indicated Miach, suspicion that he might in fact be a druid was rising with each display of authority he showed and was given with reverence. Quintus acknowledged this unspoken thought with a nod of his head. "We will have to watch this development closely."

All turned to the front of the room when Oisin walked up and held up his hands. "Everyone we can start the meeting for the determination of a mill and additional roads put forth by the Romans here at the back," he turned and indicated the Romans lined up on the back wall, "We can ask them questions if needed. Now let me turn this over to the leaders here in Gosbecks, to Cathmore, Ronan and of course Miach."

Cathmore strode to the front and proceeded to get everyone's attention. "Good day to you all, thank you for coming to the meeting. We would like to determine the number of people that are for or against the mill. Now it will bring in more business if we do have a mill here in Gosbecks but the flip side is we will have to pay for the new building and hire those with the expertise to run it. There are several people from Camulodunum who have generously given their time to us to discuss the cost of the mill and how that would affect us should we go that way. Let me introduce you to a miller from Camulodunum, this is Ultan who will talk to you about the mill and its cost."

A short, round, bald man stepped up to the front and smiled an oily smile. "Good day to all of you. I am Ultan, one of the millers from Camulodunum. I've been working as a miller for seven reaping seasons and can tell you it is a good investment. The amount of wheat I can grind is amazing. If a farmer comes in with a normal reaping amount of wheat, say ten baskets full of wheat to be ground, I can grind it in one morning and only charge him one twentieth of the ground wheat. On a daily basis I can grind up to forty baskets of wheat. The normal cost is about one twentieth of the wheat brought in to grind. Some farmers have more, some less but all are ground with that cost. The first year we had it slightly higher to recoup the cost of the building but it was still only one fifteenth of the cost to grind the wheat. I imagine your mill will start out at that amount but not be higher. The more farmers that use the mill the more the cost will drop." He sat down after his speech and folded his arms over his rounded belly content with his speech for the people of Gosbecks. The crowd murmured as the import of his words went through the populous. It seems they didn't realize the amount of tax that would be levied on the farmers each time they went in to grind their wheat. One twentieth was easier to realize than one fifteenth which seemed a lot to some of the smaller farmers.

One of them stepped forward and asked: "If the farmer only has five baskets to grind what would the amount be to that farmer, would the amount be higher or the same?"

"With only five baskets it would be higher but one way around the higher amount is to pool the surrounding farmer's amounts to be ground. So if you were able to get at least two or three or more farmers to pool their amounts and get it up to twenty baskets then the amount would be one twentieth again. The farmers would then negotiate between themselves how the amount would be paid between them," Ultan said smiling again. This prompted a renewed discussion around several groups in the crowded room.

Another man stepped forward to ask: "If the discussed payments have a dispute from within this little pool or cooperative of farmers who would resolve the problem?"

"There must be an advocate here who will listen to the problem. Do you not have one?" Ultan asked. Several people said yes and more nodded affirmatively to answer the question. Miach stepped forward and said: "I would be willing to arbitrate these disputes between farmers." The crowd of people smiled and calmed down knowing their resident druid would be their authority without having to name him as a druid. It would have been dangerous with the Romans in the room to label him as a druid. For their part the Romans took notice of this exchange. Several of them looked at Quintus but he only nodded his head imperceptibly in acknowledgement. It was obvious to them that Miach was the resident druid. They kept quiet for now but would file this bit of information away for later use.

Others in the crowd stepped forward and out of that group one woman asked: "How long will these extra fees are imposed? Would they lessen once the building is paid for?"

Ultan smiled again and said: "They will lessen as soon as the capital is paid off on the building."

"Have you paid off your capital investment on your mill?" asked another merchant.

"My mill is very large so the answer is no, I have not paid off the capital investment but by the next ten reaping seasons it should be completely paid off. My mill has a grinding capacity of forty baskets per day, much bigger than your mill," Ultan said and still maintained his oily smile on his face. This elicited more discussion between the farmers and business men in the room.

Ronan stepped forward and asked: "So the capital investment of your mill will take how long exactly to pay off?"

Ultan looked slightly disgruntled at the question but still maintained his oily smile: "It will take a full twenty reaping seasons to pay off the capital investment of building the mill." A dissatisfied murmur erupted from this latest revelation from Ultan. More people displayed their disappointment with the answer to how long they'll be under the Roman yoke if they voted to approve the building the mill.

Cathmore stepped forward and said: "Does the Roman moneylenders have anything to do with the terms of payment? Can you actually negotiate better terms before the building is started?"

Ultan started sweating slightly but still held his oily smile "You can negotiate with the moneylenders but they usually come in after the building has already been completed and you need capital to get the whole process started. You generally need capital to start the whole process of grinding the wheat and you'll need to have back up replacement parts to keep the mill functioning. Once the mill is completed you'll need to have backup parts for the water wheel and the mill stone, lumber to make repairs and capital to pay for the labor to fix any needed repairs. Bank on at least one full year's expense up front which the moneylenders are happy to forward to you."

"No wonder you'll take twenty growing seasons to pay off the cost of building the mill. It sounds as if you might never get out from under the foot of the Roman moneylenders if by this time you still haven't been able to pay it off yet. Should there be a major storm or gods forbid a fire you'll still be under their boot," Cathmore said to Ultan. Cathmore wrinkled his lips in disgust at the whole situation. The people standing next to him nodded their agreement and looked at Ultan for his response.

A rich looking merchant asked: "What about the cost of an emergency regarding an altercation between tribes or another altercation that damages the mill. Who would be stuck with the cost of that expense?"

Ultan was no longer smiling when he said: "You would have to go to the moneylenders for some type of payment which is called insurance to pay for the damage. I do not know what rate they would charge you for this additional monetary insurance." This garnered more murmured discussions between the people, a lot of the farmers where shaking their heads as they looked at Ultan.

"So there would be additional costs if there is an unforeseen circumstance that prevents Gosbecks from paying off the mill?" asked Ronan who before this discussion was leaning toward approval of building the mill. This elicited more disapproving mutters from the crowd. More looked at Ultan with repugnance on their faces at the rate he kept coming back to the Roman moneylenders for additional costs for the regular upkeep of the mill.

"Why would we want that enormous cost of a new mill?" asked Ealga, Niamh's mother with revulsion over the whole affair. She spat on the floor to show her distaste.

"Because with a mill Gosbecks will be a more profitable settlement," Ultan said.

"Who would it be profitable for exactly, for us as the investors or the Romans as the moneylenders?" Ealga said

Ultan started sweating more profusely and wiped his bald head with his hand. He said: "It would be for those that invest in the mill because they will get the investment of a new piece of capital equipment for the town. It will be a new reason to move more capital investments such as new factories to Gosbecks. You have a thriving market day here and more merchants will come after the mill is opened just as more farmers will come to grind their wheat. If you go with the mill the Romans will also start building better roads for Gosbecks, you'll have roads that no longer wash out during rains. They might even build some better bridges for you too, ones made of stone instead of timber. You have several streams and a good river flowing through this area that will need a good stone bridge." This engendered more discussion between the members of the crowd. The murmurs were slightly more upbeat sounding than the previous ones.

"We could still get more merchants with just are regular market day. We are close enough to fertile farms that would need a mill," Niamh said from the back of the room. "We could still build the mill and get the additional bridges as well. The merchants will hear about the mill and come to our market day to see it and the new bridges. It might have the advantage we are looking for." Her remarks had a settling effect on the crowd, there was more murmuring but it wasn't the negative type, more positive.

In the front a man stepped forward and asked: "Will the moneylenders give us a good deal on any problem that might come up with the mill, say if there is a fire or maybe a flood because of too much rain?"

"I don't know for sure if the money lenders will give you a good deal, they are in it to make money so I would assume they would. You could work with them to see if they would facilitate some kind of payment plan and the time to pay it back, say instead of ten years into fifteen years to pay them back. They will want their money back so they'll work with you. You might want to talk to more than one money lender to see if you can get some competition going on between the two of them[139]," Ultan said with alacrity, still sweating

---

[139] http://www.mariamilani.com/ancient_rome/Ancient%20Roman%20Trade.htm http://www.unrv.com/government/provincialgovernment.php http://www.mariamilani.com/ancient_rome/ancient_roman_jobs.htm

but not as much as he was earlier so now he only had sweat on his upper lip.

The crowd started talking amongst themselves for a moment and one lady stepped forward to say: "So we would have more than one money lender to deal with if there is a problem? Couldn't we just shop around for best rates from the Roman money lenders? Why would we want that?"

Ultan started sweating more profusely at her questions. "They all are in it to make money; it is up to the people of Gosbecks to make the best agreement with them. You might want to elect an advisory board to discuss the terms of any contract, especially ones with the money lenders."

"So we are talking about more meetings and councils to decide whether or not to get a mill? It seems just like a peace treaty between the tribes, with so many ups and downs to negotiate," Ronan said from his place near the front.

"Yes, it is just like that," Ultan said. "Gosbecks will want to treat the negotiations with the money lenders just like a delicate peace treaty."

Miach stepped forward and said: "The decision of whether or not to build a mill is fraught with many perils to understand. Thank you for your very succinct discussion of the benefits of having a mill built Ultan. We will need to understand the entire amount of capital expenditure of the mill and subsequent building of bridges and roads by the Romans. It might be exactly what Gosbecks needs, to grow into a thriving community but we'll need to understand the entire cost of these buildings. If we should decide to build the mill, will it cost Gosbecks too much? Will we be in debt for fifteen or twenty years after the mill is built? And who will run it since there is no experienced miller here in Gosbecks? Will it be a transplant from Camulodunum or will we run it with an untried native of Gosbecks? And if we do bring in a miller how will we train the next person to run the mill? These are questions that will take a lot of discussions to develop a plan for. But the biggest question is do we vote for the mill or not? We should put it to the vote now. Those in favor of the mill say "Yea"." The amount of the "Yea's" was not as significant as it was when the meeting was convened. The "Yea's" were about a third of the room. "Those not in favor say "Nay", Miach said after the vote for building the mill was made. A larger portion of the room said "Nay" than before. Miach said: "The Nay's have it the proposition of whether or not to build the mill is no. The mill will not be built here in Gosbecks."

The Romans were stunned by this reversal of the decision. The room was beginning to break up and leave. Some of the bigger merchants were shaking their heads in resignation as they couldn't believe that Gosbecks had made the decision the way they did. Some of the more prosperous farmers were also shaking their heads, knowing that a mill would be the best thing for Gosbecks. The smaller farmers were smiling their approval and made their way to the door glad that the specter of the Romans would be put off for now.

"Don't they realize the mill will be built with or without their agreement?" Faber asked Quintus in Latin.

Quintus shrugged, "I don't think they all realize it now. Some of them know a mill would be the best thing for Gosbecks and when we come back to build it they will be better positioned to take advantage of the new mill." Quintus huffed and said: "Now that the decision is made we can pack up and go back to see the governor and give him their very unreasonable decision. We'll be back but they won't be happy with what we bring back with us. Go back to your places of billeting and we'll pay up through the end of the tomorrow. We'll leave the day after tomorrow for the Roman fort. We'll be back in the spring to take our place in Gosbecks." The men nodded and all began to leave the tavern. Quintus paid Oisin for their drinks and they all left.

Out in the courtyard they met up with Bebhinn and Cathmore. "Is the decision to your liking?" asked Quintus, curious to hear what they say.

"Yes, it is the only realistic decision they could have made," said Cathmore feeling very justified at the results of the meeting. "Gosbecks is too small to have a mill built here."

"And you Bebhinn, what do you think of the decision?"

"I also believe it is the only one we could have made. After hearing Ultan talk about the money lenders and how they get involved I think this is the better way to go," Bebhinn remarked.

"What about if they wait until next reaping season before they begin building the mill? It should be built in time for the next reaping season," Fullo offered as he got Janus tacked up for the ride home.

"Didn't you hear the decision was made to not approve the mill being built at all," Cathmore said with exasperation. "Gosbecks is too small to have a mill built here. We will continue grinding our own wheat."

"Fair enough," said Quintus as he mounted on Boreas and turned the horse's head back to the way they came. He and Fullo took off at a quick clip to return to the farm. Cathmore, Meara and Bebhinn stood and looked after them.

"What do you think they meant about building the mill anyway in Gosbecks, do they know something we don't?" Cathmore asked to no one in particular as they began to trudge homeward.

"I think they were just mad that we didn't jump to the idea of having a mill and Roman built roads around here. Romans come into our villages and rearrange things to suit themselves. As if the roads we have here are not good enough," Bebhinn sniffed disgustedly. "I am looking forward to the day when the Romans are out of my farmhouse for good. They come in with promises of help but in fact make more work for everyone. Do you know he suggested we learn Latin?"

Cathmore was quiet for a moment, he was looking forward to more help on his farm but he didn't say anything, knowing that Bebhinn was not to be deterred. "I understand, it is not convenient to have the Romans at our table every night. Conversation has to be curtailed or redirected into subjects that are more palatable for us and them. Watching what we are saying is very tiring."

"But at least they brought in extra meat when they came," Meara added. "It was nice to eat a choice cut of beef after so long not getting any."

"Next time Edana gets more geese I'll have her run it over to you. She went out hunting with Meadghbh and caught quite a few," Bebhinn said. "Good thing that Ailbe told her where to hunt, which side of the lake to hunt on, they were quite successful."

"So Ailbe is truly becoming a druid in his own right," Cathmore smiled. "You need to let Miach know about this ability he has, the people of Gosbecks should all benefit from his prognostication of the best places and types of animals to hunt for."

"I'd like for him to stay a young child as long as possible. He is very young still, let him grow up a normal boy for now," Bebhinn requested Cathmore. "I'd like him to get a few more seasons under his belt before he is turned over to Miach[140]."

"Alright but he will begin to get famous for his ability before you know it," Cathmore breathed harder as he used his staff to walk faster. Meara and Bebhinn had to redouble their pace to keep up with his long legs, obviously aware that he did not approve of what Bebhinn said about Ailbe. Bebhinn settled in to endure his unspoken rebuke and kept pace with him.

Faber and Coriaro returned to Lorcan's home and began to pack up their belongings. Lorcan walked over to them and asked: "So now that the decision's been made for the mill I assume you are packing up to leave?"

"Yes, we will be leaving the day after tomorrow and will like to pay up for the time you put us up in your home. Thank you for your hospitality," Faber said as he packed up his weapons and mess

---

[140] http://www.druidry.org/druid-way/resources/training-druidry http://www.patheos.com/blogs/johnbeckett/2014/10/why-im-an-obod-druid.html

kit then turned to Lorcan. "We appreciated the home. It is much warmer than the tents we were in."

"Plus we enjoyed the impromptu music sessions that we were treated to here," Coriaro said as well. He had already packed up his weapons and was working on arranging his mess kit to his approval, turning his bowl just so he could get his cup and spoon in the bag just right[141].

"Were you surprised by the vote on the mill? I was. I thought for sure a mill would be approved. We in Gosbecks need to get bigger and compete with Camulodunum," Lorcan allowed. He picked up a couple of walnuts from a nearby bag, broke them open to eat the meat inside.

"Why do you think they voted the way they did then?" Faber asked as he finished packing his mess kit and moved onto his clothes bag. He had a tunic drying by the fire that he packed into the bag.

Lorcan shrugged, "I don't know. It seems they are very reticent to get the Roman money lenders here in Gosbecks right now. That was the most discussions I heard in the area I was standing in. Most of the people were small farmers and they don't have the large amounts of wheat that needed to be ground like some of the more prosperous farms. There are so many farms that were unable to reap their fields this time around. A lot of men did not return from the rebellion."

"About what amount were the farmers not able to reap their fields this last season?" Coriaro asked.

"I'd say it was easily a good third of the farmers couldn't get all their crops in," Lorcan shrugged again. He looked sad at the reminder of all the men and women who did not return after the

---

[141] http://legvi.tripod.com/id69.html https://images.search.yahoo.com/yhs/search?p=Imperial+Roman+Eating+Utensils&hspart=att&hsimp=yhs-att_001 http://www.dailymail.co.uk/news/article-1247230/The-Roman-Army-Knife-Or-ingenuity-Swiss-beaten-1-800-years.html

rebellion. "We were required to play a lot of sad music this time around"

"War is always harsh, for those that die but also for those that are left," Coriaro said with compassion. "I have lost a lot of fellow legionaries in my time so I know what I'm talking about."

Lorcan nodded his head. "Thanks for listening to us play our music at all times of the night. You've been very good guests. I know the hours I keep are difficult but it has been that way for a long time so I'm used to it now. It seems regular to me."

"Yes we saw that all the musicians in the area come to the house to rehearse with you. Gosbecks is lucky to have you," Faber told him with a laugh. "I was fine with the late night meetings but we still had our early morning meeting to attend. It was a little difficult at first but then we got used to it."

"Now that we are going you can continue without having to worry about us," Coriaro laughed. "And I'll be able to sleep all night long even when I am assigned a night watch when we travel. I'll still sleep better."

Lorcan had the impudence to smile at this exchange and he pulled out his pipe to run a trill through the keys. "That's one last impromptu rehearsal for you." Then he topped it off with a jaunty little tune that they recognized as one that will be for the mid-winter festival. The Romans laughed and hummed along while they finished packing.

At Ronan and Fingula's farm Bundarus and Rufus let them know that they would be leaving the day after tomorrow. "Thank you for the good billet. We have been very comfortable here. Since we have one full day before we leave is there something you would like us to help you with? If you need something done on you farm we could help there," Bundarus rumbled.

"Why thank you for the offer. I think I have a few big item tasks to do on the farm, mainly repairs on the fencing around the perimeter. I'll need to purchase the timbers but that shouldn't be too hard to do. There is plenty next door at Ferdia's farm that I can buy. Yes I think doing the work on the fence would be the just what is needed," Ronan beamed at the Romans.

Rufus returned his smile and said: "I would love to work on your fence, it will keep us fit and keep in shape for the military drills we will be doing for the rest of the months until spring."

"So you're leaving soon? I am sorry to see you go." a timid Eilis said as she was carding some wool getting it ready to spin into yarn for her tartans. She looked up and smiled at Bundarus, a small smile but filled with purpose.

"Yes it is so soon but we'll be back in Gosbecks by the spring planting," Bundarus rumbled, his voice gentle as he spoke to Eilis.

Fingula said: "You are coming back then? That's good I liked what you talked about earlier when you were telling us to sell our textiles to some Roman traders. There is a seller of clothes at market day but he has not seen our wares. Ronan and I would like for you to be our agent to help sell our textiles to these Roman traders."

Bundarus smiled. "I was going to approach you about this anyway. I would be proud to represent your textiles and scarves to the Roman traders. Your textiles are good enough to be shipped back to Rome for selling there. You should be very proud. We can work out the details of my being your agent later but I would proudly represent your goods."

Ronan and Fingula hugged, beaming at their good fortune to have Bundarus represent their wares to the Roman traders. Ronan said: "Then we need to redouble our efforts to get more tartans and scarves out to sell. Fingula you need to dye more wool in the blues, yellows, and reds like we talked about. Eilis you'll need to make much more yarn in the next couple of months so keep working!" Ronan grinned and hugged Fingula again. "We are finally going to make our way in the world with your lovely textiles and scarves. We might even look into hiring some extra help."

Eilis jumped up at that with vigor. "We could hire Sadhbh to help me card more wool. She would be more than happy to work with me."

"Yes she would work well with you and you two are good friends anyway. What about Meadghbh or even Edana? They could also help especially if we get this enterprise working out," Ronan added the added profits floating about in his head.

Fingula shook her head and pulled him back to the present. "What could we possibly pay them with? The past couple of market days have been lean and we don't have enough to pay for all the dyes that I need. We should maybe get Sadhbh to work since her father is no longer around and they need the extra money but we cannot hire the rest."

Bundarus stepped forward: "I have money that I've been saving for the future, I could loan you the money for the future since I'll be your agent you need the commodities that I'll be selling. I can give you five sestertius for the capital to start. You'll be able to purchase the dyes and extra wool if you need it from others. You'll be on your way."

"You'd do this Bundarus? Alright I accept it only as a loan and I'll pay you back as soon as we sell these tartans and scarves at the next market day and beyond. Thank you!" Ronan was very overcome with the enormity of what he was getting into on the commodities market. It was something he'd always dreamt of but had no way of doing until now. Now with this little bit of capital he could move forward. Fingula was also bright eyed and was already dreaming about the increase of their wares and the better living they could now afford. A smile laced her face as she could envision it. She made plans to buy a new bigger loom[142] and the dyes she needed next market day, small increments at first but as things began to move she would increase the amounts.

At Cathmore's farm Grex and Titus let them know that they would be leaving the day after tomorrow as well but they would

---

[142] http://resourcesforhistory.com/Celtic_round_houses.htm#gsc.tab=0
https://www.pinterest.com/pin/18295942208919797/
https://www.pinterest.com/pin/18295942208919797/

be able to help out one more day if he needed anything done. Cathmore seemed to be unhappy to see them leave but he put a good face on it. "Thank you for helping out. I will take you up on one item that has needed to be fixed since I returned home from the my skirmish with a Roman squad where I hurt my arm. I have some fences that have fallen down as well as our cow barn that needs to be fixed up. Those two items would be what needs to be taken care of. You can get started on the cow barn today."

Grex smiled and said: "It would be our pleasure to start now. What exactly does the cow barn need?"

Cathmore said: "It would be best if we just go out and look at the barn now. I think the roof has a few places where it leaks, the doors need to be reset so they close better and there are the walls that would need to be looked at."

"Then let's go now so we can get the cow barn taken care of, since we've been using the barn I noticed that the fence also needs to be shored up as well," Titus said and he stood up from the table they were all at.

"Yes I forgot about that as well. It might be the cow barn is all you'll be able to work on before you go," Cathmore replied.

"We'll be able to get more done if you just give us the materials and let us get to work," Grex said.

"Yes, half of our time spent as legionaries is building, either roads, fences or bridges so this will be easy," Titus said. "At least this won't be a road or bridge, which is a back breaking endeavor. I worked on more roads than I care to talk about."

"So being a soldier isn't just about warfare? You do more than just wage war?" Cathmore asked.

"Yes we do much more than just wage war. When we were in Gaul we were constantly working on roads and our fort. Whether it was building barracks or living quarters for the officers it was building more roads. I was personally involved with forty millia passus of paved roads. We always had competitions between the centuries on how far the road would get built. I personally worked on the road from Hatra[143] to Wadi Al-Tharthar[144], and that was the hottest assignment I've ever been on." Titus related with a proud smile.

"I didn't realize that the Romans did more than just fight. When you say you build roads are you talking about the ones that are more rock than just a dirt track?" Cathmore asked seeming truly interested.

"Of course, we build roads that have a paved surface, made from interlocking stone sort of like a mosaic. They are much more durable than just a dirt track and much less bound to become a quagmire in heavy rains. They are designed to let the water run over them but not to wash out since they are designed properly to let the water flow through the substructure. The roads we built had a paved surface with gravel on top[145]," Titus opined warming up to the subject.

"I'm not sure what you mean by gravel," Cathmore asked as he stood up and prepared to leave to the cow barn.

Titus stood too and kept talking. "Gravel is small rocks that are laid out on top to give the wagons something to grip as they pass over it. They range from the size of your fingernail to small bits the size of seeds. Having the gravel on top lets the road last longer because the more it is used the smaller the rocks are ground down into the substrate."

Grex stood as well and followed Cathmore and Titus to the cow barn. Outside they went directly to they looked at cow barn critically. There they saw the amount of work was greater than Cathmore let on, more structural problems showed as the cow barn's roof was tilted to the left and was missing shingles. Also the walls of the barn didn't look to be in the best shape except for the back right corner. The fence surrounding the barn was also

---

143 http://www.roman-empire.net/articles/article-036.html

144 http://www.roman-empire.net/articles/article-036.html

145 http://www.historylearningsite.co.uk/ancient-rome/roman-roads/
http://www.history.com/news/history-lists/8-ways-roads-helped-rome-rule-the-ancient-world

in disrepair, missing some slats and falling down in other places. It was obvious that Cathmore's arm had hindered him for a long time preventing him from fixing the barn as well as other major duties around the farm. Titus and Grex looked at each other and shrugged their shoulders.

"All right now, where is you mallet and nails? We should get working on this right away. How about the extra wood you need to shore up your cow barn? Where do you have the extras?" Grex said right off the top.

Cathmore smiled and said it was all in the barn. He showed them everything they needed the materials were laid out but under a lot of dust as he had not gotten to them yet.

"See there is the mallet, saw and drill if you need to use them. Over in the bucket is the nails that you'll need," Cathmore indicated the leather bucket leaning against the stack of lumber.

"Do you have a ladder? Or we can make one quickly if you don't out of the lumber stack," Grex asked.

"I have a ladder in the barn over there, it is old but very sturdy," Cathmore pointed to an old ladder that was grey with usage but looked to be in good repair. The Romans got their mallet and saw out and began to work. Titus took the mallet and nails then started going through the lumber for usable pieces to start with. Grex started with the saw and went to the lumber as well. They discussed what needed to be done first and decided to work on the roof first. Grex got the saw out and started cutting shingles out of the lumber slats. Titus picked up the shingles and headed over to the roof to look at the areas that showed obvious signs of leaks. Cathmore showed him the worse spots and pointed out new problem areas. Also looking at the roof they determined that a supporting joist was causing all the sagging to the left and would need to be replaced at a later date since they did not have the time to do it.

Both Grex and Titus worked under Cathmore's direction for the rest of the day on the cow barn. They managed to make enough shingles for the roof and finished patching up the holes so there were no longer gaping holes in the roof. Then they began to work on the back right corner of the barn. The leaks had caused the corner to start rotting in places so they needed to replace the rotted boards. Both men worked methodically and took the direction from Cathmore quite well. By the end of the day they had fixed the roof and were almost done with the right corner. The next day would be the fence which would require much more lumber than they currently had. That evening they discussed where they could get more lumber and determined that Niamh's farm would be the best place to go get it.

"It was a good day's work gentlemen," Cathmore said at dinner that evening. "We will get the cow barn finished tomorrow and might even have time to fix one of my fences over by the south paddock."

That afternoon Quintus and Fullo got back to Bebhinn's farm and found everyone still working in the garden doing the chores Bebhinn had given to Edana and Meadghbh. They were all still gardening and harvesting the vegetables when the Romans rode up into the courtyard.

"Looks like Bebhinn gave them a lot of chores to do this day," Fullo smiled as they pulled up to dismount from the horses. The horses were used to the farm and let out happy whinnies to see their pasture. They were restive when they were untacked but pleased to be turned out. The horses whinnied and bucked when they were untacked and let out in the pasture, galloping off to the far side of the field. The men took themselves off to see where the others were in the garden. Fullo called out: "We're back from the meeting and it looks like you are still doing the chores Bebhinn gave you earlier."

Both girls turned and smiled at the Romans. Edana stood up and said: "You are correct, we are still doing the chores that Mother gave us and probably will doing the same tomorrow. How was the meeting? Did Gosbecks vote on the mill?"

Quintus stepped forward and said: "Yes they did but they voted to not go with the mill and to forego the road improvements. Not the best decision but I can respect their reasons for it. Just to let you know now that the decision has been made we will be leaving the day after tomorrow. We need to get back to our governor and let them know what Gosbecks has decided to do."

"You're leaving so soon? You should stay at least a few more days, we need to get the goat shed enlarged and the roof taken care of," Edana said with worriedly "I still have many more chores for you to help us with."

"I know but we no longer need to stay in Gosbecks. The Roman veterans will be back in the spring in time for sowing. Fullo and I will be back then," Quintus smiled trying to put a good light on their leaving.

"But I don't want you to go yet," Edana said faintly, a small frown marring her beautiful face. Meadghbh also stood and looked at Fullo with a sorrowful look on her face.

"Don't be sad, we'll still be here tomorrow to get some of the chores done. We'll start on the goat shed first thing in the morning. Do you have all the materials for enlarging and fixing the roof?" Fullo said quickly.

"Yes we have lumber and enough nails to fix it. The only thing I do not have is a saw," Edana explained. She still looked pensive and wiped her hands on the front of her tunic leaving muddy streaks on the soft blue wool.

Ailbe who had been standing off to the side and listening piped up: "They'll be back in time to help with the sowing so do not fret Edana and Meadghbh." Then he grinned and said in true little boy fashion: "Will you still teach us how to play draughts tonight? I want to learn the game and perfect it in time for you to come back in the spring and play you." Edana and Meadghbh both looked at them and offered watery smiles.

Quintus and Fullo looked at him and both burst into laughter. "Of course we'll teach you how to play draughts. You'll need to practice your wagers and strategy so when we get back we'll be able to play the game the right way. Well done young Ailbe, you managed to change sad faces into happier ones," Fullo said smiling widely. "Plus I want to see if you can tap into your otherworldly ways to win at the bets," he chuckled.

Quintus' eyebrows went up when he mentioned Ailbe being able to tap into the other realm. "Does this mean you'll be given tips from the gods as to how we'll be betting? That is so unfair! I don't know if I'll be wagering anything with you." He laughed though to ease his mock indignation.

Ailbe smirked. "I'll prove to you that I have the gods' ears, they favor me." Then he looked pensive for a moment as he thought about it. "Maybe the gods won't favor me if it's for my own benefit and not others. But I will surely try to see and play you the way it should be played." Ailbe's face cleared and he grinned.

"Then I'm really interested in how well you learn tonight," Quintus grinned too. "It is a deal. We'll teach all of you how to play draughts even Bebhinn. That way all of you can practice it until we return in the spring. You should have enough time to perfect your strategies." Ailbe, Edana and Meadghbh all grinned. They began to finish up on their gardening chore and gathered up all their clippings, putting them in the satchels and wiped their hands on their tartans leaving dirty runnels of smeared dirt. Then they all turned and made their way back to the farmhouse together.

Once at the farmhouse Edana and Meadghbh both unloaded their satchels and turned to Bebhinn who had just arrived. "We've got some but not all the snippets from your medicinal plants. We will have to finish tomorrow," Edana told her mother. "There are about four more rows of the plants that we need to harvest."

Bebhinn nodded and smiled. "I knew you wouldn't be able to finish today but we got a good head start on the tonics and elixirs with these snippets. It will keep me busy for at least twelve days preparing all of them for future use."

"Quintus told us that the mill decision was not to build. I'm sorry to hear that but I understand why. He also told us that they will be leaving to go back to their general the day after tomorrow.

But they'll be returning in time to sow this spring," Edana voiced to her mother.

"Yes I heard that as well earlier from them. At least they will be back in the springtime. We'll have plenty of work for them come that time. Are both Fullo and Quintus coming back to stay here?"

Quintus who had been listening to their exchange said: "Yes if you'll still have us we would be able to come back to your farm and stay."

Bebhinn's' eyebrows raised and asked: "You're not going to build your own home?"

"We would like to stay here to get you back on your feet since your husband and oldest son are no longer here. Then we will turn and build our own houses since we will be retiring here in Gosbecks." Quintus explained.

"How many Romans will be retiring here to Gosbecks?" Bebhinn asked, Edana and Meadghbh both moved forward to listen to his answer.

"There will approximately eighty that will be retiring here to Gosbecks. Those eighty will be bringing their families. Some will be given land to farm and others will be taking up other ways to live, some will be merchants, some will be opening taverns. It all depends on what the retiring veterans want to do," Quintus clarified. He looked at the women and expected more questions.

It wasn't long in coming when Edana asked: "Taverns? What about Oisin's tavern, one will not be enough for everyone?"

"Probably not, we Romans use taverns for several things, like for food, for meetings, for drink like at Oisin's," Quintus explained.

"Where will they get the land for their farms?" inquired Bebhinn, looking much more pensive at the thought of what might in fact be in store for a lot of residents in Gosbecks.

"We will buy the land from the present owners. There seems to be a lot of farms that are struggling because they lost so many farmers in the last rebellion. There are a lot of people who didn't finish reaping their crops this past season. They might be willing to sell and their farms will go to a Roman veteran. The farmers might even be able to stay on and be hired as laborers for the veterans," Quintus supposed. "This is of course all speculation on my part because it might be quite different when I return. There will be a lot of the farmers who will be able to get back on their feet and pay any taxes that are still in arrears."

Bebhinn fell silent at this bit of information. She was one of the farmers who were in arrears. She also thought of Cathmore who was even more in arrears than she was since he didn't have a son to help out. She needed to let him know about this bit of information. He and Miach will want to know what was coming this spring. Did they realize how many Romans would be coming this spring? It would change the face of Gosbecks and enlarge it by a full fourth of the population. There were many farmers in Gosbecks that would willingly sell their farms but what would they do instead? She didn't think they would be willing to be hired back just as laborers to the Roman veterans.

"Are the Roman veterans coming to stay or will they be moving on? Will they be bringing women with them?" She asked.

"Some will move on but most will stay. There will be some veterans who will be bringing women and children with them but most won't have any women with them. They'll come and meet different local women here in Gosbecks," Fullo told them, looking at Meadghbh. She blushed and looked away but then looked right back at him and smiled. Bebhinn saw this exchange and her heart dropped even further. She knew there was something developing between these two but now she was certain. She then turned to Quintus and saw him looking at Edana with a smile on both of their faces. She knew Edana was lost to her, to the man who killed Ailbe and Edana's father and her husband. Hatred filled her veins at that moment, a cold white fury that knew no bounds.

She was so angry she almost missed the next thing Quintus said: "We'll be fixing up the goat shed tomorrow and I'll need for you to make a list of the other duties that we will need to finish when we come back in the spring."

"I'll get the list started right now since I know the goat shed will take all day tomorrow to fix. Right now Meadghbh and I need to go get the goats from the upper pasture and bring them back to the normal paddock," Edana said to Quintus. "I'll be composing the list as I walk up to the upper pasture."

"I look forward to getting it. I will be able to leave you with some money to purchase lumber and extra materials needed so it will all be here when I get back," Quintus said.

"Thank you Quintus we'll be ready for when you get back from where you're going. I'll have everything here ready to be put into place," Edana told him.

Quintus smiled at her. "I know you'll get everything ready. Spring is an extremely busy time so I'll try to get back as early as possible." He met her eyes and gave her a more meaningful look. Bebhinn hated him even more in that instant as she observed the unspoken communication between the two. *Not my daughter* her mind screamed. She seethed as she looked at Quintus, cold fury swirled up in her veins. *I will get my revenge on you*, she silently swore. Unbeknownst to Quintus he continued to hold Edana's regard, they were in each other's orbit to the exclusion of all else.

Fullo turned to Meadghbh and asked her: "Do you want me to come along with you to get the goats from the upper pasture?"

"Absolutely, it will make this chore so much easier and more fun," Meadghbh said. "Why don't both of you come with us?" She smiled at Fullo and Quintus.

"I think we both will come with the two of you to herd your goats," Quintus laughed shaking his head. "I never would have seen myself as a herder before but I guess I am now."

"We both are then," laughed Fullo as he caught up Meadghbh in his arms and hugged her. Meadghbh laughed with him as she hugged him back. "Then let's go before it gets much later, we'll be returning in the dark as it is." So everyone except Bebhinn and Ailbe went off to go get the goats from the upper pasture.

Bebhinn was left to get the end of the day meal together for everyone. She thought of the things she could put into Quintus' food to cause him discomfort and harm but something stopped her cold. She was a healer not a poisoner, one who succors the ill, not cause it. It went against all that she was to even think that way. Bebhinn flushed red with horror at what she was thinking. *I'll have to tell Miach what I almost did when I see him*, she thought. He'd be so horrified that she would even think that way, so against her druidic healer training. Miach was her mentor and she wanted to live up to his good opinion of her. She would have to fall back on her teaching and make Quintus and Fullo an especially good dinner tonight. She resolved to get in touch with Miach as soon as possible to discuss her lapse of judgment. She turned and looked at her larder and saw it was fully stocked. She pulled out the smoked haunch of deer that she got from Cathmore earlier and went about preparing a good meal of it.

"Ailbe what about an evening meal of deer tonight, we should get a good going away dinner in the pot for Fullo and Quintus?" Bebhinn asked.

"Deer for our evening meal that sounds really good, we will celebrate their going back to the Roman governor. I'll be sad to see them go but they'll be back in the spring, in time for spring sowing. I wonder if the rest of Gosbecks realizes they will be back with more Romans," Ailbe said.

"More Romans, what exactly do you mean?" Bebhinn asked.

"They are only the scouting party for a larger group of Romans coming to Gosbecks. There will be many more Romans coming back with Quintus and Fullo when they return," Ailbe replied. He turned and petted Cabhan on the head, smoothing back the ruffled tan of his hide.

"Oh, I'll have to ask Quintus about that when they get back from their chore. I'm sure you're right," Bebhinn said as she turned to start cooking for everyone.

"I want you to point out on the way to the upper pasture all of the items you want to fix when I come back," Quintus said to

Edana as they walked to the upper pasture with their hands clasped together.

"I want you to stay more days instead of just two," Edana looked forlornly at Quintus, looking at him with sorrowful doe eyes.

"I am sorry but we must return to our main fort and give the governor a report of what has happened here in Gosbecks. That is the first thing I must do. I'll be back to stay in the spring, just for the winter season I'll be gone. Before you know it I'll be back," Quintus smiled and chucked Edana's chin with a playful cuff. She smiled half-heatedly and continued on her way to the upper pasture.

Behind them Fullo and Meadghbh were talking softly. "I want to join with you before I go. Is there a way we could absent ourselves from the rest tomorrow and go somewhere private?" Fullo murmured.

Meadghbh blushed and smiled at Fullo. "We could let the goats go to the upper pasture and do something then. Or we could stay and use the goat shed. It should be easy to slip away and be together without Ailbe or Bebhinn to know."

"Let's go to the upper pasture, we'll find a small secluded spot to lie down together," Fullo smiled at Meadghbh. "I want a memorable morning joining that will last us until I get back in the spring. It will have to do us until I get back to you."

"I know just the spot in the upper pasture. There is a quiet spot by the limits of the upper pasture on the north side. There is a small clearing with a beautiful meadow that the goats keep it cut down. It is very pretty and quiet. If someone comes looking for us they wouldn't be able to see us," Meadghbh whispered to Fullo looking at him closely.

"It sounds perfect. We'll go there first thing in the morning. I'll make sure we are the only ones to take the goats to the upper pasture tomorrow morning," Fullo crooned with a knowing grin on his face. Meadghbh didn't know what he meant but just nodded with a big smile on her face.

Ahead Edana said: "Why don't we go back to the goat shed tomorrow to join?"

"No, no more goat sheds for me. Come to my pallet later to-night and we'll join there. I do not want to use a smelly goat shed for our last time together before I go," Quintus told her quietly.

"In the house? People will hear us as we join! We made a lot of noise in the goat shed." Edana said with shock.

"We can do it much quieter and if they hear us it doesn't matter. We'll only do it once but it will be a moment to remember. I don't want to do it in the dirty goat shed again. You and I deserve better, a much cleaner place," Quintus related. "I don't ever want to join together with you in a dirty place like that again."

"But we have prying eyes in the farm house. Mother, Ailbe, Meadghbh and Fullo will all hear us," Edana pleaded. "I will feel so hemmed in if we join in the house like that, what if we find a good place to join somewhere around the farm?"

"No, the farm is dirty. I want you to be clean when we join. I'll wash and I want you to do the same," Quintus said with intent.

Edana sounded nonplussed: "The farm is not dirty it is just a farm. I don't understand what you are saying. I am clean as well I don't know why I should take a bath."

"You aren't clean. You've not had a bath since we last joined. I need to be clean as well. We Romans have baths on a daily basis. When we get back with our entire century of veterans will open a bath house for Gosbecks and everyone will benefit from daily baths," Quintus said as they walked along. "We need to be clean to stay healthy. Bebhinn will find with the bath house opened that she'll see less health problems in the population of Gosbecks."

"Daily baths will keep the population healthy? I've never heard of such a thing. In the winter we go months without taking a bath," Edana said.

"And you probably get more fevers and illnesses because of it. The Roman military moves into places and institutes sanitation to keep the fevers at bay. We can't stop every fever but we do stop the ones dealing with cleanliness. You'll see and will benefit from the better sanitation and cleanliness," Quintus smirked and pulled her closer in to him. She resisted at first then softened as they continued on to the upper pasture. Presently they got there and realized that because it was a relatively mild day the goats were spread out in the upper pasture. So they needed to go into the pasture to herd the goats. After herding them all up especially one recalcitrant black and white ram they started going back to the lower pasture then back to the farmhouse. While they were walking Edana asked Quintus one more time, "Do I really need to wash before we join tonight?"

Quintus turned and looked at her. "Of course you do, I want to smell your womanly scent, not your stink from running and gardening."

"So you're saying I smell bad?"

"Yes from normal daily chores everyone gets a certain smell. I just want you to be clean for our time together tonight. I'll also wash off as best I can, you do the same," he said.

'All right I'll wash off the grime from the past couple of days. I'll have to do it inside with Meadghbh though. Mother will be surprised to see us both wash off," Edana said.

"Maybe you can get her to wash off too," he said. "She'll be a better healer if she is clean."

"I'll see if I can't get her to do it," laughed Edana. "She probably won't though but maybe, she does wash her utensils and hands when she does her healing or birthing."

"Then she will. All good healers recognize the power of cleanliness when dealing with blood," Quintus smiled to hear Bebhinn was cleaner than her daughter. "You might want to get Meadghbh to also wash. I know Fullo will wash with me as well. Maybe we can get Ailbe to wash with us so everyone will be clean."

"I hope you do try, he is hard to get clean," Edana laughed even harder.

"We might be more successful than you think. He is easy to get to do things if he wants to learn draughts tonight. That is what we'll tell him. No bath, no game," Quintus laughed with her. They were laughing until Fullo and Meadghbh asked why and were told what they were going to do tonight. Everyone started laughing. Meadghbh didn't even put up a fight at her washing. When they got back to the farmhouse everyone separated and got ready to bathe. True to his prediction Fullo and Quintus were able to get Ailbe clean. Edana and Meadghbh had no problem getting Bebhinn to wash with them. Soon they were all clean and setting down to dinner of deer with late season vegetables. It was a good dinner for them all and Edana and Meadghbh got the put away the dishes and cleaned them in record time.

Quintus stepped forward with the game pieces. "Now we will all learn how to play draughts[146]. Fullo will leave the draught counters for you to keep practicing so you'll be ready for us when we return this spring. You can play the game in teams or individually. The betting comes in when we begin the next turn. You will get the hang of the game as we go on," Quintus set out the draught counters to demonstrate how the game was played. Everyone had lots of questions so Fullo and Quintus played a game to show everyone how the game was played. They played two full games before the others got the hang of it. The rules were opaque to understand especially when Quintus and Fullo would talk about betting. Then Fullo and Quintus had them all play in teams, Fullo as the leader of one team and Quintus as the leader of the other. Ailbe, Meadghbh and Fullo on one side, Edana, Bebhinn and Quintus on the other, and they played several games until it got quite late.

"It is a good game to play, I think we'll play it every night until you get back from seeing the governor," Edana said after the last lively game. "I know we'll be ready for you by spring."

Bebhinn shoved Ailbe off of his seat: "To bed with you Ailbe, it is quite late and we still have to get up early to do our chores,"

"I'll get to bed and will get up just in time for my chores

---

[146] http://draughtshistory.nl/origin22.htm
http://www.chesslab.com/rules/CheckerComments4.html

Mother," Ailbe said. He got up and went over to his pallet to lie down. Once there he folded his tired head onto his arms and went right to sleep, his tired little boy snores quickly sounding out as soon as his head hit the pallet. Bebhinn laughed and made her way to her pallet and sleeping area which was by Ailbe's. She changed into just her tunic and lay down on the pallet.

Meadghbh kissed Fullo good night and went to her pallet as well. Edana looked at Quintus and saw him mouth later and point to his pallet. She nodded her head yes and went over to her pallet. Edana quickly got a bowl of water and some soap weed. She quickly washed herself. The she changed into her tunic as well and lay down next to Meadghbh. "Why did you wash?" Asked Meadghbh.

"I am going to couple with Quintus tonight. I wanted to be clean." Edana whispered. Meadghbh gasped in surprise and giggled.

"Enjoy yourself."

Everyone lay down to sleep. Edana waited until she heard the deeper breathing of Meadghbh before she rose and went over to Quintus. They quietly lay down and covered up. Quintus moved her under him and he rose over her to lie on top of her, bracing his arms so he didn't crush her.

Quintus breathed into her ear: "We must be quiet so keep your moans low. Fullo is already sleeping as is Bebhinn and Ailbe. Is Meadghbh also sleeping?" He kissed her neck with little open mouthed kisses, licking his way to her throat.

"Yes, Meadghbh is sleeping," she whispered and moved her head back to give him more access to her throat. She muffled a low moan as he started to move down her tunic to her breasts and kissed them open mouthed through her tunic. He began to move her tunic up to her waist and she helped by lifting up her hips when he got to them. Soon he had uncovered her lower body and started moving her legs apart with his. He fit his body between her legs and moved one of his hands to her womanhood. He opened her labia with his fingers and found the bundle of nerves that were so sensitive. He used his fingers to find her natural moisture and moved it to her clitoris. He then proceeded to circle the sensitive clitoris, she moaned and became slightly louder as she gasped.

"Stay quiet my Edana, you must stifle the moans so we do this without noise."

She stifled her moans and pressed her lips together to keep them from opening when he continued to circle the spot that felt so good with his fingers. He moved more of her copious moisture from her vagina to her clitoris and started to find a tempo that brought her pleasure to higher heights. The feelings started to build until Edana then moaned her completion as he made her climax. He moved his mouth over hers to capture her cries as she opened her mouth to his tongue. She allowed him to plunder her mouth as she continued to feel the tremors blow through her system. He moved to get his penis free from his loin cloth and set it near her entrance.

"Stay quiet, I'm going to enter you now." He pushed into her welcoming depths. She moaned into his mouth as he recaptured hers. They began to move in rhythm slow at first then faster as he was striving towards his climax. "You feel so good, warm and wet." He began to move faster and she started to feel the pressing feeling again. They moved in unison as they each followed their urgent feelings. He waited until she found hers first then as she clenched around him he followed her over the edge to glory. They both breathed hard into each other's mouth, sharing their breath as they both came down from their mutual feelings. "This is how your parents must have joined so no one could hear," he breathed into her ear. Edana started to giggle but stayed quiet when he told her "Hush, don't wake up the others." They smiled at each other and continued to kiss, Quintus raining small kisses on Edana's mouth, face and ending on her nose. Quintus pulled out of Edana and rolled to his side taking her with him.

"I should go back to my pallet before too much longer, before we fall asleep," Edana whispered quietly.

Quintus kissed her lips and said: "I agree and good night." He kissed her for several more moments then let her go. She lifted up quietly and moved back to her pallet. She felt the result of their loving slide down her thighs. She quickly got back onto her pallet and lay down drawing up her blanket over her. She stared into the black night of the farm house, still feeling the waves of ecstasy coursing through her body from their lovemaking. "I am very happy," she said quietly to herself and turned over to go to sleep. She drifted off to sleep as she relaxed into the quiet of the night.

The next morning dawned bright, the weak winter sun was doing its' best to shine down on the earth. Everyone got up, got their morning meal and went out to do their morning chores. Edana and Quintus went to the goat shed to start work on the roof. Ailbe went to do his chores with the chickens and ducks and Bebhinn went out to finish the chores in her medicinal garden. Meadghbh and Fullo took off to turn out the goats in the upper pasture. They walked off with their hands entwined as they led the goats.

"Are you ready?" Fullo asked smiling.

Meadghbh blushed and nodded. "I am ready for the coupling. It will be wonderful."

"I want to go slow and do this the right way. For a woman the first time there is pain. I'll do everything possible to make it wonderful," Fullo told her. Not having any experience Meadghbh just nodded her head. She had heard from her mother that the first time a woman coupled with a man there was pain and blood, proof of her innocence. She was not ignorant in the mechanics of coupling having had the talk from her mother on the last Beltane festival. During the festival there were quite a few virgin women waiting to experience their first coupling. The festival was for fecundity and all couples celebrated with drink and sex. This last Beltane festival was right before the rebellion so there were a lot of new babies nine months later. Unfortunately there were not a lot of returning men that missed the birth of their children. Meadghbh and Edana didn't find any person to couple with so both sat out the Beltane festivities. Her brothers Caolin and Addis both took part in the Beltane festivities and the girl that Addis slept with Daireann had a baby boy Hugh nine months later. The little boy was a carbon copy of her brother with his dark curls and dark eyes. Daireann later met an older man and married him. Meadghbh hadn't seen Hugh in seasons, since before he started walking. She hadn't seen him since the last midwinter festival.

Now Meadghbh would couple with Fullo and possibly get with child herself. She prayed to Bres[147] the god of fertility that she wouldn't get pregnant, at least not until Fullo returned in the spring. She could see herself settling down with Fullo. They walked on until they got to the gate and ushered the goats on through to the upper pasture. They walked through the dew laden grass to the meadow, the hawthorn ringing the meadow with beautiful reaching branches that soared black in autumn's sun. There was a little brook that ran through the meadow and sang a merry tune as it ran over the rocks. Meadghbh let Fullo to a small bower, the floor thick with leaves the from fall, the hawthorn creating a secluded area. "How is this for our first coupling?" she asked.

"Perfect, this is exactly what I envisioned when you described it yesterday. Let me lay down my cloak so we can lay on something soft," Fullo said as he took off his cloak and laid it down on the floor of the bower. He then turned to her and caught her up in a sweet kiss, something gentle and not too demanding as she was suddenly shy. Their lips met, gentle at first. Fullo rained small kisses on her lips before he captured her mouth and opened it with his. They took several moments kissing and learning each other's mouth. His tongue swept in and took possession of hers. They kissed for a little longer then Fullo turned her toward the bed and lay her down, careful to take off her tartan first. She lay down with her face pensive but also wanting as they continued to kiss, Fullo raining kisses on her mouth, face and moving towards her throat.

---

[147] http://www.pantheon.org/articles/b/bres.html
http://ancienthistory.about.com/od/celtsmyth/tp/010209celticgods.htm

She lifted her head to give him more access to her throat and he took full advantage of it, turning his kisses into open mouthed wet kisses that combined sucking and licking on her sensitive throat. She moaned and lay back to give him more access. His hands began to explore her breasts, roaming over them and cupping. His fingers finding her taut nipples and pulling on them, circling them with increasing fervor and rolling them with his fingers. She pushed her full breasts into his hands.

Fullo moved his hands to her tunic and started to lift it up. She helped him by lifting up giving him access to her hips. "You have beautiful hips, nice and full. Your ass is even better, I have plenty to grab onto," Fullo groaned into her ear. She moaned as he kissed her ear, sticking his tongue into her ear and swirling it around. He moved his hands up to her breasts, moving her tunic up to uncover them. . "Your breasts are even better than your hips and buttocks, they are nice and full with dark rose nipples, I have plenty to grab onto and suck when I want to." He moved his mouth to her breast and took her nipple in his mouth and began to suck. Meadghbh began to moan even more. He then laved the nipple and moved to the other breast and began to suck. Meadghbh arched her back to put even more of her breast into his mouth. She groaned even more loudly and bit her lips. He let go of her nipple and moved further down to her lower stomach.

He then moved his hands to her hips, opened her legs and settled his hips between them then moved further down. He used his hand to go to her labia and spread her lips to open her to his view. "The best part of your body is here, all swollen with need and dripping wet. You are ready for me." He then took his finger to dip into her vagina and move the moisture of her need up to her clitoris and began to move in small tight circles. Meadghbh gasped and nearly bucked him off her hips with reaction. He was causing her to feel so much that she almost couldn't take it.

She moaned even more loudly and said: "I don't know what you are doing but it feels so good. Keep doing it."

"I will," Fullo breathed as he looked into her face to gauge her reactions. She closed her eyes and arched up into him. There was an intense feeling of urgency she felt and she wanted to follow the feelings to something, she didn't know what. "That's it, feel my hand, feel what I'm making you feel. That sensation is the best part of joining, what we all strive for." She started to undulate her hips in response to the movement of his hand. She began to feel even more urgent, wanting to reach some pinnacle but not knowing what she was reaching for. He began to move his fingers even faster, moving that bundle of nerves back and forth in a rapid tattoo. She wailed in response and quickly came to her climax. The waves of ecstasy flowed over her, her eyes rolled back into her head in response.

Fullo moved his hips into place and undid his loin cloth to free his manhood. He leaned down and whispered to Meadghbh: "Now is the culmination of all these feelings, we will join." He placed his penis into her womanhood and pushed in quickly while she was still feeling the waves from her climax. He breached her maidenhood with a quick, sure push causing her pain and she cried out in response. "That's it, that's all the pain I'll cause you, now we'll go to that fleeting feeling of completion," he groaned into her ear as he began to move slowly in her letting her adjust to the feeling of him inside her. She looked at him and started feeling the sense of urgency again. Now that she knew it was the precursor to her climax she started to move with him, undulating her hips and meeting his thrusts.

They started slowly then began to pick up speed. Fullo started pounding into her depths and angling his penis to touch her in different places inside. He found one particularly good angle and she cried out in response. He repeated the motion and she started to cry out with each of his thrusts. Soon they were both groaning in unison as he pummeled her with his thrusts. Soon she felt her climax and wailed out in response. As soon as Fullo began to feel her climax he followed her over the edge into his own. He shouted her name in response when he came into her. They were both breathing hard into each other's ears. Meadghbh began to giggle and Fullo followed her and began to laugh. "Yes, that was a good first joining. The more times we do this the better it will become. You are a jewel my Meadghbh. I shall never let you go now." Meadghbh just smiled as she looked at him. Now she understood what Edana had told her about joining, which was truly a feeling you can't describe and had to feel yourself.

She felt so relaxed and wanted to stay in Fullo's arms. She hugged him to her, running her hands up his back, to his shoulders and around his neck. She moved his head to her lips and kissed him. "That was truly amazing. I will never let you go now either." She smiled up at him. He replied by kissing her more fully and slowly opening her mouth with his tongue. They twined their tongues and languidly began to kiss again. Fullo kept them joined as long as possible until they began to feel the cold. He rolled to the side and disengaged their bodies. He felt around for her tartan, finding it her spread it over them both. Then he got next to her and held her close. "We should always come to this place now in remembrance of this first joining. It has been christened with your virgin blood so it is now sacred."

"Should we make a little alter here?" Meadghbh asked. "A place of remembrance, maybe make a small sacrifice to the gods?"

"That is a good idea. Maybe today we should bring a duck here for fecundity and sacrifice it."

"No we need to bring a rabbit from the warren. I'll show you where it is and we can take one live to kill it and make the sacrifice to Bres, the god of fertility," Meadghbh breathed.

"We could also make the sacrifice to Venus[148], the Roman goddess of love." Fullo said lazily. "Then let's do that after we take a short nap. There is nothing better than resting after a good bout of love making," Fullo whispered.

Meadghbh smiled. "So we just made love did we?"

---

[148] http://www.ancient.eu/venus/

"Definitely," Fullo breathed next to her ear and started to hum a Roman love song.

"What are you humming?"

"A Roman love song, sung between two lovers that have just culminated their love in an act of passion, just like we did. It is called 'My Lady Has Eyes of Water'," and Fullo proceeded to hum the whole song for her.

"Is she crying? Is that why it is called that?" asked Meadghbh.

"That is one good interpretation but it is because she has blue eyes, they remind her lover of the ocean."

"Can you sing the words for me?"

Fullo smiled and then sang the song in Latin which was why he didn't sing it before. His voice was good, a thin tenor but he hit the notes correctly when he sang. When he was done she smiled and asked him to translate what the words meant. He did so with several corrections to his interpretation because he didn't know the word in Celtic for some of the words in the song. When he was done she hugged him and said: "I think I love you as much as the girl in the song loved her lover."

Fullo smiled and said: "I love you as much as he loved his girl-friend. Like I said I'll never let you go." He turned to her and began to kiss her languidly. Meadghbh turned to him and returned his kiss with passion.

"Let us couple again," she breathed.

"We need to wait because you are still too tender after the first time you make love," Fullo murmured into her ear.

"But I want you again. You will make it better I know."

He smiled and turned to her again. "Alright let's have another round of love making." They then proceeded to make love with as much passion as they did the first time. Meadghbh was right. It didn't hurt much the second time either.

After a short nap they roused and prepared to go to the rabbit warren where they were able to snare a fat buck for their sacrifice to the goddess of fertility Bres and to Venus. They came back and performed the ritual, burning the rabbit carcass. Then they laced hands and returned to the farmhouse to get back to their chores. They met up with Quintus and Edana at the goat shed and started to pitch in to help. By the end of the day they had finished with the repairs to the roof. Enlarging the shed would have to wait until they returned. Edana still needed to get the materials for the enlarging project so she promised to do it by the time they returned in the spring.

The next morning they all met in the courtyard to see off Quintus and Fullo. "Please return as early as possible," Edana said to Quintus.

"We'll do our best to return early. Just have all your building materials ready so when I come back we can get started on all the projects in between sowing the fields," Quintus replied and he leaned down to give Edana a lingering kiss on the mouth. In the background Fullo and Meadghbh were both kissing with their own passion. "Please return early. I will count the days until you return to me," Meadghbh said to Fullo.

Fullo smiled and kissed her one more time. "I'll do my best to return to you as soon as possible."

Ailbe was impatient to say goodbye to Fullo and Quintus and interjected: "You both need to come back to Gosbecks as soon as possible. There are a lot of things that will need your attention when you get back."

"What exactly will need our attention?" Quintus asked as he smiled at Ailbe.

"You will need to talk to everyone about their worries. There will be a lot of unrest when you return."

"Is this your prediction? Maybe from the gods?" asked Quintus.

"No it is a certainty," Ailbe replied in his strangely hollow tone that he used when he was channeling the gods.

"He is telling you what the gods have allowed him to see. Take heed of what he says and return to is as early as you can," Bebhinn replied. "Be safe in your travels." She smiled at them and offered a farewell wave to them as they mounted their horses. Meadghbh was weeping and Edana was looking like she would start to cry when they wheeled their mounts to leave. Even Ailbe looked sad to see them leave. The men looked at everyone.

Quintus said: "We'll be back before you know it. Get ready for the sowing. We'll be busy when Fullo and I return." He looked at Edana then wheeled his mount away. He cantered off to Gosbecks to get the rest of his Contubernium. Once he got back to Gosbecks they all assembled and took off for the main Roman fort and the governor.

CHAPTER 12
PLAYING DRAUGHTS

Faber and Coriaro returned to Lorcan's home and began to pack up their belongings. Lorcan walked over to them and asked: "So now that the decision's been made for the mill I assume you are packing up to leave?"

"Yes, we will be leaving the day after tomorrow and will like to pay up for the time you put us up in your home. Thank you for your hospitality," Faber said as he packed up his weapons and mess kit then turned to Lorcan. "We appreciated the home. It is much warmer than the tents we were in."

"Plus we enjoyed the impromptu music sessions that we were treated to here," Coriaro said as well. He had already packed up his weapons and was working on arranging his mess kit to his approval, turning his bowl just so he could get his cup and spoon in the bag just right[149].

---

[149] http://legvi.tripod.com/id69.html https://images.search.yahoo.com/yhs/search?p=Imperial+Roman+Eating+Utensils&hspart=att&hsimp=yhs-att_001 http://www.dailymail.co.uk/news/article-1247230/The-Roman-Army-Knife-Or-ingenuity-Swiss-beaten-1-800-years.html

"Were you surprised by the vote on the mill? I was. I thought for sure a mill would be approved. We in Gosbecks need to get bigger and compete with Camulodunum," Lorcan allowed. He picked up a couple of walnuts from a nearby bag, broke them open to eat the meat inside.

"Why do you think they voted the way they did then?" Faber asked as he finished packing his mess kit and moved onto his clothes bag. He had a tunic drying by the fire that he packed into the bag.

Lorcan shrugged, "I don't know. It seems they are very reticent to get the Roman money lenders here in Gosbecks right now. That was the most discussions I heard in the area I was standing in. Most of the people were small farmers and they didn't have the large amounts of wheat that needed to be ground like some of the more prosperous farms. There are so many farms that were unable to reap their fields this time around. A lot of men did not return from the rebellion."

"About what amount were the farmers not about to reap their fields this last season?" Coriaro asked.

"I'd say it was easily a good third of the farmers couldn't get all their crops in," Lorcan shrugged again. He looked sad at the reminder of all the men who did not return after the rebellion. "We were required to play a lot of sad music this time around. Even some of our musicians did not return from the rebellion, even more singers too."

"War is always harsh, for those that die but also for those that are left," Coriaro said with compassion. "I have lost a lot of fellow legionaries in my time so I know what I'm talking about."

Lorcan nodded his head. "Thanks for listening to us play our music at all times of the night, you've been very good guests. I know the hours I keep are difficult but it has been that way for a long time so I'm used to it now. It seems regular to me."

"Yes we saw that all the musicians in the area come to the house to rehearse with you. Gosbecks is lucky to have you," Faber told him with a laugh. "I was fine with the late night meetings but we still had our early morning meeting to attend. It was a little difficult at first but then we got used to it."

"Now that we are going you can continue without having to worry about us," Coriaro laughed. "And I'll be able to sleep all night long even when I am assigned a night watch when we travel. I'll still sleep better."

Lorcan had the impudence to smile at this exchange and he pulled out his pipe to run a trill through the keys. "That's one last impromptu rehearsal for you." Then he topped it off with a jaunty little tune that they recognized as one that will be for the mid-winter festival. The Romans laughed and hummed along while they finished packing.

At Ronan and Fingula's farm Bundarus and Rufus let them know that they would be leaving the day after tomorrow. "Thank you for the good billet. We have been very comfortable here. Since we have one full day before we leave is there something you would like us to help you with? Perhaps fix your shuttle on your weaving loom, the one that you showed us yesterday? Or if you need something done on you farm we could help there," Bundarus rumbled.

"Why thank you for the offer. I think I have a few big item tasks to do on the farm, mainly repairs on the fencing around the perimeter. I'll need to purchase the timbers but that shouldn't be too hard to do. There is plenty next door at Ferdia's farm that I can buy. Yes I think doing the work on the fence would be the just what is needed," Ronan beamed at the Romans.

Rufus returned his smile and said: "I would love to work on your fence, it will keep us fit and keep in shape for the military drills we will be doing for the rest of the months until spring."

"So you're leaving soon? I am sorry to see you go." a timid Eilis said as she was carding some wool getting it ready to spin into yarn for her tartans. She looked up and smiled at Bundarus, a small smile but filled with purpose.

"Yes it is so soon but we'll be back in Gosbecks by the spring planting," Bundarus rumbled, his voice gentle as he spoke to Eilis.

Fingula said: "You are coming back then? That's good I liked what you talked about earlier when you were telling us to sell our textiles to some Roman traders. There is a seller of clothes at market day but he has not seen our wares. Ronan and I would like for you to be our agent to help sell our textiles to these Roman traders."

Bundarus smiled. "I was going to approach you about this anyway but you've beat me to the punch so to speak. I would be proud to represent your textiles and scarves to the Roman traders for sell elsewhere. Your textiles are good enough to be shipped back to Rome for selling there. You should be very proud. We can work out the details of my being your agent later but I would proudly represent your goods."

Ronan and Fingula hugged, beaming at their good fortune to have Bundarus represent their wares to the Roman traders. Ronan said: "Then we need to redouble our efforts to get more tartans and scarves out to sell. Fingula you need to dye more wool in the blues, yellows, and reds like we talked about. Eilis you'll need to make much more yarn in the next couple of months so keep working!" Ronan grinned and hugged Fingula again. "We are finally going to make our way in the world with your lovely textiles and scarves. We might even look into hiring some extra help."

Eilis jumped up at that with vigor. "We could hire Sadhbh to help me card more wool. She would be more than happy to work with me."

"Yes she would work well with you and you two are good friends anyway. What about Meadghbh or even Edana? They could also help especially if we get this enterprise working out," Ronan added the added profits floating about in his head.

Fingula shook her head and pulled him back to the present. "What could we possibly pay them with? The past couple of market days have been lean and we don't have enough to pay for all the dyes that I need. We should maybe get Sadhbh to work since her father is no longer around and they need the extra money but we cannot hire the rest."

Bundarus stepped forward: "I have money that I've been saving for the future, I could loan you the money for the future since I'll be your agent you need the commodities that I'll be selling. I can give you a sestertius for the capital to start. You'll be able to purchase the dyes and extra wool if you need it from others. Plus you'll be able to buy a new shuttle cock that you need for weaving the textiles. You'll be on your way."

"You'd do this Bundarus? Alright I accept it only as a loan and I'll pay you back as soon as we sell these tartans and scarves at the next market day and beyond. Thank you!" Ronan was very overcome with the enormity of what he was getting into on the commodities market. It was something he'd always dreamt of but had no way of doing until now. Now with this little bit of capital he could move forward. Fingula was also bright eyed and was already dreaming about the increase of their wares and the better living they could now afford. A smile laced her face as she could envision it. She made plans to buy a new shuttle cock and the dyes she needed next market day, small increments at first but as things began to move she would increase the amounts.

At Cathmore's farm Grex and Titus let them know that they would be leaving the day after tomorrow as well but they would be able to help out one more day if he needed anything done. Cathmore seemed to be unhappy to see them leave but he put a good face on it. "Thank you for helping out. I will take you up on one item that has needed to be fixed since I returned home from the rebellion. I have some fences that have fallen down as well as our cow barn that needs to be fixed up. Those two items would be what needs to be taken care of. You can get started on the cow barn today."

Grex smiled and said: "It would be our pleasure to start now. What exactly does the cow barn need?"

Cathmore said: "It would be best if we just go out and look at the barn now. I think the roof has a few places where it leaks, the doors need to be reset so they close better and there are the walls that would need to be looked at."

"Then let's go now so we can get the cow barn taken care of, since we've been using the barn I noticed that the fence also needs to be shored up as well," Titus said and he stood up from the table they were all at.

"Yes I forgot about that as well. It might be the cow barn is all you'll be able to work on before you go," Cathmore replied.

"We'll be able to get more done if you just give us the materials and let us get to work," Grex said.

"Yes, half of our time spent as legionaries is building, either roads, fences or bridges so this will be easy," Titus said. "At least this won't be a road or bridge, which is a back breaking endeavor. I worked on more roads than I care to talk about."

"So being a soldier isn't just about warfare? You do more than just wage war?" Cathmore asked.

"Yes we do much more than just wage war. When we were in Gaul we were constantly working on roads and our fort. Whether it was building barracks or living quarters for the officers it was building more roads. I was personally involved with forty millia passus of paved roads. We always had competitions between the centuries on how far the road would get built. I personally worked on the road from Hatra[150] to Wadi Al-Tharthar[151], and that was the hottest assignment I've ever been on." Titus related with a proud smile.

"I didn't realize that the Romans did more than just fight. When you say you build roads are you talking about the ones that are more rock than just a dirt track?" Cathmore asked seeming truly interested.

"Of course, we build roads that have a paved surface, made from interlocking stone sort of like a mosaic. They are much more durable than just a dirt track and much less bound to become a quagmire in heavy rains. They are designed to let the water run over them but not to wash out since they are designed properly to

---

[150] http://www.roman-empire.net/articles/article-036.html
[151] http://www.roman-empire.net/articles/article-036.html

let the water flow through the substructure. The roads we built had a paved surface with gravel on top[152]," Titus opined warming up to the subject.

"I'm not sure what you mean by gravel," Cathmore asked as he stood up and prepared to leave to the cow barn.

Titus stood too and kept talking. "Gravel is small rocks that are laid out on top to give the wagons something to grip as they pass over it. They range from the size of your fingernail to small bits the size of seeds. Having the gravel on top lets the road last longer because the more it is used the smaller the rocks are ground down into."

Grex stood as well and followed Cathmore and Titus to the cow barn. Outside they went directly to they looked at cow barn critically. There they saw the amount of work was greater than Cathmore let on, more structural problems showed as the cow barn's roof was tilted to the left and was missing shingles. The walls of the barn looked to be in the best shape except for the back right corner. The fence surrounding the barn was also in disrepair, missing some slats and falling down in other places. It was obvious that Cathmore's arm had hindered him for a long time preventing him from fixing the barn as well as other major duties around the farm. Titus and Grex looked at each other and shrugged their shoulders.

"All right now, where is you mallet and nails? We should get working on this right away. How about the extra wood you need to shore up your cow barn? Where do you have the extras?" Grex said right off the top.

Cathmore smiled and said it was all in the barn. He showed them everything they needed the materials were laid out but under a lot of dust as he had not gotten to them yet.

"See there is the mallet, saw and drill if you need to use them.

---

[152] http://www.historylearningsite.co.uk/ancient-rome/roman-roads/ http://www.history.com/news/history-lists/8-ways-roads-helped-rome-rule-the-ancient-world

Over in the bucket is the nails that you'll need," Cathmore indicated the leather bucket leaning against the stack of lumber.

"Do you have a ladder? Or we can make one quickly if you don't out of the lumber stack," Grex asked.

"I have a ladder in the barn over there, it is old but very sturdy," Cathmore pointed to an old ladder that was grey with usage but looked to be in good repair. The Romans got their mallet and saw out and began to work. Titus took the mallet and nails then started going through the lumber for usable pieces to start with. Grex started with the saw and went to the lumber as well. They discussed what needed to be done first and decided to work on the roof first. Grex got the saw out and started cutting shingles out of the lumber slats. Titus picked up the shingles and headed over to the roof to look at the areas that showed obvious signs of leaks. Cathmore showed him the worse spots and pointed out new problem areas. Also looking at the roof they determined that a supporting joist was causing all the sagging to the left and would need to be replaced at a later date since they did not have the time to do it.

Both Grex and Titus worked under Cathmore's' direction for the rest of the day on the cow barn. They managed to make enough shingles for the roof and finished patching up the holes so there were no longer gaping holes in the roof. Then they began to work on the back right corner of the barn. The leaks had caused the corner to start rotting in places so they needed to replace the rotted boards. Both men worked methodically and took the direction from Cathmore quite well. By the end of the day they had fixed the roof and were almost done with the right corner. The next day would be the fence which would require much more lumber than they currently had. That evening they discussed where they could get more lumber and determined that Niamh's farm would be the best place to go get it.

"It was a good day's work gentlemen," Cathmore said at dinner that evening. "We will get the cow barn finished tomorrow and might even have time to fix one of my fences over by the south paddock."

That afternoon Quintus and Fullo got back to Bebhinn's farm

and found everyone still working in the garden doing the chores Bebhinn had given to Edana and Meadghbh. They were all still gardening and harvesting the vegetables when the Romans rode up into the courtyard.

"Looks like Bebhinn gave them a lot of chores to do this day," Fullo smiled as they pulled up to dismount from the horses. The horses were used to the farm and let out happy whinnies to see their pasture. They were restive when they were untacked but pleased to be turned out. The horses whinnied and bucked when they were untacked and let out in the pasture, galloping off to the far side of the field. The men took themselves off to see where the others were in the garden. Fullo called out: "We're back from the meeting and it looks like you are still doing the chores Bebhinn gave you earlier."

Both girls turned and smiled at the Romans. Edana stood up and said: "You are correct, we are still doing the chores that Mother gave us and probably will doing the same tomorrow. How was the meeting? Did Gosbecks vote on the mill?"

Quintus stepped forward and said: "Yes they did but they voted to not go with the mill and to forego the road improvements. Not the best decision but I can respect their reasons for it. Just to let you know now that the decision has been made we will be leaving the day after tomorrow. We need to get back to our governor and let them know what Gosbecks has decided to do."

"You're leaving so soon? You should stay at least a few more days, we need to get the goat shed enlarged and the roof taken care of," Edana said with worriedly "I still have many more chores for you to help us with."

"I know but we no longer need to stay in Gosbecks. The Roman veterans will be back in the spring in time for sowing. Fullo and I will be back then," Quintus smiled trying to put a good light on their leaving.

"But I don't want you to go yet," Edana said faintly, a small frown marring her beautiful face. Meadghbh also stood and looked at Fullo with a sorrowful look on her face.

"Don't be sad we'll still be here tomorrow to get some of the chores done. We'll start on the goat shed first thing in the morning. Do you have all the materials for enlarging and fixing the roof?" Fullo said quickly.

"Yes we have lumber and enough nails to fix it. The only thing I do not have is a saw," Edana related. She still looked pensive and wiped her hands on the front of her tunic leaving muddy streaks on the soft blue wool.

Ailbe who had been standing off to the side and listening piped up: "They'll be back in time to help with the sowing so do not fret Edana and Meadghbh." Then he grinned and said in true little boy fashion: "Will you still teach us how to play draughts tonight? I want to learn the game and perfect it in time for you to come back in the spring and play you." Edana and Meadghbh both looked at them and offered watery smiles.

Quintus and Fullo looked at him and both burst into laughter. "Of course we'll teach you how to play draughts. You'll need to practice your wagers and strategy so when we get back we'll be able to play the game the right way. Well done young Ailbe, you managed to change sad faces into happier ones," Fullo said smiling widely. "Plus I want to see if you can tap into your otherworldly ways to win at the bets," he chuckled.

Quintus' eyebrows went up when he mentioned Ailbe being able to tap into the other realm. "Does this mean you'll be given tips from the gods as to how we'll be betting? That is so unfair! I don't know if I'll be wagering anything with you." He laughed though to ease his mock indignation.

Ailbe smirked. "I'll prove to you that I have the gods' ears, they favor me." Then he looked pensive for a moment as he thought about it. "Maybe the gods won't favor me if it for my own benefit and not others. But I will surely try to see and play you the way it should be played." Ailbe's face cleared and he grinned.

"Then I'm really interested in how well you learn tonight," Quintus grinned too. "It is a deal we'll teach all of you how to play draughts even Bebhinn. That way all of you can practice it until we return in the spring. You should have enough time to perfect your strategies." Ailbe, Edana and Meadghbh all grinned. They began to finish up on their gardening chore and gathered up all their clippings, putting them in the satchels and wiped their hands on their tartans leaving dirty runnels of smeared dirt. Then they all turned and made their way back to the farmhouse together.

Once at the farmhouse Edana and Meadghbh both unloaded their satchels and turned to Bebhinn who had just arrived. "We've got some but not all the snippets from your medicinal plants. We will have to finish tomorrow," Edana told her mother. "There are about four more rows of the plants that we need to harvest."

Bebhinn nodded and smiled. "I knew you wouldn't be able to finish today but we got a good head start on the tonics and elixirs with these snippets. It will keep me busy for at least twelve days preparing all of them for future use."

"Quintus told us that the mill decision was not to build. I'm sorry to hear that but I understand why. He also told us that they will be leaving to go back to their governor the day after tomorrow. But they'll be returning in time to sow this spring," Edana told her mother.

"Yes I heard that as well earlier from them. At least they will be back in the springtime. We'll have plenty of work for them come that time. Are both Fullo and Quintus coming back to stay here?"

Quintus who had been listening to their exchange said: "Yes if you'll still have us we would be able to come back to your farm and stay."

Bebhinn's' eyebrows raised and asked: "You're not going to build your own home?"

"We would like to stay here to get you back on your feet since your husband and oldest son are no longer here. Then we will turn and build our own houses since we will be retiring here in Gosbecks." Quintus explained.

"How many Romans will be retiring here to Gosbecks?"

Bebhinn asked, Edana and Meadghbh both moved forward to listen to his answer.

"There will approximately eighty that will be retiring here to Gosbecks. Those eighty will be bringing their families. Some will be given land to farm and others will be taking up other ways to live, some will be merchants, some will be opening taverns. It all depends on what the retiring veterans want to do," Quintus clarified. He looked at the women and expected more questions.

It wasn't long in coming when Edana asked: "Taverns? What about Oisin's tavern, one will not be enough for everyone?"

"Probably not, we Romans use taverns for several things, like for food, for meetings, for drink, for music like at Oisin's," Quintus explained.

"Where will they get the land for their farms?" inquired Bebhinn, looking much more pensive at the thought of what might in fact be in store for a lot of residents in Gosbecks.

"We will buy the land from the present owners. There seems to be a lot of farms that are struggling because they lost so many farmers in the last rebellion. There are a lot of people who didn't finish reaping their crops this last season. They might be willing to sell and their farms will go to a Roman veteran. The farmers might even be able to stay on and be hired as laborers for the veterans," Quintus supposed. "This is of course all speculation on my part because it might be quite different when I return. There will be a lot of the farmers who will be able to get back on their feet and pay any taxes that are still in arrears."

Bebhinn fell silent at this bit of information. She was one of the farmers who were in arrears. She also thought of Cathmore who was even more in arrears than she was since he didn't have a son to help out. She needed to let him know about this bit of information. He and Miach will want to know what was coming this spring. Did they realize how many Romans would be coming this spring? It would change the face of Gosbecks and enlarge it by a full fourth of the population. There were many farmers in Gosbecks that would willingly sell their farms but what would they do instead? She didn't think they would be willing to be hired back just as laborers to the Roman veterans.

"Are the Roman veterans coming to stay or will they be moving on? Will they be bringing women with them?" She asked.

"Some will move on but most will stay. There will be some veterans who will be bringing women and children with them but most won't have any women with them. They'll come and meet different local women here in Gosbecks," Fullo told them, looking at Meadghbh. She blushed and looked away but then looked right back at him and smiled. Bebhinn saw this exchange and her heart dropped even further. She knew there was something developing between these two but now she was certain. She then turned to Quintus and saw him looking at Edana with a smile on both of their faces. She knew Edana was lost to her, to the man who killed Ailbe and Edana's Faber and her husband. Hatred filled her veins at that moment, a cold white fury that knew no bounds.

She was so angry she almost missed the next thing Quintus said: "We'll be fixing up the goat shed tomorrow and I'll need for you to make a list of the other duties that we will need to finish when we come back in the spring."

"I'll get the list started right now since I know the goat shed will take all day tomorrow to fix. Right now Meadghbh and I need to go get the goats from the upper pasture and bring them back to the normal paddock," Edana said to Quintus. "I'll be composing the list as I walk up to the upper pasture."

"I look forward to getting it. I will be able to leave you with some money to purchase lumber and extra materials needed so it will all be here when I get back," Quintus said.

"Thank you Quintus we'll be ready for when you get back from where you're going. I'll have everything here ready to be put into place," Edana told him.

Quintus smiled at her. "I know you'll get everything ready. Spring is an extremely busy time so I'll try to get back as early as possible." He met her eyes and gave her a more meaningful look. Bebhinn hated him even more in that instant as she observed the unspoken communication between the two. *Not my daughter* her mind screamed. She seethed as she looked at Quintus, cold fury swirled up in her veins. *I will get my revenge on you*, she silently swore. Unbeknownst to Quintus he continued to hold Edana's regard, they were in each other's orbit to the exclusion of all else.

Fullo turned to Meadghbh and asked her: "Do you want me to come along with you to get the goats from the upper pasture?"

"Absolutely, it will make this chore so much easier and more fun," Meadghbh said. "Why don't both of you come with us?" She smiled at Fullo and Quintus.

"I think we both will come with the two of you to herd your goats," Quintus laughed shaking his head. "I never would have seen myself as a herder before but I guess I am now."

"We both are then," laughed Fullo as he caught up Meadghbh in his arms and hugged her. Meadghbh laughed with him as she hugged him back. "Then let's go before it gets much later, we'll be returning in the dark as it is." So everyone except Bebhinn and Ailbe went off to go get the goats from the upper pasture.

Bebhinn was left to get the end of the day meal together for everyone. She thought of the things she could put into Quintus' food to cause him discomfort and harm but something stopped her cold. She was a healer not a poisoner, one who succors the ill, not cause it. It went against all that she was to even think that way. Bebhinn flushed red with horror at what she was thinking. *I'll have to tell Miach what I almost did when I see him*, she thought. He'd be so horrified that she would even think that way, so against her druidic healer training. Miach was her mentor and she wanted to live up to his good opinion of her. She would have to fall back on her teaching and make Quintus and Fullo an especially good dinner tonight. She resolved to get in touch with Miach as soon as possible to discuss her lapse of judgment. She turned and looked at her larder and saw it was fully stocked. She pulled out the smoked haunch of deer that she got from Cathmore earlier and went about preparing a good meal of it.

"Ailbe what about an evening meal of deer tonight, we should get a good going away dinner in the pot for Fullo and Quintus?" Bebhinn asked.

"Deer for our evening meal that sounds really good, we will celebrate their going back to the Roman governor. I'll be sad to see them go but they'll be back in the spring, in time for spring sowing. I wonder if the rest of Gosbecks realizes they will be back with more Romans," Ailbe said.

"More Romans, what exactly do you mean?" Bebhinn asked.

"They are only the scouting party for a larger group of Romans coming to Gosbecks. There will be many more Romans coming back with Quintus and Fullo when they return," Ailbe replied. He turned and petted Cabhan on the head, smoothing back the ruffled tan of his hide.

"Oh, I'll have to ask Quintus about that when they get back from their chore. I'm sure you're right," Bebhinn said as she turned to start cooking for everyone.

"I want you to point out on the way to the upper pasture all of the items you want to fix when I come back," Quintus said to Edana as they walked to the upper pasture with their hands clasped together.

"I want you to stay more days instead of just two," Edana looked forlornly at Quintus, looking at him with sorrowful doe eyes.

"I am sorry but we must return to our main fort and give the governor a report of what has happened here in Gosbecks. That is the first thing I must do. I'll be back to stay in the spring, just for the winter season I'll be gone. Before you know it I'll be back," Quintus smiled and chucked Edana's chin with a playful cuff. She smiled half-heatedly and continued on her way to the upper pasture.

Behind them Fullo and Meadghbh were talking softly. "I want to join with you before I go. Is there a way we could absent ourselves from the rest tomorrow and go somewhere private?" Fullo murmured.

Meadghbh blushed and smiled at Fullo. "We could let the goats go to the upper pasture and do something then. Or we could stay and use the goat shed. It should be easy to slip away and be together without Ailbe or Bebhinn to know."

"Let's go to the upper pasture, we'll find a small secluded spot to lie down together," Fullo smiled at Meadghbh. "I want a memorable morning joining that will last us until I get back in the spring. It will have to do us until I get back to you."

"I know just the spot in the upper pasture. There is a quiet glen by the limits of the upper pasture on the north side. There is a small clearing with a beautiful meadow that the goats keep it cut down. It is very pretty and quiet. If someone comes looking for us they wouldn't be able to see us," Meadghbh whispered to Fullo looking at him closely.

"It sounds perfect. We'll go there first thing in the morning. I'll make sure we are the only ones to take the goats to the upper pasture tomorrow morning," Fullo crooned with a knowing grin on his face. Meadghbh didn't know what he meant but just nodded with a big smile on her face.

Ahead Edana said: "Why don't we go back to the goat shed tomorrow to join?"

"No, no more goat sheds for me. Come to my pallet later tonight and we'll join there. I do not want to use a smelly goat shed for our last time together before I go," Quintus told her quietly.

"In the house? People will hear us as we join! We made a lot of noise in the goat shed." Edana said with shock but was secretly titillated.

"We can do it much quieter and if they hear us it doesn't matter. We'll only do it once but it will be a moment to remember. I don't want to do it in the dirty goat shed . You and I deserve better, a much cleaner place," Quintus murmured.

"But we have prying eyes in the farm house. Mother, Ailbe, Meadghbh and Fullo will all hear us," Edana pleaded. "I will feel so hemmed in if we join in the house like that, what if we find a good place to join somewhere around the farm?"

"No, the farm is dirty. I want you to be clean when we join. I'll wash and I want you to do the same," Quintus said with intent.

Edana sounded nonplussed: "The farm is not dirty it is just a farm. I don't understand what you are saying. I am clean as well I don't know why I should take a bath."

"You aren't clean. You've not had a bath since we last joined. I need to be clean as well. We Romans have baths on a daily basis. When we get back with our entire century of veterans will build a bath house for Gosbecks and everyone will benefit from daily baths," Quintus said as they walked along. "We need to be clean to stay healthy. Bebhinn will find with the bath house opened that she'll see less health problems in the population of Gosbecks."

"Daily baths will keep the population healthy? I've never heard of such a thing. In the winter we go months without taking a bath," Edana said.

"And you probably get more fevers and illnesses because of it. The Roman military moves into places and institutes sanitation to keep the fevers at bay. We can't stop every fever but we do stop the ones dealing with cleanliness. You'll see and there will be benefits from the better sanitation and cleanliness," Quintus smirked and pulled her closer in to him. She resisted at first then softened as they continued on to the upper pasture. Presently they got there and realized that because it was a relatively mild day the goats were spread out in the upper pasture. So they needed to go into the pasture to herd the goats. After herding them all up especially one recalcitrant black and white ram they started going back to the lower pasture then back to the farmhouse.

While they were walking Edana asked Quintus one more time, "Do I really need to wash before we join tonight?"

Quintus turned and looked at her. "Of course you do, I want to smell your womanly scent, not your stink from running and gardening."

"So you're saying I smell bad?"

"Yes from normal daily chores everyone gets a certain smell. I just want you to be clean for our time together tonight. I'll also wash off as best I can, you do the same," he said.

'All right I'll wash off the grime from the past couple of days. I'll have to do it inside with Meadghbh though. Mother will be surprised to see us both wash off outside," Edana said.

"Maybe you can get her to wash off too," he said. "She'll be a better healer if she is clean."

"I'll see if I can't get her to do it," laughed Edana. "She probably won't though but maybe, she does wash her utensils and hands when she does her healing or birthing."

"Then she will. All good healers recognize the power of cleanliness when dealing with blood," Quintus smiled to hear Bebhinn was cleaner than her daughter. "You might want to get Meadghbh to also wash. I know Fullo will wash with me as well. Maybe we can get Ailbe to wash with us so everyone will be clean."

"I hope you do try, he is hard to get clean," Edana laughed even harder.

"We might be more successful than you think. He is easy to get to do things if he wants to learn draughts tonight. That is what we'll tell him. No bath, no game," Quintus laughed with her. They were laughing until Fullo and Meadghbh asked why and were told what they were going to do tonight. Everyone started laughing. Meadghbh didn't even put up a fight at her washing. When they got back to the farmhouse everyone separated and got ready to bathe. True to his prediction Fullo and Quintus were able to get Ailbe clean. Edana and Meadghbh had no problem getting Bebhinn to wash with them. Soon they were all clean and setting down to dinner of deer with late season vegetables. It was a good dinner for them all and Edana and Meadghbh got the put away the dishes and cleaned them in record time.

Quintus stepped forward with the game pieces. "Now we will

all learn how to play draughts[153]. Fullo will leave the draught counters for you to keep practicing so you'll be ready for us when we
return this spring. You can play the game in teams or individually.
The betting comes in when we begin the next turn. You will get
the hang of the game as we go on," Quintus set out the draught
counters to demonstrate how the game was played. Everyone had
lots of questions so Fullo and Quintus played a game to show everyone how the game was played. They played two full games before
the others got the hang of it. The rules were opaque to understand
especially when Quintus and Fullo would talk about betting. Then
Fullo and Quintus had them all play in teams, Fullo as the leader of
one team and Quintus as the leader of the other. Ailbe, Meadghbh
and Fullo on one side, Edana, Bebhinn and Quintus on the other,
and they played several games until it got quite late.

"It is a good game to play, I think we'll play it every night until
you get back from seeing the governor," Edana said after the last
lively game. "I know we'll be ready for you by spring."

Bebhinn shoved Ailbe off of his seat: "To bed with you Ailbe,
it is quite late and we still have to get up early to do our chores,"

"I'll get to bed and will get up just in time for my chores
Mother," Ailbe said. He got up and went over to his pallet to lie
down. Once there he folded his tired head onto his arms and went
right to sleep, his tired little boy snores quickly sounding out as
soon as his head hit the pallet. Bebhinn laughed and made her way
to her pallet and sleeping area which was by Ailbe's. She changed
into just her tunic and lay down on the pallet.

Meadghbh kissed Fullo good night and went to her pallet as
well. Edana looked at Quintus and saw him mouth later and point
to his pallet. She nodded her head yes and went over to her pallet.
Edana quickly got a bowl of water and some soap weed. She quickly

---

[153] http://draughtshistory.nl/origin22.htm
http://www.chesslab.com/rules/CheckerComments4.html

washed herself. The she changed into her tunic as well and lay down next to Meadghbh. "Why did you wash?" Asked Meadghbh.

"I am going to couple with Quintus tonight. I wanted to be clean." Edana whispered. Meadghbh gasped in surprise and giggled.

"Enjoy yourself."

Everyone lay down to sleep. Edana waited until she heard the deeper breathing of Meadghbh before she rose and went over to Quintus. They quietly lay down and covered up. Quintus moved her under him and he rose over her to lie on top of her, bracing his arms so he didn't crush her.

Quintus breathed into her ear: "We must be quiet so keep your moans low. Fullo is already sleeping as is Bebhinn and Ailbe. Is Meadghbh also sleeping?" He kissed her neck with little open mouthed kisses, licking his way to her throat.

"Yes, Meadghbh is sleeping," she whispered and moved her head back to give him more access to her throat. She muffled a low moan as he started to move down her tunic to her breasts and kissed them open mouthed through her tunic. He began to move her tunic up to her waist and she helped by lifting up her hips when he got to them. Soon he had uncovered her lower body and started moving her legs apart with his. He fit his body between her legs and moved one of his hands to her womanhood. He opened her labia with his fingers and found the bundle of nerves that were so sensitive. He used his fingers to find her natural moisture and moved it to her clitoris. He then proceeded to circle the sensitive clitoris, she moaned and became slightly louder as she gasped.

"Stay quiet my Edana, you must stifle the moans so we do this without noise."

She stifled her moans and pressed her lips together to keep them from opening when he continued to circle the spot that felt so good with his fingers. He moved more of her copious moisture from her vagina to her clitoris and started to find a tempo that brought her gasps to higher heights. The feelings started to build until Edana then moaned her completion as he made her climax.

He moved his mouth over hers to capture her cries as she opened her mouth to his tongue. She allowed him to plunder her mouth as she continued to feel the tremors blow through her system. He moved to get his penis free from his loin cloth and set it near her entrance.

"Stay quiet, I'm going to enter you now." He pushed into her welcoming depths. She moaned into his mouth as he recaptured hers. They began to move in rhythm slow at first then faster as he was striving towards his climax. "You feel so good, warm and wet." He began to move faster and she started to feel that pressing feeling again. They moved in unison as they each followed their urgent feelings. He waited until she found hers first then as she clenched around him he followed her over the edge to glory. They both breathed hard into each other's mouth, sharing their breath as they both came down from their mutual feelings. "This is how your parents must have joined so no one could hear," he breathed into her ear. Edana started to giggle but stayed quiet when he told her "Hush, don't wake up the others." They smiled at each other and continued to kiss, Quintus raining small kisses on Edana's mouth, face and ending on her nose. Quintus pulled out of Edana and rolled to his side taking her with him.

"I should go back to my pallet before too much longer, before we fall asleep," Edana whispered quietly.

Quintus kissed her lips and said: "I agree and good night." He kissed her for several more moments then let her go. She lifted up quietly and moved back to her pallet. She felt the result of their loving slide down her thighs. She quickly got back onto her pallet and lay down drawing up her blanket over her. She stared into the black night of the farm house, still feeling the waves of ecstasy coursing through her body from their lovemaking. "I am very happy," she said quietly to herself and turned over to go to sleep. She drifted off to sleep as she relaxed into the quiet of the night.

The next morning dawned bright, the weak late autumn sun was doing its best to shine down on the earth. Everyone got up, got their morning meal and went out to do their morning chores. Edana and Quintus went to the goat shed to start work on the roof. Ailbe went to do his chores with the chickens and ducks and Bebhinn went out to finish the chores in her medicinal garden. Meadghbh and Fullo took off to turn out the goats in the upper pasture.

Fullo holding a wool blanket took Meadghbh's hand and led her outside to the barn where the oxen were located. "We need to have quiet time for our loving." Here he placed a deep kiss on her mouth, deepening it when Meadghbh opened hers. They kissed intensely, then Fullo stopped the kiss. "Come on." He led her outside to the barn with the two bovines. Inside he moved her to the back where the hay was located and took down enough hay to create a soft bed on the ground then threw the blanket over it. He turned to Meadghbh and extended his hand: "Come here."

Meadghbh smiled and walked forward then laid down on the bed of hay. She extended her arms and said: "Come here my love."

Fullo, happy to hear she loved him, eagerly came forward laying down. He claimed her mouth once again, kissing her extremely by opening his mouth wide thrusting his tongue into Meadghbh's mouth. She moaned and kissed him back with equal fervor. Fullo began to undress her, slowly taking off her tartan, unwinding it one handedly. When it was off he continued to lean over Meadghbh obviously, nodding to het for assisting in the exercise. Next he went for her tunic, pulling the hem up from the side while he continued to kiss her. He finally pulled the tunic up over her head.

Fullo took hold of Meadghbh's breast. He loved the feel of it, reveling in its softness and the heaviness of it. He leaned down, laved it with his lips and tongue then he sucked on it. Meadghbh moaned: "Yes, I love how that feels Fullo." She took her hand and ran it through his beautiful tresses, scratching his head. Then Fullo started kissing down her, starting with her belly moving toward her womanhood. He got to her labia, separated the lips and kissed her using his tongue. Meadghbh squirmed and tossing her head, arching her back. She held his head down to herself closely. He licked her clitoris until she cried out as she burst into her climax. Then Fullo got up and put his penis into her vagina. He pushed it in hard. Meadghbh went wild in ecstasy. Then they started to move together in the age old movement of love. Fullo move back and forth and he picked her up and turned her around, entering her from behind. Since this was new to Meadghbh she cried out in surprise. Soon Fullo moved going back and forth, back and forth harder and harder. Meadghbh was so surprised at how good it felt. She began to feel that feeling of anticipation that soon culminated in a climax. Once Fullo felt her climax he finished off with his explosion.

They both were tired and sweaty. After all that work they looked at each other and started giggling. Meadghbh said: "This does get better and better the more we do this, just like you said."

"It was very good this time around. Like the next time the next and the next time. No sweetheart I'm here to talk about me leaving. I know it is very quick and is not a good thing. I know you want me to stay but I will be back in the summertime. So it is not that long, but even then I cannot wait till we are back together," murmured Fullo.

"I've known you will be leaving but it is so soon! I will miss you dreadfully. I'll wait for you,' Meadghbh said tearfully. Fullo grabbed her at this and buried his face in her neck as he gave her a bear hug.

Fullo looked up at the sun. "We need to leave now. Get your clothes back on and we'll get going.'

"I'll get ready to go with you." They began to get up and got dressed. Meadghbh was very sad. "I know you would be back in the summertime, but that seems to be so long. I would rather you stay here with me"

Fullo jumped up and grabbed her and kissed her. It was a kiss that spoke of more. "You are becoming more important to me. The more I know you, the more time I want to spend time with you. I wish to keep this going. So wait for me." Meadghbh sniffled and shook her head yes. They grasped their hands and walked back home.

CHAPTER 12
FAREWELL TO GOSBECKS

It was so early in the morning, the sun had not come out yet. Everyone was asleep, all except Quintus. He quietly got up and moved over to Edana's pallet. He stealthily lifted the edge of the blanket and slipped underneath. Moving in closely to Edana he positioned himself between her legs and got up underneath her shift. She continued to sleep peaceably. Quintus opened her legs further and revealed her womanhood. He took a deep breath to smell her. His penis got even harder at the sweet scent of Edana. He moved his face closer to her lady garden and licked her lips, running his tongue up to her clitoris. Once there he circled it then affixed his lips to it to create a suction. He then sucked and at the same time moved his tongue on the clitoris rapidly. Edana moaned half-awake feeling the erotic feelings of a sensual dream. Quintus continued to manipulate her clitoris then he moved two fingers into her vagina to test her reaction to his work. Finding her vagina warm and juicy he continued to insert his fingers rhythmically. Then he went back to work drawing her clitoris into his mouth and sucked. Edana feeling the intense feelings down there in her nether region woke up with a loud moan. She lifted her blanket and saw Quintus. Quintus smiled and murmured "Good morning Edana, how are you this morning. I hope you are feeling a little bit romantic."

Edana's emotion of stimulating and sexy feelings woke up. "I feel very romantic this morning. I wonder why?" Then Edana giggled, she lay back to let Quintus finish what he had begun. Quintus chuckled and began to worship her body. He returned to the position between her legs and began to pay her love button special attention. With every lap of his tongue Edana groaned out loud despite her attempts to keep quiet. She hovered on the edge of her climax with Quintus. Knowing just what she needed he put two fingers into her vagina and moved them rapidly. Edana bowed her body as the intense pinnacle hit her. She clamped a hand over her mouth to keep from crying out her ecstasy. After a moment to collect her thoughts that had burst from her brain as a result of her massive climax she leaned down and grasped Quintus's face. He turned and gave Edana a passionate kiss. "I will never get over that feeling," She said. She turned to Quintus so that they were chest to chest, her breast thrust against Quintus, her nipples pebbled by the feeling. He raised his hands and gripped them, rolling her nipples with his fingers. Edana groaned even more. "If you do not make love to me right now, I will cry out and wake everybody up!"

"We wouldn't want that, would we?" Ground out Quintus as he settled himself between her legs, pulling out his penis. He found her wet entrance, then with a strong thrust he pushed it in. The feeling was superb, so tight and wet. It was so perfect that he growled out "Too good!" He slowly got the rhythm going as he pushed in and out of her channel. Every push and pull was ecstasy. Soon he could not wait and started going faster and faster in a frenzy, pushing it in and out of her as quickly as possible and going at different angles. When he hit a particular angle, Edana cried out. He plunged in that angle again and again, over and over she cried out each time. He started going faster and harder, getting close to his finish but he wanted her to finish first. She was getting close to her culmination and cried out, reaching her climax. Then Quintus drove in harder and faster. Then he came as well.

They came back down to earth after reaching their heavenly limits. Edana was very happy and so was Quintus. "It gets better each time we do that!" Grinned Edana.

Quintus smiled as well "It does and it will continue to do so the more times we do it. I plan on doing it more and more with you, Edana. But I do have to tell you something. We received a message from the general that we are to return to go back west to his fort. Unfortunately we will be leaving tomorrow morning early. But I will be back in spring, in time for the sowing. I look forward to coming back to my Edana."

"Leaving so soon! Why can't it be in a week or even a month?"

"Gosbecks is going to be the place of another *Colonia*. So we will be bringing more Romans with us. We will be bringing at least eighty Romans, plus their families, so that should be about 250 extra people, if not more. It will be a good time for you to learn Latin." Quintus kissed her lips, her nose, then her forehead.

"Coming back so many people you will outnumber the people in Gosbecks two or even three to one. I will have to tell the people of Gosbecks about this," She thought a moment, "Will mother still be able to be a healer?" Edana asked.

Quintus grinned. "Of course she will be. People in the medical field are few and far between, and she is far too good at what she does. We might bring surgeons with us but she can work in town with them. I'm surprised you are not too worried about me leaving so soon."

Edana smiled sadly: "I have known that you were going to have to go back for some time, but I am glad to be back soon in time for sowing. That is a festival time. I know you will be back in time for all the Beltane festival. It is a good time to be here in the spring. On one sad note is I will miss you dreadfully better will only be for a couple months."

Quintus grabbed her and kissed her soundly. The kissing turned to more amorous kisses leading to one more bout of lovemaking. Quintus flipped Edana over onto her stomach. Then he put a pillow under her hips to raise them. He spread her legs giving him access to her lady garden again. Since she was already well lubricated he plunged into her. This angle hit her nerves in the best way. Edana moaned in ecstasy. Quintus set a leisurely pace, moving in steady strokes. Edana enjoyed the motion but then started to seek more. " Faster," she moaned. He lifted her hips up higher elevating her up off the pallet and proceeded to oblige her by moving in faster, harder strokes ramming into her sleek, welcoming entrance. They continued, their bodies slapping together. Quintus' balls pulled up in his body in preparation for climax but he needed to hold back for Edana to reach hers first.

"Come for me!" he lowly growled to release his sexual tension. His growled voice and urgent face sent her over into a climax. She saw stars. Her womanhood clenched around his raging penis which caused Quintus to redouble his efforts to find his climax. He increased the speed of his strokes. He began to ram her, he gasped but enjoyed the action exploding into her vagina. They wound down with kisses and fondling.

Slowing down they cuddled. "Where is Bundarus and Rufus? Grex and Titus? Where's Coriaro and Faber?" asked Edana.

"They are all letting their billeting places know that they are leaving tomorrow," Quintus kissed her neck, then licked it.

"Oh alright," And Edana melted into his kisses. They kept kissing which evolved into more lovemaking.

冋冋冋冋

It was midmorning when Fullo finally came up to Meadghbh. "Meadghbh, we will be moving out tomorrow morning but before that I would like to couple with you at least a few more times. Can you walk with me to the far field? We have that beautiful place where we first coupled. I would like to do that at that sacred glade we consecrated once more. We'll be back in the summer in time for harvest next year."

"Leaving! Oh my gods and goddesses! Just when it has been so nice having you around. We just got started. We just learned about each other," Meadghbh lamented.

"No, sweetheart. The general requested we return immediately. And the general is not somebody to take lightly. So you listen to him every time Quintus gets his instructions. All in all we will be an acting baggage train protection unit, a very low problem and non-dangerous job. I know Quintus is mad about this, but it is to our betterment. Otherwise, we would all be exposed to more risk," said Fullo.

"Can we meet right after lunch? Or should it be right now?"

"I think we should meet right now. That way it gives us more time to explore each of our bodies. I want to explore yours to the level of one who has total sexual mastery over you," Fullo said. He took her hand and brought it to his groin. He was sporting a hard on. Meadghbh was suddenly too turned on to be mad at Fullo's boldness. In fact she held that as part of Fullo's charm.

They just grabbed each other's hands and ran off into the pasture sprinting past the goat's pastures to the north pasture and into the glade where they first culminated their passion. They quickly started kissing, trying to get the Celtic clothes off. Meadghbh was better at getting out of her tartan and her tunic. Fullo was having more problems with the sandals so he sat down on the ground to take them off. Meanwhile, Meadghbh was able to get out of all of hers so she stepped naked up to him to help them take off his clothes. It was a seductive action that she gave him when she leaned down letting her generous breasts move forward and into Fullo's face. Fullo ogled them then grabbed his lover's breasts and kissed them with a passion. They were both panting hard. She helped him out of his loin cloth. She dropped down in front of them. She looked up at him, then grasped his penis and slowly and seductively licked it. She started licking him from the bottom all the way up to the head of his penis paying specific attention to the pre-come that was beading up out of it. Then she turned sideways, turned her head sideways, put her mouth on his penis and sucked as hard as she could.

After doing this for several minutes he stopped her saying: "No more else I will come." He roughly grabbed her and made her lay down making her knees splay outward then he shoved the discarded tartan under her hips. Fullo said: "It is my turn. Move down and spread your left and right legs outward and keep them open." He got up to her clit then sucked at it, getting a good suction with his lips. Meadghbh squealed at the feeling of intense rapture. Fullo continued to suck on it then traded his lips for his tongue licking rapidly back and forth. Meadghbh squealed some more and quickly screamed out her ecstasy.

Fullo quickly moved up her body to position himself at her entrance and pressed in pushing all the way to his limit quickly. He had to pause a moment because she felt so good, so moist, so hot and so tight. He started to move slowly, so slowly that it made them both sigh in happiness. Then once they got moving in the regular manner Fullo increased the speed, changing the angle of his thrust. Meadghbh cried out at one of his thrusts, so he repeated it again and again, eliciting squeals from Meadghbh each time. Fullo moved her legs and lifted them up over his shoulders changing the angle of his penetration, making it deeper. Meadghbh gasped in happiness enjoying the new deeper penetration and how he hit her nerves even stronger. Fullo increased his speed. Meadghbh ground out a yell and came with great gush of womanly juices. Fullo increased his speed and strength and quickly followed her. He came with a shout.

They smiled at each other. Fullo grabbed her again pulling around, then forward on her feet, turned her so he stood behind, pushed her down and took her. Meadghbh cried out at the quick entry. But it felt so good. This is a new feeling because it was also a different penetration and it seemed to hit her the right nerves over and over again. Fullo grabbed her hips and plowed into her savagely going at her again and again and again. Meadghbh felt the exquisite pleasure radiating from her womb. The only sound in the glade was the slapping of their bodies against each other and their heavy panting. With another shout Meadghbh came again. Fullo took her even faster, pressing into her harder and harder. Then with a shout he came as well.

Each of them were exhausted from all of energetic ways they had sex. They languorously laid down and got into each other's arms. Fullo kissed Meadghbh's face, her lips, her nose, and her eyes. Meadghbh was dreaming in her completion. She felt so good. Fullo surprised her when his hand started skimming across her body one more time concentrating on her breast and her womanhood. Fullo then open it up and buried his fingers in her vagina. "Say one more time," Fullo breathed in her ear.

"Yes, please." Meadghbh whispered

Then they coupled one more time this one more tender and loving, face-to-face, kissing, lazily and moving slowly. They kissed gently. Her fingers trailed up and down his back. His hand around her breasts and her belly sketching with just the back of his fingernails along her skin. This was a sexy way to make love. Both of them savored each other's body. They were able to go for quite a while. Slowly they reached the combination of completion and fulfillment.

Fullo was not one to tell a currant bedfellow he loved them, but that was a step he could take with Meadghbh. Meadghbh on the other hand was afraid to say that she loved him, even though she did love him. She was afraid he would not take it seriously, and on his way back switch his attention to someone else. He said nothing, but they showed each other, how much they care with their bodies. Kissing each other, stroking each other or in other words, showing each other, how much they cared.

☖☖☖☖

Bundarus was on a mission. He needed to talk with Eilis immediately because they had orders to return to base fort and would be leaving tomorrow morning at first light. He wanted to speak with Eilis because up until now he hadn't gotten the nerve up to talk with her to tell her of his feelings for her. He was mad about her. Her eyes, her lovely raven black hair, her laugh, her amazing talent of making the tartans, and even the cute way she blushed all made him love everything about her. He hesitated at the door not having the fortitude to knock.

Turns out he didn't have to wait long because Ronan came out of the barn and saw him. "Well Hail Bundarus! What brings you to our humble abode? Is it another order from your Roman buyers?"

"No, unfortunately it's not that. I have some sad news. We, meaning the Contubernium, will be leaving Gosbecks to return to the base fort per the General Gaius Suetonius Paulinus's direct orders. We leave tomorrow morning at the crack of dawn. I have been given the responsibility to pay you for the billeting you provided for us. I wanted to say goodbye and thank you. Plus I also would like to talk with Eilis. I have feelings for your daughter."

Ronan looked at Bundarus with wonder. He was sorry to hear they were leaving but that had been understood for a while. The news that Bundarus had feeling for Eilis was a knockout blow. Just as it rendered the athlete unconscious so too did this man's profession of love to her father. "You wish to tell her first? That is very lucky because we were getting requests for her hand in marriage already. I'm sure she will be happy to hear your interest in her. I will send Fingula to go get her. Then Fingula and I will give you the opportunity to talk."

Bundarus was excited. He would get the opening he wanted to talk with her. It seems like it was none too soon because other suitors were making the rounds to put in their arrangement. "Would you please let her know I have high regard for her. I hope she waits for me. We'll be back in the spring, in time for sowing."

Ronan's face split into a grin. " I will most certainly tell Eilis!

This is great news. We are most appreciative for your work as an agent for the sales we have received through your efforts. Marcus Domitius Afer has become our favorite buyer of tartans. Let me go get Fingula and then we'll go get the girl. Come inside. I looks like we'll be needing more help. That's not a bad place to be." With that he happily went inside looking for Fingula.

Bundarus was anxiously waiting for Eilis to come. Would she be willing to wait for him until next summer? He hoped she would. Ronan returned with everyone. Bundarus said: "Eilis can I talk to you privately? Maybe we can go for a walk?"

"Sure Bundarus, I would like that," smiled Eilis. She followed him out and down the drive. Eilis looked at Bundarus curiously.

Bundarus feeling her regard started to sweat. He needed to get the information out before he lost his nerve. "Eilis, we just got our orders to return to base fort. We leave at first light tomorrow morning. I wanted to tell you I have fond feelings for you." At this admission he blushed. "What I mean to say is I really hold you in the highest regard. I will be returning next spring. Can you wait for me? I know this is asking a lot of you, but I think you'll be happy if you did."

Eilis looked at Bundarus with a serious expression. "You're telling me to wait and not to listen to my suitors? I need more protestation of feelings than 'fond feelings'. I need 'you love me' in order not accepting the men seeking companionship."

Bundarus felt the full extent of Eilis' ire. "I'm sorry. Let me rephrase that. I would like to ask you to save yourself the problem of seeing who is going to pair up with you. I want to be that man. Over the past few weeks my regard for you has increased exponentially. I want you to think of me as I think of you each and every minute of the day."

Eilis looked at Bundarus. Any indignation that she had vanished. She saw him as a man with deep feelings. "Well, will you keep the faith on your end?"

"Yes I will."

"Then you have my word that I'll keep the men at bay. I'm glad we had this discussion," said Eilis. She blushed and looked more beautiful for it.

Bundarus then did the first thing that came to him. He slowly reached for Eilis, cupped her face then leaned in for a kiss. It started out chase, his lips just brushing hers. But then Eilis opened her mouth and put her tongue out, opening his mouth. Tentatively she entered his mouth, to twine with his tongue. Bundarus groaned, his penis filling with a rush of blood and took control of the kiss. He bent her over his arm and kissed her with passion, his tongue dominating hers. Soon they were kissing with abandon, the only sounds were of their passionate moans and their panting breath.

Bundarus knew they needed to stop or else he would mount Eilis. In a haze of passion he broke the kiss. "Stop this kissing else you will be ravished by me. Tell me you want to finish this."

"Finishing meaning having joining as couples do?" Eilis panted.

"Yes." Bundarus hoped fervently she would say yes.

Eilis was a religious girl. She would not have casual sex without the blessings of the gods She felt compelled to need to have it sanctified by telling Bundarus. "I know you want the goddess of marriage to have sex but I believe you have to have a union sanctified by Miach and Brigid, the goddess of the home. I want to be married before we couple.'

Bundarus felt instant frustration at her refusal. Then he got his lust under control. "I understand." He put his arms around her and pressed his forehead to hers. "I will abide by your wishes." He made his heart slow down, was glad his undergarment kept his raging hardon from Eilis' gaze. "We should return to your house. I want to pay Ronan and Fingula for billeting Rufus and I. Rufus should be here anyway because he wanted to say goodbye."

With that they returned to the house. Rufus was indeed there talking with Ronan and Fingula. "Well hail Rufus. I heard the sad news that you are leaving tomorrow. I'm very sorry to see you go," Eilis said with feeling.

Rufus smiled sadly "Thank you for the sentiment. I will miss you," he looked at Eilis with feeling. When he noticed Bundarus' angry regard at his interest he said: "I mean all of you." He made the effort to look at Ronan and Fingula.

"We know what you mean," Ronan said. "You'll miss the excitement of market day and all the amazing deals we make!"

"Yes, that is exactly what I meant," Rufus said with a guilty glance at Eilis.

"Why don't you all come eat the end of the day meal with us?" asked Fingula.

"Yes, we would like that," put in Ronan. "An impromptu celebration to see you off."

"All right, we'll do it," said Bundarus.

Fingula and Eilis went to make the meal and the men stayed in the common area. They discussed the reason for the *Contuburnium* to leave Gosbecks. "The reason we're leaving is we need to gather up the veterans with their families and take them to Gosbecks," explained Bundarus.

"That means about 200 to 250 new citizens of Gosbecks will be coming. I highly recommend you learn Latin," Rufus said.

"200 to 250 new citizens? That means you Romans will outnumber the native Gosbeckians by two or three to one. We will be outvoted in every decision!" Ronan exclaimed reaching the same conclusion as Edana did earlier.

"It will be incumbent upon you to negotiate with your politicians to change it. I have experience in your ability to work around the law.," explained Bundarus. Ronan didn't look that happy about the turn of their conversation.

The ladies called for them to come into the dining area and they all had a very good midday meal.

𐃘𐃘𐃘𐃘

Titus and Grex entered the main room of Cathmore's farm. He and Grex needed to let them know that they would be leaving tomorrow to go back to the General Gaius Suetonius Paulinus's fort out west. They would settle up the earnings of Cathmore from the time they had spent staying with them. Titus also wanted to ask him about Aine. He wanted to ask Aine to wait for him. He had grown to like the way she looked and also the way she acted. He enjoyed her funny personality and her easy smile. He hoped that he would get her to stay available, so that he could have somebody when he got back from the general's fort to Gosbecks.

"Well hail Meara. How are you today?"

Meara turned around and smiled because she always had a soft spot for Titus. She enjoyed his easy wit and ability to make everyone laugh. "I am quite well, how about you. It is good to see you again. To what do we owe this great honor?"

"We come bearing sad tidings. We are to leave for our general's fort tomorrow. We have the money to settle up with our time with you and Cathmore. We also want to say goodbye to Aine and Flann."

Meara was sad, she had gotten to be used to Titus and Grex staying with them and all the extra work the two did for them. There is still work to be done on the barn but that would have to wait for a later time. "I am very sorry to hear this, we had really begun to enjoy your company. Also all the extra work you did around the farm was much appreciated. I'll go and get Aine and Flann right now. Wait here."

Titus was very happy about this because he would get to talk with Aine. Also, it would be good to say goodbye to Flann. He had a soft spot for Flann. She reminded him of his little sister. It was also going to be sad to seek the end of their time with Cathmore, Meara, Aine, and Flann. He enjoyed the time here because they were so interesting to him and at night they would get together and do sing. The singing was sublime. He thought Flann had the gorgeous voice, a nice contralto. *I just wish I could've gotten the opportunity to talk with Aine, but I will now,* thought Titus so he was happy. The girls walked in the room with Meara..

"So what is this you are leaving us?" Said Aine. "It was getting to be so nice to have you guys here. You help us out on the farm so much. And there is so much more to do."

"Our general has called us back to his fort in West." Titus said with sadness. "We will leave first thing in the morning tomorrow. We wanted to let you know how much we enjoyed our time with you and with your wonderful family. I also want to settle up our time. We owe you a certain amount. I have it here. I also asked to talk with you, Aine. Just to let you know I find you a particularly wonderful person and would like to get to know her better. I really like you."

Meara was surprised at this. "So you like Aine? Are you willing to offer her marriage, is that what you're asking? I would prefer she marries a good Celtic man. But you have been so nice and so steadfast and dependable that I might be able to look upon you as a future son in law." Meara was secretly horrified that this Roman would like to marry Aine. But because it was Titus she we would make an exception.

Soon Cathmore came in from the fields. He looked up and were greatly surprised to see Grex and Titus. "We have some big news to give you. The Roman general's soldiers sent to Gosbecks is called back to their fort. But we will be returning in the spring of next year in time for sowing. I would like to talk with you Aine if you have the time. I like to walk outside with you to speak privately."

"All right, that is fine with me," Meara looked hard at Titus and Cathmore having missed the previous conversation just nodded his head.

Titus and Aine went out to the outside hearth and stopped. Titus took Aine's hand and looked into her eyes. Aine was surprised. "I think the constant time spent with you, Flann, your mother, and your father made us get to know each other quite well. I found the time spent with you particularly pleasant. I would like to spend more time with you when we get back in the spring. Please wait for me. I do not want you to tie yourself down to me, but I will tie myself to you."

Aine just looked at him. "Well, then have a nice trip. I'll see you in the spring when you return."

Titus was sad. He was hoping for Aine to fall into his arms and say take me away, but this did not happen. "Well, let me go and say goodbye. It has been a lot a fun. I will be back in the spring to keep this job going. Period."

Titus excused himself and said he was sorry and that he would be thinking about her all the time he would be gone. Aine said nothing much to Titus's grief.

◰ ◰ ◰ ◰

It was nighttime in Larkin's house, like normal. Faber and Coriaro were awake as usual. Extreme exhaustion hit for Coriaro and Faber so they went to bed as early as they could which was around midnight. They got to sleep a couple hours but then were woken up by something unusual. It was quiet for once but then there was some overheated harsh whispering. It woke Coriaro up first. Listening to the whispering he understood it was about the human sacrifice that happened at Samhain. He quickly hit Faber to wake him up

"Coriaro what the fuck. I was just sleeping!" Faber said harshly.

"Faber, be quiet and listen to what this these guys are saying. They are talking about the human sacrifice." Coriaro whispered.

Coriaro and Faber turned and listened to the whispered conversation. Like Coriaro had said they were talking about the human sacrifice last Samhain. Just harsh whispering that sounded like they were angry. They overheard: "Think you dolt. I have two Roman soldiers sleeping in this room. And they might hear you! Now what are you talking about?" Larkin said.

An unknown person severely whispered: "The thrice killed sacrifice is not working. My crops are not growing like everybody else's. I demand another one be made."

"I do not think we can do that. The thrice killed sacrifice works for everybody in Gosbecks except for you, your farm is by the swamps. That is probably why it is not doing well," Larkin said urgently.

"I have gotten good crops before, it is just that this thrice killed sacrifice did not work. We need another willing victim to be killed by garroting, stabbing and bludgeoning. I demand another one!"

"Quiet! You wake the two soldiers! They will reported back to their Centurion Quintus, if you do not be quiet. We told them that that body on the bonfire was gentleman that died of a fit and not a human sacrifice. That is all they have been told by the whole village per Miach's order. So the more you say right now, the worse it is because they do not know anything about the thrice killed sacrifice. Be quiet," dark and harshly whispered Larkin.

"I demand it! If it is not a thrice killed sacrifice then maybe a bigger one should be held. Maybe the one using multiple sacrifice victim's in the wicker cage. We should do that one, because it will be more efficacious and we can get more out of it. Maybe even get rid of the Romans in the first place. Yeah, I like that one better!"

"There hasn't been anything like that for years. We just had to kill Declan in the thrice killed manner of garroting, stabbing and bludgeoning. It is the most humane way of doing it and it was the most beneficial way." Larkin said satisfactorily

"It did not help me! My farm is still not producing anything. The crops are still not growing. My wheat is not growing. My vegetables are not growing. My cows have no grass to graze on. Nothing is growing. It is as of the Druids have placed a curse on my farm."

"There is no such thing as a druidic curse like that! It is probably something in the soil. You were advised before to move and counseled before to look into getting another plot of land. You just refused to do anything about it. It is because of your laziness that you are set in that spot?" Harshly whispered Larkin.

"Do not be putting this back on me. I have been a true member of Gosbecks and a good member of this community. I want to keep my farm, where I am close to my wife's grave. She died the coughing sickness last year. I want to stay close to her."

A vulgar curse was heard. "I must do something about my farm. It is not that bad a plot of land, but it is a little swampy. There are better plots over on the west side of Gosbecks Larkin, I know that! I will never move because my beloved wife is laid to rest at my farm. If you won't give my message I will have to ask someone else. I was hoping it would be you because you have the best and most melodic way of talking to others in Gosbecks but I see I shall have to find someone else."

And with that, it was heard to be movement in the next area and the door open and shut. They heard Larkin curse. He turned and got ready to get for bed and lay down.

Coriaro got up and went over to Faber then whispered into his ear: "Now we have exactly what happened. It was a human sacrifice that we saw last Samhain and was called thrice killed victim, whatever that means. We at least have that question answered. But now we need to know who did it and what was the reason. When we get ready to go. These we can have this to tell to Quintus."

Faber whispered: "We are very lefty lucky to have heard that interchange."

〓〓〓〓

That morning, Coriaro and Faber struck out after getting a bleary-eyed sleep. When they got to the tavern which was the meeting ground for the *Contuburnium* base. They sought out Quintus. "Quintus, we had an illuminating night. Larkin and an unidentified person were talking about the human sacrifice. They called it the willing victim thrice killed sacrifice. Declan was the willing victim and was killed three times. We know how and what was done to the victim but not the *why*. By garroting, stabbing and bludgeoning the willing victim was killed. This person wants to do another one. Larkin did not agree with him so they argued. It seems that there is going to be another human sacrifice!" And excited. Coriaro told Quintus.

Quintus was amazed. All this time they had heard nothing but this whispered conversation sounded the affirmative that the human sacrifice did occur and Quintus was glad to have it confirmed. "So they talked about a thrice killed sacrifice? I wonder what that meant. There seems to be so much more that we need to find out. But good job. I am glad you guys heard this, this is the confirmation that we have had that human sacrifice did in fact occur. Unfortunately, now it is too late to do something about it, but when we get back can. This went on and draw out specific scenarios of what the thrice killed means and if they will actually do it again. Good job Coriaro and Faber."

"I just hate the fact that we did not get the identity of the second person. It would make finding out exactly what he meant so much easier. He sounded like another musician or somebody that comes to the door knowing that Larkin late night hours. He seemed to be very ignorant of the Romans. Despite the fact that he kept talking about Romans as a terrible ruling class." Said Faber. He wanted to speak like those in the patrician class.

Quintus smiled and said: "Well, everybody get up and get on the horse and let us get away. The sooner we get going, the sooner we will be back."

Fullo came over after listening to a portion of the whispered conversation between Quintus Coriaro and Faber. He sidled over and got between Faber and Quintus. "I heard a little bit about what you were talking with Quintus. Did you find out anything about the human sacrifice?"

Coriaro and Faber smiled and said: "Yes," in unison. "We overheard two people talking. Larkin and another unknown person. They said that there was a thrice killed sacrifice last Samhain So there was a thrice killed human sacrifice. The unknown man talked about the need to do another one because the last sacrifice did not seem to cover his farm. He said his farm was located near a swampy area and so nothing grew. I think it was just natural, but he did not."

Fullo grinned. "So we do have evidence that the human sacrifice happened. I knew it, the people of Gosbecks were so good at covering up the fact that there was a sacrifice. Miach probably helped cover up the situation and offering that explanation of a human that had a fit died. We know better. This is really good news. Now we have something to come back to investigate."

Faber agreed. "Now I cannot wait to get back here and continue our investigation. He said something about the thrice killed sacrifice needs to be performed again, but what does that mean thrice killed? The Celts always have new and vigorous way to kill somebody."

"Yes, I know what you mean. Did they ever talk about what the thrice killed means, I mean the reason for needing to perform one?" Asked Fullo.

"No, we never did. He kept saying thrice killed as if we knew what that meant and the unknown person kept saying they needed another one because his farm. It did not work so was not a complete spell. I would like some of the mumbo-jumbo."

Coriaro said: "Since we know that this unknown person has of farm near Gosbecks he will probably be easy to find out who that was. Of course it might be more of a problem if he somehow dies. Seems the Celts are very good at convenient deaths. Do you remember about Janice? That was the slave that was supposed to see or witnessed a murder, and she was summarily dispatched."

Fullo nodded: "I heard about that. It was under Claudius's reign. I hope with the current emperor's not so shady but I am not sure. So far he seems to be going in our direction, so maybe were lucky."

Coriaro said: "Let us leave that up to Quintus to see where it goes with this. He is a smart guy. I'm sure he is going to come up with the way to investigate this thrice killed victim sacrifice might even be able to get the appropriate information."

"That would be the best." Said Fullo

"So Quintus, what you think about all this. The thrice killed victim, and the fact that this unknown farmer wants to do another sacrifice," said Coriaro.

Quintus looked down, he was deep in thought. Then he looked up and said: "I think we have something here. We should go further and investigated when we get back to Gosbecks."

The men then settled down and continued on their long journey back to base fort in the west. Quintus became deep in thought. *A human sacrifice, a thrice killed victim, Samhain, and the ritual bonfires. This is all something to think about indeed. I want to find out what role Miach had in the whole affair, is he in fact a druid?. I also want to know how much power he had over all the people in Gosbecks. What role does the thrice killed victim have in the Samhain ritual? I also hope that Edana had nothing to do with this horrific ritual. I like her so much, possibly love her. I want to return to her…*

CPSIA information can be obtained
at www.ICGtesting.com
Printed in the USA
BVHW071023281119
565084BV00001B/12/P

9 781480 880559